To my

Thank you very much for
all your help and support.

I hope you enjoy this
little story.

Your Friend.
CADDEN

AKa.
michael Grr

The Falling

Free Fall

Caden's Journals

CADEN

authorHOUSE°

AuthorHouse™
1663 Liberty Drive
Bloomington, IN 47403
www.authorhouse.com
Phone: 1 (800) 839-8640

© 2015 Caden. All rights reserved.

No part of this book may be reproduced, stored in a retrieval system, or transmitted by any means without the written permission of the author.

Published by AuthorHouse   12/18/2015

ISBN: 978-1-5049-6454-8 (sc)
ISBN: 978-1-5049-6453-1 (e)

Library of Congress Control Number: 2015919640

Print information available on the last page.

Any people depicted in stock imagery provided by Thinkstock are models, and such images are being used for illustrative purposes only. Certain stock imagery © Thinkstock.

This book is printed on acid-free paper.

Because of the dynamic nature of the Internet, any web addresses or links contained in this book may have changed since publication and may no longer be valid. The views expressed in this work are solely those of the author and do not necessarily reflect the views of the publisher, and the publisher hereby disclaims any responsibility for them.

Acknowledgements

I would like to express my deepest appreciation to a number of people who saw me through this book. I am grateful to all who provided support, allowed me to talk things over with and pick their brains, read my interpretations, offered comments, and assisted in the proofreading and editing.

Thank you to my classmates and friends from my senior physics class of 2012. Your inspiration and creative ideas were very important in publishing these journals.

I would like to acknowledge and thank my professor at Wyoming University, Dr. Jim McCarthy, for his personal thoughts, guidance and wisdom with these journals.

Most of all, I would like to thank my girlfriend, Erika, for her limitless support, understanding, and love throughout this long and arduous project. Without her many hours of proofreading and inspirational ideas, I do not believe that I would have had the courage or strength to publish these extraordinary journals.

Prologue

Many classic stories begin with the words *once upon a time*, but this isn't one of them. Not because the herein events were not important or significant. They were. At least I think they were salient. "Once upon a time" tales usually have happy endings; this may or may not. I'll let you decide.

Although the following events might seem absurd, please try to keep an open mind. There is much contained in these journal entries that is nothing short of amazing. There are countless things humankind is blinded from and oblivious to in this Universe and especially in others. Most people live their lives completely unaware of the rest of this world and other universes. Most humans live their lives in a tiny cocoon of safety and assurance that things are as they seem to be. These uninformed people have no idea what really exists "out there."

Believe me, I should know. I was, in fact, one of those people. I was maintaining a normal life, living a stable life day after day, believing that one plus one always equals two, without exception.

That is, before it all started to fall apart. Before I found it and realized that my world wasn't my world after all. My own reality began to slowly unravel when I found it. Or maybe it found me. It's difficult to say. An out-of-time journal written by a man I didn't think I had ever known. At first it wasn't like Moses parting the Red Sea or Isaac Newton's apple-and-gravity revelation, but as I began to read this ridiculous journal, I had the strange feeling I somehow knew the impossible to be possible.

I tried to keep my own journal of the following events as best I could recall and from certain messages that were personally communicated to me. Today I still question my own sanity. In short, what follows is a manuscript of the strange and bizarre events that fell upon Michael Cardazia and Erika Nirvona.

Who am I? Well, that's not really important—at least not at this point. Suffice it to say that I had some part in the following events. Some readers may be uncomfortable with that, so if you prefer to give me a name, just call me Caden.

Whether you believe the stories contained within the journals or my interpretation of them to be true isn't important. Rather, if you find this journal (even if you think it is a fictional story), I implore you to take it straight to the CIA. I'm not sure if there's anyone you can trust within that organization anymore, but it would be better than the alternative.

I have very little time left, so before my time runs out, please do what you can to prevent *him* from getting his hands on this document. The macabre individual known as Dr. Shelly is not to be trusted under any circumstances as you'll learn in the ensuing journal entries. That is, of course, if you decide to read on. If you choose to walk away, I understand. In fact, it's probably the safest thing to do.

He could not return to living full-time with the Dursleys, not now that he knew the other world, the one to which he really belonged.

— J.K. Rowling

Introduction

Dissemblance: Everything works out in the end. If it hasn't worked out, maybe it's not the end.

Even as an ankle biter, he had a strange feeling he lived in the wrong time and a spurious place. Throughout high school and college, this perception of his disconnection agonizingly endured. Although there were times the feeling abated, it never completely vanished; it remained always in the background of his essence. Other times he felt mired in a sea of stagnant molasses, which contributed to a feeling of being mundane, of being just one ant in a large anthill with no individual purpose and no identity. There were times when Michael felt that, if he closed his eyes and let go, he could easily be somewhere else. Sometimes he would let his imagination run amok and imagine he was a king, or at least a prince, somewhere else in another time and place.

There were occasional times he wished this feeling would come true, that there was an exciting other life to which he belonged, like something in a grandiose Hollywood blockbuster starring a twenty-million-dollar-a-film leading man. However, most of the time he felt a complete disassociation with this world. Nonetheless, he knew that he would never truly wish for this alternate life because of people he would miss, especially his "better half."

Michael Cardazia was a forty-seven-year-old high school science teacher. He taught science to children who lived within an impoverished inner city. During his sophomore year of college, he had contemplated medical school, but he lost his desire after his father, Leon, passed away at the age of forty-seven.

In so many aspects, his life was perfunctory: he grew up in a middle-class neighborhood and society, went to college, married, and divorced. Like many, he felt as if his life was in a rut day after day.

Michael was neither affluent nor impoverished. He owned a house—or, rather, the bank to which he paid a monthly mortgage owned the house. Michael never had children. He drove a common compact car, a Toyota Corolla. Although he exercised regularly, he had a slight chronic limp in his left leg due to a herniated disk.

Occasionally he used an antique cane from the early 1900s that he had inherited from his great-grandfather, whom he was named after. The cane was made of Brazilian rosewood. A beautiful carving of wolves decorated the entire shaft, and the handle, which was made from rosewood, was encrusted with blue diamonds. Most of the time he didn't require the support of the cane; rather, he carried it around because he liked the craftsmanship and antiquity of the cane. His great-grandfather had been a cardiologist, and he'd had the cane with him when he died at the age of forty-seven from a heart attack during a game of golf.

In general, most facets of Michael's life were mundane. According to the early journal notes, Michael was the poster child for ordinary. He would not be considered a prototypical protagonist.

Francis Scott Fitzgerald once said, "Show me a hero and I'll write you a tragedy." That's the thing about heroes; you never know when one will emerge. Sometimes they develop from the most unlikely sorts of people. Christopher Reeves once stated, "Heroes are usually ordinary people who find the strength to endure during harsh times." But Bernard Shaw might have been the most poignant when he remarked, "You cannot be a hero without being a coward."

Michael may have been boring and not a classic hero, but there were still a few uncharacteristic aspects of his life. Michael was the lead singer and part-time guitar player in a band named According to Her. The band had been formed when he was in college, and most of the guys stayed together and played gigs once or twice a month just for kicks. The band played mostly classic rock, but every so often they threw in some more modern material from groups like the Foo Fighters and Blink 182 (usually surprising the audience).

Still, he always had an inescapable, unearthly feeling that he was an anomaly. It was a gut feeling that he was destined to have lived somewhere in the distant past or future, or somewhere else in the Universe, he wasn't sure which. The only thing that felt certain was that he wasn't meant to be living in the present, which seemed absurd to him and probably would to anyone else—if he dared to tell them.

Michael also suffered from two intermittent fears. Inexplicable anxiety overwhelmed him when he was driving on certain highways. There is no word relating directly to a fear of driving on highways, but the closest word is *hodophobia*, which is simply a fear of driving in general. Yet, he didn't mind driving for the most part.

He thought that maybe some wordsmith should make up a phobia name for this particular kind of fear; this certainly seems easy enough. After all, there seemed to be a name for just about every kind of phobia, wasn't there? There were some really strange phobia names like *anablephobia* (fear of looking up) or *cacophobia* (fear of ugliness) and even *consecotaleophobia* (fear of chopsticks). Who could be afraid of chopsticks unless Chuck Norris or Bruce Lee was using them? Anyway, the least they could do was invent a phobia name for a fear of driving on highways. It often occurred to him that perhaps he should pursue more hobbies since he knew of these names.

The other phobia he experienced related to driving over bridges. Fortunately, there was already a term for this phobia so he wouldn't have to worry about inventing one. It turned out that gephyrophobia was a relatively common phobia. Who knew? The derivation of the word *gephyrophobia* is perfectly straightforward if you know Greek—*gephyra* is bridge, and *phobos* is fear.

Although Michael had sought therapy to alleviate his phobias, no treatment or medication seemed to assuage them. This fear made no sense, since he had no inherent fear of cars, roads, or bridges. The level of panic also varied; sometimes it was almost crippling and other times not so much. Again, this seemed to be illogical. He was sure that Mr. Spock could relate.

Michael remembered that *hodo* is the Greek word for road. Maybe that's why there wasn't a specific phobia word for driving on large highways. There were no highways in ancient Greece, just roads, and in the modern world there seemed to be some kind of unwritten rule that all phobia names must come from ancient Greek words. Michael made a mental note to give up his idea of creating a phobia name for highways and really concentrate on *getting a life!*

The other peculiar thing about Michael was that he always felt there was goodness about his being, and if he ever had to face the ultimate evil, goodness would prevail. Once again, none of this made any sense to him, at least not now.

Michael taught at a charter school known as Above it All Academy located in a mid-sized town in Southern New Jersey. The building was constructed at the turn of the twentieth century, primarily from bricks and stones. Such building materials were ideal for brick ovens for cooking pizzas, but not for keeping classrooms cool in the spring and summer months. The school looked more like a medieval castle than a modern-day high school. There were security cameras outside each classroom, in every hallway, and at all entrances of "the castle," as he facetiously referred to it. Security personnel armed with Taser guns and donuts were stationed at every main entrance and exit.

Each morning during his drive to school, Michael would enter the main parking lot and pass a giant sign to the left of the entrance that read New Jersey School of Character. Michael laughed each time he read the sign. Maybe there were a few characters at the school, but mostly there were hypocrisy, absolute control, micromanagement, favoritism, and administrative "spies" among certain staff.

The school was run by a head mistress who subscribed to a dystopian philosophy and a totalitarian ideology. Michael would often imagine that he was really the character Winston Smith and that the school was located in Oceania. The ghosts of "Big Brother" often permeated the hallways and classrooms. Fortunately, he was able to ignore most of the omnipresent tyranny inner party elite and escape by reading and focusing on his teaching. That's all I can say for now. You never know who is listening or watching through the many cameras in the castle.

It was nearing the end of another onerous school year when the first of the signs began to appear. Initially, these signs appeared to be wayward, almost whimsical. Later, during the last week of the school year, the signs became more coherent.

Michael's physics classes had finished the prescribed curriculum and so Michael decided to explore Einstein's theory of relativity with his senior classes. This led to a discussion of gravitational time dilation—the effect of time passing at different rates in regions of different gravitational potential. The lower the gravitational potential, the more slowly time passes.

Einstein originally predicted this effect in his theory of relativity and it has since been confirmed by tests of general relativity. This effect has been demonstrated by noting that an atomic clock placed on a jet plane is shown to tick more slowly than an atomic clock placed at rest and will eventually show different times. Perhaps a more dramatic example is illustrated through an experiment performed on the International Space Station (ISS). After the first six months in space, the crew of the ISS had aged .007 seconds less than those on Earth (the relatively stationary observers) because the station moves at approximately eighteen thousand miles per hour, much faster than the range of normal human speeds. Although the effects detected in such experiments are nominal, with differences being measured in nanoseconds, they do exist.

The natural consequence of this effect was that if time could actually be relative, could it also be manipulated? Could time actually be moved faster and slower or even forward and backward? In other words, could time travel actually be possible? Many of the students were fascinated by this discussion, except for one. He was the one student whom most observers would expect would be intrigued.

Brace Strider was also an anomaly. He was tall and thin and had a translucent complexion. He wore his long, jet-black hair in a ponytail. Brace had transferred to Above it All Academy just before the start of the school year. No one seemed to know much about him. He was a loner who displayed similar qualities to those of Robert Pattinson in the Twilight movies—minus the vampire attributes, according to some female students. Some students had tried to befriend Brace, but their efforts so far had been to no avail. Michael perceived a transcendental quality about Brace.

He was one of Michael Cardazia's smartest students, yet he seldom completed or handed in assignments. It was obvious he understood most of the concepts based on exam scores, but turning in assignments was clearly not a priority for Brace. The concept of time displacement was one that should have appealed to him, yet he seemed distracted and disinterested.

As the clanging of the bell signaled the end of class, Brace stopped at the door and asked, "Mr. Cards"—which most students called him—"is it okay if I stop in after school to talk to you about something?"

"No problem," Mr. Cardazia replied.

This seemed odd to Michael because Brace had never asked for extra help and, by all indications, understood the class work. Most notably, Brace never stayed after school for any reason.

At the end of the school day, Michael waited for Brace to stop in, still curious why the boy would want to return to class. After impatiently watching the clock for twenty minutes, Michael packed up his work and was ready to head home. Suddenly, Brace appeared at the classroom door. "Sorry I'm a little late, but it was unavoidable," Brace said apologetically.

Michael saw this as an opportunity to address his concern. "I was just about to leave, but now that you're here, I did want to talk to you about your lack of interest this week in class."

Disregarding the question, Brace instead retorted, "Mr. Cards, do you ever get the feeling you are somewhere, like here for instance, but shouldn't necessarily be here?"

An ominous feeling began to swell in Michael Cardazia. He understood exactly what Brace was saying. Instead of showing his understanding, he decided to "play dumb," which he thought he did quite well at times. "What do you mean by that, Brace?"

"I mean have you ever felt you were not supposed to be in this time and place?" Brace asked with a feverous quality. "Are there times when you sense you were meant for something else and are just biding time here, waiting for something else to happen or waiting to be somewhere else?"

Michael knew precisely what Brace was referring to, but paused and stared down at the floor for a moment. An aberrant feeling began to seep into the pit of his stomach. Finally, he turned to Brace and said, "How could you have known?"

Brace was not standing there anymore; he had somehow vanished into the preverbal "thin air." On the wood floor where he had stood seconds earlier was a scrap of paper. It was all that was left behind after Brace performed his best Houdini impression.

Michael ran into the hallway looking for Brace, but caught only a glimpse of Mr. Jacque, an elderly school janitor. Although the man had been employed at the school for the past twenty years, no one knew his first name; he simply went by the name Mr. Jacque. Mr. Jacque and

Michael Cardazia had started working at the school on the same day. Mr. Jacque was African American, probably in his late sixties or early seventies. He always kept his thin, grayish beard immaculately trimmed. Perhaps from years of laborious work, Mr. Jacque had developed a slight hunch in his lower back. But his most memorable quality was the huge smile on his face. Most would agree it was hard to picture Mr. Jacque without a grin.

Hastily, Michael asked, "Mr. Jacque, did you see where Brace ran off too?"

"Mr. Cards, I have been sweeping and mopping the hallway for the last ten minutes or so, and I didn't see anyone enter or leave your classroom in that time."

"Are you sure, Mr. Jacque? Absolutely sure you didn't see anyone?"

Mr. Jacque pulled out a gold pocket watch. Its color appeared worn from age; it was definitely an antique. He peered down at the time and said, "I'm sure. I have been right here in the hallway for the last ten minutes, and there was nobody but me and my sweeper."

"That's a beautiful watch. May I see it?" Michael politely asked.

Mr. Jacque proudly handed over the watch and said, "My great-great-grandfather owned this watch during the Civil War. It's been passed down to the men in my family from one generation to the next."

Michael carefully looked over the pocket watch. It was fairly heavy, possibly solid gold. The face of the watch was painted to resemble a solid oak round table. At each of the hour places was the image of an armor-clad knight, a medieval warrior. The second hand was in the form of a blue-and-red, shimmering, jewel-encrusted sword. The hour and minute hands were in the form of two silver chalices, one large and one small. On the back of this elegant timepiece was the engraved and enameled image of an ethereal lady floating slightly above a crystal-clear, blue lake.

"It is exquisite. The detail is amazing," Michael said as he handed the watch back to Mr. Jacque.

"Thanks. They certainly don't make things like they used to. John, my great-great-grandfather, passed the watch down through the men in my family. There was some chatter in my family that he was a Civil War spy for the Yankees and he acquired the watch during one of the battles. This pocket watch is also rumored, in certain factions of my family, to have been forged just before the start of the war by a necromancer. It's supposed to possess mystical powers, although I have never been able to crack any of its magical secrets."

Michael laughed. "I'm not a big believer in magic either. I like magic shows, but I'm always thinking there must be some explanation. Even if you don't figure out how to conjure up any of its magic, you don't see too many beautiful timepieces like this one anymore. Anyway, if Brace happens to come back, or you see him, please let me know."

"Will do, Mr. Cards." Carefully placing the watch back in his top pocket, Mr. Jacque began to whistle a tune that was vaguely familiar to me as he went back to attending to the floors. Then he stopped and turned to me. "By the way, Mr. Cards, have you checked the security cameras? Maybe they'll show where Brace wandered off to."

"Thanks! You know, that never occurred to me. I will check with Mr. Holmes."

Michael went back to his classroom and looked at the scrap of paper left behind after Brace's departure. The crazy thing about the paper, as if Brace disappearing without a trace wasn't bizarre enough, was now it didn't seem normal. He noticed the paper was very thin and different from standard paper; it was more of a brownish parchment. And no letters or sentences were written on it, at least not in a traditional sense. Rather, he saw a series of mysterious symbols or signs:

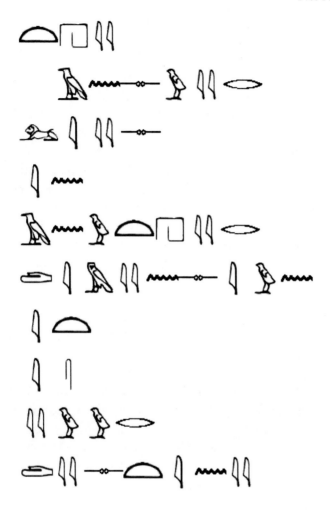

What language could it be? With its unusual symbols, it didn't resemble any modern-day language. Still, this writing did seem remotely familiar for some unknown reason. Michael couldn't recall why it seemed vaguely familiar. *Probably the beginnings of senility,* he thought to himself. He decided he would do some research on the puzzling symbols at home.

Besides, he was running late to meet Erika Nirvona, his longtime girlfriend. Erika was a year older than he, but looked like someone in her early thirties. She was five six and had long, brown hair that matched her big brown eyes. Erika was slim and had an athletic figure. She often displayed a doleful but beguiling smile that could entrance even the most hardened of the pragmatic unromantic. Yet she seemed completely unaware of this allure. In short, she could be quite stunning when she wanted to be, and just plain beautiful when she didn't care to impress. Michael had been instantly attracted to her when they'd first met a decade earlier.

It had been early June about ten years earlier, and he'd been slated to attend a charity benefit for homeless animals sponsored by Last Chance Adoption Center (LCAC). The dinner and dance was being held at the Aquila Run Golf Club. Michael had always had a special interest in helping animals, even as a child. His mom would often kid him that he got along better with kids, the elderly, and especially animals, than his own peers. At Above it All Academy, he was often referred to as the "Animal Teacher."

It had been arranged that Michael would attend this charity event with Missy, his childhood girlfriend who had recently contacted him after fifteen years. But, due to an unforeseen commitment, Missy was unable to accompany him. As it turned out, Missy's unavailability was the best thing that could have happened.

When Michael walked into the restaurant, he'd seen Erika across the room. It was as if the words to "A Long December," written by Adam Duritz and immortalized by Counting Crows, made perfect sense for the first time in his life: "All at once you look across a crowded room to see the way that light attaches to a girl." As luck would have it, there had been an empty seat next to Erika. He'd contemplated how to approach her, wondering if she was alone or attending with someone else. He decided to take a chance introduce himself. They'd spent much of the remaining evening talking.

Michael had found that they shared a number of interesting coincidences: both had been born on the eleventh day of the month; his mother and her ex-husband's mother had the same birthday; Michael and her sister shared the same birthday; her sister died at the same age as Michael's father (forty-seven). And, in the world of social media frenzy, they were likely the only two people under the age of fifty who had never looked on Facebook or tweeted, twittered, or texted.

Thankfully, they both knew how to e-mail. Michael contacted Erika the following day and asked her to dinner. Ever since their first date, not a single day had passed in which he hadn't seen her or at least talked to her on the phone.

There was no psychic or fortune telling machine that printed out a card in the imaginary town of Pico Mundo that read, "You are destined to be together forever," as happened with Oddie Thomas and Stormy Llewellyn in a Dean Kontz novel, but there was a quiet, unspoken bond that was there all the same, a bond that seemed to be the strongest power he knew on Earth. It was an endowment that kept him grounded when he felt that, if he just let go, he would drift away to another world.

Erika had mentioned when they first met that she worked for the federal government. However, for obvious reasons, she had neglected to mention that she was a classified employee. Her main headquarters was located at the George Bush Center for Intelligence in Langley, Virginia.

> Washington is a city of Southern
> efficiency and Northern charm.

> —John F. Kennedy

Journal Entry 1

DC, Here We Go

Journal note: From this point forward, "I" and "me" in my journals refer to Michael Cardazia account of the journals that I have found and interpreted - Caden.

It was ten years later, and she was coming directly from work to meet me at our favorite restaurant, La Rosata. It was a family-owned and operated restaurant renowned for exquisite Italian food, comfortable surroundings, and reasonable prices. And no, I haven't received any compensation for this brilliant advertisement, although a free appetizer once in a while would have been nice.

When I arrived at the restaurant, she was already waiting for me at our favorite table, over which, on the wall, painted in cursive script was this quote: "Life is too short to drink bad wine." Ironically, neither one of us drank much alcohol, let alone wine.

Erika was punctual and efficient. She was not a person fond of public displays of affection, although in private she was warm and affectionate. Gently she placed a kiss on my cheek as I sat down.

In addition to being beautiful and intelligent, she was keenly observant. Once, while having refurbishing work done in her house, she noticed a small flaw. The workmen kidded that she must work for the FBI because she had noticed something so small. I remember biting my tongue and thinking, *Close, but not exactly.*

It was great being with someone so smart and cognizant; however, it sure did make it hard to put anything over on her. For example, in the future, throwing a surprise party for her fiftieth birthday would never be a possibility. But there was plenty of time to worry about that, or at least I thought there would be.

Our favorite waiter seated me. Kent was a bit of an odd man. He was tall and thin. With a ghostly complexion, he looked like a young Fred Gwynne in his role as Herman Munster. Kent was partially deaf in his left ear and tended to talk rather loudly. He was wearing his usual black tuxedo and white bow tie with a purple handkerchief he told us had been his father's when he was maître d' at the Tavern on the Green in New York City, a proud fact he mentioned almost every time we sat at one of his tables.

Kent was both pensive and emotional. Often, he would hug Erika and me when we entered the restaurant, muttering things like "Thank God it's you two" and "I don't think I can deal with people tonight." Maybe he thought we weren't real people?

I always thought Kent's chosen profession was a bit of a conundrum, because it seemed to me that dealing with people on a daily basis would be—and this is just my personal opinion—a requisite for being a server in a restaurant. But Kent definitely marched to the beat of his own drummer. Though he was a bit peculiar, he always made us feel welcomed.

"Michael," Erika said, "I have some good news for you."

I was thinking that I like good news, especially compared to bad news. "What is it?"

As if she really didn't know how I'd reply, she said, "What are your favorite cities to visit?"

"That's easy: Las Vegas and Orlando."

You know, what happens in Vegas stays in Vegas, like losing your money. And I love Orlando because everybody loves Disney World, and we have been there at least ten times—Erika probably twenty times. She could be a Disney Mom. Believe it or not, there are actually moms who have been selected by Disney to be Walt Disney World panelists because they have demonstrated an excellent knowledge of the Walt Disney World Resort. They are familiar with the parks, resort hotels, dining and entertainment, shopping, and recreational activities, and they can offer help and tips to make vacation planning quick and effective for those who are not so familiar. Or so the website says.

"And, of course, Washington DC," I added. That was my kind of town with amazing museums. "Are we going back to one of these cities?" I asked hopefully.

"I have to go to DC for work for three days in July, and I was thinking maybe you would like to come with me."

It took me about a nanosecond to think, *A free room at a luxurious hotel, and I can visit the very cool museums while in the company of Erika.* The Air and Space Museum is my favorite; I believe everyone should see it. Well, it took only another nanosecond for me to answer, "When do we leave?"

"I have to be in DC from July second to the fifth, so I thought it would be fun to be in our nation's capital on the Fourth of July. They are supposedly having a unique parade, and the president and vice president are rumored to be planning to attend the festivities. Talk from the water cooler, so to speak, is that it is supposed to be spectacular, and I want to see it firsthand."

Between September and June (the school calendar year), I could not accompany her when she traveled. But if she had to go to DC in the summer, it would be like a mini vacation for me. Though she had to work during the day, I could visit the attractions our nation's capital had to offer, and I knew there was plenty to do and see in DC. It occurred to me that Washington DC might want to consider hiring me as a consultant in their tourism department. Just a random thought. (There will be many of them in this journal.)

The George Bush Center for Intelligence is the headquarters for the CIA. Okay, so I was dating a spy, but it wasn't James Bondish and all that is portrayed in the movies. Her work didn't involve flying all over the world to exciting and exotic locales, and saving the world from super criminals. Those movies showed the hero getting the girl. Well, in this case, getting the guy. Besides, she had already gotten me long ago. It was pretty routine CIA stuff.

Although much of the work was obviously important, it was not always exciting. I think that's why people love the movies so much, because most of our lives are tedious and routine. Hollywood must have realized this a long time ago and made a gazillion dollars and countless stars understanding this need in people. I remember reading a quote from Elvis Presley. He said, "When I was a boy, I always saw myself as a hero in comic books and in movies. I grew up believing this dream." Maybe most of us felt the same. Maybe that was part of the problem.

Although it is not common knowledge, the United States has carried out intelligence activities since the days of the Revolutionary War, but only since World War II have they been coordinated on a government-wide basis. President Franklin D. Roosevelt appointed New York lawyer and war hero William J. Donovan to become the first coordinator of information, and then, after the United States entered World War II, head of the Office of Strategic Services. The OSS was the predecessor to the CIA and had a mandate to collect and analyze strategic information. After World War II, the OSS was abolished (according to public records), along with many other war agencies, and its functions were transferred to the state and war departments.

President Truman was the first president to officially recognize the need for a postwar, centralized intelligence organization. Truman signed the National Security Act of 1947, which established the CIA. The CIA became responsible for coordinating the nation's intelligence activities and correlating, evaluating, and disseminating intelligence affecting national security.

CIA employees are classified so the public doesn't know who they are—I have probably committed a federal crime by divulging Erika—or how many there are. It is estimated that approximately twenty thousand people work for the CIA, but the actual number and budget are classified. The CIA is sometimes referred to euphemistically as the "Other Government Agency" or "The Agency," particularly when its operations are an open secret— basically a governmental secret that is widely known but one that the agency won't admit to. I am not revealing any classified information by writing about this—at least I hope I'm not.

Within "The Agency" is a wide range of career opportunities. There are positions that most of us would never even think about, such as a CIA truck driver, packer/crater, and warehouseman or warehousewoman. Imagine being secretly classified as a truck driver or crater. There are also more exciting and covert positions like those related to science, technology, weapons, and cybersecurity. There is field agent work, and there are the clandestine service divisions.

I could try to embellish the truth about Erika and write that she worked in one of those glamorous divisions, but I was a Boy Scout, and honesty would have been the first merit badge I would have earned, if they actually had that badge. The truth is, she was somewhere in the middle, working in the support services division as a human resource administrator. This was not exactly Laura Croft material, but her job was still classified and vital in many ways. This is as much information as I can divulge without risking possible imprisonment with a cellmate named Bo or Billy Bob.

The idea of a mini vacation was really appealing, especially since we were at the end of the school year and everybody was looking forward to the summer break. To be honest, I had completely forgotten about the note Brace had left with me before he disappeared. I had meant to tell Erika what happened in school but got distracted. Maybe it was one of those nights when she decided to look so stunning I forgot about the disappearance incident and the yet-to-be-deciphered note.

We were talking about the plans for our upcoming trip when a cell phone rang. I checked my pockets and she checked hers, but neither of our phones was ringing. Instead, it was a phone wedged under the tablecloth of the booth in which we were sitting. I picked up the cell phone, which was an older model—even older than mine. The caller ID read, "California." I answered the phone, but no one was on the line. Only the sound of static.

"Who's calling us now?" Erika joked.

"See for yourself." I handed her the phone.

She listened for a moment. "It's definitely static."

"Funny, I don't know anyone called static, do you?"

Erika quickly snapped back. "Very funny. What I mean is, although it sounds like static, there seems to be a definite pattern repeating, almost as if it's a signal or some kind of code."

She handed the phone back to me, and I listened, "I see what you mean. I do think it is some kind of message and not just white noise."

Kent came over to check on us, so I gave him the cell phone and explained what had happened. "I'll see if I can find out who left the phone here," he obliged.

He returned a few minutes later and said, "I asked the boss, and no one has contacted us looking for a missing cell phone. None of the other waiters or waitresses remember seeing the phone. We carefully clean the tables and booths every night, and no one noticed it before."

"I guess someone must have lost it earlier today," I said.

"That's just it. I checked, and no one sat here today. You are the first people to sit in this booth today. But here is the strange part—I checked the phone, and there don't seem to be any recent calls. In fact, the most recent calls were not even made in the past decade."

"That doesn't make any sense," Erika contemplated.

"Right," Kent replied. That's why I called a buddy of mine at the phone company. According to his records, this phone has not been in use since 2001.

"Weird," intoned Erika.

"I'll send the phone to my buddy," suggested Kent. "Maybe he can do some phone company magic and figure out who owned it."

"Are you sure?" Erika offered. "We don't want you to have to go through too much trouble. I know some people at work who would be able to look at it to save you the effort.

Kent was not bothered. "No trouble at all. You guys know that you're my favorite customers. If anything comes up, I'll let you know next time you're in."

Not wanting to compromise her position and explain how she could get the information, Erika decided to let it go. "Well, Kent, if you're sure it's not too much of an inconvenience," she answered.

He gave a Herman Munster smile. "Not at all."

After finishing dinner, we went back to her place and took a walk around the neighborhood. It was a beautiful summer evening with very low humidity and temperatures in the low seventies, just the way it would be if I could control the weather or move to San Diego. We talked about the trip and our plans for the weekend as we walked among the blooming flowers and trees, which were flourishing from the summer rains.

While walking, Erika kept stopping to pick up pennies. This was not atypical. She would find pennies all the time, and she believed they were signs from her deceased sister. She found them everywhere we went—and they were always tails up. Although I was not a big believer in the psychic world, I began to rethink my position after seeing the frequency in which these coins turned up. They'd be in places where no one would ever expect to find pennies, or any coins for that matter.

After finding eleven pennies, which was an unusual haul even on a good day, I asked to see a couple of them. She handed me four pennies, all of which, I discovered upon examining them, had been minted in 2001.

"That's a little odd," I remarked slightly out of breath as we started our clamber up the last hill of our neighborhood walk.

"What's odd?"

"All of the pennies you handed me are from the year 2001. Were they all tails up when you picked them up?" I questioned.

She looked at the remaining seven pennies in her hand. She gave me a curious, inquisitive look.

I remarked, "Let me take a wild guess. All of those pennies are also from 2001 and you found them tails up as well."

"Yes. That really is weird. There's no way I would randomly find eleven pennies in a row with the same date, all tails up. Maybe my sister is really trying to tell us something."

"It could have just been a coincidence."

"Really," she said disdainfully.

"Sorry, bad joke. The odds of finding eleven coins in a row tails up alone would be over a thousand to one. But to find all of them that way, and for all of them to have been all minted the same year? Well, the odds would have to be something like a gazillion to one."

"Maybe someone is trying to tell us something about an event that happened in 2001. What do you remember about 2001?" she asked.

"Well, Vanilla Ice was thrown in jail after allegedly ripping out some of his wife's hair," I said, trying to add some humor to the conversation.

"Yea, I don't think that's it. Anything else?"

"Well, the human genome sequence was revealed to the world," I bragged, displaying my knowledge of DNA research.

"Interesting," she said. "I remember something about a major earthquake in India that killed over twenty thousand people."

I chimed in, "There were the terrorist attacks on the World Trade Centers that year as well."

She began to realize we might be off track. "That's true. It could also be that the year doesn't refer to an event but something completely different."

"So maybe Apple introducing iTunes in that year has nothing to do with finding these pennies?"

"Exactly," she replied with a slight tone of annoyance in her voice.

We finished our walk in eerie silence. I'm sure we were both thinking the same thing—was there any connection between the eldritch finding of the eleven pennies and a decade-old abandoned cell phone at dinner? Was the year 2001 significant, or did it have a different meaning all together?

Back at her house, I remembered about Brace and was going to mention the incident at school when Erika's mood changed from inquisitive and curious to affectionate and passionate. I've never been one to question good fortune. Once again, I forgot about the prior events at school. I simply got swept up in the moment as we retired for the evening.

Everybody's worried about stopping terrorism.
Well, there's a really easy way: stop participating in it.

—Noam Chomsky

Journal Entry 2

Joseph and 9/11

June 20 was the seniors' physics final exam and last day of
the school year for the students. For some reason unknown
to everyone, the teachers had to come back the next day
to check out. The checkout process took a maximum of
twenty minutes to complete, but there were inevitably
always several teachers who took four or more hours.

Anyway, every student showed up for the final exam
except one—Brace. After the late bell rang, I checked
the school's information system for a home number. There
was a contact number listed for Brace, so I dialed. After
five rings, a raspy voice answered.

I said, "Hello, Mrs. Strider. This is Mr. Cardazia, Brace's
physics teacher. I wanted to let you know that he did not
show up for his senior final exam. I was calling to see if
everything is all right with Brace. Is he feeling ill?"

After a momentary pause, the woman on the other end
said, "Who are you calling about?" I repeated that Brace
was missing his final exam, which had been scheduled
for that day. She cleared her throat and spoke with a
despondent tone. I could visualize salty tears rolling down
the creased skin of her cheeks. "There is no one here with
that name, at least not anymore." There was a brief pause

as she regained her composure and continued. "A long time ago I had a son who went by that nickname, but he used it only around me and my deceased husband. His birth name was Joseph."

"I'm sorry, but I am a little confused. Could you repeat that?" I asked.

"Mr. Cardazia, is this some kind of a sick joke?" I knew that some of the seniors considered my final exam to be too easy—almost a joke—but I was boggled by her response.

I tried to remain focused. "I am sorry to surprise you like this, and Brace—I mean Joseph—is going to pass the class even without taking the final exam. I thought you should know about his absence from school and the fact that he missed his exam."

This time there was an even longer period of silence and then she blurted out, "How did you get this number, and why did you really call me?"

"I looked in the school records for your phone number. As to the main purpose of my call, Brace has been acting strangely recently, and when he missed the final exam, I thought I should call and let you know. I know Brace is a loner, but recently he seems to be more distant than usual."

Another very awkward, long moment of silence followed. As I sat dumbfounded, I started to get that gothic creepy feeling that something was wrong. It's the sensation you get when you're watching a horror movie and the macabre music starts playing just before someone dies.

"I don't think you understand, Mr. Cardazia," she sternly replied.

There are many things I don't understand in this world, like why terrorists murder people in the name of heaven and why we could send a man to the moon but could never develop a good instant coffee, but missing school and a final exam seemed cut and dried to me. "Mrs. Strider, I really do seem a little lost here. I know I probably sound a little stupefied, but could you please elaborate for me?"

She started to speak and got choked up again, "Mr. Cardazia, Joseph died ten years ago along with his father."

A number of thoughts and antic feelings flooded my mind. When I began to clear my head, I started to say that Joseph was a senior in my physics class and I had known him for the past year, but she cut me off. "Ten years ago we lived in Cape Cod, Massachusetts. Brace and his father were passengers on the United Airlines Flight one seventy-five to Los Angeles on September eleven, two thousand one."

All I could think was, *How could that be?* But she continued. "My husband, Alexander, was offered a promotion in his company, but it required him to relocate to Los Angeles, California. We were considering the offer and moving to Bell, California. Alexander wanted to be sure it was the right decision for us. He wanted Joseph to see the area before making a final decision. I couldn't make this trip with them; besides, I had already been to California with Alexander several times looking at schools and neighborhoods. Joseph had always dreamed of visiting Disneyland. Alexander thought it would be a good opportunity to surprise him, just in case he turned down the job offer." Her voice began to once again crack and trail off.

There are moments in life, thankfully rare, when someone or some media outlet informs you that something quite shocking, bizarre, and seemingly impossible has happened. At that point you don't know what to think or how to react. I can only imagine what most people were thinking and feeling on November 22, 1963, around 12:30 p.m., when they heard the news of the assassination of President John F. Kennedy. *Camelot had fallen.* For me, this was one of those times.

"I am so sorry, Mrs. Strider. I really can't even imagine what to say." I really couldn't. How could anyone?

"Mr. Cardazia," she sternly stated, "I don't have anything more to say, so please don't call me again." She hung up the phone.

What I was thinking? What the hell was going on? How could her story be true or make any logical sense? Mrs. Strider was claiming Joseph and his father were two of the victims killed in the 9/11 attacks—the same Brace, or Joseph, who was a senior at my school and had been in my physics class this past school year. Unless Brace was a ghost—and I don't recall ever meeting a ghost—I couldn't come up with any explanation.

I recovered momentarily from my miasma of thoughts and remembered what Mr. Jacque had said: "Did you check the security tapes?" Most of the time I resented the Stalag atmosphere of the Castle and the countless cameras, but for once I decided to use them to my advantage. I went down to the cave—that's what Mr. Holmes called it—to look at the videotapes.

Mr. Holmes was the head security officer at the school. His parents were huge Sherlock Holmes fans, so much so that they legally changed their name from Jackson to Holmes shortly after they married. They'd had only one child before they died in an automobile accident. Of course, they named him Sherlock. I'm not sure if it was a blessing or a curse to be named after a fictional character.

"S," I said as I walked into the cave. (I called Sherlock *S*). He was monitoring all the cameras. The cave was nothing more than a small basement office littered with all kinds of high-tech security surveillance and listening devices. S had at his disposal an arsenal of equipment that would have made the fictitious, quirky, but interesting MI6 Bond character, Q, very envious. The school might not have had the money to pay its staff a competitive salary, but it spared no expense when it came to security and monitoring devices.

"M!" he said, using the name he always did when we talked. I sometimes thought we were trapped in a bad James Bond sequel movie (because there were no bad James Bond movies—at least up until Roger Moore left). "What can I do for you?"

"I was wondering if I could see some video footage taken outside my classroom yesterday between 2:25 p.m. and 2:35 p.m."

"Did you get her approval?" he asked.

"Oh, you mean Ms. Addanc. Yes, she was fine with it." Ms. Addanc was our head mistress.

He gave me a dubious look but started fishing through the digital video chip.

"I know it's here somewhere because I just had it out a minute ago. Ms. Addanc's office called looking for the same chip. Ah, yes, here it is. I didn't get a chance to send it to her office yet, so let's take a quick peek before I send it."

He plugged the chip into his security screen, and we began scrutinizing the tape.

We saw Mr. Jacque sweeping and mopping the floors as he usually did. An occasional student walked by, but there was no sign of Brace. The footage ended, and there had been no visual sign of Brace entering or leaving my classroom. There was only a slight hint of a barely perceptible image that might—or might not—have been Brace. It appeared I was the only one able to see this possible specter in person.

"Maybe I can help," suggested S. "Are we looking for something in particular?"

"No, I was just curious about something. Are you positive these chips were not substituted or tampered with in any way?"

"Of course not! Nobody but me would have that access or that authority," he said indignantly.

"I'm sorry, S, but I needed to double check on something. Thanks. You have been a great help." I decided to leave before I insulted him any further.

As improbable as this story was beginning to seem (the story Brace's mom told me and Brace's apparent near invisibility in video cameras), I decided to follow up and see where it would lead me. I turned on my computer and looked for any information about the 9/11 attacks. The ages of the victims on those forsaken flights ranged from two to eighty-five, with a number of unknown ages.

Of course, there were no passengers listed under the last name Strider. What was I even thinking? Brace's student information card claimed he was born in 1993, which would have made him eight years old at that time. There was only one child on the flights—a girl—who had been eight years old. Additionally, there was only one male child from Massachusetts, and he had been two years old. It was possible, but highly unlikely, that Brace and his father were among the unknowns.

Okay, maybe I was crazy for even thinking about the possibility that what Mrs. Strider had told me was true. The story about Joseph being Brace and being killed in the 9/11 attacks couldn't possibly be true. At least that's what I told myself. Still, there was no record of Brace on any of the ill-fated flights. Yet, his mother would have no reason for making up this story. Why would she? What possible motive could she have for concocting such a horrific story? On the other hand, if the events were true, who was the senior in my physics class whom I had known for the past year as Brace Strider?

What should I do? What should anyone do? I didn't really know what to do, but for some reason, and I don't know why, I decided to start to keep a journal—a small diary of the events that had begun to transpire. I would keep a log of the events just in case more weird and unexplained things happened. If nothing else, I joked to myself that maybe I would have some material to transform into an apocryphal story someday.

I still had some time before the end of the school day and school year, so I decided to see if I could link together any of the information I had read. Only two flights left Massachusetts that day, flight AA 11 and UA 175. Of those two, only flight UA 175, which crashed into the South Tower, had children aboard. Maybe the fact that the passenger list did not include the last name Strider could be explained. Maybe Mr. Strider had used a different last name, a pseudonym. Or perhaps Mrs. Strider kept her maiden name, and Brace used it instead.

However, I couldn't explain the lack of corresponding ages of the children on board. Unless Brace was one of the unknowns or had aged at a different rate than normal people. Those seemed to be the only two explanations that might hypothetically explain Mrs. Striders' story. However, even if Brace was one of the unknowns or had aged at a supersonic rate, how could he have died back then and still be in my physics class all year until the final exam? Of course, the ghost conspiracy theory was beginning to look better and better.

The school bell was about to ring—one of my favorite bell rings of the entire year. Okay, I'll divulge a little secret. No matter how much a teacher likes children and teaching, no matter how many teacher-of-the-year awards adorn a teacher's desk, there isn't a teacher or student who doesn't like summer vacation. Trust me. As much as I miss hearing the wide gamut of teenage complaints about school and life, as much as I love hearing "I am sorry. I wasn't listening. Could you repeat that?" (countless times), I could gladly wait until next September to once again hear those cherished words.

Before leaving for the summer break, I wanted to say good-bye to Mr. Jacque. I had not seen him since the day Brace left me the note. I checked all of his favorite hallways. I even checked one of his preferred hiding places where I had caught him one afternoon reading *Gone with the Wind*, his favorite book. After a fruitless search, I stopped down to the boiler room.

I asked his boss and longtime friend, Mr. Jenkins, if he had seen him. He told me abrasively that Mr. Jacque had not been to work for the last couple of days. He had not called in sick, just hadn't shown up for work. Mr. Jenkins had tried calling Mr. Jacque's home phone number, but discovered it had been disconnected. He called the apartment building manager but was told no one had rented that particular apartment for at least a decade. It was almost as if Mr. Jacque had completely disappeared or had never existed in the first place.

"Mr. Jenkins, didn't you find this story a little fishy?" I inquired.

"Of course I did! He was a friend of mine, you know. That's why I went over to his apartment building. According to our records, he lived in apartment number eleven. There was a buzzer security system, and luckily one of the tenants was just entering the building when I arrived. I intended to knock on his apartment door and see if anyone would answer."

"I bet you knocked and no one answered, right?"

"No, it was a little more complicated than that," he said. He seemed a little confused but, after composing himself, he continued, "I couldn't find his apartment."

"So, the apartments were numbered, but it was hard to know which apartment was apartment eleven?"

"No, I mean … yes, that's just it. I'm no fool, you know. All the apartments were clearly labeled from one to twenty except for one. There was an apartment ten and an apartment twelve. Hell, there was even an apartment thirteen. But there was no apartment eleven on any of the floors!"

A lot of rock bands are truly a
legend in their own minds.

—David Lee Roth

Journey Entry 3

Band on the Run

It was several days after the end of the school year and a
few days before my trip to DC with Erika. Our band was
playing at Who Knew on Saturday night. Who Knew
was a small bar and popular restaurant located in a New
Jersey shore town called Margate, originally known as
South Atlantic City. Margate was positioned just a few
miles south from its more famous and world-renowned
sister city, Atlantic City, hence the original name.

This small town has a population of approximately six
thousand residents. Margate is the kind of town where
bars open until 5:00 a.m., streets flood with a drop of
rain, there are twenty-five-mile-per-hour speed limits, and
there's an army of cops waiting to welcome visitors and
enforce that statue. However, there were at least three
donut shops located within the center of town—a Dunkin
Donuts, a Krispy Kreme, and a local donut shop, which
was rumored among the local enforcement personnel to
have the most delicious product. Obviously, major crime
wasn't an issue for the town. Even with all those small-
town "charms," Margate was still a popular affluent shore
community, and people flocked there in droves during the
summer months.

Margate's most famous and longest-standing resident wasn't even a person; rather it was a pachyderm. Lucy the Elephant, six stories tall, had been constructed of wood and tin sheeting in 1882 by James V. Lafferty. She had been built in an effort to sell real estate and attract tourism to the area. Lafferty was the first-known person to come up with the idea of an animal-shaped building. Lucy is still the oldest example of zoomorphic architecture existing today, at least according to a random *Jeopardy* question. The first was built in Margate. This structure, whose original name was "Elephant Bazaar," was dubbed "Lucy the Elephant" in 1900. She still stands sixty-five feet high, sixty feet long, and eighteen feet wide. She weighs about ninety tons and is made of nearly one million pieces of wood.

Over the years, Lucy has served as a restaurant, a business office, a cottage, and a tavern, which closed as a result of Prohibition. A popular rumor is that Marco Reginelli, a New Jersey mobster and under boss of the Bruno crime family, once used Lucy as a hideout and even conducted mob business with other gangsters in what is now the first-floor gift shop. Another popular story is that Lucy once was a hotel for the rich and connected, but neither story has ever been confirmed or denied.

What is known for sure is that Reginelli eventually extended his influence to the resort area of Atlantic City. In the late 1940s, he built the 500 Club, a nightclub, in Atlantic City. In the early 1950s, the 500 Club frequently presented singer Dean Martin, who first performed with comedian and future partner, Jerry Lewis, at the club.

Lucy had fallen into disrepair by the late 1960s and was scheduled for demolition. However, instead, she was moved several blocks from her original location and refurbished as a result of a "Save Lucy" campaign in 1970. Lucy even received a designation as a National Historic Landmark in 1976.

On my first date with Erika, I took her to see Lucy because she had mentioned the night we met that she had never seen her and always wanted to "meet her." So naturally, I took Erika to" meet her" after dinner.

Who Knew was located a block from Lucy and the beach, away from most of the other bars in the town. The joint had an interesting dichotomy. The upstairs was an expensive restaurant known for its excellent selection of fresh seafood and steaks, while the downstairs, truth be told, was a classic dive. On a typical weekend night, it could literally take a half hour to wedge one's way in between the endless waves of people to travel from the front to the rear of the bar. The walls were fashioned from old oak that still bore the names of former patrons carved into it. The actual floor, rarely seen, was covered with shards of broken glass, filth, and muck. And just for a touch of ambiance, the men's room was equipped with a trough in lieu of the customary urinals found in most establishments. The smell was putrid.

In short, it was the kind of bar people first visited in college and instantly and inexplicably fell in love with. Maybe it was because the essence of Who Knew wasn't about glitter and glitz; rather, it was about substance and having fun. Because the bar was so diminutive and packed, the atmosphere was very informal, and patrons had no choice but to meet and talk to people. It was standard practice to dance and sing with strangers who became very friendly before long.

On nights when there were no bands playing, Who Knew featured a DJ who would play songs patrons would not typically expect to hear at a bar. Theme songs from old TV shows like *The Jeffersons*, *Gilligan's Island*, and cartoons like *George of the Jungle* were a staple of the regular set of songs. All of these factors—the packed-in crowd, unusual songs, and old-style look—contributed to the fact that its clientele was faithful.

Our band, called According to Her, was playing Saturday night. We band members had met during our freshman year at Penn State, except for Austin Rattler. I was born in Camden, New Jersey, and grew up in Cherry Hill, New Jersey. Although not called Cherry Hill until 1961, it was originally settled by the Lenni-Lenape Native Americans who coexisted peacefully with the first settlers from England and the Quaker followers of William Penn who arrived in the late seventeenth century. I guess I remember a little too much of US History II. And they say our educational system is falling.

Steve Knight had been my best friend throughout childhood, and we both attended Penn State University. He was our lead guitar player. Steve was very talented and probably could have had a career in music if he had decided not to attend law school at the University of Pennsylvania. Although the music world might have lost out, it was convenient having free legal advice when I needed it. He was married to Jenny, and they had two children, a boy and girl—just above the national average of 1.83 children per household.

Jackson Hewitt was our drummer by night and our accountant by day. With his name, he'd have had to grow up to be an accountant, right? He loved working with numbers and was excellent with mathematical equations. It was unfortunate he didn't like to gamble, because he probably would have cleaned up in Atlantic City. I did my best to try and get him interested in the casinos, but to no avail. Jackson, with his soon-to-be-ex-wife, Janice, had three daughters.

Prentice Styles, our keyboard and piano player, was the most intelligent member of our group. He would never tell us his actual IQ, but I did catch him sneaking out one night to attend a Mensa meeting. Prentice was considered to be a virtuoso pianist, having played from the age of five. Instead of pursuing a musical career, he decided he preferred saving lives more, and after attending John Hopkins University and Medical School for what seemed like twenty years, he became a surgeon.

Austin Rattler was our bass player and oldest member. He had been born and raised in Amarillo, Texas. Austin was divorced and had a son. After college, Austin became a bail enforcement agent, otherwise known as fugitive recovery agent or, sometimes, "skiptracer." (This last name was my personal favorite). A little known fact (because that's what I do as a teacher—provide info) is that bounty hunting is legal in only two nations: the United States and the Republic of the Philippines. Other countries do not recognize the concept of bounty hunting and consider it kidnapping, and therefore a criminal act. They use law enforcement agencies to recover fugitives accused of crimes. Go figure.

Our band met Austin during our senior year spring break trip to South Padre Island, Texas. After dinner during our first night on the island, we went to The Casablanca Lounge. This "gin joint" was set up to look like Rick's Café. It was a piano bar with an authentic 1930s Pleyel piano. The bar was filled with curved arches, a sculpted bar, balconies, balustrades, and beaded and stenciled brass lighting fixtures that cast luminous shadows, especially of the potted plants, on white walls.

We had been there for only a few minutes when a dispute arose between five rednecks and a guy who looked like a cowboy. Before I knew what was happening, Steve and Jackson jumped into the fray, so Prentice and I followed. For whatever reason, these Southern clodhoppers didn't like cowboys and had started a fight with Austin.

Austin was very grateful for our assistance. Even though he turned out to be a University of Pittsburgh Panther, a longtime rival of our beloved Nittany Lions, we all became friends, and he became the last of the original members of our band after our bass player left.

So there you have it—a band made up of a teacher, a lawyer, a bounty hunter, an accountant, and a surgeon! Not quite The Fab Four, partly because we were five and partly because we didn't have the following of the Beatles, but we did have our own little set of groupies. Our performances weren't exactly like Tom Jones concerts with women throwing their underwear on stage at us. But there was always hope.

We were nearing the end of our first set of Bruce Springsteen music (since this was New Jersey, we had to play some Bruce, especially at the Jersey Shore) when I noticed a doppelganger of Brace sitting at a table behind Erika. Since I didn't believe in ghosts—at least not at this point—I was somewhat aghast. Sitting with Brace was an older gentleman in a grey flannel suit. Something about this gentleman exuded familiarity, wisdom, and ancientness. I had an eerie feeling that I had met this older gentleman before.

The shock of seeing Brace was mind blowing. The mystery guy he was sitting with was a little older, actually a lot older, than our usual crowd. It wasn't as if our groupies and fans were eighteen and nineteen years old, but this guy looked ancient—like Methuselah—and seemed out of place.

As soon as the song ended, I jumped off stage just like a rock star, reminiscent of Tom Cruise in *Rock of Ages*, and ran over to the table. Erika stopped me and said, "Good set, but do you guys have to do three Bruce songs? Wouldn't two be enough?" She had never been a big Bruce fan.

"I'll take it up with the guys," I promised. She gave me a wink, which always paled in comparison to one of her smiles.

"Erika, did you notice the people sitting at the table directly behind you?"

"Yes. There were two young couples sitting there. Why?"

43

Once again I was having one of those eldritch moments in which I see things that no one else seems to see. "Just curious. I'll be right back," I said.

She looked slightly surprised. "Off to meet your other girlfriend?"

Sarcastically, I replied, "Yeah, you know me. I'm a player."

I waited for a laugh or even a "that's corny" line, but I just got a suspicious look, so I continued explaining. "Actually, I thought I saw someone I needed to talk to, but he seems to have left. It's a strange story; in fact, it really doesn't even make sense to me, so you'll probably think I'm off my rocker. I'll be back in few minutes. I'll try to explain, even though I'm not really sure about it myself. I promise."

She rolled her eyes and gave me one of those "do what you have to do" looks. She smirked. "Say hi to what's-her-name for me."

"Seriously, you're the only girl for me, and always have been ever since I met you," I said in a staid tone. I meant that. I would never cheat on her. She had been in an unfortunate marriage and had been unfairly treated. I had too much respect for her to ever hurt her. She deserved better than what she got the first time around. Maybe I wasn't blessed with an overabundance of admirable traits, but loyalty and honesty were two that I did have. In the Boy Scouts, I definitely would have earned those two badges before anyone else in my troop, assuming they existed.

I gave her a quick kiss and ran out the door. There was a sudden chill in the air, and it was just starting to rain, which meant it wouldn't be long before the streets flooded. I shivered a bit and looked around. I saw Brace and the older gentleman heading toward the beach. I yelled at them to stop, but they ignored my pleas and kept walking.

Margate, the South Jersey shore, can be very tranquil at night. As a kid, I would listen to the waves gently crash against the shoreline and pretend that, when I grew up, I would become a secret agent and save the world. Instead, I became a high school science teacher, which I guess would be kind of close in a bizarre, backward universe. The rhythmic undulation of the waves would work better than warm milk and tryptophan, and in no time, I would be dreaming of my covert double-oh missions, saving the world, getting the girl, and … Well, I guess the rest is self-explanatory.

The Margate beaches and the people who visit them are nothing like the way they are portrayed on MTV's *Jersey Shore*. There isn't the drama and fighting that the less-than-critically acclaimed, mind-numbing show portrays. People here actually have real names—not like Snookie. What kind of name is that anyway? I have never ever met anyone named The Situation. I've met only real people who enjoy beautiful beaches in the summertime.

Eventually reaching the beach, I ran onto the sand, quickly scanning the shoreline for Brace and his mysterious friend. There was no one on the nighttime-cooled sand but me. There were two sets of footprints, which I assumed were theirs but could have been made by anyone. The footprints were barely visible and led toward the water. The slight summer breeze had already begun to erase them, blowing light crystals of sand that partially covered parts of their imprints, which radiated down the shoreline.

The possibilities began to formulate in my mind. First, maybe I was crazy and had imagined seeing Brace and the unknown familiar guy and all the weird things that had happened lately. This craziness was a distinct possibility. Second, Brace and his companion could have run really fast down the beach beyond the scope of my vision. This was unlikely, unless they were bionic, especially for the older man, and this option represented another whole set of problems I wasn't ready to deal with. Lastly, they could have walked straight into the ocean and disappeared. Also very unlikely.

Taking off my sneakers and rolling up my jeans, I slowly walked ankle deep into the Atlantic Ocean. The rough waves seemed to lessen. They became gentler as the water began to warm and assuage my heightened state of awareness. My vision began to burn and flash with vibrant colors as I blinked with increasing frequency. Eventually the conflagrant eased, and I was able to see clearly into the ocean.

The phrase "seeing is believing" ran through my mind. I vaguely remembered the words having some biblical reference, but I wasn't really a religious man. As I looked into the water, I saw a spectacular holographic image of a neoteric city surrounded by a giant gate made of gold and emeralds. I didn't recognize anything I was seeing. I was, however, able to rule out any place on Earth that I had seen. The vision was ephemeral. Suddenly, a large wave came out of nowhere and knocked me down. I coughed and spit out a modicum of salty water.

My walk back to the bar was short in distance, but seemed endless. I was wet from being knocked over by the wave and confused by the disappearance of Brace and his companion. But the worst part was going to be trying to explain what happened without seeming completely out of my mind. When I got back to the club, Erika was talking with Steve and Jenny. Erika turned toward me and said, "Quick date, huh?"

"Well, you know me. I like to cut to the chase." (This phrase originated from early silent films. It was a favorite catchphrase of, and thought to have been coined by, Hal Roach Sr. Isn't Wikipedia great?) "Can I talk to you alone for a minute?" I asked her.

She looked at me with bewilderment. "I just realized you are wet. Did you go swimming without your bathing suit? Even the Polar Bear club doesn't start until the wintertime, and I believe they wear bathing suits."

"You know, it seems like my corny jokes are starting to rub off on you."

A look of concern came over her face, and not just because she realized that my corniness might be rubbing off on her. "Michael, what is going on? Did something happen out there?"

"Not exactly. Let's talk outside."

As we walked outside, I began to tell her the story. She was a good listener, as most good spies are. I began by telling her about Brace and the cryptic note he left behind—and my inability to decipher it. I recounted my phone conversion with Brace's mother in which she claimed her son died on one of the planes during the 9/11 tragedy. I told her that I had seen Brace and an older gentleman sitting behind her after our performance instead of the young couples she saw sitting there. I heroically described the chase scene during which I had bravely followed the elusive pair onto the beach before they mysteriously disappeared. I described the vision of a foreign city appearing to me in the middle of the Atlantic Ocean. Conveniently, I left out the part about being knocked over by a wave and choking on seawater; it didn't seem to fit the heroic story. I just basically spilled my guts. (Believe it or not, I really don't know where that expression comes from.)

She thought for a moment. "Michael, there were four people sitting behind me, two young couples. There wasn't a teenager and an older guy sitting there. I know you have a really creative mind and have an overactive imagination at times, but I don't know why you think you saw them or why Brace's mom claimed he died years ago. And I don't understand your vision of an imaginary city floating in the ocean. Are you all right? You're not having a breakdown, are you?"

Another one of Erika's best qualities was her ability to not beat around the bush. (This is another great phrase, which actually evolved from the earlier literal meaning. In bird hunts, some of the participants roused the birds by beating the bushes and catching the quarry in nets when they flew up in alarm.)

"Well, I have considered that possibility along with early dementia sprinkled with jimmies of insanity, but I don't think I imagined those things. Besides, being a science guy," I half-heartily explained as I tried to convince myself, "I have to believe that there has to be a reasonable and verifiable explanation."

She gave me a dubious look along with a smile of reassurance and said, "We'll figure it out together, but your band is about to start the second set, and it would be helpful to have their lead singer with them on stage."

"You're right, as usual," I said. I turned and adroitly darted back to the makeshift stage in the rear.

She gave me an angelic smile as I looked back at her, and soon I was back on stage singing "Monkey Wrench" to the bewilderment of our older fans and the delight of our younger ones. Music has a way of making people forget their worries. Before I knew it, the evening was finished, and we were heading back home.

But I, being poor, have only my dreams;
I have spread my dreams under your feet;
Tread softly because you tread on my dreams.

—W. B. Yeats

Journal Entry 4

Visions and Dreams

It was around two in the morning I think, because I could never remember if I set the time on the VCR/DVD player correctly. (Where's a five-year-old when you need one?) I was home after dropping Erika off at her house. Before I could go to sleep, I had to feed Bachelor, my male cat. He was a black tabby who loved to eat. To say he was a very unusual cat would be an understatement.

Bachelor would eat any kind of human food—cookies, pizza … just about anything. He was actually—and I really believe this—a dog trapped in a cat's body. I could hold him in my arms just like a baby—all his paws up in the air. He would even play fetch. He reminded me of what James T. Kirk said about Mr. Spock in *Star Trek II, The Wrath of Khan*: "Of this I can say of my friend, he was more human than anyone I knew."[1] Okay, big surprise—a science guy who is also a big-time Trekkie. I'm not the kind who dress up as a Klingon or a Star Fleet officer and go to Star Trek conventions, but I did watch—and knew the name of—every original episode. Also, I don't speak

---

[1] *Star Trek II, The Wrath of Khan*. Dir. Nocholas Meyer. Writers Gene Roddenberry, Harve Bennett, Jack Sowards. Paramount Pictures, 1982. Film.

any Klingon. Of my friend, companion, and pet, I can say this: "Bachelor was more dog than any dog I ever knew."

I turned on the TV, ate half a sandwich, and started watching an infomercial. Let's face it, a guy will watch practically anything on TV, especially when it's late and there's something to eat. I was lying on the couch when the phone rang. I answered. The whispery voice was somewhat familiar, but I couldn't quite recognize it: "It is your destiny. It is what you were meant to do." The line disconnected. There is nothing like a weirdo calling in the middle of the night to get you looking forward to the coming day. I made a mental note to start checking the caller ID before answering the phone after midnight.

The next thing I realized was that I was not in my house anymore. I was somewhere in the middle of outer space. I wasn't cold, even though it can get quite chilly, especially at night. After all, the temperature of space is just a few degrees above absolute zero. And I could breathe, or at least the lack of oxygen in space didn't seem to have any effect on me.

Not to intentionally sound like Carl Sagan, but it seems as if there are billions and billions of stars. There was an amazing display of vibrant colors from blue to red. There was a collage of different star types—red giants; super red giants; yellow, white, and red dwarfs; and neutron stars were splattered as far as I could see.

In the background suddenly there appeared a giant hourglass. Instead of sand, it was filled with small glass spheres. There were numbers, which I took to represent years, etched on the glass spheres. The hourglass was right side up, and the marble-like objects were rising upward from the bottom to the top, and not downward as one would expect. The numbers, in reverse order, passed by slowly at first, but began to increase in speed until I could no longer discern them.

While this was occurring, the stars and galactic materials were changing as well. The number of stars and galaxies decreased in correspondence to the dates on the upward-falling marbles. I got a sense that the vastness of space was decreasing exponentially as well. The walls of space began to close in on me, and a very slight feeling of claustrophobia kicked in.

For the most part, I had never suffered from claustrophobia. I could walk into a closest and close the door without anxiety. I could put a blanket over my head, ride Disney's Mission: Space roller coaster in the dark, and could even stand in the middle of a huge crowd. Although I really, really hated being inside a closed MRI machine because it feels like being inside of a coffin. (Not that I have ever been incased in a coffin—at least not yet.) I think that's normal for most people—not liking to be confined in a closed MRI machine or being encased inside a coffin.

The relocation of the marbles inside the hourglass continued for an indeterminate amount of time with the synonymic loss of stars and galaxies. For the first time, I intuitively understood that the Universe—or what was left of it—was becoming rudimentary as it spiraled toward its infancy. Eventually, this process slowed as the last of the marbles reached the top.

The claustrophobic aura left me, and I found myself outside of nothingness peering inside at something. The Universe, which had once been vast and seemingly unlimited, was now condensed into an extremely hot, dense, single point in space. If I hadn't been a scientist, I would have been thinking that the whole experience was pretty cool, a possible idea for a Disney ride or attraction. But since I am a science guy, I wondered if this was my own interpretation of the beginning of our Universe, perhaps the big bang?

I wondered if I was going to meet God himself—or herself. Personally, I had always believed if there was a God, it's just as likely the God would turn out to be a woman and not a man. Actually, it would probably be more likely for God to be a woman and not a man, but I'll save my reasons for another time when it is more relevant.

At some point, the scene dissipated. Disappointed that I hadn't met God, I found myself riding an Amtrak train. The conductor announced next stop—New Carrollton, Maryland, which would be followed by Union Station, Washington DC. The train was only partly full; however, the passengers were a collage of humanoid-like people. The ticket collector guy/girl (I never know what to call them) was collecting and punching holes in the passengers' tickets. The collector walked past me without asking for my ticket, which was good because I didn't have one.

I surveyed my surroundings to get a closer look at the people—or human-like beings—sitting in front of and behind, me. They all appeared to be humanistic except for one genetic variant or mutation. Some of the passengers had an extra appendage or lacked one. I noticed that some of the passengers were missing or had an extra sensory organ—an extra ear or eye, for example. Still others had what could only be described as gill slits on different parts of their bodies.

In addition to their unique features, they all were wearing translucent watches, each with an hourglass image embedded in the center. It looked as if the hourglass was inverted, and the sand was moving upward and not downward, similar to what I had seen in space moments earlier. The bands were made of some type of metallic substance; I didn't recognize the material. They were encrusted with precious jewels that spelled out the letters G-O-T-U.

As I looked toward the front of the coach, I saw Erika standing and talking with some very important-looking people who were dressed to the hilt in full military garb. Erika was dressed in a black jumpsuit with a multitude of pockets and zippers, looking very spyish, reminiscent of Angelina Jolie in the movie *Mr. and Mrs. Smith*. The one exception was that Angelina wore an evening gown, and Erika wore a black jumpsuit, but that's not the point. Now most people would be thinking, *What the hell is going on?* But I was actually thinking, *She looks really good as a spy.*

I walked up to her and tried to speak with her, but she didn't notice me because, as I was beginning to understand, these were all dream sequences. I was not really there. I had that feeling we sometimes have when we are in the middle of a dream, and we get the sense maybe the experience isn't real. We rarely stop to think it may be a dream. We go along with it unless it's a nightmare, and we do all we can to wake up. Well, I was stuck in the middle of it, and it didn't seem like a phantasm. Besides, like most dreams, it seemed vividly real.

Erika was holding some kind of chart or map and pointing at the center. The document appeared blurry, so I guess my dream didn't want me to know what it was. The military men nodded in apparent agreement and handed Erika a folder with the words *Highly Confidential* printed in large letters on the front. (Great, my dream let me see that part).

The conductor announced, "We have now arrived at Union Station. Please detrain carefully. Have a great day, and thanks again for riding with us." The train smoothly rolled to a stop.

I found myself standing in the center of Union Station. A giant screen appeared and started displaying historical facts about Union Station. Following is a small historical bonanza of Union Station facts.

On October 27, 1907, Union Station officially opened its doors at 6:50 a.m., when the Baltimore and Ohio Pittsburgh express train arrived.

In 1909, President Taft became the first president to use the presidential suite, which was built so that the president and other very important people could enter the train apart from the general population. (It must have been an awfully big suite.)

Over the years, many famous dignitaries were officially greeted in these rooms, including King George VI and Queen Elizabeth II of England, King Albert of the

Belgians, King Prajadipok of Siam, Queen Marie of Rumania, and King Hassan II of Morocco.

A public/private partnership funded the $160-million restoration of the station per legislation enacted by Congress in 1981 to preserve Union Station as a national treasure. At the time, it was the largest, most complex public or private restoration project ever attempted in the United States.

Geez, even in my dreams I provided interesting, but otherwise useless, trivia. I guess that's why I always wanted to be a contestant on *Jeopardy* or *Who Wants to be a Millionaire?* One would think that the giant screen would provide some useful information—like, what is the dream about or what does this all mean? No, that would be too much to ask, even in my own dream. It seemed I just couldn't get away from the minutia of facts, even in my fantasies. The screen stopped broadcasting, and I was walking somewhere on the streets of Washington DC.

This was to be my last stop before I woke up. How did I know this at the time? Well, as I was walking, I saw a person. Though I couldn't see the face, the individual was carrying a sign that read: Last stop before you wake up. I guess dreams do sometimes provide useful info after all. I continued to walk, and I stopped at 511 Tenth Street, in front of Ford's Theatre. This was the scene of the fatal shooting of Abraham Lincoln.

I walked inside the theater and was politely greeted by a gentleman dressed in a park ranger uniform. He motioned me to follow him. This seemed to be the part of the dream in which people could actually finally see me. He said, "Welcome, Mr. Cardazia. Follow me."

"Excuse me, Mr. Park Ranger. This question may be a waste of time, but can you tell me what any of this is about?"

He smiled and said, "My name is Turbo, and I cannot answer all of your questions, only some—maybe. However, I can tell you that this isn't a waste of your time."

So, he could hear me also. That seemed to be promising.

"Turbo, like the charger and tax?" I joked. He apathetically nodded yes, so I continued. "What do you mean this isn't a waste of time?"

Turbo was tall, well over six feet. He appeared to be a lugubrious and gloomy character. One eye was cloudy, and his hair was thin and scanty. It clung damply to his long and narrow forehead. His movements seemed almost shambling. He spoke with a deep, resonating voice. The park ranger accoutrements—hat, badges, tie, shoes, and uniform—seemed to be foreign to him, and I got the feeling that his normal attire was much different and that his present outfit was for my benefit.

It struck me that maybe Turbo had a dry sense of humor, perhaps even drier than mine. In a way he reminded me of Lurch, the butler from *The Addams Family*. I expected him to say "You rang?" or "Uh-h-h-h-h-h-h-h-uh!"

Instead, he explained, "It is true that this is a dream, and dreams are not exactly reality. However, sometimes our dreams actually provide information, albeit in a symbolic language. In some cases, although it is not the norm, a few select individuals can dream of the possible outcomes of undetermined future events."

"So, you are saying the events in my dreams are, in a symbolic way, clues to what is going on here, and that I am physic?"

Turbo retorted, "As to the question of you being able to predict the future, I cannot say. I myself am not physic, but I am saying that some, but not all, of the events in your dream are pieces of information that are part of the answers you are seeking to the questions you have."

We then entered a room that resembled a small museum. On display were artifacts related to the theater and the assassination of Abraham Lincoln. Hanging on the wall was an enormous picture, underneath which was the following inscription:

> What is now Ford's Theater was originally a house of worship, constructed in 1833 as the second meeting house of the First Baptist Church of Washington, with Obadiah Bruen Brown as the pastor. In 1861, our founder John T. Ford bought the former church and renovated it into a theatre and called it Ford's Athenaeum which was destroyed by fire in 1862. It was rebuilt the following year and when the new Ford's Theatre reopened in August

1863, it had seating for 2,400 persons and was dubbed a "magnificent new thespian temple."

I will leave no stone unturned: The origin of this phrase is not important unless you are into Greek mythology. My dream left no trivial fact or bit of information out of the story.

Turbo motioned for me to follow him, and as I did, we walked to a position directly across the street from the theater. (Isn't the transportation system great in a dream sequence? You get from here to there in a blink. No waiting in lines or going thru TSA inspections.)

We were now inside 516 10th Street, the Petersen House, which is the nineteenth-century, federal-style row home where, on the morning of April 15, 1865, President Abraham Lincoln died after being shot the previous evening at Ford's Theater. The house was built in 1849 by William A. Petersen, who was a German tailor. (Again, not important).

As we walked into the back bedroom where Lincoln died at 7:22 a.m., I looked into a mirror in the hallway and didn't see my reflection—at least not my current one. Instead, I saw a much younger version of myself—a nineteen-year-old man, the age I was when my father passed away. Turbo and I entered the bedroom, and I noticed a silhouetted, doppelganger glowing image of a very tall man lying on the bed.

Turbo began to spit out a few more facts, almost sounding like a computer with no emotion: "In 1896, the government bought this house for $30,000." (The price was not necessary, but he told me anyway.) "As of 1933, the National Park Service has maintained it as a historical museum, recreating the scene at the time of Lincoln's death. The bed that Mr. Lincoln occupied and other items from the bedroom were sold to Chicago confectioner Charles F. Gunther and are now owned by the Chicago History Museum." (Again more information than I needed, especially since it was my dream.) "Similar pieces have taken their places." He paused, and the inflection of his voice changed, became more passionate. "This is the important part." (He must have been reading my mind.) "The bloodstained pillow and pillowcases *are* the original ones used by Lincoln himself, the morning he transmuted."

I closed my eyes for a second and made a mental note to remember that piece of information because it was a possible clue—or at least part of a clue—that might help me unravel what all of these odd experiences meant.

"Turbo, does Mr. Lincoln's death have anything to do with me or the strange things I have been seeing and experiencing lately? And, what do you mean *transmuted*— don't you mean died?"

Before giving me an answer or another riddle, Turbo vanished, and I was left standing in the room alone. The last thing I noticed was that now there was a picture hanging above Lincoln's smallish bed. It was a picture of a physician. The name J. G. Sotos was engraved on a brass plaque on the bottom of the frame.

The next thing I was aware of was that Bachelor, my cat who is really a dog trapped in a cat's body, was meowing for his breakfast. It must be 5:00 a.m. already, and he hadn't eaten in an hour or two. I thought to myself, *I really have to stop watching infomercials late at night and eating just before bed.*

The only way of catching a train I have ever discovered
is to miss the train before.

—Gilbert K. Chesterton

Journey Entry 5

Train Keep a Rollin'

It was the morning of July 1, and Erika and I were taking
the Amtrak train from Philadelphia to Washington
DC. Although not quite as historic as Union Station in
Washington, Philadelphia's 30th Street Station does have
some interesting history worth mentioning. Here it goes:
30th Street Station opened in 1933. It is the main railroad
station in Philadelphia, Pennsylvania, and a major stop
on Amtrak's Northeast and Keystone corridors. In 2010,
approximately 3.8 million passengers used 30th Street,
making it the third busiest Amtrak station in the system.
In fact, the station is listed in the National Registry of
Historic Places.

The station design was influenced by the Northeast
Corridor electrification, which allowed the tracks to pass
beneath the main body of the station without exposing
the passengers to the soot that was produced by the early
steam engines. The station itself also included a number
of innovative features, including a pneumatic tube system,
an electronic intercom, and a reinforced roof with space
for the landing of small aircraft. I guess this somehow
comes in handy, with all the planes landing at the train
station.

The 30th Street Station was even a movie star of sorts when it was featured in the opening scene of a very popular 1985 thriller, *Witness,* starring a post–*Star Wars* Harrison Ford and pre–*Top Gun* Kelly McGillis. I think that was her big start in the movies, but that's not important.

Erika picked me up around 7:00 a.m. since the train was to leave at 8:45 a.m. Because she had to work over the next few days, her travel day was her only non-work day and her only chance to enjoy the sites. We decided to get to Washington early and make the most of the day together. She offered to drive to the station, and I gladly accepted. (As I wrote earlier, I don't enjoy driving on certain large roads, as they create anxiety for me. Maybe the reasons will become clear to me later on.)

During the ride, I sat very quietly, which is unusual for me.

"Honey, what's wrong? You have that look again." Her voice was most compassionate.

"It's stupid," I lamented, but continued explaining. "The feeling that I get sometimes on certain bridges and highways. I don't know if it's a panic attack or anxiety. It bothers me because I know it is totally illogical, and there is no reasonable explanation behind it. And the worst part is that sometimes I'm afraid it will never go away and will always be a part of me. That makes me feel so weak—like a coward!"

She looked at me with sympathetic eyes. "I don't think it makes you weak or has anything to do with being a coward. It's just a part of you, like the feeling that you have always belonged somewhere else. Your therapist said it might never completely go away. Maybe it's just something you have to accept."

And there it was—the word *accept*. It was the one concept I had struggled with most in life, and one we both grappled with. Acceptance. Maybe it was one of things that had bound us together so closely and so quickly. In our own ways, we each struggled with that aspect of life. I knew that she understood acceptance (or the lack of it) every bit as much as I did.

Suddenly, I didn't want to talk about it anymore. Like most people, I tended to shy away from things that hit home the hardest, so I quickly changed the subject. I decided to mention the research I had done the night before regarding the number eleven. "Anyway, did you know that the number eleven is a very interesting number?" I wanted to ignore the kidding, for both our sakes. Well, mainly my sake.

"Nice redirect," she said with a wink. "I guess I'm not the only one who doesn't want to talk about certain sensitive topics." She chuckled. "Yes, it's a cool number. We were both born on that day so it must be phenomenal, maybe even epic."

I tried not to laugh too hard. "Right, and you remember on our last walk we found exactly eleven pennies, which were all minted in two thousand one."

As if she was reading my mind, she said, "Michael, what are you really thinking about?"

I figured it was best to get to the point, "Do you remember Mr. Jacque? You met him at one of the Back-to-School nights."

"Of course! He was making sure the floors were squeaky clean for the parents. We talked briefly, and he seemed very nice. I do recall thinking there was something about him that seemed unusual, maybe even out of place. I noticed he had a beautiful pocket watch. He proudly showed the watch to me and claimed it was from the Civil War."

"Yes, he showed me the same watch also. It really is an exquisite piece. I asked him about it, and he told me a similar story. Anyway, he disappeared from school on the last day, and no one knows where he is."

Erika seemed surprised. "He just quit his job?"

I could offer no explanation. "No, he just disappeared as if he never really existed." I recounted what I had discovered. "There appears to be no record of him. His boss tried to call and went to his last known address to find that his apartment number didn't exist anywhere in the building."

"Did Mr. Jenkins ask the apartment supervisor why there was no apartment eleven but there was a ten and a twelve?" she probed.

"You know, I never thought to ask that question," I said wryly. "I don't have your spy instincts. But don't you think that is very weird?"

"*Ghostbusters* weird," she said, and we both laughed.

She smiled. "You were about to enlighten me about the great number eleven?"

"Right, I almost forgot." (At this point I figured she probably regretted asking.) "It is considered a master number—a double-digit number of the same number, like twenty-two, thirty-three, forty-four, and so on. In numerology, the significance of the number—one in the case of eleven—is doubled."

"So?" she asked sounding completely disinterested.

"No, that's not the important part. I just figured I would throw that in."

She gave me one of those get-to-the-point looks, so I did. "Eleven is also known as the psychic's number. It's the most intuitive of all numbers and represents illumination and deep insight." I could tell I had begun to grab her interest and decided not to waste the opportunity to ramble on. Besides, she believed in the psychic world a lot more than I did.

"Go on, Sherlock, what other nuggets did you uncover?" she prompted me.

"In numerology, elevens tend to be very sensitive, charismatic, and inspirational."

"Yes, you can be a little sensitive at times, and I, of course, can be quite charismatic," she said playfully.

"The number also acts as a channel for information between the higher and the lower realms of spiritualism.

Ideas, thoughts, understanding and insight come to elevens without their having to go through a rational thought process," I continued.

"You might have a point. I'm not sure anyone would accuse you of being the most logical or rational," she playfully added.

"Touché. Anyway, in order to find fulfillment and happiness, elevens have to focus on bigger goals beyond themselves. You know, not lose sight of the forest for the trees, so to speak."

"Why do I get the impression you're referring to me now?" she asked somewhat defensively.

I tended to forget how perceptive she could be. I hated that. "Here's the part I'm sure you will agree applies to me," I said. "Elevens seem to develop slowly and need more time to mature and prepare themselves for the bigger goals and challenges they need to face."

She smiled. "Don't be too hard on yourself. Men tend to be more like big, dopey dogs," she said, stealing one of my more famous excuses.

I laughed. "You know it's true. Anyway, the article said one of the major challenges for elevens is to develop confidence in their abilities, and that's also the key to unlock their enormous potential."

"We do have great potential, don't we?" she said proudly.

"I like to think so. But there are also potential pitfalls since elevens often walk the edge between greatness and self-destruction and have a tendency to indulge too much in self-criticism."

She sighed remorsefully. "You do have a point. I know I am too hard on myself. But I have always been that way, even as a child."

"Maybe one day you can change that," I said reassuringly. "But here's the part that really hits home—with me anyway. Many elevens often feel alien, or out of place, confused, and lacking direction. We also tend to be dreamers."

"No doubt, that's you to a T," she responded.

Before I could go any deeper into my research, we arrived at the station. Since we were early and I didn't feel like talking about elevens any more, which I am certain made Erika happy, I changed the subject and began to recount the strange dream I'd had the previous evening. I got to the part about the crank phone call when I lost focus—big surprise.

The weird thing was, I usually didn't have many strange dreams, at least not the kind that I can remember. Most of my dreams are typical guy stuff, like making a last-second catch in the end zone to win the Super Bowl or being James Bond and saving the world while winning the girl's heart. My dreams were not usually deep or hard to interpret; they were the "big, dopey dog–type" guy dreams.

I didn't want her to think I was any crazier than she probably already figured, especially after my lecture on the number eleven, so I begin talking about my dream by trying to relate the experience to her dreams. "Erika, you know how sometimes you have dreams that come true?" And she did. As I mentioned earlier, she was a lot more in tune with the psychic world than I was. She had an uncanny "ability" to find tails-up pennies wherever we went, including the one time when we found eleven during an evening walk in the neighborhood (probably a sign from her sister, she thought). Sometimes she would dream of an event, and it would come true.

She would tease me saying that, if she died before I did—unlikely if I had an inkling of where this story was eventually heading)—she would send me a sign from heaven. But she recognized that I was so oblivious to any psychic happenings, I would probably not notice. I would laugh and tell her she was right, so she'd better make it something very obvious and unusual.

"Like what?" she had asked during one such discussion, and I came up with a far-fetched idea: "You could make the Penn State football team win the National Championship."

She had just smirked and replied, "I'm not a miracle worker."

I decided to get back to the subject and brought up once again my bizarre dream of the night before. She looked at me quizzically because I don't often mention dreams to her let alone bring them up again. She asked, "Well, what did you dream about last night? The number eleven after the weird call?"

I laughed and then told her about floating in space and watching what appeared to be the creation of the Universe.

"You are a science teacher, so dreaming about an event in science wouldn't be that weird."

"True, but I have never dreamed about the big bang before or about floating around in outer space," I replied. Then I continued with even stranger details. "After the creation of the Universe, I was riding on an Amtrak train with mutant humanoid people who were wearing strange watches." I described their features in detail and mentioned that she had also been there looking like a spy and talking to military bigwigs. "Oh, and by the way, before I forget to mention it, you looked really hot as a spy."

She blushed slightly, laughed, and responded, "Michael, most of what I do at the agency doesn't involve spy stuff."

"Yes, but on occasion you do visit military bases as part of your job responsibilities."

"I suppose there are some cases that require me to visit military bases, but there are no mutant-like people there, unless of course you include some of the generals," she retorted.

"That part of the dream doesn't seem to have any relevance to my life except that I used to teach biology and genetics.

Anyway, the part of the dream that really sticks with me is meeting Turbo and visiting the Petersen House."

She tried to rationalize. "You have always been interested in the Civil War and Abraham Lincoln."

"True that," I said, sounding like one of my students as she rolled her eyes at me. "But I really think Turbo was trying to tell me something about Lincoln and a guy named Soto."

"Okay, so, in your dream, you met a fictional guy named Turbo who looked like Lurch from *The Addams Family*, and he gave you information about an event that occurred a hundred and fifty years ago." She seemed to be getting impatient. "Doesn't that sound a little unbelievable, even to you?"

"You're probably right," I said. She usually had good instincts. I find many women do have a sort of "woman's intuition" that men lack. Women have ESP; men had ESPN.

"I'm sure it means nothing," I said. "Just my vivid imagination filtering into my dreams. Besides, we're here now and have plenty of time to pick up our tickets. You made really good time getting here," I said complementing her.

"Well, for some reason traffic wasn't too bad this morning, but you never know, which is why I suggested an early start."

"That's fine. It just gives me more time to read or do a crossword puzzle while we wait for our train."

"Great," she said, surely glad this conversation was coming to an end. I think she was being sarcastic, but I learned there are times when it's best to let things go with women. Maybe I was smarter than the average guy after all.

Once again, our luck was holding out, and the line of people waiting to pick up their train tickets was minimal. Erika was not the type of person who could sit still for very long, and she was checking train arrivals and departures. Luckily, I didn't have the same affliction. After we got our tickets, I picked up *Angel: A Maximum Ride Novel*, the seventh book in that series by James Patterson. We found seats in the waiting area, and I became distracted by the exciting world of avian mutant teenagers.

Before I knew it, Erika alerted me that the line for the train was forming. It was her rule that, the closer to the beginning of the line we could be, the better seat we could find—even if there were two hundred or so empty seats to choose from. Consequently, we found seats together on the train with nobody sitting next to us. I had come to realize she was also usually right even when I thought she was being silly. However, this is where our luck ended. At the last minute, a couple entered our train car with a young infant. Not surprisingly, he screamed and cried the entire ride to Washington. Even though I never had kids of my own, I like children. That's why I'm a teacher. However, this infant had a pair of excellent lungs, and I couldn't read peacefully or concentrate enough to do a simple magazine crossword puzzle, which never turned out to be simple, and I usually gave up after ten minutes.

When Erika had finished the work she was doing on her laptop, I thought we were going to discuss our plans for the day. Instead, she blurted out, "Maybe you should have been an author or a publisher instead of a teacher. Anyway, I looked up the name J. G. Sotos."

I put down my book and gave her my full attention as she explained. "There are a number of people with that name, but there is a particular John G. Sotos who is a cardiologist in Palo Alto, California. He heads a medical device company. Besides being a physician, he has a particular interest in rare diseases and is somewhat of an amateur historian. I also found a reference that says he's the current medical advisor to the Fox TV show *House MD*, but I guess that's not important." Right there she sounded a little bit like me, which was a scary thought.

She continued, "I think this is the part that will really interest you. He believes Lincoln was dying of cancer at the time of his assassination and would have been unlikely to survive a year. He published his report in a 2008 book, *The Physical Lincoln*. The rest of the information is technical, so maybe it would be best if you read it yourself." And she handed me the laptop.

I began to scroll down and read: "Sotos believed Lincoln had a very rare genetic syndrome called MEN 2B. He postulated that this condition accounted for Lincoln's great height and for many of the president's other reported ailments and behaviors. Soto thinks cancer, an inevitable element of MEN 2B, killed at least one of Lincoln's four sons, three of whom died before age twenty.

MEN 2B is short for "multiple endocrine neoplasia type 2B." In 50 percent of the cases, patients inherit the disease from a parent. Soto believed there was a decent chance that Lincoln's mother, who died at age thirty-four, may have had it. In the remainder of cases, the mutation appears spontaneously in the sufferer, who can then pass it on to his or her children.

One of MEN 2B's many manifestations is neuromas, or lumps of nerve tissue, on the tongue, lips, and eyelids. Although there are no pictures of Lincoln's tongue, his lips have a bumpy appearance in photographs. The hint of a lump on the right side of his lower lip is even visible in the engraved image on the five-dollar bill.

These growths can also occur in the intestines and can cause constipation and diarrhea. Lincoln suffered with lifelong constipation, and briefly during his presidency, he took mercury-containing pills called "blue mass" to relieve it.

Soto concluded that several things pointed to Lincoln having cancer. Countless observers commented Lincoln became thinner during the time he was in the White House. Three months before he died, in April 1865, at age fifty-six, he fainted while getting up quickly from a chair. He had periodic severe headaches as well as cold hands and feet. All are symptoms of pheochromocytoma, an adrenaline-producing tumor that is one of the two MEN 2B–associated cancers.

Other arguments for the diagnosis include Lincoln's famously sad face and his predilection for lounging horizontally whenever possible. Soto hypothesized those were signs of weak muscle tone, sometimes seen with MEN 2B.

I put down the computer and handed it back to her.

"It said that a simple blood DNA test could prove or disprove his theory, right?" she asked.

"Yes, and there are a number of Lincoln blood samples they could get the DNA from, assuming these samples would still be viable after a hundred and fifty years. The problem is, we don't have the technology yet to extract enough of a sample without damaging the artifact."

"So, right now there would be no way to ascertain if Lincoln did have that rare genetic disease," she recognized.

"Not right now, but maybe in the future. You have to admit, it is bizarre for me to dream about Lincoln and Sotos, especially now that we see a possible connection."

"It is really, really weird. Beyond *Ghostbusters* weird," she replied as we both chortled.

"But let's say—hypothetically—that you could find the necessary technology to test Soto's theory without destroying the small amount of available blood. Or that you could steal some of Lincoln's blood without getting caught or destroying it to prove or disprove Soto's theory. What does this have to do with you?" she asked.

"That is the million-dollar question, and I'm wondering the same thing. This probably sounds stupid, but I was considering that my interest in the Civil War is more than a coincidence. Maybe somehow I'm tied to Abraham Lincoln and the Civil War."

She gasped. "You mean like he is your long, long, lost relative or something? You think Abraham Lincoln could be related to you?"

"No, but technically I could be Lincoln or John F. Kennedy reincarnated," I boasted.

"What are you talking about?" she replied sounding impatient with the notion.

"Sorry, it was just a bad joke. What I mean is, maybe there is a connection between me and that time period," I answered trying to diffuse the situation.

We both pondered that thought in silence as the train pulled into to Union Station and we disembarked. After waiting in a cab line that meandered outside Union Station, we hailed a taxi and were taken to our hotel. We decided to get all-day metro passes. I consider myself a Metro aficionado, and I knew from experience that the subway was the best way to get around the city—fast, efficient, and the train lines are color-coded.

The Washington Metropolitan Area Transit Authority (Metro) began building its underground system in 1969 and finally opened in 1976, with more than fifty-one thousand people riding free on opening day. It is an underground monorail-like system that covers over 106 miles within the District of Columbia and surrounding areas. The rail lines, some running over and under each other, are distinguished by their colors—red, orange, green, blue, and yellow. It is truly an amazingly efficient system with wait times usually no more than five minutes.

The fence around a cemetery is foolish,
for those inside can't get out and those
outside don't want to get in.

—Arthur Brisbane

Journal Entry 6

Arlington

Erika sounded slightly exhausted. "Michael, how much can we do in one day? Let's pick two or three places to visit and not drive ourselves crazy."

Since she had never been to Arlington National Cemetery, we decided to make that our first stop.

"Okay," I proudly said, instantly showing off my metro skills. "We will need to take the blue line to get there. The closest station to our hotel is just two and a half blocks away."

She smiled, playfully stuck her tongue out at me, and said, "Show off."

Arlington National Cemetery is an eerily solemn and beautiful place. It was established during the American Civil War on the grounds of Arlington House, formerly the estate of the family of Confederate General Robert E. Lee's wife, Mary Anna (Custis) Lee. Interestingly, she was a great-granddaughter of Martha Washington. The cemetery is situated directly across the Potomac River from the Lincoln Memorial in Washington DC.

Many famous people were buried at Arlington including astronauts, explorers, literary figures, chief justices, sports figures, and two presidents, Taft and Kennedy. Erika was awestruck by the seemingly endless identical white headstones. It was almost surreal as the sun bounced off the white stones. They were lined in perfect rows as if the soldiers were still standing at attention.

Passing through the visitor center, the entry point into the cemetery, we walked down Roosevelt Drive. There we saw the burial sites of Admiral Byrd and Daniel "Chappie" James Jr., the first African American officer in the United States military to attain a four-star full general rank. Next to him was Rear Admiral Richard Evelyn Byrd Jr., who is generally credited for being the first explorer to reach the North and South Poles by air, though only the South Pole claim has ever been supported.

We backtracked slightly and made a quick right onto Weeks Drive toward the gravesite of John F. Kennedy. At his site is the Eternal Flame, which burns continuously. He was the first person to be given such an honor. His wife, Jacqueline Kennedy, insisted the Eternal Flame be placed at his gravesite. She lit the flame with a lighted taper. Ironically, the flame was temporarily extinguished when a Catholic school group visiting the site poured, rather than sprinkled, holy water directly onto the flame. I can't begin to imagine the explaining that someone had to do to those overseeing the cemetery.

Former President Kennedy is buried here along with his wife, Jacqueline, his unnamed infant daughter who was born and died on the same day, and his infant son, Patrick, born prematurely and who died two days later.

Silently we glanced at each other, probably thinking the same thing: How might the world and our lives been different if JFK had never been assassinated? What if Camelot had lasted a little longer and Lee Harvey Oswald hadn't been there that day—assuming that you don't subscribe to conspiracy theories.

I had always believed that changing even small events in history could have substantial effects on the time line. Therefore, changing a major event could have an even greater impact and an enormous effect on the time line. Of course, there are some who believe in pre-destiny. They believe that everything is "written in stone" and all we can change are insignificant events while the overall outcomes are predetermined. I wasn't one of those people. Instead, I believe in free will and free choice where not everything is written in stone and that we—

"Michael, isn't JFK's brother Robert buried near here?" Erika asked breaking my periphrastic train of thoughts.

"Yes, he is the next site over. The last time I was here, I overheard a tour guide saying Robert was buried at night, which is extremely rare, although I don't know why," I added trying to sound scholarly.

"Hmm, something you don't know about DC," she said with the wink of an eye.

We walked over, and I pointed out Robert's site.

"His site is very modest compared to his brother's," she commented. "They could have done a little more to make it noticeable."

I nodded in agreement. "I thought the same thing the first time I saw his gravesite. It's almost as if you could walk past it and miss it completely."

We walked back down Weeks Drive heading toward the amphitheater to observe the passing of the guard ceremony at the Tomb of the Unknown Soldier. Visitors gather just before the top of the hour to observe this ritual. Since 1937, this solemn event has occurred every thirty minutes, twenty-four hours a day, and 365 days of the year, regardless of the weather conditions. I described to Erika the extreme measures the soldiers who guard the tomb must endure to hold this "prestigious" position. "Although I cannot confirm what I am about to tell you is completely accurate, I did read that, to be accepted as a tomb guard, a soldier must memorize and recite, error free, the entire thirty-five-page historical informational pamphlet about Arlington National Cemetery."

"That is absurd."

"Wait, it gets better. According to my limited sources, during the first six months of duty, a tomb guard must live in the barracks under the tomb and cannot talk to anyone or watch any television. They spend off-duty time studying the hundred and seventy-five notable people laid to rest in Arlington National Cemetery. The guard must memorize who they are and where they are interred. Every guard spends five hours a day getting his uniform ready for guard duty."

"Is that all? They don't have to reinvent the wheel or win the Nobel Prize?" she responded.

"No, I don't think so," I said before realizing I was being stupid, because her comment was obviously a joke. "But they cannot drink any alcohol, fight, or swear in public on or off duty for the rest of their lives."

"And if they do any of those things, what happens to them?" she questioned.

"They are stripped of their wreath badge, which is considered extremely prestigious, as fewer than six hundred were ever awarded. Oh, and there is one more thing. To be a guard, a soldier must be between five eleven and six four and have no more than a thirty-inch waist."

"I guess that means you can't apply then," she said playfully.

"You mean all those hours at the gym haven't paid off?"

"Yea, right. I was mainly referring to how you tend to read things, like labels, recipes, and everything else!" she said, flabbergasted."

I wasn't so sure, but I had to admit that, even being a teacher, I didn't always read things carefully, as I often preached in class, in an effort to save time. I decided not to inquire any further as she continued. "Old wise one, if what you say is accurate, why would anyone endure this brutal training? That is malarkey. I think such strict training would make them crazy anyway."

I tried to rationalize. "Well, maybe they feel it makes them stronger soldiers if they can get through the program. It's a guy thing, being tough and all."

She smiled coyly and said, "Men. Sometimes I just don't get them."

I bit my lip. "Oh yeah, women are much easier to understand."

"Point taken," she admitted.

I was a bit shocked, since it was very rare that I won a discussion, mostly because I didn't deserve to win, but nevertheless, I felt victorious.

As I looked at the tomb, I saw three Greek figures sculpted into the east panel of the white marble of the sarcophagus. I pointed at the stone Greek figures. I was about to ask Erika another inane question, but she knew me too well, and she finished my thoughts. "Do you mean the Greek figures representing Peace, Victory, and Valor?"

I looked at her dumbfounded. "I guess knowing your Greek gods is standard CIA training stuff."

She was forthright in her reply. "They didn't make us learn about Greek gods at the agency. Those figures are mentioned in the pamphlet we picked up on our way in. It helps to actually read, you know."

She was right. Sometimes I neglected to read, especially when I was trying to assemble a toy or furniture that looked to be simple. It invariably takes me forever to figure out how to assemble the item, and I eventually break down and read the instructions. This is probably a guy thing.

I felt stupid, "Are there any other interesting tidbits I forgot to read about?"

She knew I loved useless trivia, so I am sure she continued mostly for my benefit, "Well, it says that Army Sergeant. Edward F. Younger, who was wounded in combat during World War One, and highly decorated for valor, made the selection of the Unknown Soldier of World War I from four identical caskets at the city hall in Chalons-sur-Marne, France, October 24, 1921. Sergeant Younger chose the unknown by placing a spray of white roses on one of the caskets. He picked the third casket from the left, although it doesn't state why. The chosen Unknown Soldier was transported to the United States aboard the USS *Olympia*. Those remaining were interred in the Meuse Argonne Cemetery in France."

She continued with a wry smile, "Did you know that there are also unknown World War Two, Korean War, and Vietnam War soldiers buried here, adjacent to this monument?"

"I knew there were more than one, but I didn't know there were three more. I guess that makes sense. You know how much I hate trivia, but go ahead and tell me about the others."

She smiled and continued, "There is one more thing that you would probably find interesting as a science teacher. According to the pamphlet, the remains of the solider buried in the unknown tomb for the Vietnam War were exhumed in 1998. Based on mitochondrial DNA testing, scientists identified the remains as those of Air Force First Lieutenant Michael Joseph Blassie, who was shot down near An Loc, Vietnam, in 1972. Ever since then, it was decided the crypt that contained the remains of the Vietnam unknown soldier would remain vacant."

"Wow, that's interesting, I didn't know any of that."

"See, you really don't know everything about DC," she gloated.

During the changing of the guard, I notice that the guard who was leaving the amphitheater dropped something on the ground.

Erika noticed it too. Thank goodness. Maybe I'm not completely crazy. "Michael, did you see the guard drop the piece of paper?"

"Yes. I don't think he realized he dropped it, and I bet that never happens."

Apparently, we were the only two who saw this, because everyone else walked right by the fallen paper. I picked it up, but the writing on it didn't make any sense to me. It was a random bunch of letters thrown together haphazardly.

Erika anxiously wanted to know about it. "What does it say?"

"I'm not sure. It's just a group of random letters."

"Let me take a look at it. Maybe it's a code. I had a basic course in deciphering codes," she said.

"So you really are a spy," I prodded her amusingly.

She rolled her eyes. "It was just an elective. Now do you want me to take a look or not?"

I handed her the paper, and we scrutinized it together. The first line read 'Ufwtpe Ayy Szavtyd.' The second line read 'opnetzy zyp.'

"Hmm, this looks like there is some sort of pattern to these letters. There are spaces between some of the letters. Also, the first letter of each 'word' in the first line is capitalized. I would guess each letter group represents an individual word. Maybe the name of someone or something. This pattern looks familiar to me, if I could just remember which code form it was."

"There are about a hundred different codes to choose from. How in Mnemosyne's name could you remember all of them?" I wondered out loud.

"Who is Mnemosyne?" she questioned.

Trying to sound smart, I explained, "She was the Greek god for memory. I only know this because her name came up when I was reading one of my fantasy books and—"

"That's it!" she interjected. "Not Greek, but Roman. I think it relates to Julius Caesar," she replied.

"Great, but I have no idea what you are talking about. Please explain," I requested hastily.

She grinned. "Now you know how I feel when you ramble on about some new scientific discovery or ask me who sang the song that's playing on the radio," she replied. But she graciously continued her explanation. "In cryptography, it's known as Caesar's Cipher. He developed a simple code and used it to send secure messages. It looked familiar to me because it was one of the first codes they taught us at the CIA. The instructor indicated it is one of the most simple and widely used encryption techniques."

"Okay, how does it work?"

"All the letters in the plain text are shifted down in the alphabet by an unspecified set number. For example, in the word dog, if the shift number is five, the three letters would shift down five spaces and the word dog would be spelled I-T-L. The trick is to find the magic number."

"I think I get the point. It's similar to a gene shift within a genetic mutation," I said.

She gave me one of her stern looks and continued. "I think so, but they left Genetics 101 out of my courses at the academy. Let's focus on what the shift number would be and skip the biology lesson."

"Let me think," I said. "It would probably be an obvious number because I'm guessing someone or something wants us to solve the code since we are the only two who saw the note in the first place."

As if a light bulb went off, she jumped in, "How many pennies did we find on tails during our walk?" she asked.

"Eleven," I reiterated.

"And what are our birthdates?"

"Eleven," I stated once again.

"And what is ten plus one?"

"Eleven. Hey wait, what?" I confusingly replied.

"I'm just playing with you, but I'll bet that's the magic number. Let me see the note again."

She started writing down a bunch of letters. I heard her mumble, "Working in reverse, U would be J and F would be and U ..."

Finally she finished the first line of words and said, "Who is Juliet Ann Hopkins? I never heard of her."

I shook my head unknowingly.

"Okay, let's look at the second line." I looked at the letters 'opnetzy zyp.' "Notice there are no capital letters within the two separate words. That leads me to believe that it is not any proper type of name," she said. She started writing down the letters again from their shifted letters, and scribed two words. She handed me the paper. "It says 'section one,' so maybe we should take a walk down to that section of the cemetery," she said. I nodded in agreement.

It was a typical hot, hazy, humid east coast summer day. She liked the warm weather much more than I did. I would often tease her, calling her NaNook and telling her she could never live in Alaska and become a hockey mom like one of its former governors. But even she was hot and sweaty today.

Fortunately, section one wasn't too far away, relatively speaking. We hustled out of the amphitheater and made a left onto Wilson Drive, passing by the gravesite of Joe Louis known as "The Brown Bomber." He held the title longer and defended it more times than any other heavyweight boxer in history. Since he was a sergeant during World War II, Joe did not technically qualify for burial at Arlington until President Ronald Reagan waived the requirements for him.

We continued to wind down and around Wilson Drive passing the memorial for the crew of the Space Shuttle Challenger and the Iran Rescue Mission memorial. Toward the end of Wilson Drive, we turned left onto Meigs Drive and soon find ourselves in section one.

It was obvious this area was dedicated to Civil War veterans. Erika stopped and picked up a penny.

"Another penny from heaven?" I asked.

Erika looked surprised and said, "Maybe. But I don't think this one is from my sister."

She handed me the coin. I noticed that it was slightly faded but in good condition for being an Indian head penny minted in 1890.

"Michael, this is really weird. I know I find pennies all the time, even wheat pennies occasionally, but I've never found one this old."

"I know. Something tells me that we could be on the right track."

"Maybe you're not as crazy as I was beginning to think you were," she said.

"Or maybe, after you've been with me so long, my craziness is rubbing off and making you a little barmy yourself."

We looked at each other and laughed—a little nervously.

As we continued down the path, one of the more interesting graves we came across was that of Abner Doubleday, who was erroneously given credit for inventing baseball. A little-known truth about Abner is that he was a Union general, and he fired the first shot of the Civil War in defense of Fort Sumter. He also played a pivotal role in the early fighting at the Battle of Gettysburg. Later in life, he secured a patent for the cable car railway that still runs today in San Francisco. Yet there was never proof he was involved in inventing the game played by the boys of summer.

After searching for what seemed like an eternity, but in reality was only ten minutes, we were about to give up looking for Juliet's site due to heat and time constraints when Erika noticed a small silver tabby stray cat walking by. I carefully walked over to the cat, slowly knelt down, and extended my hand. The cat reminded me of Dusty, a rare silver tabby I had adopted from a shelter many years ago. Dusty spent the remaining eleven years of her life with me and Bachelor living a pretty spoiled life. This beautiful cat in the cemetery pushed her head against my hand and started to purr. She rolled over, and I rubbed her belly. A field mouse briefly appeared about ten yards away, and the cat was off, chasing it into the next section.

"Michael, do you see the name of the headstone next to you?"

I looked up and saw the name and date, Juliet Ann Opie Hopkins, May 7, 1818 – March 9, 1890.

We looked at the penny that we had just found moments ago.

"According to the inscription, she died in 1890. Don't you think it's unusual that the penny matches the year she died?" Erika asked.

"A couple of weeks ago I probably would have thought it was odd, but I have started to expect creepy things," I responded.

We both look up at the sky as if waiting for lightening to strike; it didn't.

At first she didn't say anything, which was a little unsettling for me. Finally she spoke. "Now I'm really beginning to believe you are not as crazy as I thought."

"Thanks. I think. Wait, you were really thinking I was seriously crazy? On second thought, don't answer that question," I said. "Okay, we found her site but for what reason?"

There was nothing there except for the headstone, the plot area, and the Indian head penny we had found.

"I don't think it was just a coincidence that we were led to her grave. I think even the cat was part of it," she said.

"There has to be some connection between Ms. Hopkins and all these bizarre events," I concluded.

"I'm not sure, but perhaps Ms. Hopkins is related to your dream and all of the other weird things you have been experiencing. We can do some research on her later when we get back to the room," she said.

"What about the National Air and Space Museum?" I asked.

She looked at her watch. "Do we pass the museum on the way back?"

Being a self-proclaimed metro expert I stated, "Coincidently, we do pass that stop on the metro."

"Well, it's still early; I guess we could stop on the way back to the hotel."

"Sounds good to me. You know that's my favorite museum of all."

"I know. You tell me all the time," she said warily.

As we were leaving, we made a left onto Sheridan Drive and walked by another prominent resident of Arlington. "Erika, since we are going by anyway?"

She gave me one of those "okay" looks, but the look also said, "Let's be quick about it."

I stopped only briefly to read the plaque. Pierre Charles L'Enfant was a major in the US army who served under General Washington at Valley Forge during the American

Revolution. He was very instrumental in the history of Washington DC. He designed the plans for the city.

Sweaty, thirsty, and a little tired, we trudged back to the metro stop.

While we were waiting for our train, she said, "I bet you're hungry."

I may not have written it down, but I am always hungry.

The metro arrived within five minutes, "Gotta love this system," I remarked.

We got off at L'Enfant Plaza rather than the Smithsonian stop, because it's closer to the museum. Most non-metro experts wouldn't know this. Exiting the station, we made a quick left, and my eyes caught sight of a Pot Belly restaurant, but we decided to postpone eating for the time being.

This name does not refer to a pig or a big fat guy; rather, it refers to a restaurant chain that makes warm and delicious sandwiches and nice salads. The Pot Belly chain was started in 1977 as an antique shop located on Lincoln Avenue. As I remembered this, I realized that it might be another Lincoln connection, but I kept the thought to myself. The antique shop owners began selling sandwiches to boost business.

The National Air and Space Museum is the most-visited museum in the world; millions visit each year. Although the present building was constructed in the 1970s with the establishment of the National Mall, the museum has a long and rich history. On June 16, 1861, the secretary of the Smithsonian Institution instructed Thaddeus S. Lowe to inflate his balloon on the future site of the National Air and Space Museum. That flight was the first demonstration of aerial reconnaissance in American history, and led to the establishment of a balloon corps for the Union armies, the nation's first military aviation unit, which was used to spy on confederate troops.

This fabulous museum maintains the largest collection of historic air and spacecraft in the world, including mind-blowing displays such as the original Wright brothers' 1903 Flyer, the *Spirit of St. Louis*, the Apollo 11 command module, and a lunar rock sample that visitors can touch. It is also a vital center for research into the history, science, and technology of aviation and space flight. It is a really, really cool place.

Our first stop was Gallery 209, which is an exhibit featuring the Wright brothers. There are a number of reproductions, such as the 1899 kite and the 1900 and 1902 gliders, which were all instrumental in creating the 1903 *Wright Flyer*. Incredibly, the 1903 *Flyer* on display is the original plane and not a reproduction. This was the first heavier-than-air, powered aircraft to make a sustained, controlled flight with a pilot aboard, and hence the first documented flight in history. Additionally, this gallery includes an original Wright St. Clair bicycle built in the brothers' shop. Only five are still known to exist.

I ask Erika, "How would you like to touch the moon?"

"You would do that for me?"

"Of course I would. Not much I can do about the sun—it's too hot. But I know where a piece of the moon is."

"Lead the way, Mr. Air and Space Guide."

I consider myself an Air and Space Museum aficionado. Along the way we passed the original *Spirit of St. Louis*, which is officially known as the Ryan NYP ("Ryan" for the manufacturer, Ryan Airlines, and "NYP" for New York to Paris). This plane was flown solo by Charles Lindbergh on May 20–21, 1927. It was the first non-stop flight from New York to Paris.

Being very observant, Erika turned to me and said, "I don't see any front windows, only side windows. How did he see forward?"

"I am not sure. Maybe he had some kind of periscope. I do remember a guide once telling the group that he was obsessed with extra cargo weight, so much so that he cut off the tops and bottoms of his flight maps."

"That is pretty obsessive," she commented.

We continued down the museum's grand entry hall, featuring The Milestones of Flight. This exhibit showcases an awesome collection of historic aircraft and spacecraft that represent epic achievements in aviation and space flight. At the bottom of the entry hall is where two of the most incredulous artifacts are located.

Erika asks, "Is that really a piece of the moon?"

"Assuming the Apollo astronauts landing on the moon wasn't a hoax (I don't want to get started here on those outrageous conspiracy theories), I believe it was brought back during the Apollo 11 Mission. Go ahead and touch it."

"It feels smooth and polished," she remarked.

"You would never know it came from something like 230,000 miles away," I continued. "If you look up slightly to the left—"

She quickly cut me off, "You mean the Apollo 11 Command Module *Columbia* that carried astronauts Neil Armstrong, Edwin 'Buzz' Aldrin, and Michael Collins on their historic voyage to the Moon in 1969?"

"Have you been studying science behind my back?"

Sheepishly she continued, "If you look closely, you can still see the burn marks on the underside of the craft caused by the friction of re-entry back to Earth."

I beamed and thought to myself, *That's my girl!*

The museum was crowded, but we were able to visit most of the displays. Amazingly, nothing abnormal happened. No weird notes or strange people—or cats. For a few moments, we were able to forget about the strange events that had been occurring.

Since food was now becoming definitely more important to me at that moment, I decided we should dine at the Old Ebbitt Grill, a DC landmark and personal favorite of mine. It is Washington's oldest, most historic saloon, founded in 1856. Ebbitt's guest list reads like a Who's Who of American history. President McKinley is said to have lived there during his tenure in Congress. Presidents Grant, Andrew Johnson, Cleveland, Theodore Roosevelt, and Harding supposedly refreshed themselves at its stand-around bar at one time or another.

During its history, Old Ebbitt Grill acquired animal heads (supposedly bagged by Teddy Roosevelt) and wooden bears said to have been imported by Alexander Hamilton for his private bar. The Victorian interior conjures images of old saloons at the turn of the twentieth century. The antique clock over the revolving door at the entrance is an heirloom from previous locations, and the marble staircase with an iron-spindled rail was salvaged from the National Metropolitan Bank, the oldest National Bank in the District of Columbia, which was once located next door.

There is an old mahogany bar reminiscent of the turn-of-the-twentieth-century saloons. Antique gas chandeliers and fixtures provide light for the main dining room. The wooden crossbeams on the ten-foot ceilings are accented by a style of pinstripe stenciling popular at the turn of the century. It is the perfect place for anyone who has an affinity for history or antiques. In addition to the atmosphere, the food is good too.

"We should probably wait until we get back to research Ms. Hopkins, because it gets really crowded there after five thirty in the afternoon," she suggested.

We were early dinner eaters anyway, and I hated waiting in lines, so I agreed. As we arrived, a distinct smell engulfed us. It was an odd combination of beer mixed with oysters, shrimp, and fried crab cakes. Although the restaurant was just beginning to get crowded, there was a table available in the rear, near the oyster bar.

"What looks good to you, besides me?" I teased.

"You know that's corny, don't you?"

I nodded. Surprisingly, I realized I tended to be corny at times. Although a curse, at least it did entertain people— well, some people. Okay, it probably only amused me and an occasional student of mine.

"I know this will be a big surprise, but I think I'll get the lasagna," she said. She almost always ordered the same thing. I was the more adventurous one when it came to food.

I remember once we took an exceptionally long red-eye flight to Las Vegas. When we arrived at four in the morning and had few dining choices, we ate at the California Pizza Kitchen, and I ordered the duck pizza. They guaranteed that you could exchange any pizza for another if you didn't like what you ordered. It was a daring choice and, not surprisingly, I exercised that exchange option.

That night in Washington, however, I was more conservative and ordered the crab cakes, an Old Ebbitt Grill specialty.

Our waitress, Brandy, was sweet but chatty—the type who is really nice but really talkative. During dinner, Erika asked me what my plans were for the next day while she would be working.

"I thought I would stay local and visit one or two of the Smithsonian museums at the National Mall. But before that, I want to visit Ford's Theater and the Petersen House," I responded.

"Are you hoping to find some clues at Ford's Theater and The Peterson House relating to your dream?" she asked.

"No. I just like visiting them. Well, I'm not really sure to be honest."

"I have to be at work early. I guess you'll eat breakfast across the street from the theater at the Waffle House," she added.

"You can always read my mind." We both laughed.

She muttered something about how it's not really that complicated, but I just pretended not to listen.

During the meal, I noticed a woman seated alone at a table, catty corner to ours. I probably wouldn't have noticed her except for three things. She was constantly staring at us, she was dressed oddly (like someone from the nineteenth century), and no staff ever approached her table. I asked Erika if she noticed her.

"Do you mean the woman dressed oddly who has been staring at us since we sat down?" she responded.

I should have realized that, if it was obvious to me, she would have noticed.

"Since you're a spy, what's your expert opinion?" I asked.

"Shhh, not so loud, and I am not technically a spy anyway," she scolded me.

I used a lower tone of voice, "Sorry, but what do you think we should do?"

"There are no laws against looking at people and dressing like an antique, but maybe you could walk over and ask her if she needs any assistance."

Since her instincts were usually very good, I figured I would give it a try. With the grace and elegance of a Clydesdale, I got up and nearly bumped into a waiter carrying a large tray.

"Excuse me, Miss. I noticed no one was coming over to your table, and I was wondering if I could get a server to assist you."

She wore a long black cape draped over her shoulders. Her grayish hair was pulled back under a white knit cap. She looked to be in her late forties or early fifties. "Please sit down for a moment," she requested, and I obediently complied. "You can call me Opie."

The name sounded familiar, but I couldn't remember why. "Listen Miss Opie—"

She stopped me. "No, just Opie."

I started again. "Opie, we noticed you were staring at us, and we were wondering why."

"Michael," she began. Now, this gave me a chill because I hadn't yet mentioned my name. She continued, "There is a reason that recently you have experienced some odd occurrences, shall we say."

Opie had an old Southern accent, reminiscent of someone from the Deep South. It wasn't so much the accent that struck me but the antique quality to it. She sounded the way I would imagine a character from *Gone with the Wind* would sound.

"How could you know that?" I asked.

She smiled reassuringly. "It's time that I be getting on, but don't worry, I'll see you again somewhere down the road a bit. Some things might make more sense by then."

I started to say something to her, but she got up and started walking toward the door. I noticed she had a distinctive limp. I walked back over to our table and sat down.

"You look nonplussed and a little ashen, Michael. What did she say?"

"Well, she said that her name was Opie—and not Miss Opie."

"What?" Erika interjected.

"Never mind. That's not important. She said everything is happening for a reason, and it would all make sense eventually.

"Is that all? Anything else?" Erika asked.

"Just that she had to leave, but that I would see her again," I explained.

Now it was Erika's turn to look perplexed. She suggested we enjoy the rest of our dinner as best we could, and research Ms. Opie on her laptop back in the hotel room.

While we were walking back to the hotel, Erika stopped in her tracks as if having an epiphany. "If I am remembering correctly, wasn't Opie the name on one of the graves we saw at Arlington this afternoon?"

Now I remembered why the name sounded familiar. "You know, now that you mention it, I think you're right," I responded.

We got back to our room at around seven. Our room number was 411, which was Erika's birth date. Weird huh?

She opened her laptop—standard CIA issue of course—and googled the name Juliet Ann Hopkins.

"What does it say?" I asked impatiently.

"She was a Civil War nurse and matron. She was known as the Florence Nightingale of the South, and on July 1, 1862, during the Battle of Seven Pines, she was shot in the leg twice while rescuing wounded men from the battlefield. The injuries required surgery, which left her with a permanent limp. After the war, she and her husband returned to live in Mobile, and Juliet's humanitarian sacrifices became widely known. She became a living legend. Sources estimate Juliet and her husband donated somewhere between $200,000 and $500,000 dollars to the Southern cause. Her husband died in 1865, and she moved to New York, where she lived the rest of her life in relative poverty. This is interesting—she was so highly regarded by the entire nation that she was buried with full military honors at Arlington National Cemetery and—"

With that, Erika stopped in mid-sentence, and this time her face became ashen. She turned the computer around and said, "Oh my God, Michael, look at her picture!"

We both stared at the computer screen with our jaws dropped wide open. The picture looked identical to the old woman we had seen in Old Ebbitt Grill. It was, no doubt, the same woman I had just spoken with at dinner.

A waffle is like a pancake with a syrup trap.

—Mitch Hedberg

Journal Entry 7

Waffles and Pyramids

The alarm rang at 7:00 a.m. because Erika had to be at the agency by 8:00 a.m. She gave me a soft kiss and said, "Good morning, Mr. Snore-Head. Did you sleep okay?"

I tended to snore—not like a bear, but loud enough that it was disruptive. Okay, so maybe I was part bear. "Yes, I slept pretty well, but oddly enough, I don't remember dreaming. Or at least I don't remember any of my dreams, if I did dream at all last night."

Erika hopped off to the bathroom to get ready for work.

I'd have thought, after the strange week I had been experiencing, that I would have had a lot of dreams— weird, strange, maybe even nightmarish dreams—but nope. At least nothing that I could remember.

"I had some doozies myself last night, but I have to run," she said. She was ready to leave. "I'll tell you about them at dinner. I'll meet you back here around five thirty." She kissed me again gently on the cheek and then left for work.

My plan was to visit Ford's Theater before I went to the museums. The theater didn't open until nine, so I had time for a nutritious—or at least a full—breakfast before beginning my day. I never skip a meal, and if I am forced to skip one, it will never be breakfast, which I always eat like a king.

The Waffle House is located across from Ford's Theater. It is quite an interesting place, to say the least. There is a newspaper clipping from *The Washington Post* pasted outside the window that reads: "Legend has it that Mr. Lincoln really wanted to dine here that bad night, but the missus refused to sit on stools that swivel, so they went to the theater across the street instead."

The funny thing is that the article does not say which Mr. Lincoln, so everyone just assumes that it is Abe they were referring to.

Eating there is a plethora of fun. The outside looks very old, and maybe a bit shabby to some, but they shouldn't be fooled. Although the food is simple, it is surprisingly good and ample. The owner, James Dubay—aka Jimbo— is usually very talkative and funny. This is definitely not a tourist joint—far from it. Almost all the customers are locals who add to its charm and friendly ambiance.

James, as some of the locals call him—although I always felt he preferred Jimbo—was a short, stocky, muscular guy. He wore thick Coke-bottle glasses. I tried to tell him once about a little invention known as contact lenses, but he would have none of it. He also wore a red Confederate bandana on his head. This was a valiant attempt—with minimal success in my opinion—to mask his grey, thinning hair. He had lost most of his Southern drawl; he used it on only a few select occasions, mostly for gags.

Jimbo loved to laugh and tell stories about the glory days of the Old South to his customers.

He was from a small town called Homer, which was named after the famous Greek poet. Homer is located in Claiborne Parish, Louisiana. Even today, the town has less than four thousand residents. All forty-eight states are divided into counties except for Alaska, which is divided into boroughs and census areas, and Louisiana, which is divided into political subdivisions known parishes, the local government equivalent to counties.

On a number of occasions during breakfast on that particular morning, Jimbo talked proudly about his hometown of Homer, which was established just before the start of the Civil War and was strongly pro-Confederate. A confederate soldier's statue stands proudly in front of the parish courthouse. Although it appeared he had adapted well to this northeastern city, I always got the impression that Jimbo had never forgotten where he came from.

Jimbo left Homer with his two young girls shortly after his wife and parents were killed during Hurricane Andrew. Another strange coincidence—they were buried in one of Homer's cemeteries called Arlington Cemetery. A cold chill ran down my spine as I thought about my own experiences yesterday at Arlington National Cemetery.

I ordered my usual egg white veggie omelet with a short stack of waffles. While I was eating my waffles, which were especially light and fluffy that day, I noticed a copy of *The Daily Evening Star*. On the front page of the newspaper was an article highlighting one of the newer exhibits at the National Museum of Natural History, which would be ending this week. This exhibit was dedicated to the Great Pyramid of Giza. Passes for this exhibit could be obtained at the Smithsonian Castle.

The Castle was the first of the Smithsonian buildings. Construction began in 1847, and the building was built in phases, with the last one completed in 1855. Architect James Renwick, Jr. designed the Castle to be the focal point of a picturesque landscape on the National Mall, reflecting a Gothic Revival style with Romanesque motifs. The façade is built with red sandstone from the Seneca quarry in Seneca, Maryland. (I guess I spent a little too much time reading the free pamphlets in these museums).

I read there was a secret passage built behind the library bookshelves that contained some rare books and magazines. It has been reported that one copy of the Gutenberg Bible—worth between $25 and $30 million—was stored in the passage. The passage also claimed a near perfect copy of the comic book, *Amazing Spider Man #1* first published in 1963. This is considered to be the rarest comic still in existence, at least according to *The Simpsons* TV show, which I personally find to be a very reliable source.

A crypt just inside the north entrance houses the tomb of James Smithson. Ironically, he never visited America while he was alive; he arrived only in death. I guess his visit became somewhat extended.

The article also mentioned that the Great Pyramid of Giza was considered to be one of the Seven Wonders of the Ancient World. It is the oldest and only "wonder" that has remained intact. The article also briefly mentioned the other six Great Wonders, but that's not important now. Besides, with today's technology, it is relatively easy to google just about any kind of information, or so people tell me.

Jimbo was just finishing one of his long-winded Southern stories with one of the locals. I asked him about the exhibit, knowing that he was a big supporter of the Smithsonian. "Hey, Jimbo, have you had a chance to visit the Great Pyramid of Giza exhibit at the Museum of Natural History?" I inquired.

"What's that?"

I forgot that he was a little hard of hearing in one ear. I spoke a little louder and focused on his good side, "The Pyramid of Giza exhibit, have you seen it yet?" I repeated.

Surprisingly, he said, "Not familiar with that exhibit. Where did you see it mentioned?"

"Look, right here on the first page of *The Daily Evening Star.*"

"Which paper?" he asked again.

I showed him the front page of the paper, and he looked perplexed, "I have never seen that newspaper. Where did you get it?"

"I found it on the table where I was sitting. I've been reading it while enjoying some of your especially delicious waffles."

"Hmm, now that I think about it, there was a newspaper called *The Washington Star* that went out of business some thirty years ago, but I don't recall one called *The Daily Evening Star,*" he replied quizzically.

I laughed. "No, it is definitely called *The Daily Evening Star,*" and I pointed to the name of the paper.

He told me they had just recently installed a computer system for billing purposes, although he thought the old fashioned way was "fine and dandy" with him. This new system had Internet access. He offered, "Why don't we type that name in and see what comes up? I spend sixty-six dollars a month on this dang computer anyway, might as well get my money's worth."

I thought I was technologically challenged, but Jimbo made me seem like a computer whiz. By the time I had finished my third cup of coffee (I love coffee), he had figured out how to turn the "dang machine" on, and he had looked up the name of the newspaper. Looking dumbfounded, he said, "Maybe you ought to read this."

You would think I would begin to expect weird things by this time, but I was once again nonplussed as I read the screen: *The Washington Star* was founded on December 16, 1852, by Captain Joseph Borrows, who initially called the newspaper *The Daily Evening Star.* It would be renamed several times before becoming *The Washington Star* by the late 1970s. In 1853, Texas surveyor and newspaper entrepreneur William Douglas Wallach purchased the paper. As the sole owner of the paper for the next fourteen years, Wallach built up the paper by capitalizing on reporting on the American Civil War, among other things."

Okay, so here's the kicker besides the fact that *The Daily Evening Star* was published only between 1852 and 1854. On August 7, 1981, after 130 years, *The Washington Star* ceased publication and filed for bankruptcy.

"Michael, what's the date on the newspaper?"

I showed him. The paper was dated last week.

He pondered for a bit, then laughed half-heartedly. "You're playing a gag on old Jimbo, right? You got that newspaper made up as a prank?"

I was going to tell him that it wasn't a joke but decided against it. After all, why get him involved and worked up over something that I couldn't explain? "Yeah, Jimbo, you got me. This was to make up for the last prank you pulled on me. Remember?"

Jimbo smirked and said, "I remember. I got you good last time."

Last time I was in town visiting, Jimbo talked me into doing a favor for him. He had supposedly met this great girl, Sara, and he wanted to ask her on a date. The problem was that Sara was a little uncomfortable going out with Jim the first time alone. She suggested a sort of quasi double date. She had a good friend, and she asked Jim if he could find someone to be her date, just for the night. Somehow, he thought of me.

I wasn't thrilled with the idea, but Erika was not the jealous type, and being a compassionate sort, she suggested I go. She said Jim had been alone long enough after his wife died and, as a friend, I should help him out. She trusted me and knew I would never do anything to jeopardize our relationship. So, I was Jimbo's wingman.

According to Jimbo, Sara suggested that we meet at her house in Foggy Bottom before going to Patty Boom Boom's, a trendy New Orleans–style club located near her house. Jimbo mentioned that the girls liked to drink a little and asked if I would make a pitcher of my famous piña coladas when we got there, before we left for the club. Even though I didn't drink much, my father had made the best piña coladas at the Jersey shore. Apparently, I had been blessed with the same piña colada gene.

I met Jimbo at the Waffle House, and we headed to Sara's. Jimbo rang the doorbell at the darkened house. I expected to be greeted by Sara or her girlfriend, but a large man came to the door and yelled, "So you're the scum who's been after my wife! I oughta' kill ya' both!"

The irate man pulled out a snub nosed pistol and fired point blank at Jimbo, who screamed as he collapsed on the porch. "I'm hit Mike! Run! Run for your life, Mike!"

I bolted from the doorway expecting to be shot in the back at any moment. After about a block or two, I stopped and pulled out my antiquated cell phone to call the police. Of course, the battery was extremely low, and I couldn't get a signal.

Maybe I was in a state of shock, but after a half hour or so, distraught, I made it back to the Waffle House. I was greeted by Jimbo, who couldn't stop laughing. I was never sure if Erika was in on the prank. She would never admit to it one way or the other.

I finished my coffee and said my good-byes. Jimbo could certainly talk up a storm. I headed straight for Metro Center. The east coast was in the middle of a summer heat wave. It would be the fifth day in a row above ninety-five degrees with high humidity. After all, what's a good heat wave without accompanying humidity?

Walking along Tenth Street, with sweat slowly oozing from my pores, I began to feel a slight change in the temperature. Maybe a storm was heading in, because a cool breeze suddenly appeared from nowhere, helping to alleviate the stagnant air.

As cooler winds hovered in my direction, I became more aware of my surroundings and noticed a reenactment of a Civil War event. A number of men and woman were dressed in nineteenth-century garb—including accoutrements. I was about to dismiss this scene as nothing out of the ordinary when a woman caught my eye. She looked exactly like Juliet Hopkins—aka Opie—whom we had met in Old Ebbitt Grill the previous evening.

Opie was talking to a couple of the reenactment actors. One was a slender, brown-haired woman of average height, wearing men's long pants. Another was an African American man dressed as a slave. He was wearing a straw hat and had long sideburns. It didn't appear that any of the people walking along the sidewalk noticed this collection of Civil War actors. It was as if I was the only person on the streets aware of their presence.

I walked over to them and addressed the familiar-looking woman. "Opie, is Juliet Ann Hopkins your real name?"

She grinned and responded that it was.

"Please tell me that you are named after one of your ancestors?" I implored.

"No, not that I am aware of. I am actually the original Juliet Ann Hopkins, as far as I know," she responded.

"How could you be? According to Erika's Google research, you died over a hundred and eight years ago," I blurted out.

Calmly and reassuringly, she looked at me as if to say 'relax, everything will make sense in time,' but it didn't make me feel any better.

"Google?" she questioned.

I ignored the question. "Is this some kind of elaborate practical joke? Did Jimbo put you up to this?" I asked hopefully.

She paused and then said, "By the way, Michael, this is Kate, and this is John. I believe you knew one of his relatives—his great-great-grandson, Mr. Jacque."

I shook their hands.

"So, Mr. Jacque is actually your great-great-grandson, and you are the one who gave him the beautiful antique pocket watch?"

He cordially said yes to both questions, and then continued, "Yes, it was a fine timepiece. It took an unusually high level of workmanship to create. A friend of mine would dabble in the magical arts and created it for me to repay a favor I did for him. I tried to have it passed down through the men in my family. I'm guessing this has been done, such as I wished?"

I nodded my head yes. "Does Kate have any long-lost relatives working at my school?" I joked.

A slender woman with brown hair stepped forward. She was not a particularly attractive woman, but did possess clear-cut, expressive features. She had an honest face, which I imagined suggested that she was someone you could confide in. She moved adroitly toward me. "Hello, Michael. My name is Ms. Warne—Kate Warne—but some of my close friends call me Kitty. I do not have any relatives who work at Above it All Academy."

Feeling a little embarrassed and somewhat confused, I said, "Okay then, what part do you play in my recent unusual and possibly delusional life?"

She grinned. "For now, let me just say that I previously did a little detective work and even helped save Abraham once."

"You mean Lincoln? Abe Lincoln?"

She just smiled and said that it was a pleasure to finally meet me.

Suddenly, an obvious thought occurred to me: *How could these people possibly know who I am or where I work?*

As if sensing my bafflement, Opie said, "Michael, I don't know anyone named Jimbo, and I can assure you this is not part of any setup. I know that this must seem very confusing, and I am not at liberty to explain all the details. But I can tell you this—life and death are not as clear cut as most people would have you believe."

"Could you possibly be a little bit less specific?" I quipped.

She pondered a bit, limped a few steps, and began to offer a slightly more detailed explanation:

"The universe is made up of energy, and every living entity is composed of this energy. As a science teacher, you know energy can never be created or destroyed; it can only change forms. Therefore, in the most elementary of senses, living organisms composed of this energy can never really be destroyed or die. Living and dying are just different stages of the energy cycle. Remember, Michael, some things happen for a reason, even things that seem strange to you at the time."

"Are you talking about collective or cosmic consciousness?"

"Well, in a manner of speaking, yes. There is a connection between both universes and between individuals from both universes. A number of distinguished Earth scientists believed in this possibility," she elaborated.

"A connection between both universes! What other universe are you talking about?" I questioned, now even more confused.

With that, they vanished. I mean they literally vanished. One second there, and then poof! Gone. And, no, I wasn't thinking *Ghostbusters* weird—just *Ghostbusters* gone!

There are some people who knock the pyramids
because they don't have elevators.

—Unknown Author

Journal Entry 8

Pyramids and Chambers

I decided to walk the eight blocks to the Museum of
Natural History. I needed time to think and clear my head
just a bit. Seeing "living" ghosts does that to me every
once in a while. I was starting to really question my sanity.
Why were these unexplained occurrences happening to
me? After all, I lived a relatively mundane and boring
life! It is true that I've always had a bit of an imagination,
but this was getting ridiculous. Still, it seemed like going
to the museum to see the Great Pyramid was the right
thing to do. I wasn't completely sure why. It was just a
gut feeling.

In a strange way, I was somewhat comforted by what
Opie had said about life and death. I had never really
been a religious person, and I'd been even less so after my
father's death, but I always felt that I had a strong spiritual
connection to the world. I considered myself more of a
spiritual person than a religious one.

What really seemed to comfort me was a renewed feeling
of hope. In a certain way, I had always had a pragmatic
view of death. In my way of thinking, there were only two
possibilities. The first possibility is that we die and there
is nothing. If that's the way it is, and there is nothing,
we won't know anything or feel anything, so why worry

about it? If there is truly nada, we won't feel sad or lonely or miss anyone. While this makes sense from a scientific point of view, the spiritual side of me felt disappointed to think there was a 50 percent chance of nothingness forever. The other possibility is that there is something beyond death. Whether that means there is a heaven or utopia—or hell—I am not sure, but at least there would be something beyond emptiness and nullity. Even if Opie and her friends were figments of my delusional imagination, her words had bolstered my hope of some nirvana instead of an unending abyss of nothingness. I guess that was the spiritual side of me kicking in: spiritual side, one; pragmatic science guy side, zero.

I arrive at the Museum of Natural History, which is located in an area known as the National Mall. I'm sure there is some plausible explanation for the name of this area, still I have always wondered it is called The National Mall when there is really nothing to make you think of a mall—no stores, food courts, or expensive department stores. Just as I have always wondered why a driveway is called a driveway when you really park your car on it. And a parkway is called a parkway when you drive on it instead of parking.

Anyway, there wasn't the usual large crowd normally present in the summer months at the Smithsonian. As I entered the building, emptying my pockets and walking through the metal detectors—standard routine after 9/11—I started to think about Brace and his role, if any, in the aberrant *de novo* events which now seemed to have become a daily occurrence in my life. Could there have been any truth to what Brace's mom had told me about his demise? If so, how could that make any sense? I believed

Caden

I might get some answers within the Great Pyramid of Giza, or at least that's what I wanted to believe.

I determined there was nothing indicating an exhibit for the Great Pyramid of Giza. However, there were some interesting exhibits, such as an exhibit about the *Scarlet Knight*—or RU27—an autonomous underwater glider that, in 2009, followed the path Christopher Columbus took as he returned to Spain from New Jersey. Since I was a graduate of Rutgers University, it did catch my attention even though it was not what I was looking for. There was also an exhibit entitled More than Meets the Eye, which seemed to be really apropos given my recent experiences; it really reinforced the idea that even I couldn't make up what had been going on.

Although these exhibits seemed a tad ironic to me personally, I decided to continue to the second floor. There were only two floors, and since the Great Pyramid of Giza exhibit, my main reason for visiting, wasn't located on the first floor, my Charlie Chan instincts told me it had to be on the second floor.

There were some implausible exhibit names like "Against All Odds" and "Are We So Different?" But I could find nothing on the Great Pyramid of Giza. There was, however, one exhibit called "Eternal Life in Ancient Egypt," and once again my detective skills suggested that might be the one I wanted.

As I walked into the exhibit, my Spidey senses kicked in. Okay, so maybe I watched too many cartoons as a kid (and an adult), but I felt as if I was in the right place.

The walls were adorned with displays of mummy masks through time, reflecting the changing styles of coffin decoration. The oldest mask dated back to Amenhotep III (ca. 1388–1212 BCE), and the most recent mask, painted in a Greek style, dated back to 50–200 CE. Although these masks were oddly captivating, they were not my primary objective.

I continued down the corridor into the first room on the right. It focused on the mummy-making process. It was a step-by-step guide, and it included a mummy dating to about twenty-two hundred years ago. If it was a book it would be called *Making Mummies for Dummies*. A giant plaque read: "Scientific study indicates that he ate little meat, and his lungs contained soot, probably inhaled while tending fires." Even as a science guy, I was often amazed by what we could glean by analyzing remains from so long ago.

The adjacent room contained grave treasures. These small fortunes were intended to provide the deceased with the spiritual and physical support needed for a smooth passage into eternity. There was a mummy dating back to the period of Egyptian history that began with Alexander the Great's conquest of Egypt and ended with the death of Cleopatra. It was decorated with a richly painted gilt mask made of *cartonnage* (which is like papier-mâché, only with linen instead of paper). The mask bore various symbols that linked the deceased man with the god Osiris, his resurrection, and his elevation to king of the world of the dead.

Although fascinating, this wasn't what I was looking for either. After searching all of the rooms of this exhibit and having no luck, I was about to give up when I saw it. It was something that seemed to be really, really out of place. It was a framed picture of the movie advertisement for *Gone with the Wind*, and it was hanging on the wall next to a mummy mask. Somehow I had missed this picture before, but I felt that it had to be a sign of things to come.

As I moved closer to the picture, I noticed there were some hieroglyphics written at the bottom of the frame. Suddenly, I remembered the note Brace had left me. I reached into my pocket and found the note, even though I didn't remember bringing it with me to DC. These symbols were almost identical. The only difference was that these hieroglyphic symbols were fashioned in a golden kind of Braille. As I traced my fingers over them, I instantly became cognizant of what I had been looking for—the Great Pyramid of Giza exhibit became visible only to me.

I walked into the main entrance of the pyramid, which was made of massive Tura limestone blocks and stood around fifty feet high. It led to a cramped horizontal passageway. As I continued along the corridor, crouching, as it was only about three feet high and wide, I realized the passage was sloping slightly downward at a small angle. This passageway led to a lower chamber. The corridor was dimly lit with torches. Dirt was strewn across most of the floor, and a plethora of cobwebs adorned the walls. After inching along about ninety feet, I noticed another ingress, which appeared to ascend and lead to other chambers.

I slowly continued downward where the passage leveled off after a little more than three hundred yards. Trekking another thirty feet, I finally reached the lower chamber. It appeared to have been cut into and below the bedrock. The air was stagnant and malodorous. The room in which I found myself appeared to be unfinished, and there were no signs to indicate what its original purpose would have been. The room appeared barren except for a few small sealed chests, each with a strange symbol on top. I was unable to open the chests, and I got the sense they were not important.

The only thing in the room, other than these strange chests, was a collection of creepy insects and reptilian life forms that slithered across the earthen floors of this chamber. A quote from Dr. Henry Walton Jones Jr. in *Indiana Jones and the Raiders of the Lost Ark* entered my mind: "Snakes. Why did it have to be snakes?"[2] I quickly decided there was no reason to stay.

Relieved to have left the lower chamber, I slowly ascended back up to the main entrance; the fetid smell thankfully receding with each step. Eventually I reached the egress that led to the ascending chamber or chambers. I continued to huddle along the cramped passageway until I entered what is known as the grand gallery.

Someone, or something, must have had a quirky sense of humor, because as I entered, I heard the song "Walk Like an Egyptian" by the Bangles playing in the background—I think. The grand gallery appeared to be a continuation of the ascending passageway, but it was much more open— around twenty-five or thirty feet high at the entrance, and at least seven feet wide. To the left there appeared to be another walkway and entrance, probably leading

[2]   *Indiana Jones and the Raiders of the Lost Ark*. Dir. Steven Spielberg. Writers Lawrence Kasdan, George Lucas. Paramount Pictures, 1981. Film.

to the queen's chamber. The blocks of stone in the walls were beveled inward by a couple of inches on either side. There were seven steps leading to the top of the grand gallery, which appeared much narrower at the top. The roof appeared to be comprised of slabs of stone laid at a slightly steeper angle than the floor of the gallery, so that each stone fit into a slot cut in the top of the gallery like the teeth of a ratchet. Just before the roof, there was another passageway leading to another chamber, probably the king's chamber.

I decided to look in the first chamber. As I entered, there was a tremendous shake and rattle, and the floor began to shift and sway. Before I could retreat to the opening that led to the grand gallery, with a thunderous racket, one of the colossal limestone blocks fell, thereby blocking the exit. There were shattered chunks of limestone surrounding me and a thick chocking dust cloud appeared from the ruble. Instantly, I was trapped, with only one option remaining—to continue forward and hope there was another way out. With a futile gesture, I pulled out my cell phone only to confirm there was no signal.

Forlorn thoughts overtook me. The old saying "trapped like a rat in a cage" crossed my mind. I took a deep breath and concentrated. I thought to myself, *I am a teacher. I teach teenagers, so I am used to disasters. I can handle this.*

There was sufficient air thanks to tiny airshafts that had been circumspectly incorporated by the ancient builders. Moving forward, I would not suffocate. Food and hydration would eventually become an issue, but not immediately, as I had a protein bar and a bottle of water with me in my backpack.

It was a conspicuously puzzling situation. Going back the way I had come was impossible. The only option was to proceed carefully forward past the broken limestone. I entered the chamber next to the ingress of the grand gallery. It was clear that it was the queen's chamber; I knew this because there was a giant plaque at the opening identifying it as such. Actually, the plaque was written in red hieroglyphics, but it seemed that I was suddenly and mysteriously able to decipher hieroglyphics! *Maybe there's something in the air causing me to hallucinate, or perhaps I have acquired a new super power that gives me the ability translate ancient languages.*

Maybe with my newly discovered abilities, I would be able to decipher Brace's message. I took it out of my pocket. As I looked at the symbols, I realized that I was able to change the symbols into words. It read: "The answer lies in another dimension; it is your destiny." I wasn't exactly sure what to make of the message, but it did seem to go along with the general theme of my recent life. I folded up the note, put it back in my pocket, and explored the chamber.

The chamber, which had a gabled roof, was made up entirely of polished limestone. There was no evidence of a queen, or that there ever had been the intention of burying a queen here. The walls were bare and devoid of any writing; however, there were three strange objects arranged in the center of the floor: a miniature granite sphere, a tiny wooden slat, and a miniscule copper object in the form of a swallow's tail. I was not sure what their markings meant, but I put them in my backpack. I have learned from years of going to yard sales that you never know what objects you might find that could come in handy one day.

Exiting the queen's chamber and reentering the grand gallery, I made one last-ditch effort to see if I could retrace my path back to the entrance of the exhibit. But this was to no avail. The entrance was completely blocked by a gargantuan stone. My only recourse was to investigate the last chamber, the king's chamber. There was a small aperture at the top left corner of the grand gallery, which I deduced must lead to that chamber.

Upon entering the royal chamber, I was partly relieved and nonplussed to see a familiar figure within the chamber. Turbo, the Lurch-like guy from my dream, approached me as I entered the main compartment. He was now dressed in ancient Egyptian garb—a long linen pleated kilt along with leather sandals. His lips and fingernails were painted with a reddish dye—henna most likely. He also wore a fancy wig comprised of what looked to be real human hair. His eyes and eyebrows were enhanced with black kohl. Apparently, Turbo liked to dress the part— whatever the current role was. My suspicions seemed to be confirmed; Turbo had a dry sense of humor. "I am pleased you found the king's chamber. We were starting to worry about you," he began.

"We?" I inquired.

"The overseer and Brace, of course," Turbo nonchalantly replied.

So Brace really did exist, and I wasn't totally crazy. That was a good thing. I think. But I wondered about the overseer.

Apparently reading my mind, Turbo continued, "I'm sure you are confused and feel bedeviled, but if you follow me, the overseer will explain."

Logic dictated (Mr. Spock would have been proud of me) that my only recourse was to follow Turbo and hope the overseer would explain what the hell was going on. He led me to the king's chamber, which was entirely lined with alabaster-colored granite. The flat roof was made up of nine colossal slabs of stone and looked to be slightly unstable. Above the main roof were five separate vertical chambers with separate flat roofs, except for the last chamber, which had a pointed roof. Turbo explained that these were relieving chambers intended to safeguard against the possibility of a roof collapsing under the weight of the stones above the king's chamber. Finally, he had given me a piece of information that was actually comforting, and not just extra fluff.

But I felt that comfort too soon. Turbo continued speaking and informed me that the first four compartments, in order, were referred to as the Davidson's, Wellington's, Lady Arbuthnot's and Campbell's compartments. The highest chamber was apparently nameless. All the chambers remained unfinished, as they apparently were never intended to be seen. However, there was some sort of mason's mark on the outside wall of the Campbell's compartment. Turbo referred to the markings as pertaining to the Guardians.

As we entered the main compartment of the king's chamber, I spotted Brace. He was wearing a silvery jumpsuit. He was talking to an elderly gentleman—the same one who had disappeared with Brace on the Margate beach. He was probably the overseer. The overseer was wearing a violet robe. He had a white mustache and beard, suggesting an ancient quality of wisdom and of being out of time.

They were both standing next to the largest object in the room, a large granite sarcophagus with a broken corner. It was not evident if this tomb contained any resident, and I wasn't about to inquire.

As I approached, Brace gestured hello, and the overseer extended his hand and said, "Hello, Michael. My name is Enoch, and I think I can fill in some of the missing blanks."

Imagination is the beginning of creation. You imagine what you desire, you will what you imagine and at last you create what you will.

—George Bernard Shaw

Journal Entry 9

The Other Big Bang

"I am sure this must all seem unsettling to you," Enoch began, "but I can offer you an explanation. Of course, only you can decide if you find it reasonable. Why don't you sit down." He gestured to some benches along the wall. "This all might sound a little dubious; however, I assure you that everything I tell you is true."

"Enoch, is it? I'm hoping your little disappearance with Brace at Who Knew wasn't a commentary on my band," I joked.

"The music wasn't my cup of tea, but yes, it was most pleasing. Now, if you would please take a seat, I will elaborate."

"It doesn't seem like I have much of a choice, so go ahead. I'm listening."

He mumbled something about there always being *choices* as he walked over to the left corner of the room where a small bar suddenly became illuminated. Enoch reached behind the structure and pulled out a turquoise-colored bottle. He filled four glasses with a clear liquid. "Will you join us for an aperitif?"

Of course I declined. "Sorry. I gave up drinking last week," I quipped.

He lamented, "Pity. This particular elixir is rich in nutrients that nourish the body besides tasting delicious, but no matter. Perhaps in time." He settled on one of the benches. I settled on a facing one.

"Michael, have you ever experienced the sensation or feeling that you belonged somewhere else and not on Earth at this time?"

I didn't answer, but he must have seen the look of intrigue on my face, because he continued. "I see that you understand. You know there is a perfectly logical explanation for this sensation, this feeling of not belonging and disconnect."

"Okay. I'm listening."

"In addition, have you experienced an illogical fear or phobia that you can't explain or understand?"

I chimed in, "You mean like driving over certain bridges or along certain highways even though I don't have a fear of driving in general?"

"Yes, that is certainly one of the side effects some of us have experienced here on Earth."

"Here on Earth?" I repeated.

Enoch looked at Brace and Turbo; both nodded in agreement. Enoch cleared his throat and began again. "Let me try to explain. As you probably know, the Universe is composed of both light matter and dark matter, the latter sometimes referred to as anti-matter."

"Isn't most of the universe composed of this dark matter?"

"That's fairly accurate. A little more than eighty percent of all the matter that appears to be contained within this Universe is composed of dark matter," Enoch said.

"And isn't all this theoretical speculation? Because, if I remember correctly, we can't directly observe this dark matter?"

Enoch smiled. "Although it's true that the dark matter cannot be seen directly, it can be detected by emitted or scattered electromagnetic radiation as well as by its gravitational effects on visible matter. I can assure you that it is quite real."

As I looked at Enoch skeptically, he continued, "There are really two types of anti-matter—baryonic and non-baryonic. Baryonic dark matter, which is the minority of all dark matter, forms massive halo objects that form connections and slight interactions with light matter."

"So, basically, you are saying that matter and anti-matter can interact without annihilation?"

"In rudimentary terms, yes. The minority of dark matter can come in contact with light matter, but it is slightly more complicated than that."

I was slightly befuddled, but I encouraged him to continue.

"Non-baryonic dark matter makes up the major portion of dark matter. This matter is not formed from atoms, at least not in the traditional sense. It is formed within light matter and baryonic matter. This major portion is made from neutrinos, axions, and supersymmetric particles, which don't exist in the light-matter universe. This non-baryonic matter did not contribute to the big bang or the big bang nucleosynthesis of this universe."

I tried to coalesce what Enoch was implying. "Are you saying that there are really two separate and distinct universes, one composed of matter and one composed of anti-matter?"

Enoch looked slightly pleased. "Not exactly. The other universe has a different ratio of anti-matter to normal matter. No single universe could exist completely of only one type of matter; there must be some kind of balance for stability. The other universe is larger than this universe because it is older; it has had more time to expand. As you know, the nature of universes is to expand until they begin to collapse back on themselves and start all over."

"You mean another big bang, don't you?"

"Yes, that is correct. The other universe, known as the Zero Universe, existed billions of years before this universe existed. At first, only the Zero Universe existed in this dimension, but after billions of years of expansion, the outer fringes of the anti-matter universe became unstable. To counterbalance this instability, another big bang occurred, which created this universe. To simplify things, we can call this newer universe, Universe Earth. In a rudimentary sense, the newer universe forms an outer backbone or skeletal framework for the outermost fringes of the older universe, and the reverse is also true. Pure matter cannot occupy the same exact region in space as anti-matter without cataclysmic results. However, from a structural and stability standpoint, both universes have become dependent on the other's existence."

"Who or what created these universes?"

"I am not at liberty to tell you at this point, and frankly, I am not sure it would make any sense if I did, but please let me continue," Enoch replied. "As you know, this universe, as it is with most universes, started with an explosion, a big bang as Earth scientists refer to it. The light elements, hydrogen, helium, and lithium, were created from the elementary particles during the first few minutes of the big bang. The heavier elements and particles were created within the core of stars at a later time."

"Are the elementary particles subatomic parts of the atom?"

"Yes, they are particles that have no definite substructure, meaning that they have no smaller pieces. They cannot be broken down any further. These particles—leptons, quarks, and gauge bosons—are therefore the building blocks of all matter and anti-matter. Each light matter elementary particle has its anti-matter elementary particle counterpart."

"Okay. I think I understand, but I don't see why you are telling me this or how this involves me."

"Patience, Michael. I am getting to that point."

I nodded irresolutely, and he went on, "It is common knowledge to Earth's astrophysicists that, right after the big bang, there was a period of primordial nucleosynthesis, also known as the big bang nucleosynthesis (BBN). This BBN took place just a few minutes after the initial big bang and lasted only for a very brief period. This is when the heavier isotopes of the lighter elements were created."

"Right. That is well known by most astrophysicists and *Readers Digest* subscribers," I joked.

He ignored my joke. Either he didn't know what *Readers Digest* was or didn't think it was funny. "What is not commonly known," he continued, "is that during this same time period, heavier isotopes containing matter and anti-matter elementary particles were fused together to create a number of elements containing both types of matter. These bi-matter elements eventually formed the core of the middle area or a nether region between the two universes."

I was being to get that uncanny, disturbing feeling again. I was even waiting for some weird music to play any second. It didn't, and he continued. "Although this region acts as an encumbrance between the light and dark universes, keeping direct pure matter from contacting pure anti-matter, it also provides a portal to either universe. In addition, these special elements were also incorporated into some organisms as well. Although they were rare, there were beings whose DNA contained some of these unique elements belonging to both universes."

He stopped and gave me a minute to reflect on what he had just told me. "Michael, do you see the implications of this?"

I paused for a moment. "If pure light matter and dark matter came into direct contact with each other, there would be an explosion or annihilation of both universes."

Enoch nodded in agreement.

I continued, "But I suppose if there was an entity with a mixture of both light matter and dark matter, that entity might be able to exist in both universes without causing any decimation of either realm."

Enoch glanced over at Brace and Turbo with a pleased expression.

"But I still don't understand what any of this has to do with me?" I whispered dishearteningly.

"Don't you, Michael?"

I was afraid that I was beginning to understand what Enoch was implying, but the implications seemed too farfetched, even for me.

After a brief period of silence, Brace said, "You and I, Turbo, Enoch, and a number of others are such entities."

War means fighting, and fighting means killing.

—Nathan Bedford Forrest

Journal Entry 10

Seven Pines

It was a typical Virginia morning—very gray, malodorous, and humid. It was one of the last days of May 1862—the rainy season. The torrential rains of the previous evening had softened the ground and flooded much of the lowlands of the Chickahominy River. The river became more like a capricious and slow moving stream spreading itself out into sylvan swamps, which flowed around many small islands. In its own unpredictable way, these islands created a mile-long estuaries, contoured by scenic low bluffs.

Juliet Hopkins could sense the inevitable stench of approaching suffering, pain, and death that was about to settle within Henrico County, Virginia. A native Virginian, Juliet was known to many as Opie. She was now forty-four years old and had unfortunately acquired a sixth sense about approaching battles. Although her main interests lay on the battlefield of fallen soldiers, tending to their wounds and putting some of the broken pieces back together, much of her time was devoted to running the three military hospitals for Alabama soldiers in Richmond.

Only on certain occasions was she allowed near the battle sites, as she was considered too valuable to be at risk. She requisitioned supplies, scrutinized incoming shipments from individual citizens, and inspected the wards daily to ensure the patients were receiving proper care and nourishment. Opie hired nurses; wrote letters for soldiers; handled their petitions for furloughs; collected and distributed newspapers, magazines, and books; recorded the names of the dead; and shipped personal belongings home to their families, including a carefully wrapped lock of hair from each deceased soldier.

The Peninsula Campaign (originally called the Urbanna Plan) was a major Union operation launched in southeastern Virginia during the spring and early summer months of 1862. Commanded by Major General George B. McClellan, the operation was an amphibious turning movement (transporting 100,000 union troops by water) intended to capture the Confederate capital of Richmond by circumventing the Confederate states' army in Northern Virginia.

The roads leading into and out of Richmond radiate out from the city like spokes of a wheel. The Williamsburg Stage Road was one of these roads. It crossed the Chickahominy at the Bottoms Bridge only eleven miles from the capital of the South. Along this road, the Union corps of Keyes and Heintzelamn were stationed. Parallel to this road ran the Richmond and York River Railroad, a critical source of supplies for the Confederate capital city.

Just seven miles from Richmond another road intersecting the Williamsburg Stage was known as the Nine Mile Road. Exactly at the point where these roads intersected grew a cluster of seven pine trees, giving rise to the name "Seven Pines," a name that would later be associated with one of the bloodiest battles of the Civil War. Where the Nine Mile Road crossed the railroad tracks stood the Fair

Oaks Station. A thousand or so yards beyond these pines, two farmhouses known as the Fair Oaks Farm existed amongst a grove of oak trees.

Stationed at this farm was a division of General Keys' 4th Corps from the army of the Potomac under the command of General Casey. Approximately a fifth of a mile in front of Fair Oaks Farm was the picket line, extending in the shape of a crescent moon from the swamps to the Chickahominy. General Couch's division of 4th corps lay to the rear of this line. General Kearney's division guarded the Fair Oaks railroad station.

This formed the three lines of defense for the 4th Corps division of the Union soldiers. Originally this area had been arboraceous. Now it was mostly a vast marshland. The demarcation where the proud majestic oak trees had once stood was no more. These regal trees had been cut down to form an abatis with rifle pits and redoubts for heavy artillery. The picket lines lay in the front of the few remaining uncut trees. This allowed the Union solders to see the approach of the Confederates on either side of the clearing.

Confederate General Joseph E. Johnston was seeking to protect Richmond from General McClellan's advancement. Johnston hoped to take advantage of the swollen Chickahominy River, which had split the Union forces into two main divisions, the third and fourth corps. He orders General D. H. Hill to attack the fourth division, which was isolated from the rest of the troops at Seven Pines.

As if an ominous sign, on the night before the battle, there was a deluge—one of the most violent storms in that region in over a generation. Throughout the night, the tempest raged. Thunderbolts that seemed to personally come from Thor's own hand rained without cessation. The night sky was iridescent with electric flashes, and the earth became inundated with water, which, combined with dirt, formed a thick morass. In the morning, the soldiers from both factions arose from mire- and-mud-soaked beds to complete their morning duties.

Shortly after an early dinnertime, the booming of artillery and the staccato of small-arms fire echoed across the ominous skies. John Nance Garner III was preparing to enter his first major battle. John was a member of the Texas Brigade, often referred to as Hood's Brigade. Private Garner had enlisted in the 4th Infantry Regiment along with a number of his neighbors from Detroit, Texas. This regiment was commanded by General Hill. Like most young men of his time about to fight in a war for the first time, he was filled with visions of glory and heroic victories.

General Hill and the 4th Infantry grew weary of waiting for battle and advanced to the front lines along the Williamsburg Stage Road. Hill's soldiers burst through the woods, attacking the Union soldiers that formed the picket lines at the edge of the sparse forest. At first, the Union soldiers under General Naglee's command gave way to the shower of bullets that rained down on them from the Gray uniforms. Although outnumbered three to one, the Union soldiers began to stubbornly battle back.

This conflict raged fiercely for nearly three hours. Without warning, General Rain's brigade executed a flank movement and plowed in on the Union soldiers from the left. At the same time, General Rode's brigade attacked from the right. The only hope for the Union soldiers was to fall back and make a last stand at Seven Pines where General Couch was stationed.

At Seven Pines, General Keyes' astute eye evaluated the situation and determined that a small rise of ground was the key to avoiding a complete rout of the Union lines. To reach this high ground, he would lead his men across battle lines a distance of nearly eight hundred yards. During their mad dash to reach this critical piece of land, a deadly volley of gunfire poured onto his ranks as the Gray Coats attempted to also reach this high point of land.

Unfortunately for the Confederates, General Keyes' men reached this high ground first. With this new advantage, the Union soldiers were able to unleash a tremendous volley of firepower that proved to be too much for the assaulting columns of Confederate soldiers. One of the soldiers gravely injured was Private Garner.

For reasons unbeknownst to Juliet, she had been given permission by her commander to leave the hospital and be on the front lines with the boys that day. Never one to question good luck, she had quickly accepted the offer. Besides, she had been out in the field for some time now and sensed that she would be needed very shortly. She was with General Hill's men when the conflict exploded, spraying the earthen-brown soil with bloody-red color against the background of the Blue and Gray.

As evening approached, with the river fog fast approaching, the Confederates collected their wounded and gave up the battle for the hill. The injured and un-injured spent the night in their captured camps. Although injured herself, Juliet Hopkins attended too many of the fallen Confederate soldiers, including John Garner.

Garner had been shot just above his left shoulder. He'd lost consciousness during the trip down the hill and had been carried by a fellow soldier to the base camp. Juliet realized Private Garner had also stopped breathing. She was able to successfully revive him. He was transferred to a hospital she had established in nearby Richmond where he eventually recovered.

Although it was unknown to her at the time, her purpose at Seven Pines was more substantial than she or anyone could have realized. One of the soldiers who would have died without her help was Private Garner. He survived the war in part due to the assistance of Juliet Hopkins. He later fathered a child named John Nance Garner IV.

As an adult, John Garner IV became a very important politician in the United States. He served as a member of the Texas House of Representatives from 1898 to 1902. He was elected as a Democrat to the United States House of Representatives in 1902 and was elected from the district fourteen subsequent times, serving until 1933. Garner's hard work and integrity made him a respected leader in the House, and he was chosen to serve as minority floor leader for the Democrats in 1929, and then as Speaker of the United States House of Representatives in 1931.

In 1932, Garner ran for the Democratic presidential nomination against the governor of New York, Franklin Roosevelt. When it became evident that Roosevelt was the stronger of the candidates, Garner cut a deal with Roosevelt to become his vice-presidential candidate. He was re-elected to the 73rd Congress on November 8, 1932, and on the same day was elected vice- president of the United States, making him the only man to serve as both speaker of the house and president of the senate on the same day, March 4, 1933. He was re-elected vice president in 1936 and served in that office until 1941.

It was widely speculated that Franklin D. Roosevelt (FDR) would not have initially won the presidency over the incumbent Herbert Hoover without Garner as his running mate. FDR was known as a tremendous leader in the United States. His New Deal policies helped ease the United States through the Depression years. His leadership during World War II cannot be underestimated.

All of this might not have occurred if not for the help of Juliet Hopkins. Juliet died, or rather left this planet, in 1890. It was then that she became aware of her role in this universe. She, along with Brace, Turbo, Enoch, and many others were from the older universe. They were members of the Guardians of the Universe and belonged to Universe Zero.

You cannot escape the responsibility of
tomorrow by evading it today.

—Abraham Lincoln

Journal Entry 11

Four Score and the Seven-Year Itch

I closed my eyes and contemplated what I had just been told. Could any of these manifestos be remotely true? When I opened my eyes to ask Enoch a question, I wasn't inside the Great Pyramid of Giza anymore. I was sitting back at the Waffle House. Jimbo and his top waitress, Margarita, were looking at me with concern.

Jimbo looked at me probingly and asked, "Michael, are you all right?"

"I seem to be a little confused, but I think I'm okay. Why, did something happen to me?"

Jimbo nodded and replied, "As you were leaving, you walked outside and collapsed. We carried you back inside and sat you down. You were unconscious for only a few seconds. We were about to call for an ambulance just before you woke up."

Since I never wore a watch, I pulled out my antiquated cell phone and looked at the time. Sure enough, it was still July 3, and only one minute had elapsed since I had left the Waffle House. I wasn't exactly sure what to say to them. Jimbo was a trusted friend, but it wasn't as if I could tell him what I thought I remembered just happened, or

141

where I thought I had been. They would certainly call the men in the white coats—and tell them to bring their straitjackets—if I tried. It suddenly occurred to me that maybe they should call the straitjacket guys anyway and put an end to this madness.

Against all logic and reason, I decided against this, at least for now, and thought of a plausible explanation. "When I stepped outside I felt a little lightheaded. Probably because of the waffles," I said and grinned at Jimbo. "I must have blacked out or something."

Jimbo muttered something about his waffles being the lightest and fluffiest in town.

"You went down like somebody shot you," Margarita said.

Margarita Cansino was born in Brooklyn, New York. She moved to Hollywood, California, when she was eighteen. After a number of failed attempts at acting, she moved back east when she was twenty-two and settled in Washington DC. She was now twenty-eight and had been Jimbo's longest tenured employee.

Because of her looks, I had always been surprised that she'd never made it as an actress or model. She was five feet six inches tall and weighed about a hundred and twenty pounds. Although she had changed her hair color eight times or more since I first met her, she was actually stunning, and if it were not for Erika … well anyway …

Jimbo gave her a glaring look and said, "Seriously, Mike, you should have a doctor check you out, just to play it safe."

"Of course, Jimbo, you're probably right. I'll have the doctor at the hotel check me over when I get back. I think I'm due for a tune-up anyway."

"Michael, are you sure you'll be okay to make it back on your own?" Margarita asked with a concerned look.

I wondered if Erika knew how faithful I really was to her. "Thanks, Margarita, but I'll be just fine."

"Okay, maybe another time then," she replied and went over to take an order from a family who had just walked in.

I am not sure turning down a possible offer from a pretty young lady was the James Bondish thing to do, but it was the right thing to do. Maybe I wasn't a spy, but I did kind of have my own spy anyway.

As I walked out the door, I saw Margarita glance at me out of the corner of her eye, and I thought, *In another place and time, maybe.* She reminded me of someone, but I just couldn't remember who.

Even though it seemed as if I had been trapped within the Great Pyramid of Giza for hours, it appeared that only a few minutes had transpired. Therefore, it was still morning, and too early to go back to the hotel. So I decided to hop on the metro and visit the Lincoln Memorial.

It seemed the logical thing to do since, somehow, Lincoln had been in my dream, and Turbo had said some of my dream might provide insight. The closest stop to the memorial was located at Foggy Bottom. It was still a mile-long walk from the Foggy Bottom station to the Lincoln

Memorial, but I looked forward to the walk, as I needed the time to clear my head and think.

Although it's true that I had always felt I didn't belong in this time and place, it had always been just a feeling until now. Except for being the lead singer in a college band, my life had been pretty normal until this year. Normal until Brace left that strange hieroglyphic note before he disappeared, which seemed to have triggered a chain reaction of bizarre events.

After about twenty minutes intense walking, and stopping to eat a cherry and pineapple water ice, I reached the memorial. It was located within an area known as the National Mall. The building was built in the form of a Greek Doric temple, featuring Yule marble, and contains a large seated sculpture of Abraham Lincoln with the inscriptions of two well-known speeches by Lincoln, The Gettysburg Address and his Second Inaugural Address.

The Lincoln Memorial is extremely impressive, measuring 190 feet by 120 feet and standing almost a hundred feet high. It is surrounded by a peristyle of thirty-six fluted Doric columns, one for each of the thirty-six states in the Union at the time of Lincoln's death, and two columns at the entrance behind the colonnade. Above the colonnade, inscribed on the frieze, are the names of the thirty-six states and the dates they entered the Union.

Whenever I visit this memorial, I cannot help but think how different our country's history might have been if Lincoln had not gone to Ford's Theater on that seemingly inauspicious evening. I had always been fascinated with the concept that changing one event—large or small—might lead to a chain of events that could alter the current reality. I wondered if there were multiple time lines that existed within the dimensions of our Universe.

Of course, there was always the possibility the events in the universe were already predetermined, and changing one or more events still might not alter the eventual outcome of the current time line, or of multiple time lines, if they existed in the first place. Therefore, even if the good Doctor Soto's assessment about Lincoln's terminal condition was correct, it was possible things still might be as they currently are anyway, whether or not he had been assassinated.

As I was drowning in a sea of thoughts, I heard a voice inside my head. I talk to myself all the time, so I knew the sound of my own voice. This voice didn't sound like me; rather, believe it or not, it sounded like Norma Jean Mortensen—Marilyn Monroe. Although her voice sounded childlike, it also had a very soft, sexy, feminine quality. There was no mistaking this sultry voice.

Although she was a little before my time, I had seen a few of her movies. Her voice was distinctive. Writers had used words such as *cotton candy*, *smoky*, *windy*, *lollipops*, *velvet*, *champagne*, and *lava* to describe it. One psychologist even referred to her voice as *wet*. The voice was all of these descriptive words, and it was playing in my head now.

"Hi, Michael. I think you should believe in yourself. You are not as crazy as you might think."

Hello, Marilyn, are you really the Marilyn Monroe? I said inside of my head. I guess it was getting to the point where I was not surprised by the unexpected.

"Well, of course, silly. Who else would I be?"

A most enticing and lovely figment of my overactive imagination, I responded.

"Why would you think like that?" she said, cotton candy like.

For starters, you died in 1962, I replied.

"Oh, that messy thing. I didn't really die then. There were so many crazy theories on my death. Some said I killed myself. Others thought the CIA or the Mafia was involved. The meanest ones believed that John and Robert had something to do with it."

You mean the Kennedy brothers? I interjected.

"Yes. Lots of people started nasty rumors about John and me, but we were always just good friends. He and Bobby were good men," she solemnly said. "The truth is, Michael, I just transmuted."

It suddenly occurred to me that I had a craving for lollipops and champagne. I don't even like lollipops and champagne—two things that always give me headaches.

You mean you changed from one form or state of matter to another?

"You have a funny way of saying things, Michael. But of course, you don't understand yet. You will soon."

I will, Ms. Monroe?

"Yes. Eventually we all do at our given time. Instead of Ms. Monroe, why don't you call me Jean? It sounds a little less stuffy."

Okay, Jean. What is your role in all of this craziness that has recently become part of my everyday life?

"That's easy, silly. I am one of your guides. To be more specific, I am that little voice in your head that's trying to steer you in the right direction. I am related to the gut feeling everybody has, but I'm a little more complicated. That's why you don't see me. You only hear me inside your head—at least for now."

I thought about it for a moment. If I were really bonkers, would I have the good sense—and taste, for that matter— to choose Marilyn Monroe as a companion? Would it really be that awful occasionally seeing or hearing from Marilyn? Why did John McCain pick a "hockey mom" as a running mate? Why can't anybody seem to make a good-tasting decaffeinated coffee? Okay, I was beginning to lose a little focus. I took a deep breath, exhaled, and tried to concentrate. I thought out loud in my head, *Jean, what's my next move?*

"I am cognizant that I played a dumb blonde in many of my movies, but it was just an act. Even though I never took an IQ test, I have been told my intelligent quotient would have been well above average."

I've never been one to subscribe to stereotypes, so I'm sure you are smart. For some reason, I inherently believe that I should trust you. So what should I do now?

"The reason you trust me inherently is that I am one of your specific guides. Guides play a very important role in both universes. All of these details will become suppositions in time. I know you like to read, so maybe you could start at—"

The book store! "I interjected in my mind. *That's where I should go now?*

She giggled, as only Marilyn could and replied, "Maybe they were wrong, and there is hope for you after all."

Before I could think of a witty comeback, or who *they* represented for that matter, she was gone from inside my mind. Had I somehow picked Marilyn, or had she been chosen for me? Contrary to one of her famous movies, I preferred brunettes. I guess it really didn't matter; she was with me to help me, and I focused on that point. Besides, I was sure it could have been much worse. I could have had Rosanne Barr or Rosie O'Donnell as a guide.

The bookstore was located to the right of Lincoln's statue. It was very small, almost the size of a medium closet. Since the store sold only small trinkets, books, posters, and magazines, it stood to reason that I was supposed to find and buy one of those items, although the reasons were unclear.

It made sense to just "go with the flow" as they say. Now two things occurred to me. First, who are "they"? We always say *they*, but we are never quite sure who *they* really are. Secondly, acceptance or "going with the flow" has never been one of my strong points. If we all have reasons or deals for being who we are and where we are, then maybe this was my lesson: learning acceptance for things I couldn't change rather than fighting against them. Maybe there was a little Zen in me after all.

Calmed and reassured by this thought, I entered the bookstore believing that whatever my purpose was in this store, it would become apparent to me. The books in the store were dedicated to the Civil War and the life and death of Abraham Lincoln.

At first, nothing out of the ordinary caught my eye. But if I couldn't trust my own personal guide, a legendary film star, who may have been a figment of my own mind, then whom could I trust? Undaunted, I continued to search the store. Finally I noticed a small, round table located in the left corner against the back wall.

The oak table looked centuries old. Although I doubted its authenticity, it was an excellent reproduction of a nineteenth-century artifact. What drew my attention was the oddity of the front covers of the magazines that were spread out on the tabletop. Marilyn Monroe was pictured on all of the periodical covers. The names of her movies and movie production companies were listed underneath the pictures.

I might not have had the instincts or observational powers of Sir Arthur Conan Doyle's Sherlock Holmes, but a clue of this magnitude could not slip by me. Once again I seemed to be the only person who took notice of these magazines. There were thirty-three magazines with copyright dates ranging from 1947 to 1963. They were in surprisingly pristine condition, considering the ages of some. There was one magazine that appeared to be incomplete.

Starting from the beginning, I arranged the periodicals chronologically. I started with the1947 magazine entitled *The Shocking Miss Pilgrim*, which was the film debut for Miss Monroe despite the fact that she appeared for only a few seconds in the film. As I leafed through the magazine, I gleaned only rudimentary facts and other minutiae about the film.

Six magazines into my research, I came across *Ladies of the Chorus*, which provided no information either. However, I did learn that this film was considered her first major film appearance. Very useful information if ever I get to appear on *Jeopardy* or *Who Wants to be a Millionaire*. I do like my trivia!

The majority of her films were unknown to me. Only some of the more famous titles like *Some Like it Hot*, *Gentlemen Prefer Blondes*, *Bus Stop*, and *The Seven Year Itch* were familiar to me. Other than acquiring a boatload of useless *Jeopardy* information, I was not sure what I was supposed to be looking for.

I was down to the next-to-last magazine. It was entitled *The Misfits*. Either I remembered reading a long time ago about this film, or someone had planted the thought in my brain—probably the latter—but I knew that this film was significant. Probing the deepest recesses of my mind (some would say there's not much to probe), I started to remember.

The Misfits was the last completed film appearance for both Marilyn and Clark Gable, a childhood idol of hers. Gable suffered a heart attack two days after filming and died eight days later. A year and a half later, Marilyn passed away, or rather transmuted. Remembering the picture hanging in the Great Pyramid of Giza and that Clark Gable had played Rhett Butler in *Gone with the Wind*, I figured this could be the big clue as to the magazine I was looking for.

Opening the magazine confirmed my suspicions. Inside it read "Welcome to the Travelers' Guide for Universe Zero."

We knew we were talking about spies.
I knew he knew I knew.
I was digging my own grave.

—Christine Keeler

Journal Entry 12

The Spy Who Loved Me

When I was a child, the first James Bond movie I saw with my father in a movie theater was *The Spy Who Loved Me*. After the movie, I was hooked on spies. I wanted to be James Bond. Dreams of catching the winning touchdown pass in the Super Bowl were replaced with saving the world and getting the Bond girl with great name such as Pussy Galore, Plenty O'Toole, Xenia Onatopp, or Holly Goodhead. It never ceased to amaze me what the James Bond movies got away with, especially considering the stricter censorship back then.

One of the morose transitions of childhood to adulthood is the realization that very few people become what they dreamed of during their adolescence. Even sadder is that life is never quite like the movies. As I grew up—some might debate I never did—I realized I would never be James Bond or Buck Rogers, or any of my childhood heroes. Maybe that was the real appeal of characters like Peter Pan. We all had that small child within us that never wanted to grow up, some more than others. Anyway, I guess we all have to grow up some time.

It was July 4 and our last night in the capital city. For our last supper—no pun intended—I was supposed to meet Erika at Obelisk, a fancy Italian restaurant located at DuPont Circle. It had been highly recommended by one of her colleagues at work. Personally, I have come to trust spies when it comes to dining out. It makes sense when you think about it, since they have connections and are always traveling. Learning where to get a good meal becomes paramount, besides their mission, of course.

For a change, the weather was seasonally pleasant, and the humidity was low. I decided to spend the afternoon at the National Zoo. It is one of the oldest zoos in the country; the Philadelphia Zoo is the oldest. Whenever I am in any town, I usually visit the local zoo because it is a place where I can relax and become introspective.

To reach the National Zoo, I needed to take the Metro to the Woodley Park stop. From this stop I would take two escalators to the street level and then walk about half a mile. The second escalator is very, very, very steep. The synchronized, mechanical, die-cast aluminum moving stairs ascended upward for what always seemed like ten miles to me. For anyone who has even the slightest fear of heights, this particular escalator ride is a lot of fun—yeah, right.

After an eternity on the very fun escalator, I reach the street level and immediately felt relieved, as I am not a big fan of heights either. I turned left on Connecticut Avenue. As I continued walking in the direction of the zoo, I heard my spiritual guide talking inside my head.

With a wispy voice, Marilyn began, "Hi, Michael. Did you find the item you were looking for in the bookstore?"

I thought back—or talked back, I'm uncertain of which it is. "Yes, Jean. It was hard to miss the magazines with your old movies on the front covers," I responded.

She laughed; I had to admit her laugh had a certain desirable quality to it. "I am glad you found the book. Keep it with you because it will come in handy someday."

"Okay, I guess I could do that."

"The guide also has a little magic within it. It has the ability to shrink down to the size of a penny for easy storage and carrying," Jean informed me.

"Cool! Any other magic it can do?"

"Yes. It can also become invisible to everyone but you. For these tricks to occur, all you have to do is say the words, *presto change-o,* and think about what you want it to do."

"Great. I got it. Say the magic words and think *size of a penny* or *become invisible.*"

Jean laughed. "I was kidding about the *presto change-o* part, but there is something else," she said in a velvet voice.

Now I laughed. "Of course there is."

She hesitated slightly and began, "Not everyone is who he or she appears to be. This doesn't make people bad, just more complicated."

"What are you talking about?"

There was no response.

"Hello, you still there? Earth to Jean. Anyone out there in Universe Zero?"

Again, there was no response. Apparently my guide faded in and out. Maybe it was for the best. Having someone talking inside my head—besides myself—all the time would probably drive me crazy. It would drive anyone crazy.

It was obvious she was trying to tell me something, but what? It would be much easier if guides would just tell you what they were trying to say rather than speaking in riddles. Alas, I guess it was not their way, and Marilyn seemed to be no exception.

After walking for ten minutes, I reached the front entrance of the National Zoo. The main walkway through the zoo is called Olmstead Walk. My first stop was the Asian trail, which houses seven Asian species of animals. This was the newest part of the zoo and contained the sloth bears, fishing cats, Asian small-clawed otters, red pandas, a Japanese giant salamander, clouded leopards, and giant pandas—the rarest and most popular species.

Giant pandas are now native to only a few mountain ranges in central China—Sichuan, Shaanxi, and Gansu provinces. They were once more plentiful and lived in the lowland areas, but farming, forest clearing, and other development has now restricted giant pandas to only the mountains. I wondered if man would ever stop destroying the forests and undeveloped lands. I was afraid that the line in the song "Big Yellow Taxi," written and originally sung by Joni Mitchell and later popularized by numerous artists including the Counting Crows, about "having to pay a dollar to see trees in a museum" would be our future.

It is no thunderbolt that the giant panda is listed as endangered in the International Union for Conservation of Natures Red List of Threatened Species. According to their estimates, only approximately sixteen hundred remain in the wild. More than three hundred pandas live in zoos and breeding centers around the world, mostly in China.

At the end of the trail I found myself in the indoor enclosure section of the giant panda exhibit, watching Tian Tian. One of the keepers was explaining to the crowd that Tian's name means "more and more." In the wild, a giant panda's diet is almost exclusively bamboo. In zoos, the giant pandas eat bamboo, sugar cane, rice gruel, a special high-fiber biscuit, carrots, apples, and sweet potatoes. Tian was enjoying what looked like a giant cake of fruits and water ices. I had to admit, it did look good.

His mate Mia Xiang ("beautiful fragrance") was in another cubicle. The keeper mentioned they did spend most of their time together, but it was best to separate them when Tian was eating. I guess some people would think Tian Tian was just a typical guy.

Someone tapped me lightly on my shoulder.

"Hello, Michael. I didn't know you were a patron of our zoo," Margarita said.

"Hi, Margarita. I didn't see you there."

"Well, I was tailing you, and any operative worth her gold knows how to be covert."

"You were following me?"

She laughed, "Of course not. I just happened to be here and saw you watching the pandas. This is one of my favorite places to hang out in DC when I'm not serving our delicious waffles."

"Oh, you know us men. Sometimes we are completely oblivious. You're not really a spy, right?"

She smirked. "Yeah, you guys can really be clueless. And if I really was a secret agent and I told you, I would probably have to kill you anyway."

"I guess that makes sense. Since you are here, maybe you would like to keep me company?"

"You mean a zoo date?"

Feeling a little stupid, I tried to backtrack. "Since this is your hangout spot, and you are coincidently here anyway"—I wasn't so sure about the fact she just happened to be here, thinking about what Marilyn had said earlier—"and probably know your way around better than I do, we could stay together." I felt as if I was stammering on a bit.

"I guess logic dictates that I accept your offer."

I wondered if she was a "Trekkie" also.

She took my hand and led the way. She shared with me her favorite exhibits. Margarita was very knowledgeable and had a propensity for useless trivia and mindless minutia, like me. Maybe there was more to her than I realized. After about two hours, we finished our tour and were back at the visitor center.

"Thanks, Margarita. I had a great time, and I appreciate you sharing time at the zoo with me. If you ever happen to find yourself in Philadelphia, I know a great spot at the Philadelphia zoo where you can observe the lions really close," I mentioned proudly.

"So you have connections there?" she asked.

"Let's just say I know a guy who knows a guy."

She laughed and said, "You're welcome; it was fun for me too. Maybe I'll take you up on your offer sometime."

She looked at her watch. "I guess you'll have to meet Erika soon?"

"I was going to meet her for dinner before the Fourth of July festivities tonight. You could join us. I know Erika wouldn't mind. Besides, after all the years you've worked at the Waffle House, I don't think you two have ever met before."

She gave me a very brief, almost imperceptible, look of confusion and said, "You really don't completely understand women, do you, Michael? Anyway, as much as being a third wheel appeals to me, I do have my own plans."

"Maybe I don't understand women. Is it even possible for any man to fully understand a woman?"

She thought for a moment and acknowledged, "Good point."

We said our good-byes, and I was off to meet Erika. There was definitely something about Margarita, but I knew my heart and destiny belonged with Erika in this world. Of that I was sure; I never doubted it.

Erika and I were going to attend the celebration at the National Mall. The festivities included fireworks and bands playing near the Lincoln Memorial. For the first time, the Independence Day Parade was being held at night. It was sort of a spinoff of the nightly SpectroMagic parade, a Disney spectacle that marches down Main Street in the Magic Kingdom in Walt Disney World.

I was never a big parade guy, but I did think it would be cool to witness the first Independence Day nighttime spectacular. There would also be plenty of musical acts performing before the fireworks. A number of local bands would be playing along with local musicians like Roy Clark, Shannon, and Henry Rollins.

The president and vice president were also scheduled to attend the gala. For some reason, this year's celebration was really a big deal. Naturally, for security purposes, it was highly unusual for the president and vice president to attend the same function. However, due to the recent euphoria stemming from the lack of any terrorist activity, along with the current global stability, these concerns seemed minimized. A certain lollipop-like voice and a gut feeling, however, told me this wasn't a good idea.

I had just enough time to stop back at the hotel to shower and shave before meeting Erika. She had been at the agency all day, and thought she might not have time to stop back at the hotel before dinner, so she said it would be best to meet me at Obelisk.

Since this was a rare occasion, I decided to wear a suit and tie to dinner. I am not really a suit and tie kind of guy. Let's just say I voluntarily wear a suit as often as a Philadelphia sports team wins a championship!

I arrived just a minute or two before 5:30, and Erika was already waiting for me inside. The aroma of gravy and freshly made pasta was evident as I entered. The restaurant was rather small. The quaint room was dimly lit and looked like it had been someone's living room at some point. Obelisk had a very warm and cozy feel to it. I noticed there was no music playing; the only sound came from the indistinguishable conversations from the eleven tables in the small dining space.

"Hi, Michael. You're wearing a suit! Did the Eagles win a Super Bowl?" Erika asked slyly.

"You're kidding! I have only been alive and waiting for forty-seven years. I just thought I would surprise you during our last night in DC."

"Well, you look handsome in a suit. You ought to wear one a little more often."

"Thank you. You look pretty good as well. What's the plan after dinner?"

"I thought we would listen to the president's address before the parade. We don't have to stay too late because we have to catch an early train in the morning, but I would like to see at least a little of it," she responded.

"Sounds good." (Note to self: I think I say "sounds good" way too often.) "But there is something else," I said.

"Don't tell me, some more kooky events happened to you today?"

"Well, kind of. But I can tell you about them later. What is bothering me is that having both the president and vice president together in one place is a recipe for trouble." I didn't mention to her about my private voice and gut feeling.

"Michael, the security levels are at green, which are the lowest threat levels. Besides, the agency has beefed up security, just in case. I think things will be okay."

She seemed confident; unfortunately, I did not share that feeling. I wasn't ready to talk about the voice yet, so I decided to enjoy dinner and worry later. I wanted our last meal in DC to be filled with pleasant conversation, not talk about crazy events that might turn out to be mythical, and that might, in turn, lead to my next permanent home—Bellevue.

Our waitress was congenial and friendly, though I didn't understand half the words coming out of her mouth since they were all Italian names for special grapes and foods. Erika was able translate for me. The food was excellent, and before we knew it, it was time to head over to the celebration.

As we were walking across the lawn of the National Mall toward the Lincoln Memorial where the president was scheduled to speak, Erika's cell phone rang. She almost never had it on except when she was on a job, so that immediately raised some red flags to me.

She listened for a while, and then I overheard her say, "Yes, Agent Forrester, I understand." She disconnected the call and turned to me. "Michael, I'm really sorry, but I have to do something, and I don't know how long it will take. Maybe you should head back to the hotel. It's not safe here anymore."

"What? Why? You know, you are acting like a real spy or something." I was only half joking.

"Listen, I don't have time to talk, but I promise I will explain it to you later when I get back to the hotel."

With that, she ran toward the street and hailed a cab. They never come very fast, especially during this time at night, but there seemed to be one waiting. I immediately followed and, as luck would have it, there was a cab waiting for me as well.

I told the driver, "Follow that cab!" I'd heard that line so often in movies, and I'd always wanted to say it in real life.

I heard a velvet and wet voice say, "Yes, sir." It was at that point that I realized the cab was not typical. It was a circa 1950s black Cadillac sedan. Maybe I had been fooled because it looked like a normal yellow cab when I'd entered.

The driver turned around. It was Jean, and she was wearing a cabbie's outfit. Since she was actually in a corporal form, I could hear her speak to me outside of my own mind.

After the momentary shock wore off, I heard her say, "Michael, you need to go after her and help."

"Where did you learn to drive a cab? You know what? Never mind. Jean, do you know where Erika is headed? Do you understand what's happening?"

"Yes, there are number of bad men who belong to a group called Jeezarre, which is a radical offshoot cell group of Al Qaeda. They plan on blowing up the president and vice president tonight during the parade at the National Mall."

"But that will also kill thousands of innocent people!" I blurted out in my mind.

"Exactly. That's why you have to try to help!"

"What can I do? I'm just an ordinary science teacher with no special combat training. I even run with a slight limp!"

"That may be true, but you are not ordinary. You love reading. Didn't a great wizard once say, 'It is our choices, Harry, that show what we truly are, far more that our abilities.'"

"Well, yes. Professor Albus Dumbledore said that to Harry Potter in one of J. K. Rowling's books, but that was just a story." I thought for a moment. "Hey, you're not saying that Dumbledore really exists?"

"Of course not, Sugar, that would just be silly. The point is, you need to do something to help!" After a short breath she said, "Oh, and by the way, this car was Joe D's."

"You don't mean Joltin' Joe ... I mean Joe DiMaggio?" I asked.

She said something about a wedding, borrowing this car, and how it was one of her favorites.

The following events occurred like a whirlwind so I am not exactly sure of the sequences, but I will try my best to recollect.

We arrived at the National Mall. For some unexplained reason, when I jumped out of the car, Jean picked up another passenger.

I could see Erika in the distance. I started running toward the Lincoln Memorial, the same direction Erika had run off to. The crowd was really beginning to amass, so I found myself bumping into a number of people. I even accidently knocked over an older guy, who immediately raised his cane and started cursing at me.

The president and vice president were surrounded by tall, muscular, clean-cut guys in dark suits and light-colored shirts. Their clothes and demeanor screamed Secret Service. They were already standing on a platform overlooking the memorial. The president was apparently ready to address the hyped crowd. I sensed there was very little time left before a major tragedy occurred.

I scanned the area, but I could not differentiate the good guys from the bad guys. It was just a sea of people. Even though she was presumably dropping off another fare, I said in my head, *Jean, what can I do?"* There was no response. Great. Just when I needed the voice the most, there was nothing but silence. Couldn't she drive and talk to me in my head at the same time?

Frustrated, I shoved my hands into my pockets. There I felt something small and pulled it out. It was the penny-sized version of the booklet I had picked up in the Lincoln Memorial bookstore, *The Travelers' Guide to the Zero Universe.* I must have dropped it into my suit-pants pocket with my loose change. It immediately turned to a normal-size booklet, which made it much easier to read. I have found that, with age, my eyesight has diminished regardless of how much I try to emulate Bugs Bunny and eat lots of carrots. Carrots contain a lot of beta carotene and … well … never mind.

I looked in the index and saw that there was a section called "How to Find People." I quickly turned to page sixty-two and read:

> In cases of extreme emergency, a granite
> Egyptian obelisk or sphere may be used.
> Hold the sphere upward in the direction
> of the setting sun or rising moon, think
> about the people you are looking for, and
> a rainbow of light will guide you in the

right direction and lead you to the people
you are searching for.

I remembered the three artifacts I had picked up from the Great Pyramid of Giza. One of them was a small Egyptian granite sphere. I had put it in my backpack, which was in our room at the hotel. Instantly, however, I felt something strangely heavy in my front right pocket. Conveniently, I pulled out the Egyptian granite sphere, which I was sure I had left in the hotel room. I held it straight up in an eastward direction. At first nothing happened, and I felt really ridiculous even thinking for a minute that the thing might work.

Then I remembered the second part of what the guide had said: I had to think about who I was looking for. I started to think about the bad guys. I concentrated on pictures of terrorists and Al Qaeda agents I had seen in the news. The images of Geronimo (Osama Bin Laden) and, strangely enough, Ms. Addanc popped into my visual cortex.

Abruptly, a translucent beam of light started to point outward in a straight line. It was leading me to the bad guys—I thought. Additionally, one side of the sphere started glowing and projecting images.

The first image showed Erika. Along with two guys in suits, she was frantically searching for something or somebody. The second image showed a triad of men holding a detonator device of some kind. I could see a timer, which seemed to be counting down from ten minutes. I assumed these were the abominable men Erika and her companions were looking for and that we had less than ten minutes before the bomb was detonated. It also seemed reasonable that the beam of light was leading to these men. At this point, mostly everything seemed reasonable to me.

I started sprinting in the direction of the pellucid light, presumably toward the three bad men. They were to the left of the platform where the president and all of his men now stood. The three men were dressed like tourists—big baggy shorts, DC T-shirts, and Washington Nationals baseball caps. They were trying to blend in, I guessed.

Two of the bad guys were nervously watching the perimeter of the platform. The third one was holding the detonator. Without thinking, I ran straight for him. Where were the cavalry and CIA when I needed them the most? Wasn't this the part of the movie where the good guys came rushing in to save the day, instead of an ordinary high school physics teacher with a slight limp and no combat training? Of course, that was in the movies, and this was real life. It turns out that I like the movies a lot better.

Inside of my head, I finally heard from Marilyn. She whispered, "But God hath chosen the foolish things of the world to confound the wise; and God hath chosen the weak things of the world to confound the things which are mighty." I wasn't sure if she was insulting me or trying to help me. I wasn't sure if it was a quote from the Bible but it sounded religious to me. (I later found out it was 1 Corinthians 1:27 from the King James Bible.) In my confusion, somehow I got the point: it was up to me to do something.

I had no weapon, so I reached down and grabbed a large rock. I curled my fist around it. I had seen the maneuver

167

in older cheesy B-list movies—a guy using a solid object in his fist is able to increase the force of his punch. From a scientific point of view, this made sense: increase the mass, and you increase the force. It's Newton's second law.

The creepy terrorist guy trying to look like a tourist looked up just as I connected with a punch that Rocky Balboa would have been proud of. He dropped the detonator, but suddenly I realized I had a second major problem. The device read two minutes and counting, and I had no idea how to stop it. I had always wanted to take a course in bomb squad training, but somehow it never fit into my college course schedule. I mean who has the time?

I realized that my lack of knowledge and skills in disarming bombs could possibly be a problem. I pondered this thought and picked up the detonator. Just then, I felt a crack on the side of my head and everything went dark.

A hospital is no place to be sick.

—Samuel Goldwyn

Journal Entry 13

Hospital X

I was somewhere in the Pacific Ocean on a private island. There was a cool tropical breeze blowing, and I was lying in a lounge chair on my private beach. The speakers were blaring songs from a mixed rock-and-roll collection. I was being served a tall glass containing the magical elixir known as a piña colada by one of the members of the Swedish bikini team (who were the only full-time residents on my tropical paradise—besides myself, of course). The girls served various roles: waitress, maid, butler, masseuse, etc. One of the team members was saying something about what another beautiful day it was on "Miguel Island." I wasn't really sure, as I didn't listen much while I was on this island.

I was just about to finish my tropical drink when I felt a warm, familiar hand holding mine. I heard Erika talking to me. "Michael, are you awake?"

As I slowly began to regain consciousness, I became more aware of my surroundings. I was lying in a bed. It seemed to be made up of three individual sections that could be raised separately. There were metal railings on the sides. The room was painted white everywhere. There was a strong aseptic smell in the air. There were tubes and wires hooked up to my arms and chest. I was in a hospital.

"Erika, what happened?"

"It's a little complicated but I will do my best to explain as much as I can. First, you are in a hospital, and you are going to be all right."

"What hospital? How did I get here?" I interjected.

"I am not allowed to say, because this hospital is strictly CIA and doesn't exist as far as the general public is concerned. Let's just call it Hospital X."

"Okay, I guess I understand the need to keep the name of the hospital a secret, but what happened? I remember holding the detonator, and then everything went blank. Did the bomb explode?"

"No. Everybody is fine. That typical guy macho crap you pulled out there was very, very stupid, and if you ever pull a stunt like that again, I will kick your ass. But thanks. The CIA cannot officially publicly acknowledge the event or the role a private citizen played in it, but I was told by my superiors to privately thank you."

"You and your superiors are welcome, but I was really trying to help and save *you*. What happened?"

"We were searching for three men. Somehow you knew they were planning to blow up the platform containing the president and vice president. I was with my supervisor, Agent Forrester, the one who had called earlier, and another fellow agent when I saw you fighting with three men."

"I remember hitting the guy who was holding the detonator. I picked it up, but I didn't know what to do. That's all I remember because everything went dark."

"The other two men came running toward you. One of them hit you on the side of the head with a blunt object. By the time we reached you, you had already been knocked out. We apprehended the three men and—"

"But what happened to the bomb?" I blurted out.

"Luckily, Agent Forrester is a demolition expert and was able to deactivate the detonation device a few seconds before it reached zero."

"That all seems logical, but I still have one question: How does a human resource specialist get involved in all of this spy stuff?"

"I am not sure you really want to know, but I guess that's the million-dollar question." At first she didn't answer the question. She looked uncomfortably around the room.

"You really are a spy after all, aren't you? That's so cool. I am dating James Bond. Wait, that didn't sound right. Jessica Bond or Mata Hari, if you prefer." I was just trying to break the tension.

"Stop it, Michael," she snapped back at me.

"Sorry, I didn't mean—"

She cut me off and said, "This is serious stuff you're joking about. A lot of people almost died tonight. And if we hadn't gotten lucky—"

I cut in, "And there was yours truly, of course."

"Yes, if you had not been there. Again, how is it you showed up there anyway?"

I was going to mention the Egyptian sphere and my travelers' guide, but I decided to wait. "I was looking for you. I just happened to stumble on to those guys and—"

"Convenient," she interrupted. Did she believe me? "Anyway, what's really important is that you're okay and nobody was hurt."

"Why didn't you just tell me? I always thought you had a mundane, boring CIA job."

"Two reasons," she said. "First, I was always worried that, if you ever knew, you might one day try to be a hero and pull some crap like you did today and get yourself killed or almost killed like you did a couple of hours ago. Secondly, my position is highly classified. My position and office doesn't even officially exist, even to most employees in the CIA and government. Just knowing might have put you at risk with certain people. But it doesn't really matter now."

"They—the CIA—aren't going to let me leave now, are they?"

She shook her head and replied, "I'm not completely sure, but I don't think so. They think you know too much already."

"Do I know too much?"

"Maybe, maybe not. But after risking your life last night for me and others, I think you deserve to know the whole story. However, right now Dr. Reed needs to see you and speak with you."

"Hey, I just thought of something else," I said.

"What?"

"You are a spy, and you don't even know how to text. Isn't that standard basic sleuth kind of stuff?" I mention with aplomb.

"Of course I know how to text. You're the only one left in the world who doesn't know how," she said with a wry smile.

"But I've never seen you text."

"That's because I text only on a secure CIA line."

"I can at least program a VCR or DVD player," I uttered under my breath.

But apparently not as quietly as I thought, because she heard me and gave me one of those, "you're an ass" looks before she smiled. "True, but that's not fair. Just about any guy or five-year-old, of which I am neither, can program those damn things."

"Valid point," I said, and we both laughed.

With that, a tall, slender, gray-haired gentleman walked into the room. I was guessing it was Dr. Reed because he was wearing a white lab coat embroidered with the name

"Dr. Walter Reed." I am quick like that. I leave no stone unturned. Nothing gets past this steel-trap mind.

I wasn't sure if anyone else was listening to our conversation. That's the trouble with spies. You're never quite sure of what's going on, who's who, or who might be listening.

He extended his right hand to shake mine and said, "Hello, I am Doctor Reed. I just wanted to see how you're feeling."

"You tell me, Doc," I replied as Erika shot me a dirty look.

"We ran some tests. You took a nasty blow to the head, and it looks like you sustained a grade-III concussion. My colleagues and I were worried you might lapse into a coma, but you were very lucky that you didn't."

"I was in the middle of a wonderful dream."

Erika interrupted, "Not that "I-own-my-little-private-South-Pacific-Island" dream again."

I smiled and nodded yes. (However, I don't think I had ever mentioned the part about the Swedish bikini team to Erika before). "Anyway, I felt a warm, familiar, beautiful touch and heard an angelic-like voice talking to me just before I awoke here."

Erika rolled her eyes once again and blushed very slightly.

"The important thing is that you remained awake," said the doctor. "So it seems that you'll be fine, except a possible headache later. There is one other thing though.

I am sure it's inconsequential, but we detected a heart murmur."

"I was diagnosed with a functional heart murmur as a child. But I was told it was totally benign."

"That's correct; in most cases the murmur is benign or innocent," he informed me. "There is always a very slight chance—one out of a hundred thousand—that this condition could lead to serious problems or instant cardiac death. But since you have never experienced any problems before, I'm sure you're fine."

Erika didn't look so convinced. She tended to worry more than I did. "Doctor Reed," she said, "you think that Michael is going to fully recover? Are there any restrictions he needs to be aware of?"

"That's a good point," I blurted out. "I was supposed to go rock climbing in a couple of days."

"Michael, could you please be serious just once," Erika said in a frustrated tone.

"As I said," replied Dr. Reed, "we feel very confident, based on the lab tests, that Michael will be just fine. There are no restrictions except for taking it easy for a bit. So it would be a good idea to refrain from climbing any mountains for a few weeks. And, of course, no wandering off into one of our highly restricted and classified areas of the hospital." He winked.

"You're joking, right Doc?" I asked.

He nodded his head and gave me a wry look. "Well then, let any one of my staff know if there is anything you need while you stay with us," he told me. "I have some more rounds to make and patients to check on."

"Okay. Thanks, Doc," I replied.

"I'll check back in on you later," he said leaving us alone.

"So, Erika, getting back to our earlier topic involving real spy stuff," I said. "How are you involved in all of this?"

For NASA, space is still a high priority.

—Dan Quayle

Journal Entry 14

Vomit Comet

"I was recruited by the Vomit Comet program to work for a highly covert joint venture between our agencies, the CIA and NASA," Erika said.

"Vomit Comet—I think I've heard that name before, but I don't remember where or what it means."

"Sorry, that's the CIA slang for the program. Some operatives use it to refer to this classified branch of NASA. I know the name seems out of place but I think it's just the CIA trying to be misleading about the progam. Anyway, I think they got the term from a famous movie," she clarified.

"Now I remember where I heard the term before. It was used by the film crew in the movie *Apollo 13*. I remember reading about it once, but I just thought it was a joke. Why is it called that?"

"Michael, is that really important now?"

"No, of course you're right. Continue please."

However, I found out later—much, much later— that NASA owns a modified KC-135—the military version of the Boeing 707—for astronaut training. The plane flies a parabolic path that subjects its occupants to periods of high gravity, with twenty-second segments of low gravity. The KC-135 was given the nickname the "Vomit Comet" by some NASA employees because it lives up to that nickname. Rapid changes from high to low gravity periods tend to make most people's stomachs queasy.

"Around seven years ago," she continued, "NASA contacted the CIA and proposed the development of a highly clandestine office to investigate the existence of extraterrestrial life forms. NASA had provided the Agency with some credible documents showing the existence of such entities."

"I see. So when I first met you and said you worked in human resources, you were being mendacious?"

"No. That night at Aquila Run, when we first met, I was being perfectly honest. Of course, I didn't mention I worked for the CIA, but I did work as a Human Resource Capital Officer at that time."

"Okay, so when did you become Laura Croft?"

"Funny, Michael, real funny. Anyway, it happened a couple of years after I met you. A few years ago, do you remember me telling you about the project we were doing that was classified?"

"Yes, I think so. The CIA was testing a new program that was supposed to make figuring out retirement benefits for CIA and FBI agents more efficient—just boring numbers crunching, right?"

She nodded. "When I arrived at the job site, my superior, Agent Forrester, told me a representative from NASA wanted to meet with me. I asked him why, but he didn't know all the details. Agent Forrester took me deep down through the tunnels into a classified section of the complex. He told that everything I would be discussing was considered highly classified—it was eyes-only information. We passed through three different levels of security.

"As we entered an empty conference room, Agent Forrester excused himself. As I waited I looked around the room. It was full of drawings and maps of constellations and galaxies. It looked real spacey. I think you would have loved it. Anyway, after about five minutes, a woman dressed in a NASA shirt walked in. She was in her late twenties and rather striking. I know this sounds crazy, but she reminded me of the late Rita Hayworth. She introduced herself as Captain Rita Denton."

"Sounds out of this world," I interrupted.

"I immediately noticed a pin she was wearing on her uniform. It was a large circle about the size of a silver dollar, and it had a five-pointed star in the center. The star was actually a shield with the head of an eagle on the top. Imbedded in the shield was a cross that radiated spikes in a circular direction."

"Okay, so she was wearing some kind of award. Why is this so important?"

"It just wasn't your average run-of-the-mill award. It was the Intelligence Star."

I looked confused and I guess a little unimpressed.

"You don't see the significance, do you?"

"Not really," I mumbled.

"That award is the second-highest award that can be given by the CIA. It is given only for acts of courage performed under hazardous conditions, or for outstanding achievements and extraordinary heroism. Only a few hundred people have achieved this award in the history of the agency. Naturally, I figured she could be trusted."

I nodded my head understandingly and said, "So she was a big shot. What did she want to talk to you about?"

"She told me she worked for an offshoot of SETI."

"You mean, Search for Extraterrestrial Intelligence?"

"Yes, that's what she said the acronym stood for. However, Captain Denton said there was a more covert and classified section of SETI, and that's where she worked. The section was dubbed the Vomit Comet Program."

"What does any of this have to do with you?" I asked anxiously.

"I am getting to that part. She told me her job was to try to recruit me into the program."

"No offense, Erika, but why did they choose you? You were not a spy."

"She wasn't at liberty to say. I really don't think she knew exactly why. I told her that I didn't have any formal training in espionage, astrophysics, or anything to do with outer space. Captain Denton said none of that mattered because they wanted me specifically and would provide any training I needed."

"So, Ms. Bond, I presume you took the offer."

"Again, Michael, really not very funny. I wanted to tell you, but the position was—"

"I know, highly classified. Certain-eyes-only stuff," I interjected.

"Telling you would have put you at risk. You know I had been very unhappy at my previous position. When I was a Human Resource Capital Officer, every little problem and question would be forwarded to me, and most of the questions I couldn't answer. In addition, with all the bureaucratic ineptitude and bullshit at the agency, I just got sick of it. That kind of mundane work was driving me crazy. I guess I was looking for some kind of out, and then this new, exciting opportunity came along."

"I know you were very tired at your old position and couldn't wait until you could retire, but talk about opposite ends of the spectrum!"

"It seemed like a chance for me to refresh and reenergize my career. They recruited me very aggressively, literally offering me the moon and the stars. I should have known better, but it seemed like a way out of the tedium that my job had become. It seemed exciting, and I have to admit, I was flattered that they wanted me so badly."

"I understand completely. I can't fault your decision because I probably would have done the same thing. Actually, I would have done exactly the same thing. I would have called up Ms. Addanc in a heartbeat and given her my* I'm-out-of-here-like-Vladimir speech. I just have one question—did they recruit you so that you could spy on me?"

The hour is ripe, and yonder lies the way.

—Virgil

Journal Entry 15

Time to Get While the Getting's Good

It was around 8:00 p.m., and Doctor Reed was making his final rounds for the evening. I was his last stop.

"I wanted to let you know that we will be releasing you the day after tomorrow," Dr. Reed said. "Obviously, we had no baseline test to compare your pre- and post-concussion symptoms to, but your recent MRI and CAT scans appear to be normal.

"Thanks, Doc. That's good. No offense, but hospitals are not my favorite place to hang around."

"No problem. Most people feel the same way. It's understandable, really. In any case, it was nice to have met you."

"You as well. Thanks for everything, Doc."

I was feeling much better, and since I had time, I decided to take a walk to the cafeteria for "a cup of Joe." Believe it or not, I actually remember reading why the nickname for coffee became known as "a cup of Joe." Josephus Daniels was appointed secretary of the US Navy by President Woodrow Wilson in 1913. Among Daniels' numerous reforms was the abolition of any alcoholic beverages during Navy voyages. From that time on, the strongest drink allowed aboard Navy ships was coffee. Over the years, a cup of coffee derisively became known as "a cup of Joe" among the navy sailors.

Before I left my room, I took off my hospital gown and put on a pair of jeans and a T-shirt that Erika had brought to the hospital for me. Even as a kid, I was always a rebel. In fact, I believe that I still hold the record for most ten-thousand-word disciplinary compositions written in my elementary school. Because the cosmos has a unique sense of humor, I naturally became a teacher. I headed for the elevator. Since I was in normal clothes, none of the orderlies paid any attention to me.

I was about to push the button for the cafeteria when I noticed a button marked "penthouse." *Rather strange for a hospital*, I thought. I heard Jean's voice in my head as I fought back the strange urge for cotton candy. Strange because I wasn't hungry; but most importantly, I don't like cotton candy. Now funnel cake, that's a whole different story.

"Michael, go to the penthouse and take a look at what's up there."

"Okay, but why?"

"There are bad things going on that you should see," she responded.

I pushed the button and arrived swiftly on the penthouse floor. I got out of the elevator and noticed the floor was swarming with military personnel, and scientists were milling about. It looked like a scene from the movie *Outbreak*.

Jean, I will surely be spotted and probably get in a lot of trouble, I thought. *Not that I mind trouble, but I did promise Erika that I would be a good boy.* This was never easy for me. Besides, I had promised to behave until she got back."

"No, Sugar," she said. "You will be fine. Reach into your pocket and pull out the copper swallow's tail you got at the Great Pyramid of Giza."

I did as instructed. I just assumed that it would be there, and it was. I held the copper swallow's tail, and nobody seemed to notice me. The personnel just walked by me as if I wasn't there. *I don't understand. Why are they ignoring me?*

"Because they can't see you. You really do ask a lot of silly questions."

Is it because of the effect of this object, the copper swallow's tail?

"Yes. It is actually a device we call an absorber. Since it was constructed on Earth, it works only in this Universe. When it is held, the person's body heat initiates a reaction that absorbs all of the light around that person. The light waves are completely absorbed. There is no reflection."

But with no reflection of the light waves and all the colors being absorbed, wouldn't that cause an object to appear black and not invisible?

"Normally yes, but that's where the magic comes into play," she explained.

The magic? I questioned.

"Sugar, you have to learn to trust me if I am to be your guide. Besides, things will make more sense later on."

Gee, where have I heard that before? I guess if I can't trust a cerebral-created Marilyn Monroe, who may or may not be a figment of my imagination, then who can I trust?

I followed her instructions. It made no scientific sense, but she was right. There did seem to be magic operating here. I was free to explore without being seen. There were three laboratories, all of which were marked by signs on the doors as classified. There were no signs about excluding invisible people using an absorber device, so I figured I would be okay.

I looked into the first lab. From what I could see, I surmised they were performing heinous animal experimentation inside. There were numerous cages filled with animals that didn't look normal. These unfortunate creatures had grotesque deformities. This sickened my stomach; little did I know the feeling would get worse.

It was unclear what the classes of the animals were. However, it appeared the scientists were trying to cross different species of animals together that never should have been. The animals were all suffering and appeared to be dying. In addition, some of the animals seemed to be a combination of animal and machine parts, as if somebody was trying to create animal cyborgs of varying combinations.

Although the physical deterioration of the suffering creatures made most of the animals unrecognizable, I was able to recognize one species in particular. It looked like a monkey crossed with a bat and some type of mechanical parts, possible wings. I wasn't sure what the scientists' motives were, but I could assume that they were trying to combine the best attributes of one species with the best attributes of another, and then, in some cases, add some robotic parts to create a superior animal. These twisted bastards were trying to play God by creating their own sick version of evolution.

The second lab was filled with newborn babies. There were tubes and wires implanted into each baby's wrists. The infants were identified only by alphanumeric codes. The tubes seemed to be injecting different colored liquids into their bloodstreams. It appeared the scientists here were doing genetic manipulation experiments on these children. Most of the babies stared blankly toward the ceiling. They all had glazed looks in their eyes. I had no idea where these babies had come from or what mutations the scientists were trying to create within them. This had to be illegal, even for the CIA!

The final lab contained adult humanoid beings. These people were chained to hospital beds and unconscious. It appeared they were also being experimented on, but I wasn't sure what these experiments were. However, it looked as if a number of these poor wretched souls were missing various body parts. Maybe the scientists were trying to test cellular regenerative techniques? They could have been illegally selling organs on the black market. I was at a loss for words, and my spiritual guide was nowhere in my mind to give me advice.

I didn't need to see anymore. Once back on the elevator, I began to feel ill and headed back to my room. It was clear that scientists in the penthouse section of the hospital were running abhorrent, immoral, and undeniably illegal experiments. I didn't know if these procedures were being sanctioned by the CIA or the government, but I fervently hoped they were not.

When I got back to my room, Erika was sitting there. "Where did you go?" she asked in a concerned tone.

"I took the elevator to the top level of the hospital. The penthouse appears to be nothing more than a set of despicable laboratories where scientists are experimenting on animals, babies, and some form of humanoid creatures. Erika, did you know these labs existed at this hospital?"

"Of course not! There were some vague rumors that would occasionally float around the CIA, but I really had no idea."

"We need to do something. You need to contact someone who can put a stop to this!" I pleaded.

"I will. I promise. But right now, we need to leave this hospital," she said urgently.

"No problem. Dr. Reed stopped in earlier and told me that he was discharging me tomorrow. What's wrong?"

"I overheard the hospital supervisor talking with Dr. Reed. Michael, they are not going to let you leave tomorrow. They plan on doing some experiments on you. Maybe it's related to what you saw today up in the penthouse. I really don't know, but I don't want to take any chances." She sounded despondent, and not a little afraid.

"Sounds good to me. I really don't want to stay any longer. There are too many sick people, and the hospital and the food … don't get me started—"

"Michael!" Erika interjected exasperatedly.

"Sorry, no more jokes, at least for now. What's your plan? I don't think we can just walk out of here now."

"We may have some help. Contrary to what the supervisor said to Dr. Reed, he talked to me privately and told me he's going help by pulling the fire alarm in thirty minutes. During the commotion caused by people exiting the building, I'm hoping we can blend in and escape."

"Are you sure we can trust him?"

"I don't know him well, but I think he's a decent man. Besides, we don't have much of a choice."

"Good point, and he does seem like a nice chap."

"Put these on," she said as she handed me a set of light-blue scrubs. She quickly put on a similar set. I was going to make a joke about playing doctor but quickly dashed that idea.

"Courtesy of Dr. Reed," she said. "He thought it might help us blend in more."

"Beware of Greeks bearing gifts," I mumbled.

"What?"

"You know the story about the Greeks leaving the horse outside the gates of Troy. The Trojans thought they were getting a generous parting gift," I responded.

"And your point is?"

"Nothing. Sorry. Just my cynical side kicking in again."

The fire alarms went off on schedule, and people started moving toward the exits. Erika turned to me. Reminiscent of the last words spoken by James T. Kirk in my favorite *Star Trek* episode, "City on the Edge of Forever," she said, "Let's get the hell out of here!" It was the first and only time Kirk used those words on the series, so I knew he was very serious. Similarly, I knew Erika was very serious about getting out of this hospital.

Snapping back into serious mode, which I am surprisingly able to do on occasion especially when my life depends upon it, I joined her, and we hastily left the room. Erika and I did our best to blend in with the mix of workers heading toward the front doors. It seemed to be working, at least initially.

The elevators were deactivated during the fire alarm, so we wedged our way down the two flights of stairs along with the orderlies and nurses.

"What should we do when we get out of the building?" I whispered.

"I called a colleague to meet us two blocks from the hospital. She's going to take us to Union Station. I purchased two tickets to get us back home. After that, I don't know."

It's never that easy in a movie or a written story encrypted to serve as a diary of actual events, and this was no exception. As we started to make our way out of the building, we were spotted. Two big guys in black suits and dark glasses were pointing at us. We began running toward our rendezvous point. They started running after us posthaste. It became clear we were not going to make it to the decampment car without a fight.

We stopped outside the gates of the hospital. Erika assumed a fighting pose. "I know what I said about you being a hero earlier, and all that macho crap," she hissed at me. "But forget about that for now. Michael, are you ready to fight?"

The first rule of Fight Club is you do not talk about Fight Club. The second rule is the same. Should we even be talking about Fight Club?

—Jim Uhls in *Fight Club*

Journal Entry 16

She Can Fight Too

The lead CIA agent approached Erika first. She went into some kind of karate, jujitsu maneuvers. The big guy threw a right hook, which she easily blocked. She twisted around and deposited a roundhouse kick to his chest, knocking him back a couple of feet. The big steroidal CIA muscle head thug looked slightly dazed.

"Wow, where did you learn to fight like that?" I yelled at her.

"Never mind that, watch out!"

As usual, it was too late for me. The other CIA muscle head connected a quick jab to my face as I turned around. He split my lip open, and I spit out a wad of blood. He threw another punch at me, but this time I instinctively blocked his effort, surprising myself. In my head I heard Jean giving me instructions like she was Mickey Goldmill, the trainer from the movie *Rocky*, minus the gruff voice, "He'll kill you to death, Rock!"[3]

---

[3]   *Rocky III*. Dir. Sylvester Stallone. Writer Sylvester Stallone. Metro-Goldwyn-Mayer, 1982. Film.

"Throw a punch back at him! Move! Don't just stand still!" Jean implored.

I attempted to throw a punch, giving my best Rocky Balboa impression, but I missed as he ducked. I turned to look back at Erika; she appeared to be holding her own. I didn't know where she'd learned those Bruce Lee moves, but I was very proud. It also suddenly occurred to me that she could have probably kicked my ass anytime she wanted. That made me both proud and a little intimidated at the same time.

I turned back to engage the steroidal muscle head just in time for him to hit me directly in the nose. I think he broke it, because blood started gushing out as I dropped to my knees. Apparently not finding me a worthy opponent, he was finished with me. I had wanted to take karate as a kid, but who had the time? Not finding the time was one of the many decisions in life I suddenly regretted.

My adversary turned and ran toward Erika, who was still fighting with his partner. I had to do something fast. As skilled as she was, I didn't think she could fight off both of those guys at the same time. Normally I was good at thinking on my feet. After all, I was highly trained, a professional, and a high school teacher accustomed to being on the front lines. Nothing came to mind.

Just like in the movies, minus the suspenseful music right before something good or bad happens in the scene, Jean spoke to me in the nick of time. "Quickly! In your pocket!" shouted Jean. "Pull out the wooden slat and throw it at them."

I left the slate in my backpack! I "thought" back. *It's still in my room at the hotel!*

"Are you sure? Check quickly," she insisted.

Yes, the Egyptian wooden slat was in my pocket. *When will I learn to just look in my pockets? Jean, it's just a slat—a wooden slat. Seriously, what am I supposed to do with it?*

"Hurry! Just throw it at them!" she yelled in my mind.

As I threw the object at them, it appeared that time slowed down. Erika and the two agents froze. Ostensibly, the slat was some kind of time and space freezing device. It only seemed to affect a thirty-square-foot area, but that was enough. I ran over to them and picked up the magical slat. The freezing-in-time-like-an-ostentatious-ice-sculpture didn't appear to affect me.

However, the freezing effects worked only temporarily. Suddenly time began to speed up again, and they started to revive. I picked up a nearby stone and squeezed my fist around it. I had seen this maneuver in many late-night movies. From a physics standpoint, it made sense—increase the mass, increase the force of the punch. I threw a punch as hard as I could at the first agent, knocking him out. I repeated the procedure on the second agent with similar results—except for possibly cracking a knuckle or two. I started shaking my hand.

"Michael, what just happened?" Erika asked. She was totally confused.

I whimpered slightly. "I think I hurt my hand."

"Not your hand, you big baby."

"We were fighting with those two guys—CIA agents or bad guys, who can tell these days?" I said with a wry smile.

"I know that! I meant what just happened to me and those agents?"

"Oh, I just saved your butt and the day."

"Michael!" she screamed exasperatedly.

"Jean, my spiritual guide, told me to retrieve the wooden slat that I got from the Great Pyramid of Giza and throw it at all of you. When I did, it seemed to freeze time and space. I'm not sure how it worked, but you all just froze momentarily. It was kind of funny—like a scene from a bad movie that makes you laugh but you are not sure exactly why."

"Again, Michael, please get to the point and try to make sense." She was a bit rattled.

"Sorry. I ran over and knocked out those two agents. After I picked up the slat you began to unfreeze."

"Who the hell is Jean? And the Great Pyramid of what?"

"Right. I guess I never mentioned any of that before. I will do my best to fully explain everything, but right now people are beginning to stare, so I think we need to get out of here."

"Yes, we need to make our way to the getaway car. My colleague, Captain Denton, should be waiting for us."

We ran as fast as we could. For me it was a combination of running and limping. Erika spotted the car, and we yanked open the door.

"Michael, this is Captain Rita Denton. She is the person who recruited me into the VC program," Erika said.

I stared in utter disbelief.

"No, it's not," I said.

> I wanted to be a secret agent and an
> astronaut, preferably at the same time.
>
> —David Byrne

Journal Entry 17

Space Waitress Spy

I felt something hard—the point of a gun?—stick into the small of my back. The familiar voice of Erika's colleague instructed us to get into the car.

"What the hell?" I blurted out.

Erika looked at me. "We'd better do as she asks."

We sat in the backseat next to another agent, who sat pointing the silencer of his gun at us. Erika's colleague got into the front seat, and the driver started the engine, and the car began to move.

"Rita, can you please tell me what is going on?" Erika pleaded.

There was no reply.

Erika then turned to me. "Michael, why did you say this isn't Captain Denton?"

"Because, I have known her to be someone else other than Captain Denton. Tips must be really slow at the Waffle House, huh, Margarita? Or is it Rita now?" I asked sarcastically.

Erika turned toward me and asked, "What are you talking about?"

"For the past couple of years, I have known this woman as Margarita, a waitress at Jim's Waffle House."

"That doesn't make any sense. Why would a top official at NASA moonlight—or in this case, daylight—as a waitress?"

"Maybe it does make sense. I think I might have a guess," I answered.

Rita finally turned around in her seat and faced us, "Give it a shot, Michael."

"I am guessing that the whole waitress gig was just a cover. You were probably at the Waffle House only when I was in town."

"Very good. Please continue. By the way, Margarita was my mother's first name. I occasionally borrow it for convenience."

Now Erika chimed in. "The real reason you recruited me for this position at VC was because of Michael, wasn't it?"

Captain Denton smiled. "Of course, it was much easier to keep track of Michael with you being so close to him."

"And the reason is?" Erika asked.

"Why don't you tell her, Michael?" Rita suggested.

Erika answered for me, "Because you think he is an extraterrestrial from another world."

"Yes, we have reason to suspect that he is not of this world."

"You've got to be kidding!" Erika shouted. "You can't be serious!" Apparently she'd been joking.

"Erika," I protested, "she might be right considering everything that has happened and the way I have always felt. To be honest, I'm not really sure I belong here. The only times I have ever felt right in this world have been times when I was with you. I really do feel that I belong with you. I'm just not sure where we belong." I turned to Captain Denton. "But, Margarita—or Rita—that still doesn't give you the right to kidnap us. You know in most cultures that's considered very rude. I'm just guessing here, but I would bet it's probably not cool in other worlds as well."

"We are not kidnapping you," she responded. "We just need to ask you a few questions and verify some information."

"Then we are free to go?" Erika asked.

"No, not exactly," Rita said.

"I guess I need to review my own vocabulary list and look up the definition for *kidnapping*," I quipped. "Maybe it really means something besides what I thought."

Erika gave me a look that I interpreted as, "Shut up before you make things worse."

We pulled into a government building labeled Department of Interior, which seemed a little odd. Captain Denton and the other agent exited the car and motioned for us to do the same. They ushered us into the building and walked us down a long, dark corridor. With a little persuasion in the form of two guns stuck into our backs, we did as instructed.

We passed multiple levels of increasing security checks. After the last security checkpoint, we headed into a passageway that spiraled downward into an underground complex.

"I'm sorry, Michael, I never should have taken this job," Erika apologized.

"Erika, it's not your fault. You had no idea. Besides, I know the grass is always greener and so forth."

"That's very sweet, really it is," Captain Denton interjected, "but we have reached our destination. Please enter and take a seat."

"And to think I really believed it was a coincidence running into you," I said. "And that you actually liked the National Zoo and were a frequent visitor."

Rita gave a half smile. "Actually, that part was true. I do really visit the zoo often and enjoy the exhibits. By the way, it was a pure coincidence running into you that day."

I gave her a funny look, which was intended to let her know that I doubted her sincerity, although I doubted she cared.

We entered a giant conference room littered with computers and a holographic three-dimensional star charts. It looked very futuristic and would have been very impressive under different circumstances. I probably would have been highly interested in all the science and technology. However, given this situation, I wasn't too thrilled or interested. Captain Denton sat down, and the muscle and gun stood watch over us as we remained standing. A second armed guard joined the first.

"Dr. Collins and his associates will be here in just a minute," Captain Denton remarked.

"Isn't Dr. Collins the head of genetic testing and research for the CIA?" Erika inquired.

I immediately thought about the penthouse at Hospital X, and an icy feeling coalesced in my veins. The thought crossed my mind—*Maybe Dr. Collins had something to do with the abominable experiments going on there.*

Dr. Richard Collins finally arrived. He looked to be in his mid-fifties. He was tall with an athletic build. What really stood out were his cold black eyes, which appeared to be soulless, at least to me.

The good doctor—and I use the term very loosely—spoke with a non-emotional quality that made me shiver. "It is a pleasure to finally meet you two," he said coolly.

I was affronted. "Wish I could say the same," I said, and was immediately rewarded with a jab in the small of my back by a blunt object.

"Dr. Collins, are you aware of any illegal research being conducted at the governmental hospital that Michael was taken to?" Erika asked.

"Ah, I see you have witnessed firsthand our little research programs," he answered. "There were many in the government who were against my research ideas. Some even suggested that I was crazy. But there are always those senators willing to take a leap of faith, willing to be unpopular. But they are visionaries just the same, and they let great men do extraordinary research experiments in science."

"You are really a sick man, aren't you?" I interjected.

Dr. Collins just stared right through us without any facial expression, and ignored the comment.

Erika looked at me. Then she turned to the doctor and defiantly asked, "Why are we here, and what do you want from us?"

"We want nothing from your purse Erika, but you are now a witness. You are officially involved, so we can't just let you go. Michael—he is a different story. We need to run some tests to see if he is really from another world."

"Is this some kind of sick joke? I want to speak to your superior right now!" Erika demanded.

Dr. Collins laughed and smiled like the cat that has just swallowed the canary. "Oh, I think that can be arranged, but all in good time. Let's try and stay focused on the current events at hand, shall we?"

Erika was about to say something else, but Captain Rita Denton held her hand up. Her silent message was clear: You are just wasting your time, let's wait and hear what else he has to say.

For the first time, I agreed with Captain Denton. I wanted to focus on the tests the doctor had mentioned. I had a bad feeling about them, and it wasn't because Jean was speaking in my head. It was one of those gut feelings that everyone gets in the movies just before something bad happens.

"What sort of tests?" I asked.

"Well, we need brain tissue and brain stem tissue samples for our genetic marker testing. It is very similar to the testing we perform on animals suspected of having rabies. Actually, our test was developed as an offshoot of the rabies testing."

Erika looked at me, "Michael what exactly does Dr. Collins mean?"

"In rabies testing, they have to sacrifice the animal in order to get the required amount of tissue samples," I replied. "Although I have never heard of it being performed on humans, I would assume the same terminal procedure would apply to humans."

It would be ugly to watch people
poking sticks at a caged rat.
It is uglier still to watch rats poking
sticks at a caged person.

—Jean Harris

Journal Entry 18

I'm No Lab Rat

Captain Denton turned to face Dr. Collins. "Doctor, you never said anything about killing the subjects in your research. You promised nobody would be harmed during your testing!"

"Yes, well, you see the thing about advancement in science is that sometimes you have to crack open a few good eggs to make an omelet," he nonchalantly replied.

Erika jumped up, but the muscle and the guns moved forward and motioned for her to sit back down.

"There really is no reason for these hostilities," Dr. Collins said unemotionally. "I give you my word that the testing is painless."

"Sure, I might feel no pain, but the procedure might kill me! That's a great compromise," I scoffed.

"There must be another way to verify your information," Erika said. Rita indicated her agreement.

I thought now would be a good time to stall him. I needed a chance to think of a plan to get the hell out of there. I wasn't great at making plans, although now would have been a good time to start. However, I was usually good at the fine art of stalling. I addressed the doctor. "Dr. Collins, you probably already know that I am a science teacher. Like yourself, I am always interested in the scientific process. Seeing as I won't be around too much longer, maybe you could give me a brief description of how your modified process works. I'm sure this new technique is highly innovative and probably brilliant."

I had learned from reading many fictional books that the bad guys always like to brag about how their plan works or how they will accomplish their plans for world domination. I was hoping that Dr. Collins was no different. I was right; he was your stereotypical creep with all the wonderful bad-guy traits, including bravado. He proudly began, "It is a variation of the direct fluorescent antibody testing developed to detect rabies. Of course, any type of fluorescent testing must be done postmortem."

Translation? I needed to be dead! "I see," I responded, trying to maintain my self-composure. "But how is your test modified from the standard rabies fluorescent testing to work on humans?"

"Michael," he said. "Do you mind if I call you Michael? Are you sure you're not stalling? In any case, it doesn't matter because there is no rush. Our testing isn't scheduled until tomorrow."

"Well, since I'm free for the rest of the day, I guess there would be no harm in indulging me. And, yes, since you are literally going to know me well enough to see my brain, Michael is fine."

"Michael, I guess you're right. The test uses antibodies tagged with fluorescent dye that can be used to detect the presence of genes created from the bi-matter elements we believe were created just after the big bang. These anti-bodies bind to these genes indicating their presence. Someone from Earth would test negative because there would be no bi-matter genes to adhere to, but someone from another universe would read positive when the antibodies bind to these special genes."

"That really is ingenious," I said. I had to admit, it really was ingenious—except for the part about having to kill the subject.

Dr. Collins sneered. "It is, isn't it? However, it's time for you two to go to your holding rooms. After all, it's getting late, and tomorrow is your big test day. Surely you will want to be well rested so that you perform well."

I thought to myself that this was one of the few tests I wanted to fail. I really wanted it to come up negative. But deep down inside, I knew that it would be positive. I would pass the test, meaning I would pass away.

The muscle and guns motioned for Erika and me to follow them. As we left the room, I noticed Rita talking to Dr. Collins. She was very animated, and he just kept shaking his head no. We walked down a long hallway and entered an area marked "security." One of the thugs signaled for us to enter a room marked "holding cell."

As the door shut, Erika turned to me and said, "This is very bad," which I thought was an understatement, all things considered.

"Look, no matter what happens to me, you have to find a way to get to somewhere safe and tell someone in the Agency who can put a stop to the experiments Dr. Collins is performing at the hospital."

"I will, I promise. But we—not just me—have to first find a way to get out of here before tomorrow morning."

"I might be from another planet or universe, but that doesn't change the way I feel about you. I love you, and I always have, ever since the day we first met.

""Michael, I love you too, but leave it to me to fall for the one guy not from this world."

And with that we both laughed pretty hard. I guess we both really needed the laughter.

The cell door opened, and Captain Denton and another very familiar and friendly face walked in. Rita said, "The cavalry is here."

Most of the time death just comes whether
you've said good-bye or not.

—Veronica Roth

Journal Entry 19

Death Isn't Always Good-Bye

Jimbo and Captain Denton came rushing in. *Is everybody a spy?* I thought. "Jesus, Jimbo, don't tell me you work for the CIA also?" I asked.

He laughed. "Of course not. It's actually the OSS."

"I thought that was just an imaginary agency on the much-underrated TV show, *The Six Million Dollar Man*?"

"Christ, Michael, that was the OSI not the OSS," he said.

Erika chimed in, "I thought the OSS was abolished after the war to become the CIA."

"Very few people still know of the existence of the OSS," Captain Denton replied, "but I really think we'd better get out of here now and talk about this later."

We all agreed. We ran out of the holding room, stepping over the knocked-out guard who had been posted outside our cell. As luck would have it, another guard saw us and pulled the alarm. With the alarms blaring, we made a mad dash to escape.

As we were running, I reached into my pocket and pulled out a pack of Life Savers˙, "Does anyone want a Life Saver?" I asked.

Nobody answered, so I put them back into my pocket. Anyway, I thought it was funny. I had always wanted to ask that question during a dramatic moment. *Hey, this was probably one of those moments*, I thought.

Eventually, we came to a stop since no one knew which direction to go. Just then I heard Jean inside my head talking to me. "Michael, you all need to go up the stairs to the right."

"Listen, guys, we need to go up those stairs," I stated.

"Why that way?" Jimbo asked.

"Just call it a gut feeling."

Erika smiled and instinctively seemed to know what I was talking about. "I think we should trust him."

We walked into the stairwell and climbed the multitude of stairs. We reached the top, opened the door, and walked onto the roof of the building. The good news was that we appeared to be on the top level of the complex. The bad news was that Dr. Collins and his guards were also there.

We were slightly outnumbered, but what else would you expect? The battle was on. They were all trained in the martial arts. Erika, Rita, and Jimbo were all throwing kicks and blocking punches. It was really quite a sight. I had no such training, but I did have something even better—the copper swallow's tail, which could provide a cloak of invisibility.

I reached into my pocket and held the absorber device. As I did, I became inconspicuous. What they couldn't see, they couldn't hit—at least that was the theory. With this advantage I was able to systematically knock out four of our enemy on my own, including—with great personal pleasure—Dr. Collins.

Erika and the group stared at me. "How did you disappear like that?" asked Jimbo.

"It's kind of a long story, yet crazy and interesting at times. But I really don't think we have the time for me to explain it right now."

On the right corner of the outer edge of the roof, there was a small storage unit with a door that could be locked. We dragged the bad guys to the unit and shoved them in. It felt good to lock the door.

"This shack doesn't look very stalwart," I said. "Once they wake up, I don't think it will contain them very long. They just don't make things today with the same pride and craftsmanship that was so common years ago."

Erika completely ignored the poorly timed joke. She had become good at that since she was familiar with all of my corniness, but she did support my thought. "He's right, we need to get out of here now."

"Okay, I'm almost afraid to ask," I said. "But now what? How do we accomplish that goal?"

"We jump," Jimbo replied.

"That's what I was afraid of!"

"You have to be kidding," Erika interjected. "We are at least eleven stories up. That's over a hundred feet!"

The physics teacher part of me kicked in. "Right, and with our velocity increasing about ten meters each second we fall, we would end up being a bunch of giant splats on the sidewalk."

"Actually it's nine point eight meters per second squared," Rita added.

"Sorry, physics gods. I was taking liberties with that estimate. But even at a rate of nine point eight meters per second squared, hitting the ground will leave us flatter than one of Jimbo's waffles."

Jimbo gave me a dirty look and dropped a couple of packets on the ground. He unzipped one of his side pockets and took out a small bottle of water, which he poured over the packages. A chemical reaction ensued, and the small packages turned into life-size parachutes. "The boys at the OSS lab developed these dehydrated emergency parachutes," Jimbo said.

Erika looked at the devices with suspicion. "Have they been tested before?"

"Actually, this is the initial test," Jimbo hesitantly replied.

"Of course you're kidding, right?" I asked hopefully.

Jimbo shook his head no.

"I hope that none of the lab technicians' fathers or grandfathers were working in the lab during World War Two," I quipped.

Everyone looked at me with bewilderment.

Although it was probably not the best timing, I started to explain. "Wasn't it the boys at the OSS who developed a harebrained plot to try and emasculate Hitler during the war? They tried adding estrogen into his food by bribing his gardener to spray a liquid form of sex hormones on his fruits and vegetables. The theory was that, if he became more feminine through these hormonal treatments, he would become less aggressive, and people would not take him as seriously, especially if he lost his mustache."

Jimbo was quick to respond. "Actually it was the British who came up with that idea. The OSS was just trying to help with the plot. It might have worked if his gardener had actually sprayed the hormones in his garden instead of just pocketing the money."

"And the failure of the scheme to drop glue on the Nazis, to try to get them to stick to the ground … was that also the Brits' fault?" I interjected.

"Have you been watching the History Channel again?" Jimbo joked. "Actually, that one was our fault. I have to say that wasn't one of our better ideas, but you have to admit it was quite creative."

"And stupid," Erika added. "Michael, that was over half a century ago. I'm sure the OSS has learned from their mistakes, and besides, now is not the time for a history lesson."

Dr. Collins and his men had begun to pound on the locked door of the shack. It didn't seem as if the flimsy door would last much longer.

"Are there any better ideas?" Jimbo asked. "Does anyone want to try to go back down through the building past all of the guards stationed on the ground floor?"

We all looked at each other for a second, grabbed a parachute, and strapped it to our backs.

"In theory, each of the parachutes is digitally active and is capable of monitoring our height the second we dropped," Jimbo informed us. "They should open on their own at the appropriate altitude, which should be almost instantaneously from this height."

"And if they don't open as anticipated?" Erika quizzed him.

I gave her a concerned look.

"Then it's splat, right?" she confirmed.

I nodded my head yes.

Besides being claustrophobic, I wasn't a huge fan of heights either.

The shack door burst open just as we all jumped.

Obviously, the parachutes all worked perfectly. Well, they were not exactly perfect, but they worked fairly well; otherwise, the story would end here, and that would be pretty disappointing.

Except for a few minor scrapes due to hard landings, we were able to reach the ground surface of the complex.

"I think the boys at the lab still have a few minor bugs to work out," I stated, "but all in all, that's a hell of an invention."

"You see, not all of our inventions at the OSS labs are crazy. Some actually work," Jimbo stated proudly.

Jimbo had a car waiting for us on the street. We climbed into the four-door sedan and headed straight for the Agency.

"Jimbo, so you are also a spy? How did you know where we were?" I asked.

"You don't think that it was merely a coincidence that Rita—I mean Captain Denton—worked in my Waffle House, do you?"

Erika then pieced it together. "She's a double agent, right?"

"I did work for the Vomit Comet Program but I was originally placed in that position by OSS," she replied.

"Dr. Collins lied to me," Rita explained. "He told me that, if any ETs were discovered, they would not be harmed. The OSS had their doubts, so I was planted as a double agent. When I learned Collins was going to kill Michael,

I contacted Jimbo and the OSS with a microchip that I had implanted in my arm."

"And here we are, the cavalry," Jimbo said with a smile.

Then it happened. Out of nowhere, I felt a crushing pain on the left side of my chest, and I slumped over.

Erika grabbed me and yelled, "Michael! Michael! What's wrong? Are you all right?"

Captain Denton pulled out her cell phone and dialed 911. "We have an emergency here. A man down. Possible heart attack. We are at the corner of—"

That's all I heard.

I was drifting in and out of consciousness—or something. It was hard to tell. You know in the movies when they say to stay away from the white light if you want to live, or to run toward the white light if you want to die? Well, there was no white light. Instead, there were vibrant colors and shades of light waves that were almost indescribable.

They stopped the car and laid me flat on the ground. Erika performed CPR, but it was too late. Instead of *Gone Girl*, I was *Gone Guy*, just like that.

The grave is but a covered bridge
leading from light to light,
through a brief darkness.

—Henry Wadsworth Longfellow

Journal Entry 20

The Bridge to Zero

It was surreal. I saw my lifeless body below. Erika was crying. Jimbo and Captain Rita Denton looked stunned. I felt a tremendous sense of loss leaving Erika. After our first date many years ago, not a single day had passed without some form of contact between us. Mostly, we saw each other every day, but when that wasn't possible, we at least talked on the phone.

Now I felt this close connection being ripped from me. It was as if a part of my soul was being surgically removed with icy proficiency from hers. I've always believed there are people we meet in life who leave indelible marks on our souls, imprints that can never be erased. Erika was one of those special people for me.

I wasn't sure if I was dying or transmuting, as Jean would call it. Without Erika, I wasn't even sure if I cared. The last earthly thing I remember was seeing the paramedics arriving at the scene. They were trying to revive me, but they had no success. I saw my body jolt with spasmodic contractions after each shock was applied from the electrically charged paddles. The EMTs gave it the old college try, but their efforts were to no avail.

I was gone. The final words I heard as I was leaving were, "Instant cardiac death most likely caused by a heart murmur."

It didn't seem possible. I had always been told that my heart murmur was nonfunctional and perfectly harmless. I had just survived jumping off a building with a never-tested-before parachute. I had survived countless attacks by the CIA. Hell, I had even managed to survive twenty years as a high school teacher. But there I was beginning to lose my connection with this world ... with Erika.

As I continued to rise, an ethereal feeling began to spread through me, and I realized that this wasn't death, at least not in a traditional sense. I was fully aware of my surroundings as I spiraled through what seemed to be an endless tube. Vivid flashes of lights, colors, and sounds appeared to flow past me in a stroboscopic manner, giving me the impression of being stationary. Intuitively I knew I should have felt the sensation of traveling, or to be more accurate, spiraling through this tunnel at a furious warp speed. Instinctively I was somehow aware that the normal rules for time and science didn't apply in this unnatural place.

Eventually the tunnel ended and dumped me out. It left me at a giant cross bridge that appeared to connect the two universes. It spanned as far as I could see and appeared to be made of an achromatic nebula array of gaseous materials that were, by some means, substantial, even though the normal laws of physics dictated otherwise.

This must have been the Nether Region—the area between the two universes that Enoch had described earlier. It appeared to be a self-contained environment, because I was able to still breathe normally. *Or maybe I am really dead and oxygen is not a requirement.* Supposedly, this was the portal between the two realms.

I had two choices—stay here and wallow in an abyss of disconsolateness, or begin to walk along the bridge and see what lay yonder. I chose to wallow for an indeterminate amount of time before moving on. Although childish and pointless, sometimes the human spirit needs to wallow, to feel self-pity, before picking itself up and moving on. I don't know why; sometimes it just does.

As I stood there dazed and immersed in confusion and a state of self-pity, a strange thought popped into my mind. Actually, it was a quote from a book that I had never read. Maybe it had been recited to me as a young child and stored in my subconscious, but either way I knew this passage from Lewis Carroll's *Alice's Adventures in Wonderland*. (His real name was Charles Lutwidge Dodgson; he wrote under a pseudonym. I guess that wasn't important given the state I was in). Anyway, the quote seemed strangely appropriate given where I now was:

> Alice came to a fork in the road. "Which road do I take?" she asked.
>
> "Where do you want to go?" responded the Cheshire Cat.
>
> "I don't know," Alice answered
>
> "Then," said the Cat, "it doesn't matter."

For all I knew, I was Alice. Well, not Alice in the sense that I was a young girl who fell into a rabbit hole leading to a fantasy world populated by peculiar anthropomorphic creatures, but there were similarities between our dilemmas. Maybe the wormhole that I had just transmuted through was nothing more than a rabbit hole leading into a nonsensical fantasy world filled with strange creatures.

There was a certain insane logic in what the Cheshire Cat had told Alice. I knew I wanted out of here, to get back to Erika, but I didn't know which metaphorical road to take. Should I stay here and hope for a miracle? Or should I continue down the galactic bridge? Since I didn't know the answer, it really didn't matter what choice I made.

Once again the logic of the illogical Cheshire Cat seemed to be right to the point. Did it matter? Would anything from this point matter now or anytime soon? I decided on the latter choice and continued down the Galactic Bridge road, which might turn out to be a Yellow Brick Road, for all I knew.

At the beginning of this bridge were two large iconic towers constructed of a strange metallic substance. The outside surface of the two towers was clad with stone and masonry decorated in designs and symbols that were foreign and alien to me.

There were five floors of windows on each tower. At the top of the towers were four smaller peaks surrounding one large peak. A high bridge spanned and connected the two towers. Its purpose was not immediately obvious.

I immediately thought of London Bridge before I remembered that was stupid. Most people, like me, often confuse the two bridges in London. The famous London Bridge is nothing more than an average-looking bridge—a box girder bridge built from concrete and steel, which opened in 1973. This replaced a nineteenth-century, stone-arched bridge that superseded a six-hundred-year-old medieval structure. This is what most people erroneously think London Bridge looks like today. The bridge that most people associate as London Bridge, with its antique and iconic towers, is actually called the Tower Bridge (which makes more sense), according to what a history teacher once told me at lunch. However, I guess accuracy mattered very little now.

Approaching the first tower, I notice that the door was open. Not one to overlook the obvious— well not usually—I interpreted the open door to be a sign that I should go in. There was one room on the first floor. It was dusty and spider web laden, which would have been cool at Halloween. The room contained an array of video games, accessories, and video consoles ranging from the first to the eighth generation of video gaming.

As I walked into the room, I almost stepped on a small metallic rectangular device from which protruded two small knobs. A card attached to one of the knobs read: "1947 cathode ray tube amusement device. The precursor to video game consoles."

There were boxes piled in the corners of the room. Labels on the boxes indicated that the contents were various video consoles. The first box I open was labeled "First-generation video consoles." It contained a Magnavox Odyssey, which

I had played with when I was nine years of age. It looked just as I remembered—a white rectangular box with a raised black center and a brown power cord attached to a white-and-brown reset controller box. This controller box was cracked.

Although the video console appeared damaged, I couldn't help myself. There was old analog cathode ray television set next to the box. I plugged in the Odyssey. Although there was no obvious power source available, magically, a message scrolled across the screen:

> Hello Michael,
>
> We are pleased that you have made it through the wormhole undamaged. Please follow the path through the towers, and you will eventually find us.
>
> Truly yours,
>
> Marilyn (or Jean, if you prefer)
>
> P.S.: you will know when you have arrived at the right place. Just trust your instincts, Sugar, and you will be fine.

I decided to skip the other floors and follow the suggestion in her note. Maybe I would regret that choice, but I was following my instincts.

The two towers were adjacent to one another, so I had to pass through and under each tower to continue on the path. As I walked under and through the first tower, I noticed that the towers were connected by a bascule—a sort of counterbalanced pathway. I wasn't sure of its purpose, but it appeared that it could be opened and closed to allow something to move through it, under the top of the bridge.

As I continued to walk along the bascule, I could see down through the bridge, especially as the structure seemed to become increasingly translucent. It was a spectacular site—galaxies and star clusters appeared to materialize before my eyes. They seemed to be flowing by like a rivulet of glacial matter and anti-matter materials. I continued through and followed the path past the towers. After I'd walked a thousand meters beyond the two towers, I reached a building complex.

The sign on the nearest building indicated it was the visitor and information center, which I guess is what Jean meant when she'd said, "You will know when you have found the right place." I thought, *Wow how convenient!* Actually, the sign was written in a cluster of letters that seemed to a mixture of Latin and Hieroglyphics—letters and symbols. For some strange reason, I was able to interpret its meaning.

As I entered the building, I noticed a mirror hanging on the wall. I looked into the glass and saw myself, but as in my earlier dream, I didn't look forty-seven years old. I looked like I was nineteen. *Maybe this place isn't so bad after all.*

I walked into the first room and saw four familiar faces: Enoch, Brace, Turbo, and Jean. They were all sitting at a round table. The peculiar thing was that I instinctively knew each of them, although they were not the same ages they had been when they appeared to me back on Earth. They all looked younger, some more so than others. Enoch stood up and motioned for me to sit down. "I am pleased that you were able to join us," he said.

"Am I dead or alive?" I asked.

I'm stuck. I'm stuck in yesterday, and you're tomorrow.

—Rebecca Donovan

Journal Entry 21

Nether Lands and Annotations

Jean laughed in a sultry tone. "Michael, you are not dead. You are just in another place, another dimension, or another universe if you fancy."

Apparently here—wherever here was—I could see Marilyn and not just hear her in my head. The amazing thing was that she looked like a very young Marilyn Monroe. Maybe she really was the real Marilyn Monroe.

There were a million questions I could have asked: Where am I? What just happened? What is this place? Will Philadelphia ever win another championship? But I simply asked one question, "How do I get back to Erika?"

Enoch answered, "I am very sorry, but that won't be possible, at least for now."

"There has to be a way because I love her. She is my destiny here or there or wherever I am!" I yelled back.

After all, wasn't love the strongest power in the universe, like in the movies? Didn't Prince Charming eventually end up with Snow White? Didn't Edward eventually convince Bella to marry him and live happily ever after, even though he had to turn her into a vampire and almost destroy his adopted vampire family in the process? That's how it's supposed to be—the good guys always win in the end and live happily ever after with their sweethearts.

"That might be true," Marilyn responded. "We honestly do not know because that is not determined, but for the time being, it's not meant to be."

Again an overwhelming feeling of missing Erika and longing for her seeped through my being. I could only imagine what she was feeling back on Earth. Despondently I said, "I think I have an idea, but maybe you could tell me precisely where the Hades I am?"

Enoch spoke. "I know this must be overwhelming for you, as it was for all of us when we first came here. You are in an area known as the Nether Region. It is the buffer zone and portal between the two universes."

"I was afraid of that," I half joked.

Enoch continued, "When someone from your universe leaves for the first time and enters our universe—Universe Zero—in a proper manner, they must enter through some type of bridge in the Nether Region of Universe Zero. Each person's bridge and experience is different. We are not sure why, but we think it has to do with the fact that each being in each universe is unique."

"But how did I leave Earth and get here?"

"As I mentioned in the Pyramid of Giza, people from our universe have some of the bi-matter elements that were created just after the time of the big bang. These elements are incorporated into a specific gene. This gene, known as the transmutation gene, lies inactive until it is time for the person to come to this universe."

"Does the initialization of the gene affect everyone the same way?" I asked.

"No. Some people leave the Earth because of different medical conditions brought on by this gene. For example, some people die from cancer, some from heart-related issues, and still some from a host of other ailments. Some leave quickly while others die more slowly."

"So on Earth, it appears that the person from this universe is dying, but in reality he or she is coming to this universe—transmuting as you call it?"

"Exactly," Brace interjected. "In your case, it appeared that you had suffered instant cardiac death, causing you to die on Earth but allowing you to come to Zero."

"But according to your mom," I told Brace, "you died in a plane crash and not of medical complications."

"You talked to my mom?"

"Of course. I called your home after you disappeared from my classroom and left that strange and wonderfully undecipherable note—before I acquired my ancient-language reading skills."

Brace looked a little bewildered, so I continued. "I didn't know that you were in another universe. If I had known, I wouldn't have bothered your mother. So when I called, your mom was naturally very upset, and she told me the story about how you died in the 9/11 attacks."

Brace tried to explain. "That's true—the part about being involved in 9/11, but I was dying anyway. I had an incurable blood disease known as polycythemia vera, an extremely rare blood disease in which your body makes too many red blood cells. The extra red blood cells made my blood thicker than normal. As a result, blood clots formed more easily in my body. These clots can block blood flow through arteries and veins, which would have led to a heart attack or stroke that would end my Earth life anyway."

"I'm guessing the transmutation gene led to the defect—a mutation on a gene causing polycythemia vera?" I asked.

"Right. I was told the name of the gene was JAK2. Generally the cause of the JAK2 mutation is unknown, except in my case."

"I still don't think I completely understand."

"In our universe and the Earth universe," Enoch interjected, "random chance and free will still exist. There is no absolute destiny. One tiny, seemingly insignificant event can change the course of events that no one can predict or account for. Things can randomly occur and change, depending on the outcomes of certain consequences."

"So everything being written in stone isn't how the universes really work?" I wondered out loud.

Enoch chimed in with an explanation: "Let me give you a simple, yet very complex, scenario. A young child is about to leave his house to go play with his friend. Just before he leaves, his mother asks him to take out the trash. This simple act delays his departure for a very short time, say two minutes. He performs his chore, leaves his house, and crosses the street to meet his friend. Now let's say that, instead, his mother takes the trash out herself, and he leaves his house two minutes earlier. At that exact time, a drunk driver drives down the street, and the child is killed. The child who is killed is Bill Clinton or Barrack Obama, or some other future important world figure."

"So that simple random act—taking out the trash—had the potential to completely change the outcome of history?"

"Exactly! Time, fate, and random chance are so vastly complex and intertwined that it would be impossible to account for every random scenario of every creature and have every possible outcome predetermined," Enoch explained.

"That's what makes time travel so risky, because changing even the smallest event in the past can have unpredictable and catastrophic effects on the future, right?"

Enoch nodded his head yes.

"Is time travel even possible?" I inquired.

"That's a question for another time—no pun intended," Enoch responded.

"I just happened to be on that fateful plane," Brace interrupted. "My presence was not predetermined, just random chance."

I decided to let the time travel paradigm go, at least for now. "So you don't actually have to die of medical causes to enter this universe?"

"That is essentially correct," Marilyn said. "The transmuted gene simply must be active at the time of the person's earthly demise."

"And, of course, the person must die," I added.

They all nodded their heads in solemn agreement.

"One more thing," I added. "I seem to be much younger—like twenty years old or so. Don't get me wrong, I'm not complaining about this aspect, but you all look to be different ages as well. How is that possible?"

"Actually, you're nineteen," Marilyn responded.

"The same age I was when my father died. Is there any connection?"

Marilyn laughed. "No, Sweetie. Why do you think there always has to be a connection? Sometimes it's just random chance, purely coincidental."

I wasn't sure about that.

"Yes, we can explain some things but not everything," Enoch suggested. "However, right now we have a bit of a trek ahead of us. We should get started."

I was feeling a little defiant. "Where are we going?"

"To the capital *burghal*, which you would call a city back home," Marilyn thoughtfully replied. "It is a little different from any city on Earth. Like any place, it has its positives and negatives, but overall, I think you will be able to adjust to it."

"Why?"

"Why do I think you will adjust to the city?" Marilyn asked.

"No, why do we have to go there?"

"So you can start your new life in your new home, silly," Marilyn retorted.

Close your eyes and tap your heels together three times.
And think to yourself, there's no place like home.

—L. Frank Baum, *The Wizard of Oz*

Journal Entry 22

Off to see the Wizard, the Wonderful Wizard of …

It wasn't exactly like following a yellow brick road. I hoped
there would be few great and powerful wizards to help me
find my way back home, but I doubted I would encounter
any. I would have gladly talked with Glinda or, at the very
least, a wicked witch. But there were no scarecrows, lions,
or munchkins along the way. However, without Erika,
there was the Tin Man, and that was me—no heart.

The truth was, I wasn't sure where home was anymore.
The only reasonable course of action seemed to be to go
along with the group to the burghal, which they called
Andorra. I hoped that maybe someone there could help
me find my way back home to Earth, back to her.

Enoch explained that only the beginning of the Galactic
Bridge was a controlled environment made compatible for
living creatures. Beyond the visitor center, the majority of
the path was much less habitable. There would not be air
to breathe or any heat to sustain us. We would have to
wear specially designed space suits for the journey, which
I thought was pretty cool because I always wanted to be
a spaceman—except for having to deal with the extreme
heights and all.

No mechanical transportation vehicles would function in this harsh environment so the journey would proceed by foot. And the best part—the very best part—was that there were strange creatures that were able to survive in this Nether region, and they were not always affable.

The suits had built-in transmitters, so we were able to communicate during the trek. Enoch explained the age conundrum as we walked. Time in the two universes flowed differently because each universe vibrated in a slightly different frequency. In effect, time in the Zero Universe usually moved slower, which was why a person was younger when he or she transmuted to this universe. This affect, known as the Kilter effect after its discoverer, was not the same for everyone. Some would be younger than others upon entering the Zero Universe. As of yet, Dr. Kilter wasn't sure of the reason for this phenomenon, but he was working on it.

Enoch also explained that there were many beings such as us, some famous and some not well known. It seemed that all of these people, whether famous or not, had a part to play in the history of Earth before their gene initialized and they transmuted to Zero. Some individuals were completely successful in fulfilling their roles, some were only partially successful, and still others were unsuccessful. Again, it seemed that events in both universes were not set in stone; free will did exist in both worlds. There was no ultimate book with all things predetermined in the universes. How could there be? Even with only one universe, the variables would be astronomical.

A few of the famous people from the Zero Universe that Enoch mentioned included Opie Hopkins, Marilyn

Monroe, Kate Warne (the woman I had met earlier outside Ford's theater), and Abraham Lincoln. I had always had a fascination with the Civil War and wondered if the reason for my interest was tied to a subconscious awareness of some of the characters from that time period, many of whom I found now belonged to this universe.

Enoch confirmed that Dr. Soto was correct in his assessment of Lincoln's condition. He was dying because of the Men 2B condition caused by the initialization of the transmutation gene. At the risk of stating the obvious, Lincoln's role was to keep the union together and abolish slavery. Abraham would not have lived very much longer, even if he had not been assassinated by Booth. Like Brace, he had not technically died from medical causes, but the gene had been activated allowing him to transmute to this universe at the time of his execution. Enoch explained this was just another example of random events and free will operating in both of the universes.

Just out of curiosity, I asked if John Wilkes Booth was here in Zero, but Enoch didn't think so. Most people would have been more interested in the identity of the other famous ex-earthlings, but I wasn't. I was still focused on feeling sorry for myself.

Our journey to the capital city would take approximately one day. We would have to pass through the Acituan mountain range. There were three highly intelligent and distinct species of sentient organisms that inhabited the mountain area—the Olops, the Nivlacs, and the Neurals. Collectively, they were known as the Apotheoans. Sometimes these entities were cordial with each other and visitors, and other times they were hostile. I was hoping this was one of their benevolent seasons.

Here's where it gets a little weird, as if it hasn't already been far out enough. I was informed that each of these species represented a particular aspect of human and animal personality and behavior in each universe. The Olops were responsible for a person's yearnings and desires. Nivlacs represented the conservativeness and bourgeois side of an individual. The Neurals represented a balance between the two and, thereby, represented reason and acumen.

These were thaumaturgic—supernatural and magical—beings that supposedly had a part in the creation of every being in both universes. It was this burden that occasionally drove these creatures daft and led to the disagreements. Although this seemed farfetched to me, what the hell did I really know? I mean look where I was now!

The way to Andorra was very scenic; that is, if you were a polar bear and liked the Arctic Circle and the North Pole. It was reminiscent of a whiteout with chilling blasts of wind arising out of nowhere. However, our suits provided us with stability, oxygen, and warmth. The alabaster powdery material blowing in our path was galaxy and star matter yet to be formed. It was the starkness of the buffer zone that provided stability between the two universes.

We walked for half a day before reaching the midway point of our journey. Our party stopped and set up camp for the night. By mid-morning, we would reach the Acituan Mountains, the last major barrier between the

Nether Region and the outskirts of the city of Andorra on the planet Evion.

Enoch set down a strange-looking device that reminded me of a Rubik's Cube. Instantly, a small self-contained area was established where we were able to remove our suits. This small sphere included a makeshift holographic campfire, although it was mainly for aesthetics, as there was insufficient oxygen for us to breathe and for the flames to burn. It was pleasing to the eye, though no heat was released from the fire. Strangely, the hologram provided a level of comfort for our group, and we sat around it talking. It took me back to when I was a Boy Scout and … never mind. I'm rambling.

As we ate and drank in our little life sphere, I asked, "Isn't there any way to communicate with someone on Earth?"

"No, I am afraid that's not possible," Enoch said with a sigh.

"Actually, that's not entirely true," Marilyn interrupted.

"What do you mean?" I asked excitedly.

Marilyn continued, "On rare occasions, people from Zero have been able to communicate with someone on Earth through that person's dreams."

"Yes, but there is no factual data to support this phenomenon," Enoch asserted. "And it is highly inconsistent."

This sounded promising to me. "Okay, but it has happened before?"

"Two people must have a real strong connection—they must be soul-mates," Marilyn replied. "In such cases there have been some occasions in which a person from Zero has been able to communicate with someone back on Earth. Of course, the earthling assumes that it is just a dream even though it is extremely vivid."

That was exactly what I wanted to hear. I did have that connection with Erika, and therefore I might be able to communicate with her at some point. We talked for a little longer before I excused myself and retired to my own space tent (Turbo had provided one for each of us). Besides the fatigue, I was excited to sleep, and by sleep I mean dream, and by dream, I mean communicate with Erika.

Men trip not on mountains; they trip on molehills.

—Chinese Proverb

Journal Entry 23

The Acituan Mountains

It was a quarter day's journey to reach the mountain range, so we started immediately after breakfast. Our morning meal consisted of spaceman-like mushy food and nutrients squeezed out of a tube. Yum. To reach the mountains, we would have to cross through the Ssueg Desert. It reminded me a lot of Antarctica. It was very dry, cold, and white. So white, in fact, we had to wear special sunglasses to avoid damage to our eyes.

The majority of the Ssueg was a vast wasteland. Sporadically, we would see a tumbleweed-like bush blow by. Even rarer were the Ssueg creatures that would scurry by us. These animals were reminiscent of tiny dinosaurs. They looked like Lariosaurus, Microceratops, and Nemicolopterous, tiny Earth dinosaurs that died out a very long time ago.

Although these creatures were meager in numbers, they provided food for the Apotheoans. Even though it was nothing more than Biology 101, the thought of this food chain scenario nauseated me. I tried to think of other things—pleasant thoughts like walking along the ocean at the Jersey shore holding Erika's hand.

A two-hour walk would be required to cross the ice desert and reach the outer boundaries of Andorra. About halfway through the desert crossing, a blast of wind and ice sprang out of nowhere. To keep the party together, we all held onto a single piece of rope as we moved forward. It was an arduous task, but we eventually reached the outer fringes of the Acituan Mountains.

Marilyn instructed me not to talk to any of the Apotheoans if we came across them in the mountain passes. They were neither malefic nor benevolent. Because of the great responsibility and burden they carried, their minds were set to a different wavelength than that of humanoids. Although they were interested in talking, direct communication could cause a person to go barmy and somewhat delirious.

There were two possible trails through the mountain. The first trail, known as the Nielk, was longer but less dangerous. Dnalrebmit, the second trail, was shorter but more perilous. The shorter trail was steeper and there was a greater chance of running into the Apotheoans on that route. Since time seemed inconsequential, I voted for the Nielk trail, along with Marilyn. Enoch, Brace and Turbo selected Dnalrebmit trail, being more dauntless. Even in this harsh environment, democratic majority ruled, and so the Dnalrebmit trail was selected.

For the most part, the beginning of the trek was uneventful. The trail's incline was minimal, and the pace was manageable. We encountered the occasional bantam dinosaur creature scurrying across our path. Intermittently, tumbleweed-like pieces of permafrost vegetation would blow by. It reminded me of the song, "Home on the Range," except in this case it would be "Home on the Frozen Range, where the frozen tumble weed and strange dinosaurs roam and play."

When we reached the middle portion of the trail, we ran into some of the Apotheoans. Enoch explained that they were Olops. Apparently, color was the only determining factor, as they otherwise all looked identical. The Olops were red, the Nivlacs yellow, and the Neurals were blue.

As I had been warned, they tried to talk to us. Sille, who appeared to be their leader, tried very hard to communicate with us. We all did our best to ignore them. As we continued through the middle portion of the beaten track, the magical creatures followed us.

I turned to Enoch. "Why do they want to talk to us anyway?"

"We believe it's because they want part of our memories."

"Why would they want that?"

This time Marilyn chimed in. "Their entire lives are spent creating portions of personalities for all sentient creatures that are capable of thinking in both universes. This monumental task leaves them with no time for themselves. Stealing memories from other beings allows them to create a vicarious life and escape from their responsibilities, if only for a brief moment."

I was thinking, maybe they should get Netflix! But I doubted anyone would know what I was talking about, so instead I replied, "That's a sad existence. They can have some of my recollections if they want.

"Nooo …" my companions shouted in unison.

But it was too late. Sille and his companions must have heard me. Instantly, I started to feel twenty or so minds probing my own. A crushing wave of longing and desire seeped into my consciousness. I wanted to be with Erika. I wanted my own private tropical island. I wanted to be president. I just wanted everything.

I couldn't focus or concentrate; I was overcome with a multitude of thoughts—images and memories of things I desired. It was maddening to covet so many things at one time. It felt as if my mind was being torn in different directions. I probably would have gone insane if my companions hadn't knocked me out.

Enoch stuck a needle containing a sedative into my arm. Everything went dark, and I lost consciousness. I don't remember anything after that point because everything just went blank. Apparently, my friends carried me because when I woke up, we were through the mountain and at the footsteps of the trail leading into Andorra.

"What was in that stuff?" I finally asked. I was feeling very happy.

All cities are mad: but the madness is gallant.
All cities are beautiful: but the beauty is grim.

—Christopher Morley

Journal Entry 24

Andorra

Although I was an avid reader, I had never read Charles Dickens' *A Tale of Two Cities*, unless Cliffs Notes count. I imagined that Andorra had nothing in common with London and Paris during the French Revolution. Like most people, I was familiar with the opening lines, "It was the best of times, it was the worst of times." In this case, the latter phrase seemed much more appropriate.

Andorra appeared majestic and was surrounded by a giant wall. There was a vague blue haze surrounding this great wall, which was slightly reminiscent of the Ishtar gate of ancient Babylon that I had once seen as a question on *Jeopardy*. I wondered if Alex Trebek would be proud and, more importantly, I wondered what the people of this city were trying to keep out—or maybe in. This great city was located on the planet Evion.

Evion was the outermost planet within the Cypress system. This galaxy was a lenticular galaxy; an intermediate form between an elliptical and spiral galaxy. This system was located on one side of the Nether Region; the Milky Way galaxy was located on the other side. Unlike Earth, Evion belonged to a solar system comprised of a binary star system. Most scientists believed this type of system was very rare in Earth's universe.

Evion's primary star, a bright blue spectacle, was called Micah. The secondary star was a white star known as Abda. If not for a special ozone layer surrounding the planet, which afforded more protection from the stronger ultraviolet rays, the heat from these two stars would make Evion uninhabitable for humanoid life forms. On Earth, the ozone layer consisted of three oxygen's bonded together (O_3). On this planet, the stronger ozone layer consisted of four oxygen atoms bonded to two xenon atoms (O_4Xe_2).

There were also three natural satellites orbiting Evion. Two of the three moons were inhabited. On the closet moon, Tiberon, there were nomadic settlements spread across the more habitable sections. It had a partial atmosphere, which contained oxygen in certain regions.

The second moon, Alderon, housed military and government agencies exclusively. These agencies were considered classified. The third moon, Altria, was furthest from Evion and the binary stars. It contained no known life forms, as its environmental conditions were too harsh to sustain any life. This moon was the most similar to Earth's moon.

Fully recovered now, I was able to amble on my own. Fortunately, the Apotheoans had no mind power over a person unless that person was conscious and within their limited mental range.

"Thanks for knocking me out," I quipped.

"You're welcome," Enoch answered. "Now you see why we should not communicate with the Apotheoans. Although they are neutral—neither malevolent nor congenial—they do not comprehend that trying to communicate with our species can be harmful to us."

The giant doors leading into the city were made up of a filigree of gold and diamonds fashioned into many intricate designs and symbols indiscernible to me. Here, these rare precious metals and jewels were very common and therefore very affordable. They were used in many construction projects. Therefore, I naturally wondered: Were diamonds really a girl's best friend on this planet?

This burghal was ancient by Earth's standards—about fifty thousand Earth years old. Over a million Andorrans called this city home. It was immediately obvious that their level of technology was moderately superior to the level that currently existed on Earth.

The city was a melting pot of humanoid life forms. The Andorrans were mostly humanoid in shape, but there was a multitude of slight variations. Some involved skin pigmentation, while others included an extra appendage, similar to the creatures I had seen in my dream.

Andorra was a place of contrast and extremes. There were modern and futuristic buildings interspersed among medieval gothic structures. In general, the avant-garde buildings were constructed from diamonds and platinum. They were home to businesses, research companies, and government facilities. The older structures housed the many private residents and religious sects of the city. These antiquated buildings were fancier, adorned with sculptures and creative designs similar to what one would have expected to see on buildings in ancient Greece. The outside facades were laden with gold.

In this world, science was a mixture of logic and magic. Although most of the basic laws of physics still applied in this universe, at least on a macroscopic level, what might have been considered to be magic back on Earth was considered to be a field of scientific studies in this place. Alchemy was practiced by many scientists, which would help to explain the abundance of precious metals available.

The city's government was somewhat similar to city organizational structures on Earth. At the top of the food chain was the city's mayor. Mayor Tremball had won the last four elections. It was a quasi-democracy system. Although elections were held, it was not illegal to buy people's votes. Extra votes could be purchased by the elite class. Having money was very important for politicians here. Now that I think about it, maybe it was more similar to the process on Earth than I thought.

Andorra was divided into eleven districts. Each district had its own semi-democratically elected prolocutor, the equivalent of a councilman back on Earth. These men and women answered directly to the mayor's office. There were no term limits for the mayor or prolocutors. In other words, they could stay in office as long as their money didn't run out.

Every two years, the prolocutors held a private vote to determine the head prolocutor. The chosen official would serve as the mayor's "number one" and take over the position of mayor if the mayor suddenly died or retired before the end of his or her term in office.

The current "number one" was named Weston. The impression from the group I was traveling with was that he was a seedy character and not well liked. Naturally, he was the prolocutor in the district where I would be living.

We were heading for the Processing Ministry (PM). I would be debriefed and trained for my new function here in Andorra. No one knew what my new job would be, but they informed me that it would be determined at the PM. I figured, how bad could it be? After all, I was a science teacher with a strong background in science. They would probably give me a job in a lab or in the field working on an important scientific project. At the very least, I would probably be offered a teaching position. I wondered what the schools were like here.

Andorrans traveled in vehicles capable of levitation. The roads were actually segmented lanes above the ground. Instead of fossil fuels, these transportation devices used green technology. They used hydrogen fuel that was fused together to produce helium instead of the nitrogen gas, carbon dioxide, and water vapor, which were relatively benign unless air pollution of toxic chemicals such as carbon monoxide, volatile organic compounds (VOCs), and nitrogen oxides and global warming were bothersome.

The helium emitted from the greener tech was collected and recycled within nuclear fusion plants to produce a great deal of clean energy. The fusion process was much cleaner and created more energy than the fission process still used on Earth.

After walking three blocks, we stopped at a taxi tube. With a vacuum like motion, this long crystalline structure transported us to a taxi dock. We entered a blue sedan, and Enoch scanned a card. The driver, Mack, was part machine and part humanoid, a cyborg—a cybernetic organism.

Mack had been created as a result of the cyborg program. Externally, his left arm, his legs, and his right eye and ear had been replaced with machine parts. Internally, his liver, pancreas, and left kidney had also been replaced. He mentioned that he had been an entertainment race driver before his accident. I wasn't sure what that meant, but I really didn't care, as I was getting a little cranky.

Although many of the city's taxis were fully automated, elected officials ran a program that mandated companies to leave a certain percentage of menial jobs open for human, cyborg, and android employment. Mack was one of the lucky few who had been offered a job.

In this city, the middle class had virtually been eliminated. The city was an example of extremes; there were the very rich and the very poor. The rate of unemployment was extremely high.

As we drove along the skyline, I saw merchants below in makeshift stalls selling goods and wares.

"What are those people doing?" I asked.

"It is the market," Brace replied.

Mack must have been listening because he commented, "During the first week of each month, unemployed citizens of Andorra are allowed to buy, sell, and barter goods."

"I see. It's like a giant yard sale," I said.

"A giant yard what?" Mack asked.

Marilyn smiled. "Yes, Michael. It would be this world's equivalent of a yard sale on a much grander scale."

I wondered if any of those entrepreneurs sold a reverse transmuting device or at least a magical map that could lead the way home. One never knows what one can find at a yard sale …

As we continued to fly over the city streets, I noticed a number of Andorrans entering small and mid-sized establishments. Marilyn, noticing my fascination with those people, gave an explanation before I asked. "Those are called *heuringers* and *beisls*. They are similar to the pubs back on Earth. The heuringers are larger than the beisls."

"People—I mean Andorrans—go there to talk and drink the night away?" I asked.

"Yes, and sometimes to buy and sell drugs," Brace interjected.

Mack switched off the tiny fusion-powered engine, and we coasted into the drop-off area of the ministry. Enoch scanned his card once again as I exited the taxi. The others did not get off. "Aren't you guys getting off with me?"

"We will see you soon, but right now we have another matter to attend to," Enoch assured me.

With that, they were off in Mack's taxi, and I truly felt alone, remembering one of my father's favorite songs, "Alone Again (Naturally)," by Gilbert O'Sullivan, which I was beginning to fully understand.

I told the doctor I broke my leg in two places.
He told me to quit going to those places.

—Henny Youngman

Journal Entry 25

Checkup before Processing

The Processing Ministry (PM) was a government building, and very contemporary looking. The antiseptic smell permeating the building gave me the heebeegeebees. The PM was run by a mixture of humanoids, androids, and some cyborgs. Upon entering the main lobby, I was instantly sprayed with a disinfectant mist. A full body scan beamed a ray of light through my body reminiscent of a TSA security scan at a busy airport, but slightly more invasive. Overall, it had a very warm and welcoming feel to it. I walked in looking for the welcome doormat with a floral or beach design, but there was none.

An android approached me and extended his right hand for me to shake. "Hello, Michael," he said in a very pleasing human tone. "My name is Doctor Winston."

I shook his hand. It felt real, with calluses in his palms and heat emanating from the pores of the skin on his android hand. He informed me that he maintained a constant temperature of 37 degrees Celsius. The technology was impressive. Dr. Winston continued. "If you would please follow me, we would like to give you a brief medical exam just to ensure that you are operating at peak efficiency." Courtesy, along with a tinge of humor, had apparently been programmed into these humanoid machines.

"I thought the scanning beam of light and the mist I encountered when I first entered the building was the exam."

Dr. Winston laughed. "No, that was to ensure that you were free of contagious and disease-causing germs. Remember, you did just literally come from another world."

I followed him into a room. He told me to undress and put on the blue hospital gown and wait for the orderly. As I changed and then waited, I noticed that the room was very sterile and completely white. There was a white ceramic sink, but no pictures. There was no color or anything else to suggest any semblance of humanness. The tone was coldness, efficiency, sterility, yes. But humanity? No.

After a minute or so, there was a knock on the door, and another android, this one dressed in scrubs entered the room. He said his name was Jimmy, and he was going to take me to the examination room.

We walked down a pallid corridor. I tried to make small talk with him as we walked. He told me that he had worked at the ministry for five years. He was one of the earlier models and therefore lacked the sophistication of Dr. Winston. His skin lacked pores, and he did not maintain a constant temperature of 98.6 degrees Fahrenheit. Despite the fact that Jimmy's features looked less human than Dr. Winston's, he seemed to be more human to me.

As we reached the examination room, Jimmy cordially acknowledged that it had been nice to meet me, and he left. I noticed Dr. Winston standing with two other beings. I assumed they were doctors, and they both appeared to be humanoid. The first was female. She introduced herself as Dr. Evers. She appeared completely human. The second doctor, a male, looked human except for an extra appendage. He had an extra eye, which was partially covered by a white patch. I wondered if he could sing for the band, Third Eye Blind. He said his name was Dr. Severson.

The doctors explained they were going to run a battery of tests to check my medical condition. They used scanners and, with a simple wave of their hands, were able to accurately register my vital signs such as blood pressure, heart/pulse rates, and lung capacity. This examination room contained machines that were similar to MRI machines back on Earth, but were wider and transparent, thereby eliminating the claustrophobic effect on me. Dr. Severson drew a small amount of blood through my capillaries with needles that did not have to pierce the skin. *This would be a million-dollar idea back on Earth*, I thought. *I wonder who holds the patent rights. Do they even have patents here?*

After the doctors were finished with my physical exam, Dr. Winston asked me to go to an adjoining waiting room. This room was bare, white, and barren. These quarters projected a real welcoming and homey feeling.

Within five minutes, Dr. Winston and his two colleagues walked into the waiting room. He smiled, just like a human, and spoke. "According to our tests, you are, for the most part, extremely healthy: blood pressure, 105/65;

heart rate, 58 bpm; lung capacity, over 6L; cholesterol and blood sugars well within normal ranges."

"I guess that's no surprise. I am apparently nineteen years old here," I chirped.

"Yes. There is no sign of disease or any other complications," Dr. Evers chimed in.

"I did try to do the right things back on Earth. I was kind of a Hulkamaniac—eat right, exercise, cut down on sweets, and, oh yea, say all my prayers before bed," I quipped.

Dr. Winston laughed. *These newer android models really do have a sense of humor*, I thought. *Although I'm not totally convinced that he got the joke. How could he know about Hulk Hogan?*

"There is just one thing though," Dr. Severson said. "Granted, there are no signs of illness or disease. You are very healthy and strong—except for one thing. It appears that your DNA is fluctuating."

"And this means?" I inquired.

"Frankly, we really don't know," Dr. Evers answered.

"It might stabilize on its own," Dr. Severson added. "If it doesn't, I'm sure Dr. Shelly will think of something."

Oh, you hate your job? Why didn't you say
so? There's a support group for that. It's called
Everybody, and they meet at the bar.

—Drew Carey

Journal Entry 26

Niche

Jimmy, the orderly, knocked on the waiting room door,
popped his head in, and told me he had been sent to take
me to the Assignment Chambers located on the next floor.
Within this room, Jimmy informed me that Andorrans
were given their job classifications. Jimmy himself had
been assigned his job there a little over five years ago. All
humanoids, cyborgs, and androids were matched with
their best-fit functional roles within this chamber.

In high school I read George Orwell's novel *1984*—twice.
I wasn't sure if Andorra was a dystopia society, but the
thought was beginning to creep into my mind. I was
beginning to feel a little bit like Winston Smith, being
assigned my function in this new world. In an attempt
to assuage any reservations or discomforts I might have,
I was assured my assignment would be best suited for me
and the city.

Jimmy told me that no citizen was forced to accept his
or her job. However, no one appeared to ever question
an assignment. Mostly, Andorrans seemed superficially
satisfied with their positions, even the menial ones. The
prevailing philosophy was that every task was important
and vital for optimal functioning of the city. Still,

I wondered if there were people who challenged their given assignments, and what the consequences would be if they did.

As we walked down the curvy white hallway, I asked Jimmy if he was happy with his "role." He told me that he liked to help people. As he had been told he wasn't smart enough to be a doctor, being an orderly was okay with him. He wished he was more sophisticated like Dr. Winston, but he accepted his function with grace and dignity.

He took me to a large room marked Assignment Chambers and left. I went inside and immediately noticed that this room appeared different. It wasn't as cold and antiseptic looking as the other chambers within this ministry. The room was painted with vibrant colors. A number of portraits hung on the walls, which I assumed were famous Andorrans. In the middle of the room was a comfortable-looking couch made of Andorran leather. A number of exotic plants were scattered throughout the room. Indigenous instrumental music was playing in the background; it had a strangely hypnotic sound.

I sat down on the couch and closed my eyes for a moment. I opened them when I heard someone enter. Dr. Winston walked in with a man he introduced me to as Dr. Daniel Forest, the assistant director of this ministry. He was an imposing character. He was very tall, though I wasn't sure of his exact height. He looked like he could play middle linebacker for an NFL team. As far as I could tell, he looked completely human.

Dr. Forest explained that they would ask me to perform a task, and my performance would determine my role within this society. I was required to lie down on the couch. He showed me what he called the darkling cap, which seemed to be a highly sophisticated virtual reality helmet that would interface with my brain waves. My function would be determined by the outcome of this virtual test.

I put on the darkling cap and immediately became aware that I was not in the processing room anymore. It was hot, humid, and raining. Lush green flora grew everywhere. A plethora of native insects and small animals scattered about. It seemed that I was in the middle of a tropical rain forest.

I could see a diamond pathway that appeared to lead out of the jungle. As I walked along the path, I noticed the indigenous plants and animals were different from those on Earth. For example, there were some flowers that resembled geraniums and chrysanthemums, but they were abnormal colors for these flowers. Other natural flora appeared in various colors besides green; this was probably the result of an evolutionary effect on the planet caused by the binary stars. It was as if the principal of evolution operated in both universes, which comforted me as a person of science.

Eventually, the diamond pathway led through a clearing, and I stood facing the doors of a large facility. The large neon sign on the outside of the building read Two Sun Casino. The name could have represented the binary star system, or maybe it was representative of something else. It didn't matter.

I figured, "when in Rome," so I entered the casino and realized I was penniless. I had not yet been given a monetary card, but I was hoping that my credit was good here. I was greeted by a cocktail waitress carrying what looked like an aperitif and plate with a cookie on it. She said they were complimentary.

On this planet I was nineteen, which was apparently the legal drinking and gambling age. So, I took advantage and drank the cocktail and ate the enticing cookie, which was strange because I was never much of a sweets eater. My senses became heightened as I started feeling a little lucky and slightly high. One of the pit bosses walked over to me and introduced himself. His name was Bruno, and he gave me a Two Sun card to use for only one free spin on the giant slot machine, which was located in the middle of the casino.

Any additional gambling losses would be levied against my future earnings, he explained. However, the card could be used indefinitely for food, hotel amenities, and rooms. I could eat and enjoy the entertainment and lodging free of charge as long as I wanted. Apparently this was the ultimate casino for comps. I started to wonder if this was really the Lotus Casino and if Percy Jackson and his friends were waiting for me just around the corner.

As I looked around the casino, I felt as if I never wanted to leave, and I wondered why anyone would. The place was a virtual adult Disney World. There were great acts. In fact, Frank Sinatra and Elvis Presley were performing in the main lounge. I assumed these were the real Frank and Elvis based on prior events. The pool and spa looked as if they had been created with Eden as a blueprint.

Beautiful women wearing stiletto heels were wandering around and gambling, and cocktail waitresses were offering complimentary drinks and those strangely enticing cookies.

I was enjoying the sights and sounds when Bruno approached me and asked if I would like to sit in on a number with Frank and Elvis, whose nickname here was Press. It was a no brainer. We performed a medley of "My Way," "Burning Love," and "Best of Me" (originally performed by the Foo Fighters). It was a musician's dream come true—jamming with some of the all-time great artists. The audience gave us a standing ovation. Afterward, I shook each of their hands and left the stage as they continued their performance.

For the first time, I realized how tired I was feeling. I used my Two Sun card to get a room so I could relax and sleep for a little while. Naturally, I was given room 411, which was Erika's birth date. The room was decorated in neutral, soothing colors, which gave it a narcotic feel. I lay down on the king-size bed with a thousand pillows, and immediately dozed off.

When I woke up, I was outdoors. It was cold, and a misty rain was falling. Everyone was dressed in black. As I moved closer, I began to recognize the people standing over a gravesite. I recognized the place. It was the cemetery where my father was buried, and the place where Erika and I were to be buried together one day, which I had always assumed would be in the distant future. Even though we had never married, we had talked about spending all of eternity together. Maybe somehow we were related to Goldie Hawn and Kurt Russell ... Erika was there with her two sons. My mother, stepfather, sister, and niece were also there. A number of teachers and students from my school were there as well.

As I read the small plaque, I saw that it read Michael Alan Cardazia, 1963–2010, followed by a bunch of words that were indiscernible to me. Suddenly, it occurred to me (after all, I catch on quickly) that I was at my own funeral! The rabbi was reciting a prayer. (I think it was the Kaddish, known as the "Mourners Prayer," which is spoken at funerals.) My mom and Erika were crying.

Although I am Jewish, I have never been religious. According the Jewish faith, a person must be buried as soon as possible after death, for reasons that have never been clear to me. A small plaque is placed on the grave temporarily, and the immediate family and friends return one year later to unveil a suitable gravestone and perform a small ceremony known as "the unveiling."

I tried to talk to them, but they couldn't hear me. I tried touching them, but my hand passed through them. As my arm passed through Erika, reminiscent of a ghost scene that one might see in a Bugs Bunny cartoon, I was aware of the heat and life force from within her. It was not substantial or tangible, but it was present. Initially she seemed completely oblivious to what I was innately aware of. After I made several such attempts to touch her, Erika seemed to sense my presence, because her expression suddenly changed. She stopped crying and looked around as if she could almost sense me. It was as if I was actually there but slightly out of phase with that universe.

I wasn't sure why I could see them and they couldn't see me, but was guessing I was having a dream. From my end, it seemed to be much more substantial than a dream. It felt as if my time line was slightly ahead of theirs, and that explained why I could see and hear them but they couldn't do the same.

As the funeral concluded, my sister, Andrea, pulled Erika aside. "Before you left for Washington, Michael stopped by my house and gave me this box," my sister said. "He asked me to give it to you if, for any reason, he didn't return from your trip. I asked him why he would ask me to do this, but he seemed very solemn and serious. For some reason, I felt compelled to do as he asked and not press the issue."

I watched as Erika accepted the box. She opened it and pulled out the diamond engagement ring that I was going to give her after we returned from Washington. It was a one-karat, heart-shaped diamond with smaller diamonds set in a swirling, three-tiered platinum setting.

I wasn't sure why I had felt the need to leave the ring with Andrea before I left; it was just a feeling I had—the little voices that we sometimes have in our heads giving us advice. (No, this wasn't Jean's voice; it was a pre-Jean spiritual guide voice.) Some refer to it as a gut feeling, but that never made sense to me because I never heard voices in my stomach. Maybe strange rumbling sounds, but not voices. The point was that, deep down, I'd had a strange feeling that I wasn't going to return. I wanted Erika to have the ring, which is why I had left it with my sister.

I knew Erika had mixed feelings about marriage, and I wasn't sure what her reaction would be. But I also thought, what the hell, it's been ten years, and whatever her reaction, she at least deserved a ring.

I have often observed that life has a sense of humor—bizarre at times but there anyway. No matter how she felt about marriage, she would have a difficult time turning down the ring. When you think about it, it's pretty hard to turn down a proposal from a dead guy. There is no pressure; neither are there strings attached.

"Oh, Erika! It's an engagement ring," my sister said. "It's beautiful! Did you have any idea that he was planning to ask you to marry him?"

Erika stared at the ring and started to break down. "I had no idea," she said weeping. She looked inside the band of the ring and saw the inscription: "6/9/02: My Heart, My Soul, and My One."

Andrea smiled. "Is that the day you two first met?"

Erika mustered a weak smile and nodded. Andrea put her arm around Erika, and they started to walk to their cars. Erika said something to my sister, but I began to fade from this place so couldn't hear her.

Although I was comforted knowing that Erika had received the ring, I still awoke in a cold sweat. I got dressed and went down to the casino floor. As I was meandering around, I saw the giant slot machine. There was a small line of people waiting their turn for the machine. Each person walked up and swiped his or her card. It looked to be an older-style machine once referred to as a one-armed bandit back on Earth. As I got in line and watched each person pull the arm of the slot machine, I realized that it wasn't a normal slot machine.

The reels spun and all the bells and whistles went off. The slot machine didn't pay money. It seemed that the reels consisted of occupations rather than objects, symbols, or animals. It seemed bizarre that a slot machine would determine your position in this society.

I was hoping the slot machine was just a metaphor or a form of symbolism within my own darkling cap illusion. I tried to convince myself it was just a creative way to show me my new exciting occupation. I was sure this world was too advanced to let a slot machine determine the niches of its denizens.

The guy before me pulled the arm. The wheels spun and the bells and whistles sounded loudly. When the last reel stopped, he was very happy to find that he would be working as a film director with one of the city's big movie companies. I thought that was pretty cool, and it raised my hope and anticipation for my exciting new career. I almost couldn't wait. What would I be? *Probably a rock star, a famous scientist, or a popular movie star*, I excitedly thought.

My turn was next. I wondered if this was real or if I was dreaming. I walked up to the slot machine and pulled the arm. The reels turned, the bells and whistles blared. The smoke and dust settled as my fate was determined. The reels read "custodial, custodial, custodial, wild, and custodial." So it appeared that my big function in this world, my new and exciting occupation, was to be—janitor.

"One must always be careful of books," said Tessa,
"and what is inside them, for words
have the power to change us."

—Cassandra Clare

Journal Entry 27

The Book

I slowly become cognizant. I had either been dreaming or had been unconscious. I wasn't sure which. I was on the couch, and Dr. Forest and Dr. Winston were staring at me with curiosity. I was still wearing the darkling cap, and I took it off quickly.

"How was your experience?" Dr. Winston asked.

"You don't know?"

"No," Dr. Forest responded. "You see, the darkling cap experience is different for each individual who wears it. It is the end result that is important, not the trek, expedition, or quest. Some people travel to exotic lands, others climb mountains or try skydiving, still others have a more mundane experience. It is the message in the end that is important, not the journey itself."

"Can you also have a dream within this experience?" I asked.

"No, I don't believe you can. Why?" Dr. Forest inquired.

"No reason, just curious. So my experience wasn't real?"

"Yes and no."

I loved it when my questions were answered in riddles. "Could you be less specific?" I quipped.

"It was real in the sense that your experiences were actually occurring inside of a hologram program. The events and outcomes of your experience were not predetermined but influenced by your responses to the stimuli. It wasn't real in the sense that all of this was occurring only inside of your mind," Dr. Forest explained.

"So you don't know what my trek was, and you were not probing my mind during the experience?"

Dr. Winston answered with a wry smile. "Probing the mind during the darkling cap hologram could cause cerebral neuronal damage, and we wouldn't want that, now would we?"

"Could you tell us what happened?" Dr. Forest asked.

I started to relate the story to them. I described the tropical rain forest and the Two Sun Casino. I left out the part about somehow seeing my own funeral. With a large grin on my face, I mentioned my trio performance with Frank and Elvis, at which point they chuckled. I described the slot machine and told them what the one-armed bandit's reels showed.

They both nodded in agreement and thanked me for my time. I got up off the couch. They shook my hand and started to leave.

"Wait a minute," I said. "You can't be serious. A holographic dream from a weird-looking cap determines my career here? You mean I could have lied, told you anything and you wouldn't have known?"

"Yes, we appreciate your honesty," Dr. Forest said. "But you don't have to make it sound so bad. The darkling cap analyzes your brain capacity and determines what role you would be best suited for. The cap provides a fantasy world created in the individual's own mind to present its determination of what function would be best for that individual. I think it makes it more interesting, don't you? Letting one's own mind select the function?"

"Okay, but I was a science teacher back on Earth, and I was really hoping that—"

Dr. Winston cut me off. "I'm sorry, Michael. Your job here has been determined, but I can assure that you get to work within the Science Ministry, which at least has something to do with science."

"But—" I started to protest, but they left abruptly.

Jimmy came back in the room and informed me that he was there to take me to the Book Room. He said the Book, known formally as The Book of Records, was a magical book. Within the pages of this book were the roles of people from this universe and their purposes back on Earth. After the darkling cap established a person's function, the book provided a pass code that allowed the individual to receive a monetary card and ID so they could begin their new roles in Andorra.

We reached the room, which was guarded twenty-four/ seven because of the importance of the Book. The two guards asked Jimmy for his ID. A retina laser scanned our right eyes, and we were allowed to enter the room. I wondered how it already knew my retina!

The magical book was located in the center of the room. It was placed on a podium and encased in very thick glass. There were two hand-sized indentations on the top glass surface. Jimmy explained that I should put my hands on the indentations. He went on to explain that the book had a quirky personality, a mind of its own, and would determine if, and for how long, it would allow me to read it.

I walked up to the book and placed the palms of my hands within the indentations. The thick glass dematerialized. Snow began to fall all around me, and the magical book began to glow with a tangerine color. The book languidly opened, presenting me with an alphabetical list of the names of the Andorrans who had spent time on Earth. I scanned down the list and noticed Marilyn Monroe's name.

Marilyn had been a big advocate for equal rights for minorities and the poor. Next to her name was a quote by her, "What I really want to say: That what the world really needs is a real feeling of kinship. Everybody: stars, laborers, Negroes, Jews, Arabs, we are all brothers. Please don't make me a joke. End the interview with what I believe."

The magical book told stories in an animated form. Instead of words and descriptions, I could see the people in the book and hear them talking. The characters were slightly raised from the pages and appeared in three dimensions. It wasn't exactly like a Harry Potter scene, but it was similar. There was a picture of Ella Fitzgerald recounting a story of how, if it hadn't been for Marilyn, she might have never made it in show business.

Ella was telling the reader—me—that Marilyn promised the owner of Mocambo, a popular but small jazz nightclub, that, if he booked Ella to play, she would take a front table every night Ella played. He did, and Marilyn showed up every night. The press went wild. Mocambo became very successful, and Ella never had to play in a small jazz club again. Ella went on to say that Marilyn was an unusual woman, a little ahead of her time even, if she didn't even know it. Ella didn't know that Marilyn was really from another universe, but she was sure right about the unusual part.

The page switched, and I could see John F. Kennedy talking with Marilyn Monroe. JFK began to talk about his friendship with Marilyn and how she had been very influential in some of his social policies, like the Equal Pay Act of 1963 prohibiting arbitrary discrimination against women.

In addition, JFK promised to end racial discrimination during his administration and appointed forty African Americans to administrative federal positions, including five federal judges. No other president had previously done this. Although he was assassinated before the Civil Rights Act of 1964 was passed, he was largely responsible for that legislation, which helped lessen racial discrimination in the areas of housing, education, and voting. I now knew what Marilyn's purpose on Earth had been. Her real purpose wasn't to be a famous movie star, but to be a movie star who was able to influence and help other people. It was because of her fame that she had been very influential in efforts to end racial discrimination. She had been a major advocate for people's rights.

The pages about Marilyn began to slowly close. I noticed the names of other famous people, like Opie Hopkins, Kate Warne, Abraham Lincoln, Frank Sinatra, and Elvis Presley as the index page passed by.

I was not sure of the importance of Frank Sinatra's or Elvis's time on Earth, as the magical book breezed past their data. However, the book stopped on the name Kate Warne. I vaguely remembered meeting her with Opie in Washington DC. The information was sketchy, but it did provide some tidbits. Kate was credited with being the first female private eye during the Civil War era. She had been instrumental in uncovering the Baltimore assassination plot against President-Elect Abraham Lincoln in 1861. Kate was also involved with undercover intelligence work for the Union during the war as well as some postwar espionage activities. Interestingly, Kate died of pneumonia shortly after the Civil War, but I was guessing that the transmuting gene kicked in after she accomplished her role on Earth.

Apparently, the book decided that my time was over. The book closed its pages and the thick glass reappeared. A monetary card along with ID materials appeared on the glass surface.

Jimmy smiled at me. "Looks like your time is up. What did you see?"

"You didn't see and hear the pages?"

"No. Only the person viewing the book can see what's inside. Anyone else in the room is put into a state of suspended animation while the book's pages are open."

If they had told me I was the janitor and would
have to mop up and clean the toilets after the show
in order to play, I probably would have done it.

—Bruce Springsteen

Journal Entry 28

I Prefer To Be Called a Custodial Engineer

The term *janitor* originated from the Latin word *Janus*.
Thank God that I had four years of Latin in high school;
I was beginning to see my efforts finally paying off. Janus
was the ancient Roman god of beginnings and transitions.
He was the keeper of gates, doorways, endings, and time.
Janus had two faces because he looked to the past as well
as the future. A janitor is considered to be a keeper of a
place, and was therefore named after Janus.

I remember a colleague telling me once that the most
important person to befriend in a school is the janitor
because, if you ever needed anything, he (or she!) always
knows how to get it for you. This important status wasn't
comforting to me now.

I wasn't a teacher anymore. That was from another
world—actually, another universe. I felt like the old man
in Aesop's fable wishing for death. Ironically, I had always
thought about new challenges and changing my career,
but I guess the old saying was true, "Be careful what you
wish for because you just might get it." Not that there was
anything wrong with being a janitor. I had just always
thought that, if I changed professions, it would be to

become a rock star, an international spy, or some other glamorous profession along those lines.

Before taking me to my new apartment, Jimmy was going to drop me off at the Science Ministry. I needed to meet with my immediate supervisor and receive my new responsibilities. Jimmy had some quick errands to run and asked me to wait for him in the lobby of the Processing Ministry.

I had been waiting for only a short period of time before Jimmy arrived and greeted me. "Hello, Michael. How are you feeling?"

"I'm all right, Jimmy, I guess. I just thought that my position would be a little different, that's all."

"I understand. I always wanted to be more like Dr. Winston, but I was given this position, so I try to make the best of it."

I nodded and got into his car. It wasn't fancy or new. Actually it was more like a jalopy, but he seemed proud of it. Even though it wasn't the most desirable of Andorran automobiles, the technology was superior to any car in my former world. All of the functions were voice activated and keyed to a specific voice or voices. Only Jimmy—or those to whom he had granted access—could operate the vehicle by using the complicated voice-identifying software program. On the one hand, it seemed a little inconvenient, but on the other hand, it did cut down on car thefts. There were no indications that crime was an issue here, not even the low-level, ordinary misdemeanors and minor felonies we dealt with back on Earth.

Jimmy instructed Suzie, his car, to turn on her engine and go to the Ministry of Sciences. It was common practice for people in this city to give names to their devices, especially the larger ones. Suzie elevated into a driving lane above the buildings.

Suzie even addressed me! "Hello, Michael Cardazia. Could I pour you some jamocha?" Before I could respond, she explained that, on Evion, jamocha was the closest thing to Earth coffee. The glove compartment opened and displayed a steaming "cup of Joe" that smelled vaguely like coffee. It would probably take some getting used to on my part. Like many people from my former world, I was slightly comatose and mostly incoherent before my first cup of morning coffee.

"Hazelnut creamer and one artificial sweetener, right?" Suzie rhetorically asked.

"How did it—I mean how did *she*—know how I like my coffee?"

"Didn't the doctors explain the ID card process to you?" Jimmy asked.

I shook my head no.

"It's simple. Your ID card has all of your personal information encrypted on it. Suzie was able to scan your card and see that you like coffee—and what you like to put in it."

I must have looked a little befuddled, because he continued, "During the darkling cap experience, the cap probed your mind and personality. It recorded your personal information, including likes and dislikes, on a memory chip, which was later implanted and encrypted onto your ID card."

Do all machines have this program built into them? I wondered.

As if he could read my mind, he said, "No, not all machines can read ID cards, only certain ones. And, no, androids cannot read the ID chips, if that's what you're thinking," Jimmy replied.

"I'm sorry. I didn't mean to offend you or imply—"

But Jimmy cut me off. I kept forgetting that the androids had feelings and emotions. "That's okay. I guess that was a logical question, and you are still very new to this place."

Suzie announced, "Ministry of Sciences, next stop. It has been my pleasure to drive you. If this is your final destination, please de-car on your right side. We realize that you have a lot of driving choices, so we appreciate your business and look forward to driving you again."

Jimmy said, "I paid extra to get a personality chip for Suzie that has a sense of humor, but it was worth it, don't you think?"

I nodded. "Yes, I guess she's been watching too many commercials."

"Commercials ... you must mean promos. Here we call the ads on TV promos, which are short for promulgations."

"Well, whatever you call the TV commercials, we sure don't have anything like Suzie back on Earth."

"Thank you, Michael. I'll take that as a compliment," Suzie chimed in.

I thanked Jimmy and Suzie and walked into the building. The Ministry of the Sciences was the largest of all the Ministries on Andorra. It was the most modern of all the buildings and ministries. I wondered why they even needed janitors in a place like this; I assumed they would just have a robot cleaner.

Once again, I was sprayed with a mist and scanned with a beam of light as I entered the main lobby. There was a revolving octagonal check-in desk in the center of the room. I walked up and gave my name to one of the cyborg security guards. He asked me to have a seat and said that the director would be along in a minute.

As I settled into the plush leather couch, I looked around and noticed there were no beams or columns supporting the five floors. They appeared to be suspended without any structural support. The architects here had apparently perfected some anti-gravity device. This type of science was beyond any technology back on Earth. In addition, there were no stairs or elevators; rather, there were glass tubes that seemed to connect the levels of the building.

After five minutes, two men walked over to me. One man appeared human; the other was a cyborg. The first man was the director. He was dressed in a vested three-piece suit and tie. His suit was freshly pressed, and he was groomed immaculately. Everything about him screamed efficiency, order, and for some strange reason, hedonism. The second man wore a one-piece, light-blue jumpsuit.

"Hello, Michael," said the man in the suit. "My name is Dr. Shelly—Victor Shelly. I'm the director of this facility, and this is Walton, my assistant." I had been expecting to meet just my immediate supervisor and not the top dog. "We are very pleased to have you on staff. I realize that you are probably a little disappointed in your position, but I can assure you that every job here is considered to be a vital cog for the well-being of Andorra."

Dr. Shelly was a Peterbilt sort of a man—tall, lean, and muscular. What stood out to me was his face. He was ruggedly good looking and reminded me of someone who might ride a Harley Davidson. However, he emanated an aurora of coldness and lack of any human emotion. Probably the thing that bothered me the most were his cyanide blue eyes, which seemed devoid of humanity.

"Thanks," I said. "Custodial work obviously would not have been my first choice, but I'll do my part for the greater good. Since I was a science teacher back on Earth, maybe sometime you could explain how your science and magic mix together here."

"Yes, maybe sometime we could do that. I just wanted to meet you personally and welcome you. But for now I'm going to have Walton show you around and get you familiarized with your new duties. If you have any questions, please direct them to him. I have to run now— some loose ends to tie up, so to speak, but we will talk again soon," Dr. Shelly assured me.

A cold chill ran along my spine as he talked about loose ends. Instinctively (even without the creepy music that plays in a horror movie to let you know something is wrong) I knew there was more to the good doctor than he was letting on. Maybe I had watched too many cheesy movies. Or maybe it was that my psychic powers, which had never been significant when I was on Earth, were more acute in this world.

Walton took me to the custodial office to issue my custodial engineer badge, which really said Janitor, and my light-blue jumpsuit. All the janitors wore this as a representation of compliance and sameness. He showed me the work log schedule and where to scan my monetary card after each shift. I was shown the employee room, which we were allowed to visit during break periods. The employee room felt a little more Earth like, with vending machines and 3-D plasma holographic televisions.

He looked more like a typical cyborg. His left eye, right arm, and both legs were mechanical. He told me that, internally, his circular and respiratory systems were human, but the remaining systems, including the skeletal, were machine parts. His brain was mostly human but there were some machine neuronal parts synergistically fused together with human neurons.

He seemed like a decent guy, I mean decent cyborg. He showed me around the floors and pointed out my responsibilities. It was my job to mop the floors, dispose of and recycle the trash (almost everything was recycled on Andorra), and do some general cleaning. Additionally, since I was a science teacher, I was put in charge of the non-recyclable chemicals that were to be disposed of from the lab rooms on the second and third floors. One good thing about this world was at least it didn't appear to be a wasteful one, like Earth was.

My ID would allow me entrance to the first three floors. The fourth floor was maintained by a handful of the select janitors, and Walton did not mention what was going on within the rooms on that level. He did not mention the fifth floor at all. In fact, there appeared to be no access point or entry level to it.

I started to ask Walton what took place on the mysterious floors, but he just ignored my questions and acted as if he hadn't heard me. In my world, they would call it selective hearing, and I know most men were good at it; apparently so were cyborgs. After he finished showing me the floors, he brought me back to the main lobby and told me that Jimmy would be back shortly to take me to my new apartment.

I thanked him and began to wonder if it was more than just a coincidence that I had ended up here as a custodial engineer.

My apartment was robbed and everything was replaced
with exact replicas …
I told my roommate and he said, "Do I know you?"

—Steven Wright

Journal Entry 29

Crash Pad

I needed to get some fresh air so I decided to wait for Jimmy and Suzie outside the building. The weather on Andorra was a little warmer than it was on Earth because of its two suns, but it was still pleasant since it was their autumn season. Evion was similar to Earth in that it had both a rotational aspect that provided day and night, and a revolution period that provided a changing of the seasons. Being a creature of habit, I imagined I would have missed day and night and the newness of the seasons, so I was modestly comforted that these planetary phenomena were similar in both worlds.

In front of each of the ministries was a waiting area where people could sit and wait for their rides. There was a Victorian-style park bench, which I thought was odd given all the technology of this ministry. I sat down and waited for my ride. I looked up. Above me was the hustle and bustle of air cars and taxis zooming past in perfect harmony. Often I had dreamed of belonging somewhere else, and now that I was, I missed Earth. I missed Erika most of all. *Be careful what you wish for …*

In middle school we read a short story called the "Monkey's Paw" by W. W. Jacobs. In this story, Mr. White is given a monkey's paw by a friend who acquired from a "holy man" in India. His friend tells him that the paw is a mysterious talisman and will grant three wishes. His friend warns of the danger and responsibility of having these three wishes. Mr. White's friend's last wish is for his own death.

Mr. White does not heed the warning of his friend. He learns the hard way that wishes come at an enormous price for interfering with fate. His first wish is for two hundred dollars to make his final mortgage payment. He receives this money as compensation for the death of his son at work. Against his better judgment, his wife convinces him to wish for their son to come back to them. After a knock on the door, Mr. White realizes that his son, having been mutilated and buried for over a week, would be grotesquely deformed, so uses his third wish for his son to remain dead. *Be careful what you wish for …*

In the end, Mr. White had three wishes granted to him. After he used those wishes, all he had to show for them was a dead son, a wife who went crazy, and the two hundred dollars, which he needed to pay for his son's funeral. *Be careful what you wish for …*

Still, I didn't care. Consider me Mr. White or any literary tragic fool. All I knew was I had to find a way home, a way back to Erika, regardless of the price. That's what I thought.

I heard Suzie's voice. "Arriving Science Ministries, all aboard, watch your step."

"Hey, Jimmy. Hi, Suzie. I appreciate the ride."

"We're going to take you to your new living quarters," Jimmy stated. "It's not much to look at, but it is located in a desirable section of the city. There are plenty of restaurants, theaters, museums, and clubs within walking distance of your flat. There's even a beautiful park located close by."

"That sounds perfect. In what part of town is it located?" I asked.

This time Suzie responded. "The lower eastside, known as New London. They have some of the nicest parking garages around. The spots are spacious, and the parking lines are perfectly marked. And the underground parking … don't get me started, it's just—"

"Suzie," Jimmy interrupted, "I'm sure Michael doesn't want to know the details of the parking facilities in New London."

"Actually, Suzie, that does sound very interesting," I said. "But first I was wondering how I would get to work."

"Until you are able to afford an air car, there are two ways," Jimmy answered. "There's an extensive underground train system that runs under the city. Second, there is a metro airbus system that also runs near your apartment."

I still wasn't thrilled with my job, but at least I would be able to get to it. As we approached my new home, Suzie slowly came to a stop in front of the building.

"Welcome to La Castle," Suzie blared out.

The name on the building was Babylon Gardens. Jimmy explained that a number of buildings in this city had been named for ancient structures back on Earth. My new dwelling was huge. The building extended straight up as far as the eye could see. Suzie mentioned that there were two hundred floors. Located on the roof of the building was a lush garden, which received plenty of sunlight from the two suns.

My apartment was located on the twelfth floor and was number eleven on that floor, making my apartment number 1211, which was my birth date back on Earth. Again I wondered if this was a weird coincidence or if someone—or something—had an ironic sense of humor.

Jimmy wanted to show me the apartment. Suzie went to the garage to talk with some friends (other cars, I presumed) while she waited. In order to enter the apartment building, a retinal scan and fingerprint verification was required. The apartment was ultramodern.

There were five rooms in total: kitchen, living, dinning, bedroom, and bathroom. In the living room was a universal flat-screened, 3-D holographic television that did not require special glasses for viewing. It was possible to view channels on other planets as well as certain television programs from Earth, depending on the celestial events occurring at the time of viewing.

The furniture in the rooms was equipped with anti-gravity selections. This made it possible to sit or lie up to a foot above the furniture without actually touching the piece. Even the toilet was equipped with an anti-gravity device, which I thought was really weird and unnecessary. All the appliances in the kitchen were voice activated.

Jimmy explained that my ID card allowed me to program the apartment door to allow access to whomever I wanted by initially programming their retinal and finger print scan. After showing me around the apartment, which only took five minutes, Jimmy excused himself and said he would see me soon.

I walked into the bathroom. Above the sink was a metallic medicine cabinet. I opened the shiny door and found a wide range of vitamins and pills. Accidently, I knocked over a container. When I picked it up, I noticed that the label identified the contents as Retacine. The back label indicated that these were sleeping pills. The label warned that two pills were the limit, and a higher dosage could lead to respiratory failure and death.

Taking the bottle from the bathroom, I sat on the foreign bed. I could take a handful of these pills and go to sleep forever—no more worries. I was kidding myself; my chances of getting back to Erika were remote at best. I knew that I didn't belong on Earth, but I also knew that I didn't want to live here without her.

Since I wasn't a vampire, the so called "true death" often mentioned in a series back on Earth called *True Blood* would be my fate if I continued on this course of self-pity, unless there were really vampires in this world.

Before I realized it, the bottle was popped open, and a little pile of small, red pills was in my hand. I looked at them and swallowed hard. My eyes watered. I was conflicted. It would be so easy just to give up and sleep, end the pain.

I thought of Jennifer Aniston, not because I liked her as an actress or even because I enjoyed the television show *Friends*, but because of something I remember her saying once: "The greater your capacity to love, the greater your capacity to feel the pain." Often I find myself thinking of random and bizarre thoughts at the strangest moments—like now, when I was contemplating killing myself. Luckily, I often find an idiosyncratic logic to these seemingly random thoughts. She was right. If you could love deeply, you could feel pain equally as deeply and still be all right. Maybe that's what humanity is all about.

There was just one problem with giving in to the "true death." Actually two problems. First, I wasn't a quitter. Second, quitting meant there was definitely no way in hell that I could get back to Erika if I took these pills, at least not in this life. Being agnostic, I wasn't sure if there was a heaven, and if there was one, that would be forgiven. I couldn't take that chance.

I squeezed the pills in my hand and threw them against the wall. I screamed in frustration, which felt unfamiliar and astoundingly good.

In the bedroom I found a credenza containing Andorran clothes. They were exactly my size, no alterations needed. I changed out of my Earth clothes, which I had been wearing since I transmuted. They really were beginning to stink, so I would definitely want a shower before changing into the new clothes, which were a welcomed sight.

The clothes were an unspectacular combination of solids and stripes. There were long- and short-sleeved shirts. There were shorts and long pants. All of the clothes had an insignia of the Science Ministry on the bottom right corner. I put on a silver short-sleeved shirt and blue long pants.

Since I wasn't scheduled to start work at the Science Ministry for two more days, coupled with the fact I had nothing planned for that evening, I decided that I would meet some of my neighbors. Jimmy told me that 1209 was vacant at the present time. So I started with 1207 and knocked three times, but there was no answer. I moved on to the next apartment.

I knocked on apartment 1205, which also happened to be my dad's birth date, and a surprisingly familiar looking face appeared when the door opened.

I only hope that we don't lose sight of one thing—
that it was all started by a mouse.

—Walt Disney

Journal Entry 30

Famous Neighbors

Walter Elias Disney answered the door and greeted me. His hair and mustache were dark. He looked younger than I remembered him. He was probably in his mid-thirties, but I still instantly recognized the face. The man extended his right hand and said, "Hello, my name is Walter, but my friends here call me Elias."

I suddenly recalled that he was born on the same day as my father, December 5. When I was a young child, my dad did a great impersonation of Donald Duck. It's funny the things you remember, even in another world.

"Hello, Mr. Disney. It's a pleasure to meet you."

When I was younger, I would watch *The Wonderful World of Disney* on Sunday nights with my family. I had visited Walt Disney World with Erika many times as an adult. She and I always admired Walt Disney and were big fans of his accomplishments.

"Please, call me Elias."

"Okay, Elias. I just moved in a couple doors down, and thought I should meet some of my neighbors."

"Why don't you come in for a cup of coffee, and we can chat a bit. You do drink coffee, don't you? I don't care for the name *jamocha*. I still prefer to keep some names and traditions from Earth. I guess it makes me feel better."

I entered his apartment. The basic layout was the same as mine, but he'd had time—since 1966—to add his own personal touches. His apartment had a personal theme to it. There was a framed flyer for Laugh-O-Grams studios mounted on his kitchen wall.

"I just brewed a fresh pot of coffee; it is a little stronger with more of a citrus taste. I noticed you were looking at the flyer on the wall."

He poured me a cup. "Thanks. I was wondering what Laugh-O-Grams was."

"That was my first studio back in Kansas City. Our cartoons were popular, but I wasn't very good managing money so it went bankrupt. It wasn't a total loss though because it gave me the motivation to move to Hollywood with my brother Roy. Even some of our failures can be motivating factors for our future successes."

I guess believing in magic and a special mouse would make anyone an optimist by nature.

Elias pointed to a scrapbook located on the coffee table in the living room. He motioned for me to bring my cup with me, and we sat on the sofa. I open up the book and started leafing through it. There were a number of pictures and scripts from the Alice Comedies.

"We started the Disney Brothers Studios in 1923. The Alice Comedies were fairly successful for us. I met a young ink-and-paint celluloid artist at the studios named Lillian; she was very astute besides being an excellent artist. You know, I was going to originally name the mouse Mortimer, but Lillian convinced me is sounded too pompous for the character we were working on. Based on our success with Mickey, I believe she was right. She was right about a lot of things. I eventually married her, although it did take a little convincing on her end." And, with that, he choked up a bit and stopped speaking.

I told him that I understood how he felt. I started talking about Erika, my connection with her, and my desire to get back, somehow, someway.

Before we both became too depressed, I changed the subject. I noticed a picture frame sitting on the coffee table—or jamocha table as it was probably referred to here—of Elias shaking the hand of an executive-looking guy in a plaid suit.

"I see you don't recognize that man," he said. "Well, he was a little before your time. His name was Joseph Michael Schenck, and he was a friend of mine."

The name did ring a bell. "Didn't he have something to do with some of your early movies?"

"You have a keen mind for trivia," he said with a smile. "Joseph was the first president of United Artists. He believed in me enough to distribute a couple of my early Mickey Mouse movies." He thought for a moment as if he was remembering his former life on Earth. "Joe was an interesting guy. We eventually parted ways, but he became one of the most powerful and influential people in the film business. Joe fought to establish equal pay rates for animals used in filming, and more representative speaking roles for women and African Americans."

"Sounds like he had an important role on Earth. Did he transmute here by any chance?" I half-jokingly asked.

Elias laughed. "No, he was not like us. Anyway, he wasn't perfect. Joe got in a little trouble with some union bribery scheme and tax irregularities, shall we say. He eventually was sent to prison."

"Well, I guess nobody's perfect. What happened to him?"

"The old dog was friends with Harry and was presidentially pardoned from prison after only four months."

"You mean, Harry Truman?"

"I believe there was only one president named Harry, at least up until the time I left Earth. Have there been any Harrys since?"

I shook my head, "No Harrys. But we have had a Barack."

"Interesting. Anyway, after Joe was pardoned, he immediately returned to the film business. He became very friendly with someone I believe you know as your guide."

"Jean? I mean Marilyn Monroe?"

"Yes. He and Marilyn_became very friendly. Some considered her one of his "girlfriends." You see, Joe liked the ladies. Marilyn always claimed that their relationship was strictly platonic."

"I'll ask her the next time I see her."

He continued, "He was helpful in her career, getting her a very small part in Fox's *Scudda Hoo! Scudda Hay!* He even convinced Harry Cohn at Columbia to give her a contract after Fox dropped her."

Once again, I was struck by how the threads of life connected together, how the acts of one person could lead to a chain of events that connected so many people, even if they were unaware of these threads. If not for Joe Schenck, maybe Walt's and Marilyn's lives might have been different, and many other lives as well, including mine.

"Anyway, he was basically a good man even with his flaws. But he believed in me and in Marilyn."

"I'm sure a lot of people believed in you. After all, you are Walter Elias Disney, a legend back on Earth."

He gave me a look I didn't understand. "Thanks, but that was another life. Here, I'm not a legend."

"I wasn't famous back on Earth, and I'm not famous on Evion either. Here, I'm just a custodial engineer, which I'm told is a vital and necessary cog. But it is far from being a legend," I said with a wry smile.

A ceramic statue of a rabbit sitting in a bookcase caught my eye. The rabbit was black and white and looked a little bit like Mickey Mouse.

Elias said, "That's Oswald the Lucky Rabbit. He was the precursor to Mickey Mouse."

"Yes, I know. I've seen *One Man's Dream* at MGM studios."

Elias looked dumbfounded.

It occurred to me that Disney World wasn't completed until 1971, five years after Walt's death, and MGM wasn't opened until 1989. As I explained to him all about Disney World, I saw the sheer excitement and happiness in his eyes.

"Elias, can I ask you a question that I have always wondered about?"

He nodded yes.

"I know this will probably sound trivial to you, but once when I was watching *Who Wants to be a Millionaire,* the million dollar question was, "What were the last words Walt Disney wrote before he died?" The answer was supposedly Kurt Russell. Is that really true and, if it is, why?"

"What is *Who Wants to be a Millionaire*?"

"It was a very successful quiz game show that aired on a Disney-owned television station in the late 1990s." I stopped because the rest really wasn't important.

"Wow, my old company owns another theme park and a major network? I guess the company really has grown since I left. Anyway, I was always working and thinking of new ideas, even on my deathbed."

He paused and took a sip of the hot jamocha. He told me again that he preferred to call it coffee, and the more I thought about it, I guess I did too. "It took a little getting used to," he said. "But I think you will find after a while, you really don't miss Earth coffee, at least not too much."

He thought for a minute. "Anyway, what was I talking about? Oh yes, a good question—why did I write down the name Kurt Russell right before I died? As I was lying in the hospital bed, I had a dream that was so real; actually it felt more like a vision. Elvis Presley came to me and told me he would like Disney Studies to make a movie about his life. He named a few people who he thought could portray him well, and the last actor he mentioned was Kurt Russell. He had briefly met Kurt in 1963 during the filming of *It Happened at the World's Fair*. (That was the year that I was born, I'm sure that was just a coincidence, like everything else.) Kurt was only eleven years old at the time, and his part was uncredited, but he still left an impression on Elvis. That's the last memory on Earth that I had. Next thing I knew I had transmuted and found myself on Evion."

"That's weird. I do remember Disney signing Mr. Russell to a long-term deal, and he did end up playing Elvis in a Disney movie," I said.

Elias finished his coffee and placed the cup on the table. He looked at his watch and cordially said, "It has been a pleasure talking with you, but I have to get ready for work now."

"Elias, if you don't mind me asking, what job was assigned to you here on Andorra?"

"I am an emergency room physician. I did drive an ambulance after World War One, but I was told that had nothing to do with my current assignment. It was just a mere coincidence."

I used to believe in coincidences and random chance, but I found myself questioning the notion these days. "Wow that is an important job. They made me a janitor, which is not so important unless the trash piles up. Then you're in high demand," I said.

"Well, Michael, you never know. Life has a strange and sometimes magical way about it. You might find out one day that your job ends up being important. Things have a mysterious way of working out sometimes. After all, Disney was all about magic for me."

I doubted the part about things having a magical way of working out, at least for me. But I thanked him for his hospitality and turned to leave.

"The gang is getting together tomorrow night at Terra Firma, a popular Andorran night club located three blocks from here, and Abe is performing," Elias blurted out.

"The gang?" I asked hoping for clarification.

"The gang includes those people who spent time on Earth before coming to Andorra. The gang members all live in this building. I think you have met or even know some of our members already," he answered.

"You mean Jean and Opie Hopkins?"

"Yes, and Frank and Elvis," he replied.

"They all live here?"

"Actually, Frank Sinatra is directly across from you in apartment 1212. Marilyn Monroe is in 805, Elvis Presley lives in 108, Juliet Hopkins in 507 and Abe is in—"

I cut in because it finally occurred to me, "Abe? You mean Abraham Lincoln is in 212?" I interjected.

Elias nodded yes.

I finally realized, coincidently or not, our apartment numbers corresponded with the month and day we were born. I also wondered what would happen in the case of two or more people who shared the same birthday. Then what, dual apartments? I really didn't care and was sure the Andorrans had some logical solution to that issue. Besides, I obviously had bigger problems to worry about—like how to get home to Erika.

"I just have one more question, and then I'll let you go."

"You want to know how I acquired all of my memorabilia from Earth."

Maybe he really did have some magical powers or psychic abilities. Or maybe my thoughts had become very transparent.

"Yes. My apartment is nice, but it's missing that homey feel. I have none of my own stuff, just what was supplied to me by somebody—the Ministry I'm guessing."

"I know a guy who can help you with that. We can talk about it later when you're more settled," he replied.

I didn't press the question and thanked him before returning to my apartment.

I had a little time before meeting "the gang," so I decided to try to get some sleep. There were two reasons for my desire to sleep. First, I began to realize that I hadn't had a lot of sleep since transmuting, and I was damn tired. Second, I remembered Marilyn talking about how sometimes we could communicate with people on Earth through our dreams. So I figured, what the hell, it was worth a try. It might have been a long shot, but if President George W. Bush could win the presidential election twice, then maybe anything was possible.

I was lying in bed, as I had not yet become used to the sensation of hovering above the mattress, trying to clear my mind and relax. Random thoughts raced through my mind, and I couldn't get the idea out of my head that Kelly Clarkson had been wrong on two accounts. First, "Sleeping in the bed alone," didn't make it warmer. It made it roomier, but certainly not toastier. Second, "What doesn't kill you," doesn't necessarily make you stronger. It makes you angrier, more pissed off, sadder, more depressed, and sometimes more desperate.

Eventually my mind cleared, and I began to drift off. I was concentrating on Erika and talking with her as I started to lose consciousness. Although the doctors had assured me that dreaming was very unlikely during the darkling cap experience, I was sure that I had dreamed about Erika and almost communicated with her. It had seemed so real, and it had felt as if she was aware of my presence. Sure, I had been watching my own funeral, but at least I had felt connected back to Earth. I wasn't sure if it would work with normal sleeping and dreaming without the darkling cap, but thought it was worth a try.

After some time passed, a foggy haze appeared and a misty rain fell from an overcast sky. I saw Erika and my family standing around the casket that had been buried a year ago. A fresh gravestone was being added to the gravesite. I couldn't see the name, but I sensed that it was me in the coffin. It must be the one-year anniversary of my passing. I mentioned earlier about not being religious, and although the ceremony had little meaning for me, it did provide another opportunity for family and friends to gather and remember their loved one—me.

It also got me thinking. If these were really dreams that connected me to Earth, then it appeared that time moved at a different pace in the two worlds. What was a day or two for me here seemed to be a year on Earth. I wondered if this time flow was sequential or random. Less importantly, I wondered why it was always raining on my dead self in my cemetery dreams.

The scene shifted from the cemetery to Erika, dressed in brown-and-white pajamas. She was sleeping in her own bed and appeared to be tossing and turning. Her sleep seemed shallow and troubled.

I walked over to her bed and tried to speak, but no words came out—or she couldn't hear the words. I was unable to determine which. I tried a different approach. My hand gently passed through her body as I tried to touch her. Although I was unable to communicate with her, I got the sense that Erika was somewhat aware of my presence. She awakened from the light sleep and placed her hand on the exact spot on her shoulder that I had touched. A strange expression appeared across her slumber-land face. For a brief moment, I saw a look of hope and recognition in her eyes, but the moment dissolved. As I felt the dream begin to fade, I noticed some coins on her night table next to the bed. Somehow, I was able to knock to the floor a dime and a penny that had each been minted in 1963. I was pretty sure she would get the connection. She might think it was her sister until she looked at the years and the fact the value of the coins added up to eleven and each coin was minted in the year 1963. Suddenly, I awakened in a pool of sweat, frustrated but hopeful after my latest attempt to communicate with her.

I hadn't been able to directly communicate with Erika, but it had been only my second attempt. Maybe with practice, I would be able to get through to her on some substantial level. Although only briefly, she did appear to be aware of my presence. I had to remain confident and optimistic. It was my only hope of remaining sane.

I've discovered a way to stay friends forever
There's really nothing to it.
I simply tell you what to do
And you do it!

—Shel Silverstein

Journal Entry 31

The Gangs All Here

Elias had informed me, as I left his apartment, in my living room was a digital GPS phone book I could use to locate the nightclub. The phone book produced a 3-D holographic image of a large lion, reminiscent of the Nittany Lion, the mascot of Pennsylvania State University. This lion instructed me to make a right out of the building, walk two blocks, turn left, and walk straight into Terra Firma.

Terra Firma was located at the bottom of a three-story building. There were two bouncers checking off the names of people entering the bar as if it was an exclusive Hollywood nightclub that top celebrities would patronize. I wasn't sure if I was on the "A list," but one of the bouncers swiped my ID card and ushered me inside. Apparently, I had some influential friends.

Terra Firma was decorated like an Earth world history book. The entrance was adorned with pictures of Egyptian pyramids and sphinxes. A bevy of ankhs was affixed to the entrance of the club. Also at the entry was a large golden statue of Anubis, which gave me the creeps because, as I remembered from my World History 101 class, Anubis was the God of the Dead in ancient Egypt. It had the head of a jackal. Real nice. Anubis did make for a great first impression if you were into the gothic look. Although I did like the whole Twilight and *True Blood* concepts, goth just wasn't my thing.

The first portion of the interior of the club was bedizened with ancient Roman and Greek heirlooms. A life-size model of Aphrodite (the God of love, beauty, pleasure and procreation) and Pan (the God of nature, the wild, and sexuality) guarded the entrance into the interior; somehow this strange pair seemed to fit together.

There was a porcelain sculpture of an ancient Greek known as Menander. The inscription below this figure read "Time is the healer of all necessary wounds." Again, the cynic or realist in me—I could never tell which was which—began to ponder those words. Although I understood their wisdom, I doubted their truth. I started to wonder what kind of a club this was, but as they say, "when in Rome …"

The interior was softly lit with an orange-yellow hue provided by Greek Byzantine oil lamps. Greco-Roman bronze medical instruments were strewn across the walls. I noticed Greek and Roman vases placed on shelving units mounted throughout a portion of the walls. Large oil paintings depicting Roman and Greek life were artfully displayed along the remaining portions of the walls.

Speakers attached to the corners of the room were playing loud music. For some odd reason, I would have expected music matching a similar ancient theme played by instruments such as violins, mandolins, or even a giant harp. Instead, I heard modern rock and punk music from Earth. The Care Bears on Fire was playing an old Tears for Fears song. I thought I heard Letters to Cleo singing in the background as well. But that could have been my imagination again.

I continued into the inner recesses of the nightclub and saw people I recognized sitting at two tables. Enoch, Brace, Opie, Jean, and Turbo sat at one table. Frank, Elvis, and Elias sat at the second table, where there was also an empty seat, which had apparently been reserved for me. I sat down and said hello to everyone.

Elias indicated the stage in the mid-section of the nightclub and told me that Abraham would be performing his standup comedy act in a few minutes. The darkling cap had assigned Abe the role of entertainer on Andorra. He had performed in a number of Andorran plays, which is kind of ironic when you think about it, and now he was trying his hand at comedy, a fact that was also dripping with irony.

It turned out that Andorra had a rich cultural heritage. There were art museums, floral gardens, and animal zoos. Advanced 3-D holographic television programs were available. There were sporting events, although the definition of sports was very different than it was back home.

This section of the club was decorated in a theme that reflected the American Revolutionary War period and the Civil War period. There were Colonial American Revolutionary War buttons strung along the bottom of the stage. I noticed a large framed picture of a segmented snake with the initials S.C., N.C., V., M., P., N.E., N.J., and N.Y. above the segment parts and the words *Join or Die* printed at the bottom.

A scene from an epic Civil War battle was etched into each tabletop. There were Union and Confederate cannons on either side of the stage. Pictures depicting Civil wartime structures hung from the walls. A painting of the Confederate Andersonville Prison showing the appalling overcrowded conditions hung solemnly in the center.

I sat down between Frank and Elvis. "What's with the modern music from Earth mixed with the Greek and Roman and American historical décor?" I asked.

Frank turned to me and said, "That's just Roscoe's special satellite dish tapping into one of Earth's radio stations. I don't get the music. Sounds like a lot of loud yelling, but I think Roscoe thinks it funny. You know, shock value and all."

I thought it best not to mention to Frank that I liked some of the modern, loud music. I also thought maybe there was a way to directly communicate between the worlds. Maybe I could use that technology to my advantage at some point to get a message to Erika, besides the whole dream concept.

Elvis added, "This is Abe's maiden voyage into the world of standup comedy, so the gang decided to show up and lend him our support."

"That's very nice of the gang," I said. "I guess us former earthlings have to stick together."

Elvis looked to be around my age, maybe slightly older, in his early twenties. He was wearing black pants with a black-and-white striped shirt. This reminded me of "Jail House Rock," a song he sang early in his career.

Elias explained that Elvis liked to dress in elaborate outfits that corresponded to his concerts or movie roles back home. He said, "It helps him to keep a piece of Earth with him always. Besides, Elvis is always willing to entertain and doesn't shy away from attention." I had to admit he had a point. I found him entertaining.

Ol' Blue Eyes, as Frank Sinatra had previously been known, was always the consummate performer. He was wearing a black tux with a bow tie. Next to him at the table sat an elegant black top hat. He looked relatively young, probably in his mid-forties.

Elvis continued, "I still remember my first live performance in Tennessee at the Bon Air Club with Winfield and Bill, but that was a long time ago." His voice began to trail off.

Frank chimed in, "Press does tend to get a little too sentimental at times. I think that it has something to do with the fact that he never really got past his mother's death."

I understood. I felt the same way about my own father.

"Don't get me wrong, Press is a good guy," Frank said. "It's just that sometimes he doesn't have a tough enough skin like us people from Jersey, you know?"

I remembered many numerous Friday nights in the family Cadillac with my mother and father, who loved Sinatra's music, on the way to dinner. One station would always play Frank Sinatra music; they called the show *Friday with Frank*. I suppose it was my saturation with this musical icon's music that sparked an interest for me in his life. His music, along with the fact that while Frank was in town performing at the now defunct Latin Casino club, my father once worked on Frank's teeth during a dental emergency.

Frank grew up in Hoboken, New Jersey, during the Great Depression. Although generally beloved by Hoboken natives, he returned only twice—once to celebrate its first Italian elected mayor in 1948, and once in 1984 with President Ronald Reagan. As successful as he was, Frank never graduated high school. He was expelled for rowdy behavior and also had a run-in with the law. His mother, Dolly, was arrested several times for running an illegal abortion clinic during the Depression years.

Strangely enough, Sinatra seemed to be at peace in this world, although he had struggled with mood swings and bouts of depression on Earth. One of his daughters, Tina, once wrote, "I believe that a Zoloft a day might have kept his demons away."

Actually, Zoloft was beginning to sound like a good idea for me as well.

Frank had garnered a sizable amount of attention from the FBI due to his alleged personal and professional links with organized crime and his alleged links to Carlo Gambino and Lucky Luciano. Although J. Edgar Hoover amassed over twenty-four hundred pages on Frank, the entertainer's alleged mob ties were never confirmed. What was confirmed were every foible and peccadillo in his life, including his friendships with John F. Kennedy and Marilyn Monroe.

Abe was getting ready to begin his comedy routine when I noticed that he looked exactly as he did in all the pictures I had seen of him taken just before his death. It appeared that he was around forty-four years of age and had not aged since his assassination. I didn't understand how he could have transmuted almost 150 years ago and look the same. Everyone else in the gang had died much more recently than Abraham and Opie.

I turned to Elias. "How could Abraham still look the same? He doesn't seem to have aged at all!"

"It is part of the magic," Elias responded.

I guess magic was what Elias's life had always been about. Maybe it made sense to him, but I still didn't understand. Everyone else looked different from the way they looked when they left Earth.

Elias saw the confusion on my face, and he continued. "When someone transmutes from Earth to Evion, time doesn't always phase in sequence. Sometimes time for the two universes is in sync during the transmutation, and other times it's not."

"So it's possible to leave Earth in one century and show up in this universe centuries later?" I asked.

"Not exactly, but something like that," Elias responded.

I was still a little confused as to how this would work. However, I decided to try a different question. "Can you die here on Andorra?" I asked.

Elias tried to clarify. "It's a little harder for some people to die here because some can afford the protection of magical spells, but you surely can die here."

"And if you die here, then what?"

"Who knows? I would presume the same thing that happens back in the other universe. When people die here or back there, do they go to heaven or hell or somewhere comparable? Is there just nothingness after death?" Elias replied.

"But if you do die here, can't the so-called magic reverse the termination?"

"Very rarely. There have been some legends about dark magi, but this is neither the time nor place to talk about that," he sternly answered.

I decided to drop it for now, and besides, Abe was ready to begin his routine.

Initially, Abe appeared very stiff, but he began to loosen up a little bit as the performance went along. Although he had been considered an excellent orator during his heyday, facetious routines did not come naturally to him. Lincoln had always been very serious. He probably bore the greatest weight that any United States president had to endure during his tenure in office.

As I watched him and listened to his jokes, I thought how eerily strange it was to see Mr. Lincoln in this unfamiliar capacity. It would have been like watching a snow blizzard during a Fourth of July parade. Again I was reminded that this universe had a strange sense of humor. It would have been like multiple Philadelphia sports teams winning championships in the same season, or even a single team winning a single championship. In my head I could hear Doctor Winston's words: "The darkling cap always knows best."

I was listening to Abe making a joke about a guy walking into a bar located across from a log cabin when Elvis slipped me a note under the table: "Please meet me at my apartment later tonight after the show. It's very important. Don't tell anyone. Press."

When things go wrong don't go with them.

—Elvis Presley

Journal Entry 32

Et Tu, **Press?**

After the comedy show was over, Terra Firma became like a 1970s disco. It was strange watching the spinning lights and lasers bounce off the Revolutionary and Civil war artifacts. Roscoe, the club owner, had an affinity for anything "planet Earth like," as he put it. Apparently his taste in Earth music extended beyond modern and punk rock.

Roscoe (it seemed no one knew his last name) was from the neighboring planet Rencin and had moved to Andorra on Evion as a teenager. Frank told me that, after turning eighteen, he left his family and entered The Trades (but he didn't tell me what that was). After a few years there, he scored big and left the business. He bought this club, which was originally known as something else but nobody knew the previous name. A year later, renovated and refurbished, the club opened under the name Terra Firma.

Roscoe was the height of Wilt Chamberlin and had three arms, two on the right side. His third eye was located in the center of his forehead, slightly above the other two. He had one hearing organ on the left side of his skull. During Halloween, he didn't need a costume. I wondered if they even celebrated that holiday here.

It was during the five years he spent at The Trades, I learned, that he acquired his interest in earthly objects. Nobody in the gang would talk much about The Trades except to say it was a black-market, underground location where there existed a system of selling and bartering goods and humanoid services. I got the feeling it was taboo to talk about the underworld market in public.

Frank and Elvis had gone to the bar, so Jean came over and sat next to me. I took the opportunity to ask her about them. "So, old wise one who is my spiritual guide, can you tell me a little more about Frank and Elvis?"

Jean laughed. "You have a funny way of talking. Is there something in particular you are interested in?" She leaned in and whispered into my ear. "Or just general information, like their favorite foods or colors? As far as being your spiritual guide, that works much better on Earth than it does here."

"Right. I guess I wasn't very specific. I was wondering what their function is on this planet."

She smiled. "Always so curious. I guess that's what makes you Mister Science Guy."

"No, on Earth I was Mister Science Guy. Here I'm Mister Clean-Up Guy."

With that velvet, cotton candy–like tone she said, "Frank is a Bible salesman."

"Seriously? Does he sell the New Testament, Old Testament, King James or … let me guess—he has some copies of the Guttenberg!"

She held back her laughter. "You really have no idea what you are talking about, do you?"

"No, not usually. Is it that obvious?"

She nodded yes.

"Sorry, I guess it comes from years of teaching. I have found that even if you don't know what you're talking about, if you speak as if you do, most teenagers and, surprisingly enough, most adults will believe you. After all, George W. Bush did get elected twice."

"Who?"

"You know, the son of the father who was … oh, never mind. It's not important."

She gave me a quick wink. "You see here on Evion, "Bible salesman" is a nickname. Frankie doesn't sell actual Bibles."

It seemed as if she was going to elaborate, but she stopped for some reason. I didn't pursue the question any further.

Those of us sitting at these two tables shared a couple of drinks and told a few stories of life back on Earth. Instead of beer, the local choice for refreshment was known as *amblee*. It was stronger than beer and had a licorice flavor. As I drank my second glass, I became aware of its strangely intoxicating properties. It was at this point that the Donna Summers' song "Heaven Knows," which had always been one of my favorite late 1970s songs, started playing. Jean looked in my direction and smiled. "Michael, would you like to dance? It might help you burn off some of the amblee."

I must have looked a little tipsier than I thought. It was a no brainier. The chance to dance with a young Marilyn Monroe on Earth or Evion was a cool thing. The music was blaring, and the disco ball laser lights were sweeping the room. My head was spinning as Marilyn and I were boogieing. I missed Erika. *Be careful what you wish for …*

The amblee crept through my veins. Thoughts of Erika invaded every neuronal synapse in my brain. I felt like George Webber: "You can't go back home to your family, back home to your childhood … back home to a young man's dreams of glory and of fame … back home to places in the country, back home to the old forms and systems of things which once seemed everlasting but which are changing all the time – back home to the escapes of Time and Memory." I was afraid that maybe Thomas Wolfe was right after all.

In so many ways, I wanted to go back home. Most likely I could not go home anytime soon, and maybe I never could. I wasn't sure of anything except that I felt drained and sick. I looked directly into Marilyn's eyes and said, "I'm sorry, but I have to go."

I wanted to say "go home," but I wasn't sure where that was anymore.

"I understand. It's never easy at first, but it does get better," she said and kissed me on the cheek.

"By the way, was Joseph Schenck ever your boyfriend?" I asked.

"Who?"

"Nothing. Good night, Marilyn."

I thought of the statue of Menander who basically said, "Time heals all wounds." These words reverberated in my head incessantly. Maybe he was wrong; maybe they were all wrong. It was possible that some cuts ran too far and deep to be cured, even with time. I realized how much Erika meant to me. Maybe it wasn't scientific, but Erika was part of my DNA.

Maybe Tennyson was wrong when he penned, "Tis better to have loved and lost than never to have loved at all." In some cases, maybe it was better to have never loved at all.

I said good-bye to everybody and went back to my room at Babylon Gardens—1211. I felt the need to shower; maybe it was an act of cleansing my body and soul. The showers were sonic with a combination of compressed air and a minute amount of water. Although precious metals and gems were common on Evion, other commodities were scarce and valuable. Water was one of them.

Be careful what you wish for … I got out of the shower and dressed for bed. I poured a cup of jamocha—damn it, I mean coffee. I sat down and enjoyed feeling sorry for myself. I was ready to go to bed when I remembered the note from Elvis and ran over to his apartment—in my pajamas!

I knocked on apartment 108. Press answered the door and motioned for me to come in.

"I am sorry it's late," I said. "I almost forgot about your note."

"No worries, as we used to say back in Tupelo," he assured me.

"Don't you miss it?" I asked.

"Of course I do, but I miss Gladys the most," he sadly responded, referring to his mom.

I was depressed enough for the both of us, so I decided to change the subject. "Why did you want to see me?"

"You didn't mention it to anyone else, did you?" he questioned me.

"No, I was a Boy Scout. I can keep a secret."

"Good. Michael, I'm sure that you guessed that it wasn't random chance that you were selected to work in the Ministry of Sciences."

"I knew it! I'm supposed to be a famous actor or rock star on this planet, right?"

Elvis laughed. "Seriously, there was a reason the darkling cap selected you to be a janitor. I'm afraid that the movie star and rock star gig will have to wait. Trust me, I know.

It's not all it's cracked up to be. It doesn't guarantee happiness like you think it would.

If anyone would know that fame and stardom didn't guarantee happiness, it was the king of rock and roll, "I'm listening," I quickly responded.

"We were hoping that you could help us. I belong to an elite group known as ASAP—Andorran Secret Alliance Police."

"Wow, that sounds really cool, definitely better than cleaning toilets and mopping floors. But what does any of this have to do with me? You want me to come and work for ASAP cleaning your building instead of the Science Ministry?"

Elvis smiled. I was glad that he had a sense of humor even in the midst of his depression and sadness, which, Frank had told me, he covered up very well with his drinking and chasing the ladies.

"ASAP is Andorra's first line of defense. We collect information that reveals the plans, intentions, and capabilities of our adversaries and provides the basis for decision and action. The agency produces timely analysis that provides insight, warning, and opportunity to the government of Andorra charged with protecting and advancing her interests. Sometimes that means conducting covert operations at the direction of the council to preempt threats or achieve Andorran policy objectives."

"That's great. It sounds just like the canned mission statement of the CIA, but I still don't see what I have to do with this."

"Actually, our function is very similar to the CIA's. Anyway, we have reasons to believe that there are illegal activities going on within the Ministry of Science. We are specifically interested in the activities happening on the fourth and fifth floors. No one from ASAP has ever been able to access those floors because this Ministry is out of our jurisdiction. We need someone on the inside to help us," Press explained.

"You mean a mole or a spy, to be more precise."

"I suppose you could call it that. To be honest, it would be a dangerous job. ASAP, having no official authority over the Ministry of Sciences, would have to deny any knowledge of any covert activity. If this person—let's just say you hypothetically—were to be caught spying, you could just vanish with no questions asked."

"And by setting me up as a janitor, you figured that I might be able to access what you are looking for."

Press nodded. "As a janitor in the building, you might be able to get to places that we can't legally."

"Can you promise me a movie star career or at least a place in a rock band if I do this?"

Press looked disappointed. "Sadly, I can't promise anything. But understand that this could be very dangerous for you."

"That's too bad. I mean about becoming famous. What reason do you have for your suspicions?"

"Obviously I can't provide specific details, but we have operatives inside The Trades providing us intel."

I remembered watching an interview with a retired CIA spy on television. He said that, to be a good spy, a person needed curiosity about the world, which I had. He also said the best spies were risk takers and not thrills seekers, and I was neither. Hell, I didn't even like roller coasters except for Aerosmith's "Rockin' Rollercoaster," which I loved for some unexplainable reason, or Big Thunder Mountain Railroad at Walt Disney World. Somehow I didn't think that going on these rides came under risk-taking or thrill-seeking categories.

"I'll have to think about it," I said. "But at this point I seriously doubt I would be interested. However, let's just say, hypothetically, that I was interested. What would I be looking for?"

"Illegal and immoral medical experiments," Elvis hesitantly responded.

Science has made us gods even before
we are worthy of being men.

—Jean Rostand

Journal Entry 33

In the Name of Science

Meanwhile, back in his office on Earth, Dr. Walter Reed was lightly tapping his golden pen on his desk. The pan was engraved with his name and Latin words that loosely translated into the saying "Fortune is fickle and soon asks back what he has given." The doctor wasn't much of a gambler or a risk taker, but he did like to play the odds, especially when they were in his favor. He believed that this lessened the fickleness of fortune.

There was little doubt in his mind that he had made the right decision helping Michael Cardazia and Erika Nirvona escape the hospital. Explaining the fire alarm mishap to his superiors would be easier than having the CIA and government officials investigating his hospital if Michael and Erika had stayed. He knew they already had begun to be suspicious.

No doubt, he had definitely made the right call. Besides, Michael had already died and transmuted back to Evion just like Dr. Shelly had told him he would. A magic book had prophesied this. Michael had fulfilled his reason for being on Earth. It appeared he had simply died of instant cardiac death. Dr. Reed could provide medical evidence of his condition based on the prior testing at the hospital if anyone ever questioned him. Michael was out of the picture and presented no threats.

However, there still remained one immediate loose end, and Dr. Reed didn't like loose ends. Erika Nirvona knew too much already. The fact that she worked for the CIA made matters worse. Who knew what she had already told her superiors? It was all about damage control now, minimizing the effects and playing the odds. Whatever had been done or said was in the rearview mirror.

Besides, this loose end would be taken care of very shortly. Sure, it would be harder to explain a CIA operative's disappearance than the disappearance of the usual test subjects he acquired for his research and Dr. Shelly's, but it had to be done. He had a responsibility to science to improve the human condition. He had his orders, and following them also paid very well, as Dr. Shelly was most generous. It really wasn't about the money, although that didn't hurt.

He acquired most of his own test subjects. (He didn't like to call them people because it made it harder to do his job. He did have a conscience, after all.) These subjects came from the pool of humans that few would miss. They were undesirables, and they comprised almost one hundred percent of his test subjects—the homeless, vagabonds, prostitutes, and drug addicts. When he thought about it, he was really doing society a favor, removing the social burden created by these derelicts and vagrants.

No, he didn't need thanks from these hedonistic cities and suburbs that he helped to clean up; the promise from Dr. Shelly was more than enough. He didn't need the recognition from the taxpayers and politicians, for whom he was saving thousands, possibly tens of thousands of dollars, by removing this refuse from the streets. This world would be a better place in part for his advancements in science.

Wordsworth once wrote, "Our birth is but a sleep and a forgetting, the soul that rises with us, our life star, Hath elsewhere had its setting, and cometh from afar." But Wordsworth was a poet and a romantic, and therefore a fool. It wasn't about man's soul or where it came from; it was about where the race as a whole was going and how to improve it by making a better brand.

Charles Darwin had been a little more to the point. His methods were crude by today's standards, but he'd had the right idea. It was all about improving the product, bettering the species. Where or how the human soul came into the process be wasn't important, but the improvement, the evolution, of humankind was.

The problem with Darwin and his concept of evolution was that he'd thought that it was up to Mother Nature to take care of it. Evolution, left to its own devices, would improve humankind, but the process would take thousands or millions of years. What they were doing here was just simply moving it along a little faster. What could take eons to develop "naturally" could be reduced to decades, maybe even years, with their research and a little luck.

What they were doing on Earth and on Evion was really no different than what humankind had been doing for decades on its own. History was full of examples of men taking what they wanted in the name of religion, power, and the desire to improve their own lots in life. At least this research was for the betterment of humankind in general. People in the future would see this and truly appreciate their work. Maybe he would even be written up in future history books for his work in genetics. A Nobel Prize in medicine was certainly not out of the question.

For decades, men had no problem conducting these experiments on other species for the improvement of people. Drug and cosmetic companies had experimented on animals to improve what they considered the condition of humankind—make a prettier shade of lipstick or a more fragrant perfume. Certainly his work was more important. Humankind deserved to improve; it was in the DNA. After all, wasn't it the destiny of humankind to become as evolved as possible?

The plan was simple and plausible. Ms. Nirvona would die in a horrible automobile crash. Approximately 150 people die every day in the United States as the result of automobile accidents. These things do happen. It would be a little unfortunate to lose someone who worked for the CIA, but completely explainable by examining the statistics.

One of his waif human test subjects would be placed in the automobile, just to show the remnants of a human body in the wreckage. Of course, the body would be burned beyond recognition or identification, thanks to some extra explosives carefully placed in the auto. Samples of Erika's DNA would be swabbed throughout the vehicle and crash site, just for good measure. No one would suspect what had really happened to her.

Luckily, the exact number of homeless people in the United States wasn't known. But it was estimated that there were approximately one million people without homes, according to the Assessment Report to Congress (AHAR) that was issued annually by the Department of Housing and Urban Development (HUD). No one would notice if a few of these castaways disappeared each week, any more than they would notice a missing lab rat or mouse in one of the many laboratories throughout the country.

His underlings usually had a relatively easy time luring in these ragamuffins. Being homeless had a tendency to make people desperate and so desolate that they would be willing to believe almost any story, just to get off the streets. Acquiring test subjects was easy; in fact, almost too easy. But right now, they were not his main concern. Erika Nirvona was his biggest loose end. He would have to deal with Captain Rita Denton and James Dubay—aka Jimbo—at a later date.

Ms. Nirvona would be at his office soon. He had telephoned her two days after Michael died. He had expressed the proper condolences and social nuances associated with losing a loved one. Dr. Reed told Erika that he had some additional details about Michael's death, which he thought she would want to know. This information was classified, and he probably shouldn't relate this intel to her but felt badly about what had transpired. After all, it was because of his generosity and ingenuity that they had escaped the hospital, so he had built up her trust. She had no reason to suspect otherwise, so if she was willing to meet with him, he would share what he knew with her.

Erika would be there in about ten minutes. He would fabricate some story about how Michael's death was not from natural causes, but it had been planned. At some point, when she was engrossed in what he was saying, he would inject her with a sedative. She would be carted off to the processing center, and his job would be done. Erika would be placed among the anonymous souls scheduled for deportation to the other universe and used by Dr. Shelly in his experiments. With Erika out of the picture, he would have to worry about only Agent Dubay and Captain Denton.

We're supposed to be perfect our first day on the job and then show constant improvement.

—Ed Vargo

Journal Entry 34

First Day on the Job

I pondered what Press had told me. Was it the truth? How could I be sure? Things were not always what they seemed to be. I was a living example. Look where I was now compared to where I had been a couple of days ago.

The trouble with reality is that it's hard to be a hero. In dreams it's easy because you can't die in your own dreams, or so they say. Problem was, this wasn't a dream; it was reality. I wasn't a coward, but I wasn't really a hero either. I had helped to save some people back on Earth during the Fourth of July planned attack on the president and vice president, but that was mostly in an effort to protect Erika. I wasn't trying to be a hero, I was just lucky or in the right place at the right time.

That brought up another issue. I doubted I could ever get back to Erika, or see her again without some major help. Maybe there was some magical spell or someone in The Trades who could help. Unlikely but maybe. What I was positive of—or at least relatively sure of—was this: If I did get killed here, as I had in my previous universe, there would be little chance of getting back to her. Transmuting back to Earth by dying here seemed highly improbable. Jimmy had mentioned that transmuting was a one-way ticket.

I wasn't afraid to die. With all my phobias, ironically I never developed a death phobia. But what death meant to my chances of getting back to Erika was a fear, and that was the major factor most likely steering me away from agreeing to help the ASAP. However, I resolved to think about it for a day or two before giving Press my final answer.

The calendar was a little different here. One rotation of Evion on its axis was still called a day, but the rotation period was faster, taking only twenty hours. A week was still considered to be seven days, but the names of the days were named after the Earth's ancient Latin language.

Luna (which is called Monday on Earth) was my first day at the Science Ministry as a janitor. I would wait until Mercurius (Wednesday) night to give Elvis my ultimate decision. I thought I owed him that much.

There was an underground subway system I could take to the Science Ministry. This system was known as the Chute Tube or CT. The subway trains were very efficient and fast. Very powerful magnets caused the train to levitate slightly above the tracks. These trains were similar to, but more advanced than, the Maglev trains in Japan, which could travel over six hundred kilometers per hour and were very energy efficient.

Fortunately, there were chickens—or at least similar birds—on Evion that laid eggs, so I was able to make my usual egg white omelet for breakfast before work. The egg protein content was a little higher than it was in chicken eggs, but the taste was less palatable. I sipped my last bit of coffee, finished the last of the omelet, and headed for the CT system.

I elected to walk down the stairs leading to the CT, bypassing the elevator and escalator. For some reason this just made me feel more human. I swiped my monetary card and entered the train. There were only a few empty seats. Music was playing in the background. I could have sworn … no it definitely sounded like the Partridge Family's song "Echo Valley 26809." I looked around the train and saw various forms of humanoid creatures sitting on the train reminiscent of the dream I'd had back on Earth. Hell, maybe I was clairvoyant after all.

My job was half way across the city, but at the speed this subway traveled, it took a only minute or two. I swiped my ID, walked through the decontamination mist, and was in the main lobby of the Science Ministry.

I was immediately greeted by Walton. "Hello, Michael. Welcome to your first day at the Ministry of Science. I will take you to your post and get you started."

"Walton, right?" I knew his name, so I wasn't sure why I said that. Maybe I was testing his reaction, or maybe I was still sulking about this job. I decided he deserved better.

He nodded yes. I followed him to the transport tube, which I really didn't like. It gave me an uneasy feeling. We stepped inside and were sucked up to the third floor. There were twenty individual labs on this floor. About half the labs focused on work involving environmental and agricultural issues, such as genetic hybrid experiments with plants and crops. These scientists were trying to develop faster-growing, more-disease-resistant crops. It vaguely reminded of the boat ride in the Living with the Land tour in Epcot at Walt Disney World, except this wasn't the "happiest place on Earth" or even on Evion for that matter, according to Press.

The remaining labs were dedicated to various projects assigned by the mayor and prolocutors of Andorra. For example, Mayor Tremball had scientists in lab room 311 working on the problem of refining invisibility. Through the use of magic and science, Andorran scientists had developed rudimentary clothing and devices that allowed partial invisibility. The problem was that these devices were inefficient, required large amounts of energy, and they worked slightly less than half the time. I remembered that my invisibility device worked only on Earth.

Bethany Rice was the prolocutor of my district. In room 315, she had the scientists working on developing more efficient and faster methods of transportation. It was even rumored that the scientists were exploring the possibility of developing transporters that could beam living organisms from one location to another in a matter of seconds. Of course, this reminded me of *Star Trek*. The idea of being able to disassemble billions of atoms and exactly reassemble them—correctly—in another location within seconds seemed farfetched to me. But who was I to question this? Look where I am now. Almost anything seemed possible at this point.

Walton took me through the lab rooms and explained my cleaning chores for each lab. A few of the scientists greeted me, but for the most part, they seemed like a very serious and focused bunch as they ignored Walton and me.

The building was open twenty-four/seven, or rather twenty/seven. The labs operated on a staggered schedule, so it was best to clean and restock during a period when a lab was vacant. Walton showed me what my duties were. He showed where to dispose of the trash, where to obtain additional cleaning supplies, and so forth. My starting schedule was relatively easy. I was scheduled to work Luna to Frigg (Friday). My shift was six and one half hours long. All in all, it was a pretty simple job.

I finished my first day on the job, and it went relatively smoothly. There were no problems or incidents. That's not to say that it was fun or interesting in any way. To be honest, after I'd cleaned the first couple of lab room toilets and emptied the trash, any small bit of excitement wore off.

However, I tried to be positive, which was not one of my best qualities, and think of the work as a means to an end, a way to earn some money and pay the bills. Besides, I didn't plan to work or stay here forever. I decided that, no matter what, I was going to find some way back to Earth to Erika, regardless of the risks or costs. Luckily, tenacity was one of my strengths.

People who say they sleep like a
baby usually don't have one.

—Leo J. Burke

Journal Entry 35

Baby Makes Three

She hardly noticed at first. Erika wasn't much of a breakfast person anyway, sometimes a banana, occasionally a cookie, and sometimes nothing. The first couple of times she became nauseous in the morning, Erika attributed it to an empty stomach or some type of influenza. However, the nausea persisted along with other symptoms: fatigue, headache, and back pain.

When her menstrual cycle altered, she became concerned. The thought that crept into her mind seemed highly unlikely. She had been taking birth control pills as a precaution. The chances that she had become pregnant were, in her mind, almost nonexistent. Still, Erika couldn't ignore the symptoms. She bought a home pregnancy test, but the results were inconclusive. *Typical*, she thought. *Things never seem to be easy.*

Just to be on the safe side, she made an appointment with her gynecologist. She had occasionally talked with Michael about having a child with him. Erika had mostly raised two boys on her own and she loved children, but they had both decided that it was a little too impractical for them to start their own family at this juncture of their lives. Erika felt sad because she knew that, on some level, Michael always wanted to be a father, and she thought he would have made a good one. It was just that they had met a little too late in life for that.

As she sat in the waiting room, she thought about Michael—how suddenly he had died, how she missed him. Even death had not severed the strong connection she felt to him. She had an unexplainable, haunting feeling that Michael wasn't really dead, though she had watched him die in her arms. She had sensed Michael's presence at the funeral. And there was that strange dream she'd had several nights ago, during which she felt him touch her shoulder. Later, she'd found eleven cents on the floor—a dime and a penny, both from 1963.

She thought about the irony that she might be carrying his child, a child that Michael would never get to meet or watch grow up. All of these thoughts intermixed with anguish and sadness. In the midst of these overwhelming thoughts, she heard a voice. "Ms. Nirvona, please follow me." The nurse conducted her to an examination room. Erika thought the nurse must have been new because she had never seen her. The RN took her weight and blood pressure, jotted down a few notes, and told her the doctor would be in to see her very shortly.

After about three minutes, there was a knock on the door, and Dr. Patty Krauss entered. Dr. Krauss and Erika had been friends for over thirty years. They had met as teenagers while attending a summer modeling class sponsored by their local high school. Erika and Patty had remained friends ever since.

Dr. Krauss gave her a big hug. "Erika, I'm very sorry for your loss. I was hoping to stop by this week and see you, but now that you're here … Why are you here anyway?"

"I've been feeling a little bit off physically, and I was wondering if there was any chance I could be … you know?"

"I see. You think you might be pregnant. Have you been taking your birth-control pills regularly? And did you try a home pregnancy test?"

"Yes on the meds and yes on the test, but the results were indeterminate."

Dr. Krauss looked at Erika's chart. "Your blood pressure is a little high, and you have gained a few pounds since your last visit. Maybe we should take a quick look. You know the drill. Hop up onto the examination table."

"How will you know for sure?"

"We can take a quick blood sample and process it here in the office. It will take only about twenty minutes to get the results."

Dr. Krauss performed a quick internal exam. "Everything looks normal, so there's nothing to be concerned about physically."

"How does this blood test work?"

"If you really want to know, I can explain it relatively quickly. When a woman becomes pregnant, a hormone known as human chorionic gonadotropin (hCG) is produced by the placenta about two days after implantation. This hormone can be measured in the bloodstream about ten to fourteen days after fertilization."

"Can the test tell you how old the embryo is?"

"There are two blood tests. A qualitative test just gives a positive or negative reading. It is ninety-seven percent accurate and more reliable than a urine home pregnancy test. A quantitative test takes longer, but can give you a rough estimate of the age of the fetus and provide limited information on the pregnancy. If it's proceeding normally, for example."

"What do you suggest, Patty?"

"Why don't we run both blood tests? It's unlikely that you're pregnant, but let's be sure. That way I can give you a definitive answer and, if you are, how far along you are. I can always call you later with the more detailed information from the quantitative test, if you are pregnant."

"Okay. That sounds reasonable."

Patty drew out a needle and syringe and took two blood samples. "Why don't we make plans to get together for dinner next week, and we can catch up on everything?" Patty offered.

"That sounds great. After everything that has happened, I'm thinking about leaving the agency, and I wanted to get your thoughts. So it would be nice to sit and talk with a trusted friend. It has been such a nightmarish whirlwind since the death and funeral."

"I can imagine how hard Michael's death has been for you, so we should definitely discuss how you are feeling and where you'll go from here. Sorry to cut you short but I have a Cesarean delivery at the hospital in an hour."

"Good luck! I'll call tomorrow for the results of the test," Erika promised as she left the office.

Growing up is losing some illusions,
in order to acquire others.

—Virginia Woolf

Journal Entry 36

Growing

It was a little after lunchtime, and Erika was on her way to Hospital X to meet with Dr. Reed. He had phoned her a few days earlier and asked her to meet with him. Dr. Reed said he had some information on Michael's death that he thought she should know about. He mentioned that it was "eyes only" information, but he felt a sense of empathy bordering on guilt, and an obligation to inform her about what he had learned since Michael's passing. She thought it was strange that he would use the word *guilt*.

Very little time had passed since Michael's death, yet it seemed like yesterday as she constantly replayed the events in her head. Maybe she was in shock, because it still felt surreal. Intellectually, she knew he was gone, but spiritually she still felt the connection. That's not to say things had been easy. She had eaten or slept only minimally since that day. But the important thing was that she was still functioning. She knew Michael would have wanted that.

Erika was skeptical about her meeting with Dr. Reed, but she hoped that whatever he had to say would give her some peace and perhaps a little closure. The one thing in life she sorely lacked was inner peace. She came across as someone who had it all together: intelligent, resourceful, efficient, and relatively social. But the truth was that she lacked peace in her life. Erika showed that side of herself to very few people, but she was close enough to Michael that he saw it.

It was a two–and-a-half-hour drive back to Washington DC and Hospital X. She decided not to take the train, thinking that the long drive might do her some good and give her a chance to clear her head. She turned off her cell phone and put on some Neil Diamond music. The song "The Story of my Life" was the first to play, which was odd because it wasn't the first track, and it happened to be Michael's favorite Neil Diamond song. She continued driving somberly without noticing the coincidence. Traffic was surprisingly light, and she was making very good time. She estimated her time of arrival to be about a half hour earlier than she'd anticipated.

***

Dr. Krauss picked up the phone and dialed Erika's cell phone. The phone rang five times and then went to voice mail. "Damn Erika, I was hoping you would pick up, it's Patty. Listen, your results came back positive. You are definitely pregnant. The quantitative blood test results also came back and your pregnancy is further along than we anticipated. You are at least eight weeks pregnant. Some of the fetal cells leaked into your blood sample, it is known as Erythroblastosis Fetalis, but the name is not important. It's a little uncommon but is does happen occasionally. At this point, I don't think there is anything to worry about. Since we had these cells, we ran some additional tests. The blood work also indicated some abnormality with the fetal cells. I've sent the sample out for a more detailed analysis with a friend of mine who specializes in fetal cell abnormalities. No one here in the office is familiar with these cells. Christ! Just give me a call ASAP."

***

Erika pulled into the parking lot of Hospital X just past 2:30 p.m. Her meeting with Dr. Reed was scheduled for 3:00. She stopped in the cafeteria for a quick hot chocolate with whipped cream, which was one of her favorite hot drinks. She was just finishing her last sip when she noticed the missed call from Patty. It was nearly time to meet with Dr. Reed, so she decided to quickly return the call. "Hey, Pat, got your message. I can't believe I'm pregnant! But what's going on?"

"To be honest, we are not sure. It seems as if the fetus is healthy except for one thing."

"Well, I don't have much time. I'm meeting with Dr. Reed in a couple of minutes."

"Dr. Who?"

"No, not Dr. Who—Dr. Reed."

"That's not what I meant. Forget it. Anyway, the problem is that some of the fetal cells are growing abnormally fast."

Erika's tone became more serious. "You mean like cancer cells grow fast?"

"Yes, like cancer cells, but a little faster. We checked, and the cells are not multinucleated or abnormally shaped. In other words, it's not cancer, but it's definitely not normal either."

"What the hell does that mean?"

"We sent the cells out for a more detailed pathology report, but frankly I'm not sure. No one here is either. You have to decide if you would have the child anyway."

"With all that has happened and just finding out about being pregnant, I'm really going to have to think about everything. I have plenty of time to decide, right?"

"That's just it. You only have a few weeks—four or five at the most—to decide. Assuming the baby is still healthy and could be born viable, at its accelerated growth curve, the gestation period would be only three or four months."

Jekyll had more than a father's interest; Hyde
had more than a son's indifference.

—Robert Louis Stevenson

Journal Entry 37

Dr. Jekyll or Dr. Reed?

Erika looked at her watch; it read 3:00 p.m. She was going
to be late for her appointment. She couldn't process right
now what Patty had just told her about her baby. She
threw out her cup, walked to the elevator, and headed for
Dr. Reed's office on the fifth floor.

"Come in," a voice said when she knocked.

"I'm sorry that I'm a little late," Erika apologized.

"No, not at all. Please come in and have a seat," Dr. Reed
cordially responded. "I am very sorry for your loss, and
I appreciate you taking the time to come back to DC to
speak with me. As a doctor, I must unfortunately deal
with death on occasion, but I know it hits especially hard
when a person loses someone he or she knows or cares
about. I have been fortunate in that regard. However, I
think the information I have for you will be worth your
time, and may even provide some solace for you." *And
solve one big problem for me,* he thought to himself.

"Although Michael and I were not married, we were very
close. I really want to hear what you know."

Dr. Reed always enjoyed mixing in the truth whenever possible. "What would you say if I told you that Michael wasn't really dead and you could join him?"

"What are you talking about. I watched him die!"

"Please calm down. You have to understand that what I'm about to tell you is top secret, even for classified CIA personnel."

"How do you know about—"

Dr. Reed interrupted. "That you work for a secretive branch of the CIA known as Vomit Comet?"

Just then, two men wearing suits entered the room. Erika looked up to see that they were both pointing 6mm guns at her.

Erika wasn't shy even with guns pointed at her. Gaining her composure, she quipped, "Skipped the bedside manner training in medical school? Or is this how you treat all your patients?"

"No, just the ones who know too much. Now, if you're finished with the sarcasm, I can explain what's happening here."

Erika looked at the two men pointing their guns at her, "Doesn't look like I have much of a choice."

"We all have choices, Ms. Nirvona. It's just that some are better than others," Dr. Reed said. "For example, I chose to work in a field that would give me an opportunity to improve humankind—improve on the current model, so to speak, and eliminate some of the flaws that Mother Nature has been slow to fix. I can increase the longevity of the product ..." She glared at him with a look of disapproval. He had gotten very good at reading facial expressions, with some practice of course. "I can see that I'm wasting my time trying to convince you of my motives, so let me get to the point," he continued.

"Finally. I'm all ears."

"As I said before, Michael isn't really dead. As you know, Michael is very special. He isn't from this world exactly. When he died on Earth, he transmuted back to his own world."

"He transmuted?"

"It's a term used to explain what happens when someone on Earth appears to die but really travels back to the Zero Universe."

"You must be out of your mind. Are you for real? Let me guess, you have a hidden camera in your pen or your button, and this is some bad episode of *Candid Camera* or an MTV production of some new show."

"What's MTV? You know what? Never mind. I admit I have my own agenda, but I can assure you I'm quite clinically sane. If it makes you feel better, I took a sanity test online, and the results concluded that I am perfectly lucid. I'm willing to bet that Michael told you about our little experiments on the penthouse level of the hospital."

Erika thought about what Michael had told her. She had promised to advise her superiors at the agency. She was mad at herself. She had typed up the report and stored it on her flash drive, but with all that had happened the previous week, she had not handed it in. The flash drive was sitting in her purse.

She put on her most believable poker face and said, "I have no idea what you're talking about."

"Ms. Nirvona, I didn't get to where I am today by being gullible." He turned to one of the armed men. "Look inside her purse."

The gorilla ripped the purse from her grip and dumped the contents onto the table. Her wallet, a brush, car keys, and a bunch of other stuff tumbled out.

"Check inside the zippers," Dr. Reed barked to the thug.

Her heart sank as the flash drive fell onto the table.

Dr. Reed smirked and said, "We'll just see what's on that thumb drive."

"Now what?" Erika asked.

"Do you want the good news or bad news first?"

She didn't answer, so he continued, "The good news is that you will be joining Michael very soon."

"Okay, wacko. That sounds good. Why don't we just leave it at that."

"Come now, Erika. Do you mind if I call you Erika? You can't have one without the other."

"I suppose. And no, I would prefer that you didn't call me Erika. What is the bad news?"

"You have been selected for the processing center."

She felt a jab in her arm and then—

> Why doesn't that Devil take me with him?
> It would be much better with him than it is here.

—Eva Braun

Journal Entry 38

A Deal with the Devil

After I finished my first shift, Jimmy offered to pick me up and take me out for a drink. On Earth, I wasn't much of a drinker, but I figured there was always hope for me on Evion. I was looking to pick up a new hobby anyway, and drinking seemed to be as good as any. I was definitely young enough here to start some new vices.

As I walked outside the Ministry, I saw Jimmy and Suzie pull up to the pickup spot. I nodded hello to Jimmy.

"Hello, Michael! How was your first day on the job?" Suzie asked.

"You mean besides all the glitz and glitter, and talking to and hanging out with all the celebrities?"

Suzie laughed. "You're funny. But seriously?"

"I cleaned toilets, mopped floors, threw out garbage—basically a typical day for a Hollywood celebrity. All in all, it was fine. Nothing bad happened, so I guess that's a good thing." I tried to convince myself.

Jimmy looked over to me and said, "I know it's not what you had hoped for, but hang in there. Things do get better around here." He paused momentarily and then continued, "I thought we would stop at Terra Firma for a quick drink."

I gladly accepted his offer. "I wanted to talk to you about something anyway and start my new hobby of drinking."

Suzie dropped us off in front of the building and mentioned something about catching up with some old jalopy friends of hers across town. She would be back in an hour to pick us up.

We walked through the ancient Egyptian entrance and found a table across from a statue of Zeus. An exotic-looking cocktail waitress dressed like Helen of Troy came over and asked to take our order. She was young— probably about my new age. She had long brown hair and a kind, but relatively sad, pretty face. Jimmy ordered the local android beer on tap. I ordered a piña colada.

Our waitress, Rosalie, explained that she had never heard of such a drink. I tried to explain the ingredients, and she said she would ask the bartender to try and make one.

"Jimmy, have you ever been down in The Trades?"

"Yes. Why are you asking?"

"I would like to go down there myself and take a look around."

"Michael, I have been there before. It is a dark, dangerous place to visit. There are a lot of undesirables. Some very bad people and evil sorts down there. Why on Evion would you want to go there?"

I just looked at him and didn't say anything.

"It's about Erika isn't it? You think there might be someone there who can help you get back to her."

"Is there anyone down there who could help me?"

Rosalie returned with our drinks—Jimmy's android beer and my "sort of" piña colada. "We had to modify it a bit," she explained. "We substituted pineorange for pineapple, and we used our version of rum, but I think you'll like it. In fact, the bartender is thinking of adding the drink to the menu!"

I took a sip. "This is pretty good! A little sweeter and stronger than I am accustomed to, but I think I like it."

Rosalie smiled. "I'll give the bartender the good news. I'll be back in a bit to check on you guys."

I turned to Jimmy. "Getting back to my question, do you think there is anyone in The Trades who can help me?"

"I've heard some rumors about certain traders who dabble in dark magic. They might have some spell or some way to get from here back to Earth. But remember, Michael, you would practically have to sell your soul to one of those guys for their help."

"I don't care. I'll take my chances."

"But, Michael, when you make a deal with the devil—"

"I know the consequences can be hell. But it doesn't matter. I need to find a way back or at least try."

Jimmy looked away.

"Can you help me or not?"

"I can't condone what you want to do, but I think I can help. I never mentioned it to anyone, but I was created down in The Trades and spent many years there. I knew a lot of people and made some connections. I'm not proud of my time down there. I did some bad things. I'm much different now. Anyway, one day Dr. Winston purchased my contract from my previous owners, and I started working at the Ministry of Processing. They were very kind to me, even upgraded some of my circuitry."

"I'm sorry. I didn't know that you had such a rough upbringing."

"Don't worry about it. Like I said, very few people or androids know."

"Okay, so you know your way around down there?"

"You could say that. If you're going to go down there to try to find someone to help you get back to Earth, it would be safer if I went with you. You shouldn't go alone."

"I appreciate that, but I can't ask you to go back there."

"You didn't ask. I offered. Besides, I'm your best shot if you have any chance of getting back to Earth and Erika."

I began to feel that, in a sense, we were
all prisoners of our own history.

—Roland Joffe

Journal Entry 39

Prisoner

A brittle, cracked, blistered and scarred hand poked at her as she awoke. Her head hurt. Her CIA training kicked in. The last thing she remembered was sitting in Dr. Reed's office. Erika took a quick assessment of her surroundings. She was not alone. She was lying on a dirty floor. She was in a large room with no windows and only one thick, steel-plated door. There was a strong acrid smell of urine and vomit emanating from the room. An unfamiliar feminine voice said, "I think she's coming to."

She counted the other people in the room, there were fifteen including herself. Most of the people looked like vagabonds. They were disheveled, their clothing tattered and worn. The men smelled like soiled streets and cheap liquor; the few women, only slightly better. There was only one sink and toilet; they were not private.

There were four other females besides her. The women were dressed in high heels and black stockings. Their faces were caked with makeup and the remains of an abundance of red lipstick. Two of the women had bruises under their eyes and swollen red lips.

It wasn't long before she realized that the people in the room with her were most likely the homeless and the prostitutes who lived on the streets. They were society's undesirables, the unknowns and unaccounted-for human beings with no ties to families. These were the unfortunate ones who fell through the cracks of society and could go missing with no one noticing. Where the hell was she, and why was she here?

She considered her options. There weren't any.

One of the women walked over to her. "H, sweetie. My name is Nicky, what's yours?"

"Erika."

"Are you all right?"

"Yes, I think so except for being here. Where is here anyway?"

"Well, we have concluded that it's definitely not Kansas, so I think we are in some kind of processing center. I overheard some of the others talking about a doctor who told them they should be proud of the contributions they will make to science."

"By any chance did they mention how we would make these contributions?"

Nicky shook her head no. "They said something about transferring us, but they didn't say where they were moving us or why."

"How long have you been here?"

"It's hard to say. They took our watches, phones, and personal belongings, but I would guess only a couple of days."

Being a little distracted from the ordeal of her capture, Erika realized for the first time that her own belongings were also missing.

"What about the other people here? Do you know how long they have been imprisoned?"

"They bring us in at various times, but I would say no one has been here for longer than a week."

Erika realized the dire situation. "Well, there must be some way out of here."

"We have looked for a way to escape, but there doesn't seem to be any way out. Once a day, the guards throw us some scraps of dried-up, barely edible food and a few bottles of water. They slam the door shut immediately," Nicky said.

"And no one has told you anything? Why are you here? What was their purpose for abducting you?"

Nicky shook her head emphatically no and said, "The worst part is that nobody would miss any of us. We are all homeless, living on the streets. We have no families or at least any family that still keeps in touch with us. No one even knows we are gone, so no one even cares."

Erika whispered, "I'm sorry. I work for the government. Someone will know that I'm missing. They will look for me, and when they find me, they will rescue all of us."

The steel door creaked open, and five guards armed with automatic weapons walked into the room. A short, bald, rotund man with thick bottle glasses followed the gunmen. The man said his name was Günter. He seemed somewhat nonchalant. Erika had an instant aversion to this man; he had a mean face. His reddish face was round, fat, and exuded cruelness. Günter was holding a piece of paper, but this seemed a formality as he glanced at it only briefly before he recited the words. He had a slight German accent, which he seemed to be trying to disguise. He spoke as if he had read these words many times before.

"Excuse me," he said. "I've been asked to read this to you." He cleared his throat and continued: "I know you all must be confused and a little scared. This is the normal condition of the human spirit. Rest assured that the contribution you will shortly make will greatly enhance our knowledge of science and eventually improve the human stock."

There was something about the use of the words *human stock* that made Erika very uncomfortable. She cringed.

"Those of you wearing a blue bracelet will be staying here on Earth."

Erika looked at her wrist and noticed the orange bracelet for the first time. She quickly looked around; most people were wearing blue bracelets, except for her, Nicky, and one other gentleman.

The smallish man turned to say something to one of the guards and then continued reading: "Those of you wearing an orange bracelet are lucky. You are privileged and will get a trip that is out of this world—literally out of this world. Shortly, you will fall asleep, and when you wake up, you will be in your new destination. Once again, thank you all for your contributions."

The man turned and began to walk toward the door.

Erika shouted, "Wait! What gives you the right to hold us here as prisoners?"

The man stopped, peered into the group, and smirked at Erika, "Science. We do this in the name of science, my dear Ms. Nirvona." How did he know her name? "Humankind has been doing this for centuries—experimenting on helpless animals in the name of medical research. We have just taken it up a notch or so. For science, of course, both worlds will be a better place one day for the work we do here and there."

What did he mean by both worlds?

Erika sprinted toward the one door, but the security guards raised their weapons and pointed them at her. She had no choice but to stop. Günter and the security guards continued out the door, locking it behind them. The lights were dimmed. A minute later, a colorless, pleasant-smelling gas poured down from the ceiling. Erika tried covering her nose and mouth, but her efforts were to no avail. And, for the second time in a short span of time, everything became dark.

Weather forecast for tonight: dark.

—George Carlin

Journal Entry 40

The Trades

As we descended down a long spiral staircase, the air began to turn cool and stagnant. I had only recently begun to adjust to the warmer temperatures on the surface of Andorra. Jimmy, acting as my guide, was leading me into the depths of The Trades. I hadn't wanted to get him involved, but he would not take no for an answer. He insisted that, if I was going to attempt something this stupid, he would have to help. I found myself a bit surprised to realize that friendships between androids and humans were possible.

There were a number of entrances to The Trades located within each of the eleven districts. These secretive entrances were known only to the mayor, the procurators, and the few who had made it out of The Trades and established a life above ground. Fortunately—or unfortunately—for me, Jimmy was one of the latter.

Jimmy had a special enchanted map. It acted like a divining rod, leading us to one of the covert entrances. These gateways were located in plain sight, but were practically invisible without a magical map. Jimmy explained it had something to do with a magical mist that would "glamour", exert a type of mind control on most people and androids. Our entrance was located between a bookstore and a haberdashery.

As we approached the haberdashery, the owner walked up to us. He was an older gentleman with a grey, disheveled, scraggly beard. Mr. Cyrus was dressed in a dark-black suit with grey pinstripes. He wore a yellow button-down shirt adorned with a silk purple tie. His hair, what was left of it, was slicked back with pomade. To top off the outfit, he held a white felt fedora in his left hand as he greeted us.

"Welcome to my little store. I'm sure you will see something you like," he said with a slightly perceptible Spanish accent.

Jimmy gave him a dirty look; that is to say, if androids were capable of such looks. I had learned androids were capable of expressing some human emotion. Jimmy was especially adroit at showing facial expressions.

Jimmy ushered me forward.

"Come now Mr. Cardazia," Mr. Cyrus stated. "I have some retro clothing from the 1970s that I'm sure you would be interested in. I can give them to you for a great price—a steal really."

As we continued past him, I turned to Jimmy and asked, "Who is Mr. Cyrus, and how did he know my name?"

Mr. Cyrus pulled a small cellular device from his inside jacket pocket, pushed several buttons, and spoke into it. "Hey, boss, they are on the way down to The Trades, like you predicted."

The individual on the line must have said something disconcerting because Mr. Cyrus continued in a frantic voice, "I did try to stop them! I even invited them into my shop for some new retro clothing, but he didn't seem interested. That troublesome android hurried him along."

Jimmy nervously answered my question. "It's a long story, and I'll explain when we have some time. For now, let's just say his real name isn't Mr. Cyrus. He is not someone you want to get involved with, especially while on a quest."

"I'll take your word for now," I said as Mr. Whoever watched us with hawk eyes as we walked down the steps. It seemed there were no transportation tubes leading down into The Trades.

"Where did you get that map?" I asked Jimmy.

"When I lived here, I did a favor for a powerful augurer. To repay my deed, he gave me this map, allowing me to leave and reenter at will."

"So, the map acts like a key for entering and leaving The Trades?"

Jimmy nodded. "Leaving can be just as difficult as entering without one of these magical maps."

After descending for twenty minutes, we reached the bottom of the staircase. There was a single door made of diamonds and gold arranged in an elaborate pattern. Apparently, each entrance had its own distinctive motif, making it easier to return to the same location once inside The Trades. The amount of gold and diamonds on one of these doors would have been worth a small fortune back on Earth. There was no key lock on the door; it seemed to be solid. Jimmy told me not to worry. He placed the map squarely against the shining, sparkling door. The map glowed and sparkled, transforming into an octagonal-shaped key. Jimmy placed the key into the door lock, which had suddenly appeared out of nowhere.

The door remained closed, and a governmental holographic warning about the dangers of The Trades was displayed in mid-air in front of us. They definitely needed a new ad campaign for this place or no one would want to visit. Maybe that was the idea. After the un-Disney-like presentation ended, the door opened. We stepped inside, and the door closed behind us. I was officially inside The Trades.

I turned to Jimmy and said, "Don't lose that map."

He creased his facial muscles to form a smile. "I'll try not to."

Initially, the air seemed completely stale and glacially cold. It was at least thirty degrees cooler down there than on the surface. As we continued farther in, a warming pungent odor permeated throughout. This smell was actually pleasing. For me, it was reminiscent of the smell of the sand and spraying waves just before dusk at the Jersey shore.

For a brief moment, I was on the beach in Margate in front of Lucy the Elephant. This primo spot was crowded with sunbathers. Children were running along the shoreline laughing as the cool, soothing waves brushed up against their feet. The sand felt warm under the soles of my feet, and I could smell the salt water and see the gentle foam created as the waves gently broke onto the beach ...

I felt a hand shaking me slightly. Jimmy explained that this hypnotic scent was maintained through magic. Its intent was to distract visitors. As he was an android, the effects were minimal on him. He gave me a pill to lessen the hypnotic effects somewhat.

He explained that the marvelous smell was different for each person. Some smelled a flower garden; others imagined a tray of freshly baked chocolate chip cookies. The point was that each scent was unique and designed to remind the person of something pleasing from the past, something that would make that person never want to leave.

As we ambled, I noticed that The Trades was really a deteriorated underground city. There were cobblestone streets, cracked concrete sidewalks, and buildings that reminded me of what Earth might have looked like at the turn of the twentieth century. Automobiles were not allowed down here. Instead, there was a train system known as The Rails that ran diagonally through the city. The denizens of The Trades could use that mode of transportation. Although some locals had carriages drawn by donkey- and horse-like creatures, their main modes of transportation were The Rails and good, old-fashioned walking.

Jimmy said he could take me to the magician he had helped years ago—the one who had given him the map. He thought if anyone could help me, it would be him. Along the way, Jimmy had to occasionally remind me of our purpose there, because my mind continued to drift off to the Jersey shore even after I took the medicine.

Although the medicine helped, there were times when I could have sworn I was back in Margate listening to the waves crashing along the rocks and shoreline. I could smell the freshly made piña colada that my dad had just poured. I wanted to run into the brisk ocean, ready to body surf the next large wave. The warm sand and sun filled me with pleasant and warm memories. The smell of the salty air effused through my body until I felt the jolt back to reality as Jimmy snapped me out of it.

The magician's residence was on the other side of town. We had to walk a few blocks to reach a station point to enter The Rails. As we walked across a street known as Gibler Street, I noticed a large crowd of people and humanoid-like beings gathered together.

"What are they gathered together for?" I asked.

"That's Carnival, of course," he replied.

The area was encompassed in a bubble of warm, fragrant steam from the funnel cake deep fryers. It smelled like sweet vanilla cake batter you licked off a spoon.

—Sarah Addison Allen

Journal Entry 41

Carnival

Jimmy peered cautiously at the crowd and remarked, "Seems like a relatively tame crowd today."

"At the risk of sounding stupid"—which was really silly because, at this point, how could anything I said or observed be considered stupid—"what is Carnival?" I asked.

"During the first double solar eclipse of each month, people gather at Trade Square to barter, sell goods, and offer services. Entertainers such as musicians, clowns, and a variety of oddity acts show up hoping for donations for their live performances."

I felt obligated to ask, "You looked concerned. Is it safe?"

"Usually there are limited problems, although sometimes certain undesirables show up and cause trouble. There is no real governing body or legal system down here. Sometimes people try to take advantage of this, and trouble can ensue."

"Sounds great. No regulatory laws or governing body down here. I'll have to make sure to book my next vacation down here."

He glanced at me and said, "Sarcasm, right?"

I was going to say, "You think?" But I just nodded.

Jimmy was pleased that he had recognized the inference, as he had been working hard to understand subtleties in human language.

I looked around as we walked through Carnival. There was literally a one-man band. He played the guitar with one hand, a bass with another, the piano with his third, and the drums with his fourth arm. His voice was mellifluous as he sang a modified Frank Sinatra song, "Fly Me to Tiberon."

Down here, a monetary system of coins and paper was still used. Jimmy flipped a coin into the musician's collection jar. The man smiled with his fifty or more teeth. "Bless you, sir."

Jimmy checked his watch and said, "We have a little time before the next Rail. Would you like to wander around for a bit?"

"Sure, but I don't have any coins or paper money to buy anything."

"No worries. You can always repay me later," Jimmy replied as he handed me some coins and paper bills. He told me we had one hour to enjoy the Carnival before catching the next Rail.

I caught wind of an ambrosial aroma. There was a woman—at least I think she was a woman—selling little appetizer-like treats. I bought two and devoured them. I turned to Jimmy. "Those were delicious! What were they?"

"They are called muroidea cakes, and are considered a treat down here."

"They are pretty good. What are they made of?"

"Usually sewer rat. Or sometimes sewer hamsters or sewer mice."

I started choking and almost emptied the contents of my stomach. "Made of what?" I yelled. "You could have told me before I ate them. Did you have to mention the sewer part three times?"

"Sorry about that. Maybe you should ask me before sampling any more of the local cuisine down here."

Somehow, Jimmy's emotions and expressions seemed much more human like down there. I actually believe he enjoyed seeing my reaction to learning the true identities of the treats.

"You can be sure of that," I squeamishly replied. "Besides, I think I have now lost my appetite."

Jimmy and I continued to walk around the festivities. I noticed there were a number of people with goods spread out on blankets and tables. It reminded me of the yard sales I used go to with Erika during spring and summer weekends. Jimmy noted this was similar to the yard sales I described, except that many residents here bartered for goods instead of purchasing used items.

When we reached the midpoint of Trade Square, we encountered a crowd of people gathered around a large circular area. There were a number of gymnasts and clowns performing a variety of aerial and acrobatic stunts suggestive of a Cirque du Soleil performance.

Jimmy enjoyed the performance and left a donation in a jar for the performers. I had to remind myself that some androids displayed humanistic emotions, like kindness. I also had to remind myself to stop reminding myself.

I walked over to a well-dressed man who was wearing a three-piece suit and tie. He was approximately five foot ten and looked to be of Italian descent. This man appeared to be in his mid to late thirties and seemed out of place because of his clothing. His dress reminded me of Mr. Cyrus, the owner of the haberdashery store we had met while entering The Trades. The only thing different was the white Fedora hat—this man's was black. Most people down here wore tattered rags and clothes.

He appeared to be selling household items: a couple of paintings, mismatched pieces of furniture, small appliances, tools, and a limited selection of jewelry.

As I approached, he nodded and spoke with a thick Italian accent. "Hello, my name is Salvatore, but my friends call me Lucky."

"Hello, Mr. Salvatore. My name is Michael."

He stared at me with a puzzled look. "Please call me Lucky. Is there anything in particular you are looking for? I have many items that are useful and cheap."

"Not really. This is my first time in The Trades. I was hoping to find someone who could help me find my way home—a map leading back to another world, or some kind of magical device."

"Home, huh? Far away I'm guessing?"

"You might say that. In fact, you might say it's a world away."

"Well then, I might have just the thing for you. This gold-plated compass is rumored to be magical."

"I don't know. I really have only a few coins."

He thought for a moment and then responded, "I'll tell you what, I can't give it to you for free because I was sort of a businessman back on Earth. You know, principles and all. But I will give it to you for whatever coins you have in your pocket."

I didn't say anything at first. Was he really from Earth and would he lie to me? He looked like he could have been a gangster, but seemed nice …

Lucky continued, "Look, I'm trying to do you a favor. I can't promise that this compass will work for you. It never has for me. But the magician I acquired it from told me the compass could help to navigate a person back home if he is worthy and the cause is just enough."

Although I wasn't Don Quixote, I figured my quest was just enough all the same.

I reached into my pocket, pulled out the four coins Jimmy had given me, and handed them to Lucky. The compass was now mine. While examining it, I noticed there was ancient Chinese writing inscribed on the front. I figured it was probably an old Chinese proverb similar to those found in a fortune cookie. A few I'd received came to mind: "You are destined for great things." "You will find love when you least expect it." "He who laughs at himself never runs out of things to laugh at."

I flipped the watch over, and it suddenly transformed into an old-style pocket watch. The watch appeared to be from the Civil War time. I began to get a nagging feeling that I had seen this watch—or at least a very similar watch—before, but I just couldn't remember where.

"Good luck, then," Lucky said, and he turned to talk with another potential buyer or barterer.

Jimmy walked over to me and asked, "Do you know who that man was?"

"He said he was from Earth and his name was Lucky—that's all I know about him."

"That was Salvatore Luciano who was generally regarded as the father of modern organized crime in the United States. Lucky, as you referred to him, split New York

City into four different Mafia crime families. He was also instrumental in developing the National Crime Syndicate in the United States."

"Geez, you mean he was a real live mobster? He seemed like such a nice guy."

No, of course I can't. That's what I'd like to do. What
I can do, if I'm any sort of a man, is the next most
merciful thing. I should take her into the woods
and shoot her painlessly in the back of the head.

—Thomas Keneally

Journal Entry 42

The Factory

For the second time in less than a week, Erika woke
up in a foreign place, which was starting to make her
cross. She liked her own bed because it was comfortable
and familiar. This time though, instead of waking up
in a large room with the stench of urine and vomit, she
encountered a clinical antiseptic odor, and found herself
strapped down to an infirmary bed. There were a number
of tubes and wires running into her veins. It appeared they
were doing some type of blood testing on her.

She could move her head slightly to the right and left, but
her arms and legs were held down with restraints. As she
became more cognizant, she realized she was in a hospital
room. There were doctors and nurses dressed in white
scrubs. Machines and monitors were beeping and ringing
all around her. Since she doubted that she was back at
Hospital X, the question was, where the hell was she?

She thought she could hear music playing softly in the
background. It actually sounded like an old Kiss song,
"Hard Luck Woman," which was ironic and seemed to
be in bad taste. Maybe she was hearing things, or maybe

it was the drugs that were being introduced into her bloodstream.

There were ten people in the room with her. She recognized Nicky and the other man who had been with them when the gas poured down from the ceiling and they lost consciousness. She didn't know his name. Although they were also strapped to hospital beds, she was the only one who seemed to be conscious.

A tall man wearing surgeon's scrubs, complete with head covering and booties, walked into the room. He was muscular, thin, and had icy blue eyes. The man would have been considered good looking if not for the aura he exuded. A stethoscope hung around his neck, and he appeared to be in charge. As he deftly sauntered by her, Erika felt the same sort of chill she would expect to feel if he was a vampire. Instinctively, she didn't like him. Besides the fact that he held her and the others strapped down to hospital beds, she sensed that he had little regard for human life.

He injected a liquid substance into each of the IV bags of the unconscious people lying in the beds beside her. After a few moments, everyone appeared to regain consciousness, but could turn their heads only slightly; they were all restrained.

He cleared his throat and began speaking. "My name is Dr. Shelly. You are no longer on Earth. You have been brought to another planet that is outside of your own universe. Because you do not belong within this universe, you will be able to survive for only a short period of time before your cells become unstable and break down.

363

However, before this happens, each of you will make a major contribution to the advancement of science."

He paused then continued, "Unfortunately, these advancements in medical research require that certain sacrifices must be made. All of you, as others from your planet have done in the past, will be included in these sacrifices. Rest assured, your sufferings will not be in vain or go unnoticed in the future scientific community. Some of you, or at the very least your contributions, will be written up in a medical journal one day."

Nicky and the man Erika recognized became upset upon hearing this and struggled with their restraints. A machine hooked up to their IVs turned on and released a cerulean clear liquid into the bags. Almost immediately, the two became placid and eerily peaceful.

Softly in the background, an Alice Cooper song, "Only Women Bleed," was playing. This time, Erika didn't think it was the drugs or her imagination playing tricks on her. Dr. Shelly gave a Stepford Wife–like smile. "I do believe you have the right to know the purpose for which you are being sacrificed. We are not monsters, but rather pioneers in genetics. We are running two different highly significant programs here at the Science Ministry. Some of you will be used in experiments that attempt to enhance the durability of cellular life. It is our hope we can slow down the aging process and extend the longevity of the individual organism. I believe it's even possible to reach a state of making oneself virtually immortal against the aging process. However, this research requires the extraction of most of the cellular DNA from the subject's body. Sadly, but humanly, the extraction of this DNA requires the termination of the individual." Dr. Shelly's attitude was alarmingly nonchalant.

The doctor stopped speaking. He picked up a hot beverage from a nearby tray and took a few sips. *The evil man is looking around as if he's studying his subjects, looking for some kind of reaction from those still conscious*, Erika thought to herself.

Apparently satisfied with the hot drink and the lack of any reaction, he continued, "The rest of you will be used for parts in our cyborg program. Building cyborgs requires a certain number of human parts. Due to certain legislation and the current economic situation in Andorra, it has become an arduous task to obtain human organs for cyborg creation from our own citizens. Those of you whose DNA is tested and determined to be unsuitable for our Extension-of-Life Program will still be able to contribute toward our research. Your organs will be harvested and used to create or replace parts for our cyborgs."

Before Erika lost consciousness again, she was aware of music was softly playing. This time she was sure that she heard the Guns and Roses song, "Used to Love Her." She remembered the lyrics: "I used to love her but I had to kill her." As she drifted off into an unconscious realm, she wondered how truly mentally sick this man was.

If you board the wrong train, it is no use running
along the corridor in the other direction.

—Dietrich Bonhoeffer

Journal Entry 43

The Rails

We finished walking around Carnival and headed for the
The Rails. Jimmy mentioned that it would be a twenty-
five-minute ride on the train to reach his friend, the
magician.

"Now that I think about it, I forgot to ask you the name
of your magician friend."

"My friend's name is Merlin."

"You have to be kidding."

"Why?"

"I thought that Merlin was just an Arthurian mythical
magician created by an ancient writer and not a real
person."

"Actually, from what he has told me, he is quite real
and is a fantastic magician. He did live on Earth a long
time ago."

I tried to understand "So his legend is partly based in
truth?"

"I guess so, but you can ask him yourself when you meet him."

The train arrived. Jimmy paid a small fee for both of us, and we sat down. Each seat was individualized. The train was divided into three compartments. The first compartment housed the conductor and the engines. The second contained approximately fifty individual seats. The last compartment included a small café and bar. In The Trades, drinking establishments were called bars, just as they were at home.

Half of the seats were filled. Some of the passengers looked completely human, while others had slight variances. The majority of the clientele appeared to be poor, with tattered clothing and worn accessories. However, there were a few well-dressed men in three-piece business suits who seemed to be out of place here.

Jimmy explained that no one was quite sure who these well-dressed individuals were or why they were in The Trades. There were various rumors that they could be agents for the ASAP, part of organized crime (in other words, The Trades' own version of the mob), aliens, or a new religious sect. Since they kept mainly to themselves, they were left alone. I wondered if they were anything similar to "the Observers" on the Fox television network *Fringe*—a program I had watched back on Earth.

Although most trips on the train were short, a helmet-like hat was mounted above each seat. By wearing the hat, riders could watch programming in 3-D for the duration of the trip. Sporting events, movies, and news from the surface above were all available.

Jimmy selected the local news. He said he liked to stay informed. I chose to watch a sporting event. It was similar to a baseball game, but their version had a few major differences. For example, the pitcher and batter could have more than two arms. The field was shaped like a pentagon, with an additional fifth base, in contrast to the diamond shaped four bases in Earth's version. There were still three outs in an inning, and three strikes constituted an out, but the batter could strike out on a foul ball. A complete game consisted of eleven innings, and a weather-shortened game had to go at least seven innings. Probably the most interesting change in the game was that home field advantage was literally a home field advantage. The fans of the home team were allowed to throw a homerun ball back into the field of play. Therefore, the batter could be thrown out running the bases if he wasn't careful. I had to admit, it did make a homerun more exciting. This also made for a game that was home-team-fan friendly as well as fan interactive.

The Andorian Velociraptors were the home team, and they were playing the Tiberon Triceratops. Each team was named after a dinosaur. They played in an interstellar league consisting of twenty-four teams. There were two separate divisions, with the winner of each division playing in the Galactic Series.

We were fifteen minutes into the ride when the train came to a screeching halt, and the 3-D helmets lifted off our heads. Someone had pulled the fire alarm. The conductor's voice blared over the loud speaker: "Attention, passengers! There is a fire in the dining cart. Please exit the train in an orderly manner. We apologize for the inconvenience, but service on this train has been indefinitely suspended."

Jimmy and I detrained. He looked concerned as we started walking the rest of the way.

"What's wrong?" I asked.

"It's very rare that a fire occurs and that a train is stopped. It's almost as if someone or somebody doesn't want us to reach Merlin's house," Jimmy whispered.

He only loves those things
because he loves to see them break
I fake it so real I am beyond fake
And some day you will ache like I ache
Some day you will ache like I ache …

—Courtney Love, "Doll Parts"

Journal Entry 44

Doll Parts

Dr. Shelly and his medical staff entered the room. All of the confined patients were awake, the sedative previously administered having by now worn off. Erika had really, really, grown to hate the guy; actually, it didn't take much of an effort. Dr. Shelly had an inhuman quality about him. He talked about life as if it was disposable, especially if it could benefit scientific advancement in any way. Any sacrifices were totally justifiable as long as they improved scientific knowledge. She briefly wondered if animal testing in the name of science and medical research was really so different.

The archfiend doctor stopped by Nicky's bed. He looked at her chart and said something to one of his assistants. He leaned down beside her and calmly whispered, "According to our tests, your DNA is not stable enough to be used in our Extension-of-Life Program. Therefore, you will be placed in our organ donation program. You will greatly benefit some lucky cyborg. Please understand that this is also a very worthy program, and we wouldn't want you to feel any less important to the betterment of science."

Nicky tried to struggle, but the restraints held, and the IV machine released its calming liquid until she became docile. Two of Dr. Shelly's assistants disconnected her from the tubes and wires. They lifted her comatose body onto a gurney and wheeled her out of the room.

They were on the fourth floor of the Science Ministry. Very few had access to this floor or the floor above it. Only Dr. Shelly and his staff were permitted. Nicky was being taken to the organ donor room. Her organs would be used as parts to build special cyborgs—the next generation of cyborgs.

Once inside the organ donation room, Nicky's organs and external limbs would be excised from her body and later used in the cyborg program. Shortly after the procedure, she would be humanely euthanized. Each of the extracted organs would be outfitted with a tracking device and control chip. This would allow Dr. Shelly and his benefactor to follow these special cyborgs and, most importantly, control their actions and behaviors.

There were some bugs to be worked out, but with each new batch of cyborgs, the problems were diminished. Eventually, Dr. Shelly believed these cyborgs could be completely controlled and tracked. He estimated that, within a year, maybe six months, he would have perfected this process.

Dr. Shelly anticipated that Michael Cardazia might become a problem down the line. That's why he had one of his top cyborgs trailing him after working hours, just to be on the safe side. Mr. Cyrus had informed Dr. Shelly that Michael had found his way into The Trades and was probably on his way to meet Merlin, along with his android friend. The good doctor suggested that Rutger, one of Dr. Shelly's cyborgs, start a fire on the train to slow them down. He needed time to figure out what Mr. Cardazia was planning, especially because of his newfound friendship with Elvis, whom he really despised.

The organ extraction process was relatively simple for Dr. Shelly, as he had done the procedure numerous times before, hundreds actually. Besides, it wasn't as if the donor was going to be revived any time soon. The trick was to be careful that the organs were not damaged during the removal process, the insertion process, and subsequent activation of the tracker-control chips. Recently, the supply of donors hadn't been an issue; however, Dr. Shelly abhorred waste. He was, after all, a professional who took great pride in his surgical precision.

Unlike living organ donation back on Earth, theoretically, any body part could be extracted because these donors were euthanized during the process. Along with the typical donations of lungs, kidneys, hearts, and other organs, some cyborgs received limbs as well. Dr. Shelly could usually harvest 75 percent or more of each donor, but he anticipated that the percentage would increase over time with his research.

Nicky was a relatively easy subject to work with. Although he appalled her choice of life style—she was homeless, probably a drug addict, and a prostitute—amazingly it appeared her organs were sufficiently healthy for the transplant process. On rare occasions, he felt some level of sympathy for the people he worked on. Mostly because of her life style, Nicky was not one of these few.

He had convinced himself many times that he was doing society a favor by removing these derelicts and ragamuffins. Wasn't he saving the taxpayers on Earth a considerable sum of tax dollars? Likewise, wasn't he helping to clean up the refuse from the city streets? Dr. Shelly firmly believed this was the next logical step in evolution—survival of the fittest and the thinning out of the weak and less desirable. He didn't expect to win any humanitarian awards, but a science advancement award was definitely in his future—maybe even the Preston, the Evion equivalent of the Nobel Prize in science.

On Earth, organs could usually be stored for only eight hours, and only if they were stored in an intracellular-like preservation medium and kept cold. Here on Andorra, a more advanced version of that chemical had been genetically engineered at the Ministry of Science, vastly increasing the storage times. Some organs could be stored almost indefinitely. This advancement had been developed through the experimentation and testing of people like Nicky, but researchers had justified the practice by weighing it against the advancements they were consequently able to make in medical science.

Was it really so different than some of the advances in medical science made back on Earth by the experimentation on helpless laboratory animals? It really was just another evolution in a much more modern sense, just another rung higher on the ladder of genetic advancement.

Dr. Shelly tried not to get too philosophical during these extractions. He needed to concentrate on the task at hand. Although the procedures had become second nature to him, he had to remind himself that a simple slip or miscalculation could damage and waste an organ.

The first step for Nicky was the removal of her external limbs. Both arms and legs were already earmarked for two cyborgs Dr. Shelly was in the process of creating. Nicky would be kept artificially alive during the process; his research had shown the organs were more viable if the patient was alive during the extractions. Before he added the limbs to the donor cyborgs, he would incorporate the tracking-control chips and activate them. These chips were powered by tiny potassium ion batteries that could last up to twenty years. This was the next generation in battery technology that Earth was still a few years away from discovering.

The second step was the excision of the external sense organs. The eyes—not just the corneas——ears, and nose could be successfully transplanted onto the new cyborg. These external appendixes could be kept viable the longest. Interestingly enough, even after the removal of the limbs and sense organs, some of the patients' hearts would continue to beat, even without artificial assistance, thus technically keeping the donor alive for a short period of time.

After all the limbs and sense organs had been removed, the internal organs could be harvested. Using the internal organs was a relatively new procedure in the production of cyborgs, but one that showed great promise. Currently, Dr. Shelly had cyborgs with human livers, lungs, pancreases, kidneys, and intestines. Nicky's heart would be the first trial in human heart-to-cyborg donation.

Dr. Shelly had just finished removing Nicky's external donor parts and was ready to start the internal organ extraction when his chief nurse whispered something into his ear. Dr. Shelly quickly turned on the life support system machine. This machine could keep a person and his or her organs artificially alive for up to a week. He had to attend to a currently developing situation. The internal organs could wait. Besides, he was relatively sure Nicky wouldn't mind waiting. Not that she had a choice.

That's the scary part. I didn't know if I
should smile, crack up, scream or run.

—L. Frank Baum, *The Wizard of Oz*

Journal Entry 45

Off to See the Wizard

We departed the train and started walking toward
Merlin's residence. After approximately ten minutes, I
noticed the landscaping drastically changing as we got
closer to Merlin's. The immediate surroundings became
less city like and more Louisiana swampy. Dilapidated
concrete streets and buildings were replaced with trees
and muddy paths. Oddly, as we proceeded further farther
into the swamps, I found myself much less affected by the
air in The Trades while thoughts and images of the Jersey
shore became more distant.

The temperature was also changing— - from cold and
damp to warm and humid. Jimmy explained that this
swamp was had been created and was maintained by
Merlin's magical powers. The good news was that we were
getting closer to Merlin's house. The bad news was that I
still wasn't certain that he could, or would, be willing to
help me. If Merlin couldn't be of assistance, then I would
be back at square one.

I could be a relatively patient man, so starting from the
beginning was okay except for two problems. Without
Merlin's assistance, I had no idea who could help me.
Secondly, I had a feeling that time was running out and I
didn't want to start back at square one. I don't know why I

had this sense or where it came from, but it was definitely there. I was really starting to think that in this world my psychic powers were enhanced.

Jimmy seemed to think someone was following us and frequently stopped and looked around. My tracking and hunting skills were not as sharp as his; I saw no indication of this supposed tail. A little more than two-thirds of the way into the swamp, the muddy trail turned into a yellow brick road. Glinda was not there; neither was the scarecrow or the cowardly lion. But there was a yellow brick road leading to Merlin's house. This seemed a bit purposefully cliché.

The closer we got to Merlin's house, the more pleasant our surroundings became. It was almost surreal to see the landscape of The Trades change from the cold, dark, damp, concrete sewer, to an Okefenokee-like swamp, and then to a lush forest. The flora presence became more abundant. The forest contained varieties of what appeared to be authentic Earth oak, juniper, birch, aspen, and Scotch pine. Jimmy explained that, through some magical spell, Merlin had been able to recreate and maintain authentic flora from Earth since it made him feel more at home.

There were even small animals running through the trees above collecting a variety of nuts. These animals were larger than squirrels, but did possess similar features and apparently shared the love for nuts. Maybe Merlin couldn't create exact duplicates of Earth animals or didn't feel the need.

Small birds were singing peacefully in the trees. Their songs contained words, some of which I could understand.

Jimmy explained that some of the animals that lived around Merlin's residence were capable of speaking a language that could be understood by people. These particular birds were called musicatto birds and were used to send messages similar to the way carrier pigeons delivered written messages. Musicatto birds, however delivered messages by singing the words. Jimmy didn't know if the birds understood the messages they delivered, but they were excellent imitators and ideal messengers.

Jimmy's android ears perked up and he urged, "I think we need to pick up the pace somewhat."

"I can't hear anything, but you think we are definitely being followed?"

Jimmy nodded and we hurried along.

"Why would someone be following us?"

"Not sure. But I would guess someone doesn't want us to talk to Merlin. In any case, we probably don't want to find out."

We reached the proverbial end of the yellow brick road, which dipped into a body of water known as Dozmary Pool. It formed the boundary between the forest and the outskirts of Merlin's property. The water was a mauve color and appeared to be completely still. The lake was a mile wide, and in the middle was a small island.

Jimmy mentioned that the island was referred to as Avalon. He said there were many apple trees as well as other fruit-bearing trees there. The island was magical and produced all of its own grains and crops. There was no need for ploughs, as the island took care of its own cultivation. Jimmy was not aware if any animals or people inhabited the enchanted island, but he suspected that someone or something did.

I finally began to believe that events and myths associated with Arthurian legend might have been linked to real events on Earth long ago. If Merlin really did exist, then maybe Camelot was more than just a legend. I wondered if other legends were also based on authentic events and were kept alive in stories passed down through generations.

A small rowboat was tied up on the middle bank; it appeared to be the only way to cross the water barrier.

For the first time, I could hear the footsteps of our pursuer.

Jimmy anxiously looked at me and urged, "Hurry, untie the oars while I untie the boat. Once we start rowing, be careful not to let any part of your body touch the water."

We quickly untied the boat, jumped into it, and began to row toward the island in the middle of the lake. As I looked back at the forest, it became unclear and filmy. The air became very stuffy and uncomfortably warm.

The water looked very placid and then suddenly refreshing. "What's the problem with touching the water?" I finally asked.

"Dozmary waters are enchanted. It is rumored that anyone who touches the water will fall into a deep stupor."

"Is the rumor true?"

"Don't know for sure, and don't want to find out first hand either."

While rowing across the enchanted lake, I could see translucent fish swimming and jumping. There appeared to be a variety of different species of fish. Some of the pellucid fish had stripes and designs across their dorsal fins. They didn't seem to present a threat to us.

"Those fish are Merlin's pets. They are docile. Merlin loves animals, and he has created different sanctuaries for them here. He has other pets, which we will see soon," Jimmy said.

"I can relate. I am also an animal person. By the way, why can't I see the shoreline and the forest anymore? We're not that far out."

"It is part of the same enchantment spell that causes the water to have a hypnotic effect. It also protects Merlin's island from being seen from the forest side, unless you have the enchanted map with you."

"Why would a famous and powerful magician need to cloak his residence?"

Suddenly, the water became rippled. Someone from the shoreline on the forest side was firing some kind of metallic objects at us. The objects were missing us. Evidently, since we couldn't see the forest, they couldn't see us either. They were firing blindly into the water, hoping to hit us.

"Oh, that's why," I said with a gasp.

Do not meddle in the affairs of Wizards,
for they are subtle and quick to anger.

—J. R. R. Tolkien

Journal Entry 46

Merlin

Eventually, we reached the shoreline of the island that was Merlin's residence. We pulled the boat up onto a small beach and got out, taking care to not touch the enchanted lake water. The sand was multi-colored, all the colors of the rainbow being represented. It was spectacular to see the multitude of colors intertwined in the grains of sand.

"Are there any precautions I need to take with the sand?" I asked.

"No, it's not charmed. It's just there for aesthetics."

A path made from crushed seashells led from the beach to Merlin's door. I remembered that my father loved to collect shells from the beach and build boxes with them. I wondered if he had died normally or transmuted like me. Jimmy didn't know the answer. Maybe Merlin did.

The shelled path sloped upward for about two hundred meters then leveled off and changed from seashells to diamonds and gems. Merlin's home was a castle set upon a rocky cliff. "Let me guess. His castle is called Camelot, right?"

"Lucky guess."

I laughed and nodded in agreement.

Two large creatures came running down the cliff straight toward us. Jimmy turned to greet the two animals. "Hello Calygreyhound. Hello Freybug. How are you guys?"

Calygreyhound was the stranger of the two animals. His head looked like a wild cat's, and he had the torso of a large antelope. He had the hind legs of a lion and the claws of an eagle on its forefeet. The tail of this bizarre creature was that of a poodle. Merlin's pet also had two large wings similar to those of an American bald eagle, but much larger.

Freybug was the more normal of the two, if normalcy had any relevance here. He—I assumed they were both males—was larger than Calygreyhound. He was a little bigger than a large calf, and completely jet black. Freybug had more typical dog features and looked a little like a giant great dane.

Both Calygreyhound and Freybug ran over to Jimmy, knocking him over and licking him as they howled with excitement. They almost reminded me of big, really strange-looking dogs.

"I missed you too," Jimmy said.

"I'm assuming they know you," I said rhetorically.

Jimmy got up and brushed himself off. "These two little guys are Merlin's pets and guardians." He turned to address the pets, "Take us to Merlin."

The two animals made some kind of excited barking sound and started up the cliff to the castle. There was a carved pathway through the rocks leading up to Camelot. Even with the wizard-made passageway, the trek was a little arduous. One missed step could lead to a lethal fall amongst the cracked jagged rocks. We climbed carefully for three hundred meters with Calygreyhound and Freybug leading the way to the castle.

Camelot was constructed from a stone that was grey and bluish in color. The interior was lit with large candles stuck in metal frames that held shades made of thin, transparent horn material. Rugs with medieval designs covered most of the floors. The main entrance was wainscoted, as were with several other rooms. A large fire burned in the reception room.

Merlin walked into the room. I expected to see an older man with a long white beard carrying a wand and wearing a cobalt robe and hat. Instead, he was young, maybe in his thirties. He was clean shaven and did not carry a wand. Merlin wore a powder-blue-colored jumpsuit. He looked at me and greeted Jimmy, "Hello, Jimmy. It's been a long time. It's great to see you."

Calygreyhound and Freybug curled up in the corner by the fireplace, and each closed one of his eyes. They seemed to enjoy the warmth that the fire provided.

"Merlin, it has been too long indeed. I want you to meet my friend, Michael Cardazia. He also lived on Earth not that long ago," Jimmy replied.

Merlin extended his right hand. "Please excuse my appearance. I was just finishing my martial arts training."

"It is a pleasure to meet you, sir."

Merlin smiled. "Any friend of Jimmy's can consider himself a friend of mine as well. Please follow me into the great hall where we can talk more comfortably and share a meal together."

I began to realize I was getting hungry. The effects of the muroidea cakes had worn off, and my stomach growled. A good meal from a famous wizard would be welcomed.

We followed Merlin into the great hall. A large trestle table stood majestically in the center of the room. Wooden chairs with high, straight backs and arms stuffed with feathers surrounded this round table. I could tell the stuffing was feathers because a few were sticking out of the fabric here and there.

We sat down, and Merlin asked Jimmy, "What is it you and Michael seek from me?" Before I could answer, Merlin abruptly changed the subject and turned to me. "I hope you enjoy seafood from Earth."

"Yes, it is my favorite type of food," I quickly answered.

One of the kitchen servants wheeled in a cart of food. A feast was placed upon the table. There were lobsters, hard-shell and soft-shell crabs, and sea scallops in addition to a bevy of other seafood. Whole-grain breads and aromatic cheeses followed.

Merlin looked at me inquisitively.

I took a deep breath and said, "I was hoping you could help me with a very big problem. Jimmy seems to think that if anyone can help, it would be you."

"I do have great powers that have been enhanced in this universe, but I am still not omnipotent. What kind of help are you seeking?"

"Back on Earth, I left a girl. She was my soul mate, and I was forced to leave her suddenly—*transmuted* I have been told is the proper term. I need to find a way back to Erika. She's my life."

Merlin looked at me sympathetically and said, "There is no greater or more just cause in either universe than pure love. However, once a person has transmuted from Earth to this universe, it is not easily reversed."

I looked up, "You said it's not easy, but you didn't say it was hopeless. Does that mean it is possible?"

The Bermuda Triangle got tired of warm weather. It
moved to Alaska.
Now Santa Claus has gone missing.

—Steven Wright

Journal Entry 47

Triangles and Circles

The small, single-engine plane named *Gateway* was
making its final approach for landing on Devil's Island.
This small island was smack dab in between Florida,
Bermuda, and Puerto Rico. It was cloaked with Evion
radar-jamming technology making it virtually invisible
to the outside world.

This area was one of the most heavily traveled shipping
lanes in the world, with cargo ships crossing through it
daily destined for ports in the Americas, Europe, and
the Caribbean Islands. Cruise ships were also abundant,
and pleasure craft regularly went back and forth between
Florida and the islands. It was also a heavily flown route
for commercial and private aircraft heading for Florida,
the Caribbean, and South America. Even with this heavy
sea traffic, only on rare occasions would a plane or ship
get too close to this island and have to be "taken care of."

Devil's Island was positioned in the western part of the
North Atlantic Ocean, often referred to as the Bermuda
Triangle. It was one of only two processing factories and
portals within the northern hemisphere that provided
access into Universe Zero. The other site was located

in the English county of Wiltshire and was known as Stonehenge.

Shortly before the conclusion of World War II, Dr. Shelly's predecessor decided that these two areas would be set up as portals into Universe Zero. It was illegal in Universe Zero to use inhabitants of that universe for DNA testing and cyborg parts. However, due to a loophole in the Evion legal system, it was still illegal to use inhabitants from Earth for those scientific projects, but prosecution of such activities was difficult. The practice was still considered to be highly unethical to most residents of Evion and had to be carried out as a clandestine activity.

Given the low prosecution rate, the logical scientific step was to procure test subjects from the other universe. Processing centers would need to be established in order to ship people from Earth to Universe Zero. Devil's Island was chosen as a processing center because of the closeness of the island to the Bimini Road. Also known as the Bimini Wall, this undersea structure was technology remaining from what the ancients referred to as the great city of Atlantis.

The Bimini Wall is composed of flat-lying tabular, rectangular, sub-rectangular, polygonal, and irregular blocks that were intentionally designed to appear as geologically naturally formed rocks. Larger and smaller blocks measuring two to four meters in horizontal dimensions extended in a southwest direction creating a pronounced hook at the bottom. The larger blocks show rounded complementary edges giving the appearance of giant loaves of bread.

Both the small and large blocks were composed of carbonate, a cemented shell hash known as beach rock. This rock is native to this part of the Caribbean. What was not indigenous to this area was the Higgs Boson particles from both universes that were imbedded within the bread loaf structure of the larger blocks. These so called "God particles," nicknamed after a Leon Lederman book, were the key to transporting humans from Earth to the Zero Universe.

The Higgs Boson subatomic particle is the particle that gives mass to matter. These particles from both universes created a type of matter-antimatter field that would allow objects to be transported from one universe to the other. The processing center on Devil's Island was located close enough to the Bimini Road to tap into this field and transport animate and inanimate objects between the worlds. The effect of having these "God particles" from both universes interspersed together was to create a portal between the two universes, commonly called a wormhole.

An adverse side effect of going through the portal for someone from Earth and arriving on the Evion was the destruction of the balance of the Higgs Boson particles from the person's cells and nitrogen bases of their DNA, specifically their purine bases. This would eventually lead to mass cellular destabilization and eventually death.

This was an irrelevant detail to some of the scientists and researchers on Evion because the test subjects brought over to Universe Zero were slated for medical research and destroyed in a timely manner.

The ancient city of Atlantis had existed as portrayed in popular antiquity stories. What was not widely known was that the ancient city island was created by inhabitants of Universe Zero. The island was formed as an observatory outpost to study the Earth humans nearly ten thousand Earth years ago.

Originally there was a wormhole located on Evion that created a portal allowing access to Earth. The problem with some wormholes was they tended to be unstable and transient. Eventually many wormholes became flat-lying tabular, rectangular, sub-rectangular, polygonal, and irregular blocks and very erratic. The scientists from the Science Ministry were able to counteract this effect. They built a giant amplifier to stabilize the wormhole and keep the portal between the two worlds open. A block wall with subatomic particles—the Higgs Bose particles—from both universes was constructed. This wall was known as Bimini Road and named after the chain of small islands located in close proximity.

After many years of journeys from Evion to Earth, a massive earthquake and tidal wave hit Atlantis, killing some of the Evion scientists and observers. Contrary to popular lore, the island was not completely destroyed, but the unlucky inhabitants were all lost. After this tragedy, it was decided to stop visitations to Earth.

This decree lasted a few thousand years until scientists discovered that the Bimini Road was still able to maintain the portal between the two worlds. When the Extension-of-Life Program and cyborg programs were covertly hatched, test subjects were needed for experimentation, and a clandestine decision was made to reopen the portal.

Located in the English county of Wiltshire, just west of Amesbury and north of Salisbury, the portal was established. Stonehenge was built—a circular setting of large standing stones set within earthworks. Similar to the Bimini Road, these large blocks contained implanted Higgs Boson particles from both worlds, and they augmented the portal created by the wormhole.

Since this station was out in the open and more obvious than the Caribbean post near Atlantis, rumors were started to explain the occurrence of this odd formation. Human remains were buried at the location to suggest that the site was being used as a burial ground. In addition, the megalithic stones were arranged in a circular path and aligned with the sun and moon to suggest an astronomical observatory. Finally, animal remains such as pig parts, were also carefully placed at the site suggested sacrificial rites and a religious purpose.

These precautions seemed to work and actually led to the development of some interesting folklore. The local inhabitants were completely unaware of the true purpose of Stonehenge.

One legend known as the heel stone legend referred to a stone that lies just outside the main entrance to the Stonehenge, next to the present A344 road. It is a large, rough stone, sixteen feet above ground, leaning inward toward the stone circle. It has been known by many names, including the friar's heel and the sun stone. If someone stands within Stonehenge, facing northeast through the entrance toward the heel stone, one sees the sun rise above the stone at the summer solstice.

A rumor was started by the workers from Universe Zero living among the local inhabitants at the time that the devil bought the stones from a woman in Ireland, wrapped them up, and brought them to Salisbury Plain. One of the stones fell into the Avon; the rest were carried to the plain. The devil then cried out, "No one will ever find out how these stones came here!" A friar replied, "That's what you think!" Whereupon the Devil threw one of the stones at him and struck him on the heel. The stone stuck in the ground and is still there. Some of the people believed this tale while others doubted its validity. The truth was that the friar's heel stone was constructed with the Higgs Boson particles from both universes and set up as an amplifier for the wormhole.

Another folktale started in the twelfth century by Geoffrey of Monmouth included a fanciful story in his work *Historia Regum Britanniae* in which he attributed the monument's construction to Merlin. Geoffrey's story spread widely, appearing in various forms and in many adaptations.

According to Geoffrey, the rocks of Stonehenge were healing rocks, called the Giant's Dance, which giants had brought from Africa to Ireland for their healing properties. The fifth-century king Aurelius Ambrosius wanted to erect a memorial to three thousand nobles slain in battle against the Saxons buried at Salisbury. With Merlin's council, he chose Stonehenge.

The king sent Merlin, Uther Pendragon (Arthur's father), and fifteen thousand knights, to remove these stones from Ireland, where they had been constructed on Mount Killaraus by the giants. They slew seven thousand Irish but, as the knights tried to move the rocks with ropes and force, they failed. Merlin, using his magic and skill, easily dismantled the stones and sent them over to Britain, where Stonehenge was dedicated.

After the stones had been reinstalled near Amesbury, Geoffrey further wrote, Ambrosius Aurelianus, then Uther Pendragon, and finally Constantine III, were buried inside the "Giants' Ring of Stonehenge." This led further credence to the theory that Stonehenge was an ancient burial ground. The only truth to this legend was that Merlin was involved in the construction of the portal and the placement of the Higgs Boson particles within the stones.

Still a final legend of the Saxons and Britons stated that, in 472, the invading king Hengist invited Brythonic warriors to a feast, but treacherously ordered his men to draw their weapons from concealment and fall upon the guests, killing 420 of them. Hengist erected the stone monument Stonehenge on the site to show his remorse for his heinous deed.

Naturally, these legends helped to conceal the true purpose for the construction of Stonehenge.

The pilot in charge of *Gateway* made his final preparations for landing. The plane slowed to quarter speed, the landing gear dispatched, and *Gateway* touched down and gradually came to a full stop. All of the passengers were unconscious except for Günter and the pilot. A van arrived at the landing to take the next group of recruits to the processing center.

The sleeping passengers were transported into the back of the van. Günter looked at his newest collection of subjects. Dr. Shelly would be pleased. This new batch of derelicts looked especially healthy and promising. Günter thought it was a little warmer and more humid than usual for this time of the year; maybe he would reward himself with a refreshing tropical drink, a piña colada, perhaps?

Short cuts make long delays.

—J. R. R. Tolkien

Journal Entry 48

Bread Crumbs

I stared at Merlin, but he seemed lost in thought. He had not answered my question—was it possible to get back to Earth after being transmuted?

"Well, is it possible?" I excitedly asked again.

"There are two wormholes that provide portals from Evion to Earth that I know of, although there may be more."

"Please explain."

"A long time ago, when I left Earth and came to Evion, I worked as an independent contractor with the Ministry of Science. On Earth, I was a pretty good magician. When I came here, I found that my powers were even greater. Something in this universe seemed to amplify my abilities."

"What kind of work did you do for them?

"The Ministry of Science had discovered the two wormholes that allowed passage between Earth and Evion. The nature of most wormholes is to be unstable and transient."

"But Einstein-Rosen bridges—wormholes—are only theoretical; they really don't exist, do they?" I immediately realized that this was a foolish question. Of course they must exist. I was here wasn't I? Otherwise, how did I get here?

"I do remember reading Einstein's paper on general relativity; he was a brilliant man. However, he lacked the confidence to believe in his own calculations. He believed that these bridges could be expressed only mathematically. He thought of them as only a theoretical concept."

Intrigued, I gave Merlin a look to suggest "Go on. I understand."

"Wormholes are rare, but they do exist, at least in this universe. After all, you and I are living proof that they do exist."

"I now know they exist, but I'm not sure how they work."

"You see, wormholes are portals or passages through space that sometimes lead to other dimensions. Earth's universe and this universe can both exist because they are found within different dimensions. Both universes exist in the same general area but coexist within a different plane or what some call a different dimension. However these dimensions are found only at the end points of each separate universe."

"So different universes can coexist at the same time but within different dimensions?"

Merlin nodded. "I should also mention that these universes can vibrate within the dimensions at different frequencies, which can affect individual time sequences."

"Are there more than these two universes that exist within different dimensions?"

Merlin looked inquisitively at me but ignored the question. "To get to another universe, and hence another dimension, you would have to travel to the end of one universe. That's hardly practical, even traveling at the speed of light. Wormholes create shortcuts through space making the travel much more feasible and thus faster."

"How?"

"The simplest way to explain it would be to think in terms that each universe or dimension is connected at certain points, like a box lying on the floor. A wormhole is an opening between the two points of contact."

Merlin must have sensed that I was still confused because he continued. "Think of it this way. Suppose I had a very long piece of rope. I hold it at one end, but I want to reach the other end. Here's the wormhole analogy: instead of pulling the entire length of the rope through my hands to reach the other end, I would bend the rope, grab the other end, and bring the two points together, drastically shortening the distance. In effect, the wormhole bends or curves the space between the dimensions."

"In this case, the shortest point between two spots is not a straight line but rather a bent one."

Merlin chortled. "Sort of the idea."

"But why don't we detect wormholes back on Earth?"

"Because wormholes don't necessarily exist in two places at the same time. They can exist in only one place. Once a wormhole is activated, it must exist in both places, but only when it is opened."

"So that's why we could never detect a wormhole on Earth, because they are not always there?"

Merlin nodded.

I think I knew the answer but had to ask, "What exactly did you do for the Science Ministry?"

Jimmy looked directly at Merlin and chimed in, "Michael works there now."

"Interesting. I was hired to work with the scientists to develop a way of making the wormholes more stable and less transient," Merlin responded.

"As I remember it from my home world," I said, "although wormholes were theoretical, many scientists believed that there could be two kinds of wormholes—those that allowed travel in only one direction, and more stable ones that allowed travel in both directions." I then realized the answer to my next question. There were, in fact, wormholes that could permit travel in both directions. This obviously bolstered my hopes of returning back to Erika.

"Basically, that is correct," Merlin responded. "Schwarzschild wormholes, as they are known on Earth, allow travel in only one direction. This information was top secret. One of my less-publicized functions was to create a series of these one-way wormholes that could exist on Earth and Evion. It was a safeguard system and protect wormholes from being used by the wrong elements, so to speak."

"What would happen if a person used one of these wormholes? Would he or she be eternally stuck on Earth or Evion?" I inquired.

"Yes and no," Merlin responded.

Since I looked dumbfounded and didn't respond, Merlin continued. "You see, these one-way wormholes were designed to transport a person from Evion to another universe or dimension, but not Earth. So the person would be stuck there—wherever there was—but not necessarily back on Earth."

"So you are saying that there are really more than two universes that exist besides Zero and the Earth Universe?"

"I'm guessing Enoch explained the multi-dimensional principle when he told you about Universe Zero?"

"No. I think I would remember that conversation."

"Well, maybe it's best to keep it simple, especially for a person who has just learned he belongs to another universe. If you will indulge me, I will give you the *Reader's Digest* version of the theory." He sighed and continued. "During the time of the big bang, eternal inflation occurred. Space and time expanded at different rates. This created pockets—bubbles in space, if you will. These multiple pockets broke away and became separate universes, each with its own laws of physics," Merlin explained.

"Incredible!" I said. "Do we know how many of these dimensions actually exist?"

"No, because each of these bubbles could eventually spawn its own big bangs. An infinite number of pockets could be created from eternal inflations."

"So, basically, if a person went through one of these one-way wormholes, the chances of finding him or knowing what universe he'd ended up in would be virtually impossible."

Merlin nodded.

"I guess the writers at the Fox Network were unknowingly onto something when they created the *Mallory* and *Professor Arturo* characters," I mumbled under my breath.

"What was that?" Merlin asked.

"Nothing. I was just thinking about some television show I watched on Earth in the late 1990s. Anyway, you mentioned you also worked on wormholes that functioned in both directions."

"Yes, these wormholes, known as Lorentzian wormholes, are traversable both ways. In other words, they allow travel back and forth from the universes in both directions."

"Since I ended up here, I am assuming you were successful."

Merlin indulged me anyway, "Yes, we were very successful—maybe too successful. With the combination of my magic and scientific technology, we were able to author a stone that could amplify the signal of the wormhole, making it more stalwart."

"Where were these wormholes opened back on Earth?"

"It's been a while since I've been involved with the project, but if memory serves me correctly, one wormhole was located in the Caribbean, in an area sometimes referred to as the Bermuda Triangle. The other, which I was rumored to be associated with, was built in England at Stonehenge."

"So why can't I just go through one of these wormholes and get back to Earth?"

Merlin patiently explained, "It's not that simple. Once you die on Earth and transmute to this universe, whichever wormhole you transmuted through saves a blueprint of your atoms. If you don't return through that same portal, your atoms can become scrambled and destabilize when you travel through another gateway."

"So I just need to find out which wormhole I originally traveled through and use the same portal, right?"

"Theoretically. But how would you know which wormhole you came through? I know of only two, but I can't be sure there aren't other wormholes used in the transmuting process. It is possible you may have come through a wormhole that I am not aware of."

"That's easy. I'll just ask Enoch or Brace which wormhole I came through. They should know, right?"

"Did they actually travel with you through the wormhole? Or did they meet you in the Nether Region?"

I thought for a moment. Merlin was right. I had no idea how I got to Evion and didn't remember which wormhole I came through, let alone even transmuting through a particular wormhole. Chances were they wouldn't know which wormhole I came through either.

"Even if they were with you, wormholes tend to shift locations, so if you entered a wormhole in one location, there is no guarantee the same wormhole is still at that location. Another one could have shifted into its place," Merlin added.

"Is there any way at all to determine which wormhole I came through?"

"Well, there are certain magical devices that are able to pick up traces of a person's DNA and atoms that are emitted during the wormhole travel."

"How does it work?"

Merlin continued, "When a person travels through a wormhole, whether for transmutation or other reasons, a residual trace of the person remains. It is almost like leaving a trail of DNA breadcrumbs that can be followed later. There are certain necromantic and scientific devices capable of reading these breadcrumbs."

"What would one of these devices look like?" Jimmy asked.

"They are usually small artifacts, something that a person could easily hold in one hand. These magical devices tend to be very old. Many times they are found in pocket watches, rings, jewelry, and sometimes within compasses," Merlin stated.

Jimmy and I stared at each other. I pulled out the compass I had bought at the yard sale from Lucky Luciano and held it in front of Merlin. "Something like this?" I asked.

Everybody's got plans … until they get hit.

—Mike Tyson

Journal Entry 49

Of Mice and Men

Rutger knew Dr. Shelly would not be happy with his news. He was the good doctor's pride and joy. Rutger was the most successful cyborg built to date. He was trusted with all of the important jobs; Dr. Shelly had told him so. It was truly a rare occasion when he wasn't successful with an assignment.

He especially wanted to please Dr. Shelly because of his upcoming surgery. Some of his human parts were beginning to wear out and needed replacement. With all of the new recruits readily available, Dr. Shelly had promised Rutger some fresh new human parts.

Even though he knew the doctor would be disappointed with his news, Rutger always believed that honesty was the best policy. He dreaded making the call, but delaying the news and trying to cover it up would only make it worse. He had learned that lesson before, the hard way.

He took out his special smartphone, which allowed him to connect with the above world. These phones were one of the little projects developed at the Ministry of Science at the request of Mayor Tremball.

Anxiously he dialed and waited.

"Hello," a cool, icy voice said.

"Dr. Shelly, it's me, Rutger."

"Yes, Rutger. How are you?" Dr. Shelly nonchalantly responded.

"I'm afraid I couldn't stop them in time. Michael and Jimmy were able to cross the lake and get to Merlin," Rutger admitted.

Dr. Shelly shouted, "Tell me what happened!"

Rutger relayed the story, even mentioned that he had fired upon them on the lake to no avail.

For a brief second, Dr. Shelly paused and then said, "It's okay, Rutger. I'm sure you did all that you could. Things happen. Anyway, that's in the past. I want you to wait there and follow them on the way back. Keep me apprised of their movements."

"Do you want me to stop them from reaching the surface?"

"No, there have been some new developments, so do not harm them. Just make them a little uncomfortable. Make them feel that they are in danger, but do not kill them." And with that he disconnected the call.

Rutger thought to himself, *That wasn't so bad. Dr. Shelly seemed to be very understanding today and didn't appear to be angry.* After all, he didn't even want them killed. That was fine with Rutger. He didn't like killing. He was good at it, but for some reason, he just didn't fancy it too much.

Maybe some of the human parts he possessed were to blame for the occasional guilt he felt.

He would simply wait for Michael and Jimmy to row back across the lake and make sure he wouldn't miss them this time. Rutger would scare them a little, make them feel they were being followed, but wouldn't harm them. He'd just scare them a little, as the doctor had instructed.

***

Dr. Shelly took a deep breath and sighed. Maybe his cyborgs were not as advanced as he thought. How hard could it be to trail a human and an android companion and stop them from crossing a lake? One of his New Year's resolutions had been to control his anger—not get too mad at situations that didn't go exactly as planned. Maybe in hindsight the present situation was better anyway. Maybe he could even learn what Merlin had told his visitors.

No matter, that's what his research was all about— improving the product. He had to laugh—evolution at its finest, survival of the fittest. What would Mr. Darwin think? Would he even understand or be able to appreciate the grand scale of his work? After all, this work was a little more advanced than playing with finches and giant tortoises on the Galapagos Islands, wasn't it?

The doctor liked being in control and having all the power. Knowledge was power, and he wanted to know what Michael Cardazia wanted with Merlin. He had some guesses, but it made sense to be sure. Although he didn't know the great wizard personally, he had done some research on him. Dr. Shelly made it a priority to become familiar with anyone on Evion who had any power or could be a potential threat.

Maybe he was just being paranoid. From all that he had read, Merlin almost never got involved in the affairs of the surface dwellers of Evion. Still, the doctor wasn't a risk taker unless the odds were completely in his favor. Finding out what Cardazia was up to would increase his knowledge, and therefore the odds. Improving the odds made him feel better about taking risks.

If Merlin was going to get involved in disrupting his research, he would definitely be a very powerful adversary. The doctor would require extensive resources to deal with this problem. On the other hand, if this meeting had nothing to do with his work, then he wouldn't bother interfering.

It was instinct, or maybe just experience, that told him to check it out, to be safe. Besides, Dr. Victor Shelly hadn't managed to live a few generations past the normal life span by leaving stones unturned. He made sure that nothing was left to chance, and every detail was carefully planned for.

If by some small chance, he found out that Jimmy, Michael, or Merlin was interfering in his operation, then that interloper would be eliminated. Having the unwavering support of the mayor did have its advantages, even if the mayor was an idiot and not aware of what was going on right under his big, fat nose and ever-expanding waistline.

I poured a compass into my coffee, to
give the flavor some direction.

—Jarod Kintz

Journal Entry 50

Compass

Merlin took the compass from my hand and studied it.
"Where exactly did you say you acquired this compass?"
he asked.

"I didn't say. I bought this piece from a merchant at a sale
during Carnival," I replied.

For a moment, the compass appeared to look like a pocket
watch. I suddenly remembered why the compass/pocket
watch seemed so familiar. Mr. Jacque, the former janitor
at Above it All Academy had owned a pocket watch that
was very similar.

"This compass is indeed enchanted. In a much earlier
time, it was once known as Caliburn," Merlin said.

"So you are familiar with this device?"

"Yes. It was forged long ago on Earth. An old friend
of mine was once in possession of Caliburn. It was in
a different form back then, but I would recognize her
anywhere."

"What can Caliburn do?"

"She is a number of different things. She can be a sword or a compass. She can also be a watch or a shield at other times."

"You keep referring to it as a woman?"

"Yes. Caliburn is enchanted and carries with her the spirit of the Lady of the Lake."

"The Lady of the Lake! Of course, now I understand."

Merlin smiled. "You don't know who she was, do you?"

"Not really. I'm sorry, but my knowledge of Arthurian legends is lacking in some details."

"She—that is, the Lady of the Lake—was sometimes referred to as Viviane or Nimue. I taught her all the magic I knew. Unfortunately, power often corrupts, as it is both a blessing and a curse. Viviane could not handle the immense responsibility of her new powers. She was stripped of most of her magic and sentenced to spend eternity as Caliburn."

"That really is fascinating, but I still don't see how this helps me."

"While it is true that Viviane became corrupted, it is also true that she had a good heart. She always believed in true love. Michael, if your love is true and your cause just enough, Caliburn may be able and willing to help you in your quest."

With a renewed sense of hope, I implored him to continue.

"I'm not sure who this Lucky person is or how he obtained Caliburn, but you are in possession of her. She might listen to you."

"Please go on."

"Caliburn is no ordinary compass. She doesn't point toward true magnetic north; rather, she points toward true love. She might be able to determine which wormhole you came through."

"Does she pick up leftover DNA or traces of atoms left from transmuting?"

Merlin laughed. "Of course not. She is not scientific— she's magical! She can pick up on psychic energy. Caliburn might be able to sense what wormhole you transmuted through because of your longing for Erika. If your love is true and your sense of loss is real, she might be able to sense those strong emotions."

"How do I get her to work?"

"It's really simple. You stand straight up with your legs together, click your heels, and say out loud 'There's no place like home' three times."

"Okay, does it matter what direction I face when I imitate Dorothy?"

Merlin chuckled. "Of course not, but I have always wanted to say those words and I couldn't resist. *The Wizard of Oz* was always one of my favorite American movies—and highly underrated, if you ask me."

"Right, I knew that," I said somewhat embarrassed, because I had half believed him. "I meant about the joking part, not that you loved the movie, because I wouldn't know what movies you liked. So what can I do to get her to work?"

"You can't do anything. Caliburn picks the one she will work for."

"Can you give me any ideas about how to maybe persuade her? You know, get on her good side?"

"Sadly, no. That is part of the deal. I cannot give you any advice about how to use her."

"Why not?"

"Even great wizards have their limitations. There are just some things I am not permitted to interfere with."

"Okay. How will I know?"

"Trust me, you will know."

You don't really suppose, do you, that all your adventures and escapades were managed by mere luck, just for your sole benefit. You are a very fine person, Mr. Baggins, and I am very fond of you; but you are only quite a little fellow in a wide world after all!

—J. R. R. Tolkien

Journal Entry 51

There and Back Again

We shared one last feast before Jimmy and I were to go back to the surface. Merlin told us he rarely left The Trades for the surface world. The mythical wizard gave me a map that would help me find the two wormholes that he knew previously existed when he worked on them. He warned me there might be others that he was unaware of.

Merlin could not tell me whether the wormholes would be guarded or accessible. He could not tell me how to use Caliburn, only that I would know when—if—she worked. He could not even assure me that, if I found the correct wormhole, the gateway would allow me to transmute back to Earth.

Even with all of this uncertainty, I felt that there was at least some measure of hope. Merlin had proven to be a valuable friend and a fine host. Though I sensed he was holding back something and he had more power than I had been led to believe, I still appreciated his advice and hospitality. I had a strange feeling he would be of great help in the future.

Calygreyhound and Freybug escorted us back down the rocky walkway surrounding the castle. They playfully ran up and down the beach when we reached the shoreline. They reminded me of two extremely large puppies playing on the beach. The two big pups seemed especially fond of Jimmy as they rolled around in the colored sand together for one last time. They even seemed to have formed an attachment to me, constantly looking for me to pet them or play with them. I guess my animal magnetism extended to Evion as well.

Finally, it was time to say farewell, and they both extended their paws to shake my hand good-bye. Jimmy and I boarded our small boat and paddled back across the lake. Merlin had given each of us cloaks of invisibility to wear once we reached the shoreline on the other side of the lake.

It turned out we needed the cloaks. A big cyborg-type fellow was patrolling the shoreline, obviously looking for something or someone. My guess was he was the same guy who had originally followed us and fired his weapon at us when we were on the lake. We were able to dock and camouflage the boat before the cyborg could see it.

With the invisibility cloaks, we were able to get close enough to the cyborg for Jimmy to ID him. His name was Rutger. Jimmy didn't know him well, but knew he was an assistant at Dr. Shelly's lab.

"Why would Dr. Shelly have one of his assistants tailing us?" I whispered to Jimmy.

"I'm not sure, but it might have something to do with the mumblings about his rumored secretive project."

"What have you heard about this project?"

"Not a lot. It is highly clandestine. No one outside of a select group is supposed to know about it. I do know some people who have been on the fourth and fifth floors. Whatever they are doing, Dr. Shelly has the support of someone high up in the city government."

"Maybe it has something to do with my neighbor, Elvis. He approached me asking for my help. I'm probably not supposed to tell you this, but I trust you, Jimmy. Elvis told me he suspected that something illegal was going on and asked for my help. He wants me to do some spying in the Science Ministry."

"What did you tell him?"

"I turned him down. To be more precise, I said probably not, but I would take some time and mull over the idea before I let him know for sure. My focus was to get back to Earth—back to Erika—and I didn't want to do anything to potentially jeopardize that."

***

Rutgers' phone rang. Dr. Shelly was on the other line. "Did they return yet?" he asked.

"No, sir. I have not left my post, and I haven't seen any trace of them," Rutger replied.

"Did you ever think maybe they had an invisibility cloak and slipped by you? After all, they had just come from visiting a powerful wizard!"

Rutger hadn't thought of that. He remained speechless.

"Never mind. They have been spotted back on The Rails. Pack up and head back," Dr. Shelly ordered. There was a click and the phone went silent.

Rutger wondered how Dr. Shelly knew they had bypassed him and were back on The Rails. Maybe he had other cyborgs working on this project besides himself. Maybe he wasn't as invaluable to the doctor as he had thought. Rutger decided not to feel so dejected. He would find some way to redeem himself to the good doctor and prove that he was a valuable asset. The right opportunity would arise, and he would take advantage of it.

When choosing between two evils, I always
like to try the one I've never tried before.

—Mae West

Journal Entry 52

Caliburn Chooses

This time there were no delays or problems on The Rails.
By the time we returned, Carnival was finished. There
were no vendors or sellers. What had been a festive
atmosphere had been replaced with a dark, damp, desolate
concrete block reeking of desperation and hopelessness.

The air once again became damp and cool. The lovely,
pleasant scent that had first infected me when I entered
The Trades did not seem to be as strong. Instead, a
malodorous scent replaced the memories of the beach
and warm sand. I smelled the garbage, refuse, and rotting
food that had been present but previously camouflaged.

Maybe I was used to the seduction of The Trades by now.
Perhaps there had been something in Merlin's food that
now help me see things the way they really were down
here in the depths of the city.

Jimmy pulled out the enchanted map. It led us to the
doorway leading out of The Trades to the surface above.
When we reached the doorway, the map transformed, as
it had done previously, into a key. The jewel-plated door
opened, and we ascended to the streets above.

As we exited the building and walked onto the sidewalk, Suzie was there waiting for us. "Hi, Jimmy. Hi, Michael," Suzie blurted out.

"How did you know when we would return?" I asked.

"I've been monitoring you two since you left Merlin's. Kind of a personal GPS monitoring system using the chip in your IDs."

"I asked her to keep track of us, just in case," Jimmy clarified.

"Good thinking," I added.

Before long, we were parked in front of my apartment building.

"I don't know how to thank you for all of your help," I said to Jimmy.

"You're welcome. I have come to learn that friends help each other."

"Indeed. If you ever need anything, I'll be there for you, Jimmy."

"You never know. I just might take you up on that one day."

"I'll see you two soon," I yelled as Suzie pulled away.

I had asked Elias to take care of my mail, what little of it there was, while I was down in The Trades with Jimmy. I knocked on his door. I heard a voice telling me to come in. Elias was sitting on his couch watching an old film, *The Sword and the Stone.*

The sense of irony was not lost on me for a number of reasons. First, the film was released the year I was born. I must have read that tidbit somewhere. It was the last animated feature released while Elias—Walt Disney—was back on Earth. Lastly, because of its subject matter, I found it a little too coincidental.

"Interesting choice of films," I mentioned.

"You think so?" Elias said with a sheepish grin.

I wondered if Elias knew about Merlin's real existence. I wondered if he knew more than he let on at times. I wondered why I was being so introspective, so I quickly moved on. "I appreciate you getting my mail while I was away," I said.

"Maybe sometime you can tell me all about your little adventure. I might not be Mr. Disney here on Evion, but I still enjoy stories, especially when they involve magic."

I looked at him a little flabbergasted. *How could he have known?* He must have sensed this, because he changed the subject. "Anytime you need help just give a holler. By the way, I almost forgot. Elvis was looking for you."

I left Elias's apartment, walked down the hall, and knocked on apartment 108. The man who was once referred to as The King back on Earth answered the door. "Come in, Michael. I've been looking for you."

"Yes, Elias told me. That's why I'm here."

"I know what you said before, but I think the situation is getting worse. Something wrong is definitely going on at the Ministry of Science."

"Okay," I suggested, "just go in and arrest them or whatever the ASAP does here."

"It doesn't work that way. That Ministry is one of the more politically protected ministries. Without some documented proof, there isn't anything I can do."

"I'd love to help you, really I would. I just can't take the chance right now."

"But, Michael, you are our best hope of getting some actual proof."

I remained steadfast. "I know. I'm sorry, but I just can't."

Then something very strange happened. In my pocket Caliburn became warm. The ancient enchanted device leapt out of my pocket, landed on the floor, and rolled toward Elvis. She was glowing. When he picked up Caliburn, she began changing colors. I would almost swear she was cooing. I'm not sure how I knew, but I knew for sure that Elvis was her master, not I.

Merlin's words burned in my ear: "Trust me, you will know."

Actually, I'm an overnight success,
but it took twenty years.

—Monty Hall

Journal Entry 53

Let's Make a Deal

"What is this?" Elvis asked.

"'This' is a 'she'," I replied. "Supposedly the spirit of the Lady of the Lake is embodied within that compass."

"Michael, what are you talking about?"

I wasn't sure what would be prudent to tell Press about my escapades with Jimmy and Merlin, but decided to tell him about The Trades and Lucky Luciano. I left out the part about Merlin, at least for now. I did mention Dr. Shelly and Rutgers in my account of what happened down in The Trades. Elvis shook his head at the mention of those two names. After I told Elvis everything about those events that I thought was appropriate, he sat down.

"Okay, so how does Caliburn, I think you called her, work?" Elvis asked.

"Well, I guess I really don't know. Up until now, I thought she was my device, but based upon her reaction, I think she is meant for you."

"How do you know that?"

"Just call it a hunch."

"Then what can Caliburn do, and how do we get her to work?"

"Maybe it has something to do with the colors."

"What colors?"

"When she rolled out of my pocket toward you, I noticed flashing colors. Maybe the color changes indicate something."

"Since you seem to think that I am her master, maybe I should try something."

I nodded in agreement.

"I can ask her a series of questions for which I know the answers. I'll keep the questions to yes or no responses so we can observe the color changes, if any," Elvis suggested. He held up the compass and addressed her. "Caliburn, are we on the planet Earth?"

Caliburn flashed the color red.

"Are we on the planet Rigel?" I asked.

Again, Caliburn flashed the color red.

I looked at Elvis. "So, if your theory is correct, the color red indicates a negative response," I said.

Elvis nodded yes and again addressed the compass. "Are we on the planet Evion?" he asked.

Caliburn turned blue.

"Is my name Elvis?"

Again, she turned blue.

"Okay, so red means no and blue means yes," I assumed.

"Let's see what happens if we ask a question that Caliburn can't answer with a yes or a no," Elvis said. "What is the name of the Mayor of Andorra?" Elvis asked.

Caliburn turned white.

"What was the name of Elvis' first number one pop hit song?" I questioned.

Again, Caliburn turned white.

"It was "Heartbreak Hotel," wasn't it?" I asked Elvis.

Elvis seemed to reminisce. He smiled as he nodded.

"So we know that red means no, blue means yes, and white means she can't answer or doesn't know," I recapped.

"You mentioned earlier that Caliburn could transform into a number of different devices. We should figure out how that works," Elvis proposed.

"Good idea. Let me try something." I addressed Caliburn. "How do we get you to turn into a different device?"

She turned white.

I thought for a moment. "That wasn't a yes or no question. Is there a way for you to change from one device to another?" I rephrased.

This time she turned blue indicating yes.

"Is there a button or a knob we push?" Elvis asked.

This time the color red appeared.

"No. Well, she is enchanted. Maybe there is a magical word or phrase we have to say," I said to Elvis.

Caliburn turned blue.

"Abracadabra," Elvis blurted out.

She turned red.

"I think I have an idea. Do you have access to the Internet?" I asked Elvis.

"The what?" Press asked somewhat perplexed.

I had forgotten that Elvis had transmuted in 1977, before the Internet was widely used.

"Do you have a way to access information on the computer?"

"Yes, there is an online data information accessing system available, but here we call it the interweb," he said. He logged on, and I typed in a search for Arthurian words. A list of words associated with Arthurian legend appeared on the screen.

Elvis looked at the screen with curiosity. "Interesting. Why did you choose that search?" he asked.

"Just another hunch," I said. "Let me try something."

I held Caliburn and said, "*Wynebgwrthucher.*"

Nothing happened. I remembered Merlin's words: "Trust me. You will know."

"You try," I suggested to Elvis.

He held Caliburn and said, "Wynebgwrthucher." Almost instantly, Caliburn transformed from a golden compass to a medieval shield. The shield was divided into four sections. The top two sections were made up of red and blue squares with three lions and crowns. The bottom sections were long blue and red triangles with the same pattern.

"This is cool," Elvis said with a chortle.

"I know! Let's try one more thing," I added. "Try the word *Carnwennan.*"

Elvis spoke the word, and Caliburn changed from a shield to a dagger.

"Okay, I think I understand now," I said.

Elvis looked at me. "Please elaborate."

"Caliburn is an enchanted artifact. Furthermore, she was forged during the time of Camelot. She responds only to words used during that time period. For example,

423

Wynebgwrthucher was King Arthur's shield, and Carnwennan was his dagger."

"Good job, Michael! So Caliburn responds only to words associated with the Arthurian legend."

I nodded.

"And she changes form only if her master utters those terms."

"Yes, I think that's right," I responded.

"Caliburn, can you help Michael find his way back to Erika?"

The mythical device blinked blue.

Elvis pondered for a moment. Then he attempted his best Marlon Brando Godfather imitation. Turning to me, he said, "Okay, Michael, I've got a deal for you that you can't refuse."

It's the loose ends in which men hang themselves.

—Zelda Fitzgerald

Journal Entry 54

Loose Ends

Dr. Reed had taken care of one major headache, Erika Nirvona. However, there were still two problems to deal with. Granted, each was less of a liability than Ms. Nirvona had been, but each still needed to be dealt with. Even though Michael Cardazia and Erika Nirvona were no longer on Earth, Captain Rita Denton and Agent James—Jimbo—Dubay had helped them escape, and they needed to pay for their indiscretions.

Killing them would be easiest, but like Dr. Shelly, Dr. Reed abhorred waste. Dr. Shelly could use them for his research, killing two birds with one stone, just like the old adage. Captain Denton and Agent Dubay would be removed and, as an added bonus, their eventual deaths would improve humankind's knowledge of science; once again, a win-win scenario.

Of course, getting them would take a little more ingenuity than had been necessary for Ms. Nirvona's capture. It wasn't as if he could make up a story about having some additional information on Michael Cardazia to lure them in. Eliminating those two would take a little planning, but it was necessary. Dr. Reed decided it would be more logical to deal with the two problems individually. "Jimbo"—what kind of a redneck backward name was that anyway?—would be dealt with first.

The intelligence information had come back on Agent Dubay and Captain Denton. Giles was not cheap but he had proven to be an excellent private investigator. Besides, money was not usually a problem for Dr. Reed, especially after working with Dr. Shelly all these years.

Agent James Dubay—aka Jimbo—worked for the OSO (Office of Strategic Operations), long thought to be defunct by the general public and many in the government. His wife and parents were killed in Louisiana during a hurricane, and he never remarried. His two daughters lived with him, but they often spent time with his in-laws while he was away on a mission.

Jimbo owned a small restaurant known as the Waffle House, but this was mostly a front. Dr. Reed concluded that the restaurant would afford the best opportunity to get the agent. Giles had tailed him and established his work schedule at the restaurant. Dr. Reed would leave it up to Günter to pick the appropriate time.

Captain Denton presented a more difficult situation. She worked at 300 E. Street SW, NASA's main headquarters in Washington DC. The southwest quadrant, often referred to by locals as The Neighborhood, was the smallest section of DC. Giles' report confirmed she had met with CIA officials on a number of occasions, but her relationship with them was not clear.

Captain Rita Denton was being protected, Giles was fairly sure of it. Two men wearing dark-blue pants, white shirts, dark ties, dark-blue jackets, and tinted sunglasses were often in her background. This screamed FBI. Giles wasn't sure how the FBI had gotten involved, but it was clear that she needed to be taken care of very soon.

The NASA building was laden with security making it a poor choice for the abduction, though there was one promising opportunity. Captain Denton usually ate her lunch nearby at the United States Botanical Gardens (USBG) on Mondays. With just a little under one million visitors a year, the USBG offered a crowded atmosphere in which someone could simply disappear. A simple distraction would be needed to interrupt the G-men's concentration, but that could easily be arranged.

Günter finished his piña colada just as the truck arrived at the processing center. The group of people in the truck was especially satisfying to him. It was always satisfying when a plan was laid out and executed with efficiency. As an added bonus, there were two very special persons in this new batch of vagabonds.

***

Captain Rita Denton awoke and quickly scanned her surroundings. The others, mostly people who looked destitute, were beginning to regain consciousness. Jimbo was also there. He appeared to be the last to regain alertness. Apparently, whatever drug they used had affected people differently.

It didn't matter anyway, as long as he would be able keep up with her at the appropriate time. It appeared they were in some large processing factory, but its location was unknown to her. How long they had been unconscious was another unknown variable. They were in a large room with no windows. There was only one entrance, and it was protected by a steel-plated door. Rita gagged just a little bit, as this room reeked of urine, feces, and a helping of vomit for good measure.

The steel door creaked open, and five guards armed with automatic weapons walked in. A short, bald man with thick bottle glasses followed the guards. The man said his name was Günter. He seemed somewhat nervous and was holding a piece of paper. "Excuse me," he began. "I've been asked to read this to you." He cleared his throat and continued, "I know you all must be confused and a little scared. Rest assured that the contribution you will shortly make will greatly enhance our knowledge of science. Those of you wearing a blue bracelet will be staying here on Earth …"

The best leaks always take place in the urinals.

—John Cole

Journal Entry 55

Secret Agent Janitor

I was mopping the main hallway on the third floor of the Science Ministry. Although my primary function was to maintain the labs and hallway on the third floor, I also had access to the first and second floors.

I'd had no choice but to become a spy for Elvis. The former "King of Rock 'n' Roll" had promised to use Caliburn to help me find my wormhole back to Earth if I helped him uncover what was transpiring on the fourth and fifth floors.

When he put it that way, the Godfather aside, how could I refuse? Besides, it really was the right thing to do. There was just one problem—I had no access to those floors. I would need help, but my options were limited. There was only one person I trusted and whom I thought might be able to assist.

The previous week, while cleaning one of the bathrooms next to the lab, I had overheard one of the lab technicians talking to a fellow tech about a rumor he had heard. I guess people tend not to pay much attention to general work staff, or maybe the bathrooms were not bugged, but whatever the reason, he felt free to speak openly. As I cleaned a urinal with a certain amount of professional indifference, I overheard ... "Yes, that's what I heard from a friend, who knows a guy, who knows an associate, who said that they were doing weird experiments on *people* on the fourth and fifth floors."

His companion said, in shock, "What?" And my information provider continued, "No, he didn't know the specifics and said it was better not to ask—hush, hush stuff, you know. I think the only reason he said anything was that he was drunk at the club and didn't realize what he was saying. Come to think of it, that guy never showed up for work the next day, and no one has heard from him since." The lab techs finally noticed me and stopped talking, nodding slightly as they passed me on their way out.

Now, a week later, I was meeting Jimmy and Elvis after work at Terra Firma. My plan was to ask Jimmy for help. Even if he had no idea how to help me, I had a strange feeling that maybe he could contact Merlin, who was a great wizard who knew all about Caliburn; surely he had some magic that would work. At least I hoped so. That was plan A. And I didn't have a plan B.

Jimmy was already there when I arrived. Rosalie, our newest and favorite waitress, was talking to Jimmy. Each time we saw her, her appearance was different. She told us it was "cool" to dress up as different historical women from Earth.

Today, she was dressed as—I think—Cleopatra. She wore a simple white sheath dress. It looked to be a rectangular piece of cloth folded once and sewn along the edge into sort of a tube. The dress extended from just above her breasts to just above her ankles, and it was held up by two thin shoulder straps. She was also wearing a shiny black wig that extended to her shoulder, and had accessorized her dress with a royal-looking beaded necklace laced with pearls. "Hey, Michael," she said as I sat down. "The usual?"

"Hi, Rosalie. Thanks. That would be great."

"You know," she continued, "this drink of yours has become very popular here since we introduced it. Maybe you should ask Roscoe for a kickback." We all laughed as Cleopatra went to take another order.

Jimmy asked, "Michael, I've been researching some Earth vernacular, and I think I am saying this correctly: So what's shaking, bacon?"

I laughed. "Yes, you have it right—but it's 'shakin', bacon!' And I think you have the time reference just a little bit out of whack. Anyway, I need to ask your help with a sensitive matter. I know I'll be asking a lot, but I don't have anyone else I trust."

"I appreciate your trust in me. Why don't you tell me what's going on, and maybe I can help."

Rosalie placed a piña colada in front of me and a special drink in front of Jimmy as well. "Is there anything else I can get for you two?"

I smiled. "No, thanks. That's good for now, but check back soon."

I quickly switched back to Jimmy. "Elvis is meeting us here soon, but I wanted to talk to you first. Apparently Caliburn has decided on Elvis as her master, at least for now. I never mentioned anything to do with Merlin, just that I purchased Caliburn at a yard sale from a guy named Lucky Luciano."

"What does Elvis have to do with all of this?" Jimmy asked.

"I think this information is classified. I'm not sure, but like I said, I completely trust you. He works for the ASAP. Have you heard of them?"

Jimmy nodded yes.

"Elvis asked me a little while back to do some espionage work for the ASAP. He said they had reason to believe that there were some ... let's just say highly questionable activities occurring on the fourth and fifth floors of the Science Ministry."

"What did you finally decide to tell him?"

"Initially, I was going to decline. I wanted to help, but couldn't risk getting in trouble and not being able to get back to Erika."

"So you declined. And I assume he was disappointed?"

Nodding yes, I continued, "That's when he first talked to me—just before I enlisted your help, and we went down to The Trades. When we returned, he asked to see me again to discuss if I had changed my mind, because he believed the situation was getting more critical."

"Did you change your mind after you told him no?"

"No. At least not at first. But that's when we discovered that Caliburn chose Elvis and not me. We discovered how to get her to work, or at least partially use her."

"I think I get it. He made you a deal. If you help him, he will help you, right?"

"Yes, especially after what I overheard in the bathroom at the Science Ministry."

"Well do tell! What was the hubbub?"

"Practicing again?" I asked. He nodded. I didn't want to mention that he needed more practice in coming up with more modern sayings. At least he was trying. "Well, these two lab technicians were talking about some rumor that one of them had overheard about experimenting on people or something to that affect. They were not sure, but they seemed a little appalled and stopped talking when they finally noticed me."

"Michael, I think I get it, but I'm not sure about—"

With that, Elvis walked in and sat down.

"Hello, Michael. Hi, Jimmy," he greeted us.

I turned to Jimmy and saw a look of concern in his eyes.

I've got you under my skin.
I've got you deep in the heart of me.
So deep in my heart that you're really a part of me.
I've got you under my skin.
I'd tried so not to give in.
I said to myself: this affair never will go so well.
But why should I try to resist when,
baby, I know so well
I've got you under my skin.

—Cole Porter

Journal Entry 56

Under My Skin

Günter sneered as he headed for the exit after he finished reading his obviously canned speech. He definitely seemed like the kind of creep who enjoyed his sadistic work, Agent James Dubay—aka Jimbo—thought to himself. The five armed gunmen followed, and the steel door slammed shut.

They stood scattered throughout the concrete-and-steel processing center. All the ragamuffins and vagabonds stood shaking and confused, all except for Captain Rita Denton and Jack Dubay.

Captain Denton motioned for Jimbo to walk over to her. There didn't seem to be any cameras or listening devices. As part of their arrogance, their captors—and the question was who were they?—felt this place to be inescapable and apparently hadn't set up any listening apparatus. Just to be on the safe side, Rita wanted to speak to James quietly.

"How are you feeling?" she whispered.

"A bit of a headache, but all things considered, not too bad."

"Where were you when they abducted you?"

"I was closing the Waffle House by myself, and this balding, beady-eyed guy walked in with two big thugs. I think it was the same jerk who just gave us that bogus speech. I pretended to put up a fight with the two thugs—made them think they could go a few rounds with me. After my acting job was complete, I purposely slowed down. Before I knew it, I felt a jab in my arm, and the next thing you know, I'm here. What about you?"

"I got the feeling over the past few weeks that someone was tailing me, so I started to follow a routine. Every Monday I would have lunch alone at the USBG. It's a nice spot for a kidnapping, you know—large crowds, plenty of rooms to get lost, so to speak," Rita replied.

"Do you think they have any idea?" Jimbo questioned.

Rita shook her head no. "It doesn't seem so. They might be bad people, but they didn't seem to be overly bright. We need to talk to everyone and make sure they are out of range when it blows."

"I'll let the gentlemen know that, once we are all out, you and I won't be much help. Maybe you could talk to the ladies. They should do their best to find shelter and hide until someone can rescue them," he added.

Rita touched her left arm and felt a lump just to the right side of the bicep muscle. The small capsule appeared to be securely in place. James focused his attention on the dorsal side of his right quadriceps muscle.

As an offshoot of the joint Vomit Commit program between NASA and the CIA, an experimental chemical lab had been established. The chemical engineers had developed a new form of explosive material consisting of two elements that could be stored safely and separately. When combined later, a powerful explosive would be created.

Francium (Fr), originally referred to as eka-caesium, was discovered at the very end of the 1930s. It was long thought to be a very reactive element, but little research was done on it because of its high radioactivity, relatively short half-life, and scarcity in nature. The chemical scientists at VC serendipitously discovered that its most stable isotope, Fr-223, could be isolated and purified. Furthermore, this solid isotope could be stored in a small vial.

The second main ingredient in this concoction was Astatine (At). Discovered in the 1940s shortly after the discovery of Francium, Astatine is also a very reactive element. Although At has a much longer half-life than Fr, it was also found to be highly radioactive and scarce in nature. The chemists at VC were also able to isolate and purify At-211, its most stable isotope. Again, this solid isotope could be stored within a small vial.

A small vial of Fr-223 had been planted subcutaneously in Captain Denton's upper left arm. Similarly, a vial of At-211 had been subcutaneously planted within James Dubay's right dorsal upper thigh. Both elements were in a solid state of matter. Once the two isotopes were combined, a wetting agent would be needed to start the exothermic reaction, and the explosion would follow.

The two captives calmly talked to each of the other captives and explained their plans. There was no reason to suspect the room was bugged. Nevertheless, they tried to give the appearance of having casual conversations with their imprisoned mates. It was a slow process, but time was not an issue, at least not now. Besides, their watches and cell phones had been removed; they had no way of knowing if it was day or night.

After feeling confident that each person understood what they were attempting to do, they were ready to begin. Captain Denton extended her left arm and curled it into an L position. With her right hand she made a claw with her recently grown fingernails and started to gouge the flesh in her left forearm. A small stream of liquid formed in her eyes, similar to the reaction one has when one bites into a jalapeño pepper or cuts a strong-smelling onion.

As she continued to carefully excavate, a pool of superficial blood welled up onto the surface of her skin. At first, some of the ladies gathered around with deadpan looks. However, as Captain Denton proceeded to pass through the thin *stratum corneum* of the epidermis layer, some of the women began to gag and turn away. With one final gouge, she reached her intended target. She extracted a small radioactively insulated vial of Fr-223. Denton quickly tore a small piece of clothing from her shirt and wrapped the bloodied but superficial wound.

Captain Denton wiped her brow, took a deep breath and turned to James Dubay. "Your turn."

"Great. That looked like so much fun, I can't wait."

"James, don't be such a big baby. I thought you OSO guys were trained to be tough."

"Yeah, guy tough, but not girl tough. That's a completely different ball game. I mean you girls are tougher than we are. Think about it, no guy could ever go through childbirth."

Rita laughed. "James, just shut up and lie down on your stomach."

Feeling as if she was about to give him a physical, Captain Denton barked, "Okay, drop the pants and let's have a look."

"Go easy on me. This is my first time, you know."

Using the un-bloodied nails of her left hand, she began to bore into the upper dorsal side of James' right leg. He began to wiggle and squirm.

"Stop moving so much! You're making it worse," she ordered.

"All right, Doc, I'll do my best."

She thought to herself, *Men are such babies*. It looked as if it was going to take a little longer to excavate James's insulated vial, but it had been decided that it was less likely to be detected if the "ingredients" were hidden in two completely different sections of their individual bodies. "Doctor Denton" continued to claw into his flesh. Small rivulets of superficial blood began to dribble down the back of James's upper thigh. Rita wasn't having much success. "I don't know about this, James. They must have buried it a little deeper in you. Maybe we should give it a rest for a minute."

He gritted his teeth and yelled, "No! I just think I have a tad more flesh than you. Let's just get this the hell over with."

"Okay, James, this last layer of *epidermal stratum granulosom*. Might hurt a bit."

"The last layer of what?" he asked before he yelped like a puppy and bit down into his fist.

When I was a kid my parents moved
a lot, but I always found them.

—Rodney Dangerfield

Journal Entry 57

Parents

"I invited Elvis to join us because I thought he might
be able to help us with any information the ASAP had
accumulated," I said to Jimmy.

Elvis looked familiarly at Jimmy. "I assume that Michael
told you about our arrangement."

"You two know each other?" I questioned.

"We've crossed paths before," Jimmy responded.

"You don't seem to like me very much," Elvis retorted.

"It's not you personally. I just don't agree with some of the
ASAP polices," Jimmy answered.

I impatiently interrupted, "Now that we have dispatched
with all the pleasantries, maybe the three of us can come
up with a viable plan."

Jimmy and Elvis looked around the bar trying not to
make eye contact with each other. Rosalie stopped by to
check on us.

"Hi, Elvis, what can I get you?"

He smiled at her. "The usual."

She gave Elvis a wink and scurried off.

I looked directly at Elvis as it occurred to me. "Really, you two? Anyway, I think we all need to trust each other if you want your information and I want to get home."

The three of us looked at each other and nodded.

"Okay, Elvis, what can you tell us?" I asked.

"Not much more than I told you before. There does seem to be an increase in activity, but my operatives have not been able to ascertain exactly what's going on."

I relayed to Elvis what I'd overheard in the lavatory.

"Michael, if that's true, then the situation is worse than we thought. We need to do something right away."

"You mean me. *I* have to do something now."

"We need to find a way for Michael to gain access to those two floors without getting caught," Jimmy cautioned.

Elvis didn't seem optimistic. "The access is strictly limited, and even if he could somehow circumvent the system and gain access, there would be cameras and surveillance monitoring those floors."

"Can Caliburn help in anyway?" I asked Elvis.

"No. I have already asked her. If our color code still is working, she has indicated that there is nothing she can do."

"Jimmy, do you have any ideas or know of anyone who might be able to help?" I asked.

"Well—"

"Come on, Jimmy, we said we would trust one another," I interjected.

"I think maybe Merlin could help."

"Who?" Elvis asked.

"Merlin the Great Wizard," Jimmy proudly stated.

"You mean he really exists? No way!"

"I guess there are things that even the ASAP doesn't know," Jimmy chirped.

"Anyway, could you contact him and ask for his help?" I asked.

"Yes, Michael, he and I are actually a bit closer than you realize."

"How close?" Elvis asked.

Jimmy casually replied, "Well, he is sort of my parent."

Elvis snickered.

"Go on," I said.

"Merlin is the one who created me."

If it weren't for my lawyer, I'd still be in prison.
It went a lot faster with two people digging.

—Joe Martin

Journal Entry 58

The Great Escape

With a final plunge, Rita final extracted the vial containing At-211 from James' blood-soaked thigh. She ripped a piece of cloth from his shirt and bandaged the wound as best she could.

"It's a shame you wasted your talents with NASA and spy stuff," James quipped. "You would have made a hell of an emergency room doctor."

"And you would have made a great standup comedian. Now shut up and help me."

Together, they made sure that everyone moved away from the steel door. They mixed together the solid contents of the two vials. A liquid agent would be necessary to start the chain reaction leading to the explosion. Fr-222 had a half-life of 4.8 minutes. Once the decay started, the combination of the wetting agent and At-211 would initiate the chain reaction, and an explosion strong enough to blow open the door.

"Okay, Doc, so what do we do about a wetting agent?"

"We will need some type of bodily fluids."

"I just gave blood last week."

"No, not blood."

He looked down.

She laughed. "Not that either."

"What then, spit?"

"Exactly. Saliva is about ninety-eight percent water. The other minor ingredients—glycoproteins, enzymes, and mucus—should not affect the reaction at all. In fact, the enzymes might actually help speed up the reaction time."

James sounded somewhat relieved. "Your spit or mine?"

"Well, James, since you are a little bit more winded than I, maybe you should have the honors."

"Whatever you say, Doc."

James spit into the vial and shook it slightly. Captain Denton took the vial and carefully poured the contents into the door lock.

"We should have five minutes, maybe less because of the enzymes, before it goes boom," Rita informed James.

Rita turned to the huddled people, "Once it blows wide open, everyone should scatter. Do the best you can to hide and find shelter. Hopefully, help will arrive soon, but we cannot make any promises."

James started counting down, "T minus four minutes fifty-nine seconds …"

"James!" Rita scolded.

"Sorry. I'll be more serious."

A few minutes elapsed, and nothing appeared to be happening.

"Are you sure your boys at VC got the recipe for that explosive right?"

"Theoretically, it should have worked."

"Theoretically, but?" James questioned.

"Laboratory conditions are not always the same as field conditions. According to our calculations it should have—"

There was a loud boom. Shards of the splinted steel door were shot throughout the room. The vagabonds covered their heads and ears as they huddled in the corners of the room. The blast knocked Rita a couple of feet backward.

Jimbo ran over to her. "Are you all right?"

"I think I twisted my right ankle, but I'll be fine. Let's get the hell out of here!"

Alarms started blaring. Everyone ran out of the room. At the end of the corridor they ran through a door that was, thankfully, unlocked. It led to the great outdoors. Within the immediate proximity, they could hear the sounds of Jeep engines and snapping twigs.

"I think we need to get moving, and real fast," James blurted.

"Right!" Rita interjected. "But I think we have other problems as well. Look up there!"

The reason women don't play football is because eleven of them would never wear the same outfit in public.

—Phyllis Diller

Journal Entry 59

The Game Plan

Elvis took a sip of his usual drink. "So there are things that our files didn't include. Maybe I need to our increase our intel budget."

"Merlin created you?" I asked Jimmy. "Why didn't you say anything before?"

"You never asked me."

"Of course I never asked you directly. Anyway, do you think he can help me?"

"Actually, I already contacted him, and I'm expecting an answer very soon."

Just then, one of Merlin's musicatto birds flew in and landed on Jimmy's arm. The bird was speaking, but the words were laced together in a cacophony of music and song. It was as if the birds had created a language made entirely of music and words. I was able to decipherer a fraction of the words, but Jimmy seemed to clearly understand every musical word.

"He says his name is Clayton, and he has instructions from Merlin."

Rosalie came back to the table to check on us. "Does anybody need ... Hey! Who's your cute little friend?"

"He is Clayton, an acquaintance of mine," Jimmy replied.

"Oh, okay. Just don't let him fly around too much. The last time something flew in here ... well, let's just say the boss had a little too much fun playing target practice."

Jimmy turned to Clayton as the bird let out a yelping sound. "Don't worry, you will be fine. Continue please."

Clayton continued to sing words for Jimmy as he nodded.

"He says Merlin has been apprised of the situation and thinks that he can help."

Jimmy reached inside the tiny pouch around Clayton's neck. He pulled out a small object, which slowly began to expand. It was a solid ring colored in a mixture of blue and gray tones interlaced with the image of white wispy clouds that appeared to be in constant motion.

"This is Merlin's ring, and it will provide you with a cloak of invisibility that is not detectable with current Evion surveillance equipment."

Elvis looked intently at the ring. "Is he serious?"

Jimmy ignored the comment. "Michael, put the ring on your finger."

He handed me the ring, and I placed it on my right middle finger.

"Hey, where did he go?" Elvis blurted out.

I could see everyone and everything in the room as clearly as I had before I put on the ring. Nothing appeared to have changed, except for the fact that I was invisible.

"Good," Jimmy stated. "The ring seems to be working fine."

I slipped off the ring.

"Wow!" Elvis exclaimed. "You know the boys at the lab would love to analyze the technology in that ring. If I could just—"

Jimmy frowned and gave the former rock 'n' roll king a dirty look that stopped his speech.

"Never mind. It was just a thought," Elvis mumbled.

"Okay, Jimmy, that still leaves us with one major problem," I said.

Once again, Clayton continued to speak his mellifluous language of song and words to Jimmy. Jimmy reached into Clayton's little bag and pulled out a small container full of a heliotrope-colored liquid. "These are magical eye drops. If you place two drops in each eye, they will change your appearance to be whomever you choose. All you have to do is concentrate or envision the person you wish to appear as. Anyone you are talking to will see you as that person.

"How long does the effect last?" Elvis asked.

"The time varies with each person based on body chemistry but, on average, two drops in each eye usually last around one hour," Jimmy replied.

"What about the voice?" I asked.

Jimmy seemed a little confused.

"Does my voice change along with my appearance?" I restated.

"I see what you mean. No, your voice remains your own. Only your looks will change, so it is best not to say much."

"Unless, of course, you are an impressionist. Maybe we should give it a trial run," Elvis added.

Jimmy looked at me. "That's actually not a bad idea, just to be sure. You are probably only going to get one chance at this. And by the way, what is an impressionist?"

"Never mind. It's Elvis trying to make a joke," I replied.

I placed two drops in each eye, concentrating as I did so. I visualized myself as tall and thin. My beard covered most of the creases and lines of stress on my face, the strain from a nation that I used to bear.

Rosalie stopped back at our table, "Hey, Abraham, how are you? Where did Michael go?"

"He had a personal issue and had to leave abruptly, but he said to say good-bye," Elvis answered.

"Oh, okay. Do you guys need anything else?"

"No, we are set," I responded.

"You sound a little different, Abe. Is everything okay?" Rosalie inquired.

"Yes. I have a bit of a sore throat from my performance last week. I'm used to giving speeches, but not so much at making jokes and doing impressions."

"I'm sure you'll get used to it," she said. "Actually, from what I heard, most people liked your act. They found it refreshing and different from the typical old Andorran jokes."

I nodded to acknowledge the compliment as Rosalie went to service another table.

One final time, Clayton musically communicated something to Jimmy. Jimmy once again reached into the pouch, this time pulling out a tiny box, which expanded slightly.

"Clayton said this box is to be opened and used only in the case of extreme emergency. Merlin says that, when the time is right, you will know to use it. He has faith in you."

I turned to Jimmy and Elvis. "Gentlemen, I think we've got a plan."

All right, if the sky is falling why
doesn't it hit me in the head?

— Steve Bench, Ron J. Friedman,
and Ron Anderson

Journal Entry 60

The Sky Is Falling?

Henny Penny was in the woods one day when an acorn
fell on her head. It scared her so much she trembled all
over. She shook so hard, half her feathers fell out. Henny
Penny yelled out, "Help! Help! The sky is falling!"

Captain Rita Denton thought about her favorite childhood
story as she peered up into the sun-drenched sky. No, the
sky wasn't falling, but it might as well have been. She
squinted, rubbed her eyes, and shook her head in disbelief.
There were small monkeys flying toward them.

"Damn, those squirrel monkeys are flying straight for us!"
Jimbo yelled out.

"We need to get close to the shoreline so the agency can
pick up our signal," Rita replied.

Before being captured in DC, Captain Rita Denton
and Agent James Dubay had received injections of a
tracer solution that now flowed in their blood streams.
The protein signal was designed to last one month. This
biological signal had been designed to be located by
satellite anywhere on Earth. However, the heavy foliage
of the tropical forest was distorting and blocking the

signal. For the signal to be most effective, they needed to be near the shoreline. This would make them more vulnerable to attack by those flying monkeys, but they had no other choice.

James also looked up at the sky. The monkeys, of course, reminded him of the scene from *The Wizard of Oz* that had been terrorizing children for years. However, these monkeys appeared to be different from those in the movie. They had been modified with machine parts. *Damn, android or cyborg monkeys*, he thought. *What the hell else have these sick bastards experimented with?*

Rita pulled on his arm. "We need to traverse the jungle and begin to make our way to the shoreline."

"Those flying monkey things—whatever they are—look mean," he said.

"I know, but the trees are copious and thick. They should provide a level of protection for us from an aerial attack."

With perfect timing, one of the monkeys landed on the a few feet from them—close enough for them to read the words on its collar: Cy-Monk 1211. Three wires ran from the collar into the back of its head. Part of the creature was synthetic. Both eyes had been replaced with glass lenses. The wings appeared to be artificial. One arm looked robotic, and each hand had been outfitted with razor-sharp claws.

The cy-monk started moving toward Rita and James. James bent down and picked up a large spherical rock. The monkey sprinted away at great speed, but James threw a fastball straight at it. The monkey turned just as the rock reached it, and the rock hit it squarely between its two ersatz eyes. Cy-Monk 1211 was injured and stunned, but not incapacitated.

"All-state pitcher in high school," James stated proudly.

Rita picked up a large stick and whacked the creature behind the head, dislodging the wires that ran from the collar to the back of its cranium. "Softball batting champ in college," she quipped back. That seemed to stop the cy-monk. It slumped to the ground with a gurgling sound as electrical sparks spouted from the disconnected wires. "We need to get moving before more cy-monks decide to join the party," she added.

"No arguments here."

They ran deeper into the canopy of tropical trees. They could see the flying cy-monks circling above through the periodic openings of the canopy.

"Do we know what direction the shoreline is, or are we just running randomly?" he asked.

Rita stopped running for a moment. "Let's see if I can remember my Girl Scout training. The moss usually grows thickest on the north side of a tree in the Northern Hemisphere because the sun is less direct there. For the same reason, I'm guessing there would be more sand and fewer trees in the southern portion of the island."

"How do you know we are still in the Northern Hemisphere and not the Southern Hemisphere?"

"Actually, I don't, but we have a fifty-fifty shot, and that's what my instincts tell me."

"I have learned to trust a woman's intuition, so I guess we head in the direction opposite the moss?"

"Yes, and hope we can avoid more of these cy-monks. We got lucky with the first one, but I think they can be quite nasty."

Rita and James started to walk in the opposite direction of the thickest portion of the moss on the tropical trees. With no water, the heat and humidity of this tropical area made it necessary to find the shoreline within forty-eight hours or dehydration would set in. They had no food, but that was much less of a concern.

As they forged further into the jungle, the canopy provided both shade and covering. They continued for about thirty minutes until they saw a brick shack in the middle of their path.

"What do you think that is for?" James pondered.

"Only one way to find out," she responded.

As they approached the building, a nauseating foul stench emanated from the property.

"Man, that smell is worse than any swamp back on a hot, humid Louisiana summer day down in the Bayou Country," James quipped purposely emphasizing a Southern accent for effect and to try to lighten the mood a bit.

The building was about twenty feet long and thirty feet wide. There were no windows and only one front door made of steel or some metal that was beginning to show the signs of weathering.

"How are we supposed to get in?" James asked.

"We could try turning the handle. Maybe it's not locked."

"Seriously, you expect them to leave the door unlocked?"

Rita turned the handle and pushed the door open. "Men! They always make things more complicated than they need to be." She smiled and mumbled something about Occam's razor.

As they entered the strange house, their faces turned ashen. It was like a sepulcher. Dead bodies were hung by the ankles from wood beams that ran horizontally toward the rear of the building. There must have been twenty of them! Many of the bodies had putrefied and decayed to a point beyond recognition. Some were infested with maggots and worms.

The stench intensified as they searched the room. James began to dry heave, as there was little in his stomach to get rid of.

"Be careful, James. You don't want to lose any more water. Maybe you should wait outside."

"Sorry. I'll be fine. Besides I don't think there's much left in there to lose anyway."

A twisted and distorted look of horror was frozen on the faces of the corpses that had not yet decayed. Among the cadavers was evidence of missing body parts including eyes and arms. It was apparent these people had been used as unwilling organ and tissue donors or something even worse.

A large ash-colored cabinet was bolted to the left side wall. James opened the cabinet doors to reveal a smorgasbord of surgical instruments. Medical saws, scalpels, and other incising tools were labeled and carefully arranged on the metal shelves. It would have made a great set for the Saw movies except this wasn't a movie, he thought.

"Rita, what do you make of all this?"

"I'm not sure, but it looks like these people were being used for some kind of sick experimentation, possibly organ donation as well. I don't even want to think about any other possibilities."

"Whatever the reason, this place is really starting to give me the creeps. I think we should get moving toward the beach," he said.

"Of course you're right; we can always investigate further when we return with help."

A millipede scrambled across the floor. James was about to squash it but stopped.

"You know, you would have made a good Hindu," Rita remarked.

"A what? Why?"

"Never mind. Let's get moving."

They stepped outside and closed the rusting metal door.

"I think that we have company," Rita moaned.

"Well, I'll be a monkey's uncle," James replied.

At every party there are two kinds of people—those who want to go home and those who don't. The trouble is they are usually married to each other.

—Ann Landers

Journal Entry 62

Party Like It's …

Like most ingenious plans, at least initially, mine was relatively simple. I would get to know Dr. Shelly's schedule and then would impersonate him with a little help from Merlin's magic. He had unrestricted access to both the fourth and fifth floors, so no one would question his presence.

Unfortunately, Dr. Shelly was a workaholic. He seemed to work around the clock. However, a golden opportunity had presented itself. Next week was the Ministry of Sciences annual formal black-tie ball and fundraiser hosted by the city council. Mayor Tremball and his city council needed to raise funds for their scientific projects, which were being conducted on the second and third floors of the Ministry. The price of science was not cheap, and the taxpayers of Andorra could not be expected to foot the entire bill; most of it, but not all.

In an attempt to appease the citizens and voters, the mayor and city council decided to host a fundraiser at the Ministry of Science once a year. The city's most influential businessmen and affluent families were invited at a hefty cost per plate. Additionally, tours were given of the second and third floors in hopes of drumming up additional monetary pledges of support.

As a sign of camaraderie, all non-working employees were graciously expected to attend the affair. This applied not only to the medical personnel, scientists, and lab assistants, but also to the support staff such as the custodial engineers, including me.

There would be a number of guest political speakers along with the keynote speaker, Dr. Shelly himself. During Dr. Shelly's harangue, I planned to slip out, impersonate him, and do my best Sherlock Holmes impression. I estimated his speech would last for about twenty minutes. Figuring another ten minutes of questions and answers and a brief meet and greet afterward, I guesstimated I had an hour to investigate the fourth and fifth floors.

We were allowed to bring one guest, as stated in my invitation. Since I had no girlfriend and had made no attempt to meet anyone in Andorra, I decided to ask one of the guys. Taking Elvis would be a little suspicious, since he worked for ASAP. Similarly, Jimmy felt that bringing an android to one of these functions might raise some questions. Brace, Enoch, and Marilyn were off to Earth bringing in a new recruit. Abe was booked to perform his comedy at a local club that evening. This left only one choice—Elias. He affably agreed to accompany me to the benefit. Since most of the employees were bringing a guest, I figured I should as well.

Given his position as an emergency room doctor, he would naturally have an interest in science, which made for a perfect cover story if anyone inquired. Besides, having an accomplice might come in handy.

I was not a formal kind of guy and therefore had only two suits and a couple of ties back home. Obviously, I didn't own my own tuxedo as Elias did, so I had to rent one from Today's Essence. This store was similar to Today's Man on Earth, but it catered to beings with multiple appendages as well as two-armed and two-legged beings such as myself. I had to admit, I did look somewhat dashing in a tux.

After I picked up the tuxedo, Elvis and the scientists at ASAP made a slight modification to it. They replaced the top button of the shirt with a tiny digital camera that was virtually undetectable, even with advanced scanning equipment at the Science Ministry. The camera was equipped with an advanced form of Wi-Fi technology and would be activated when I blinked three consecutive times with my right eye.

I knocked on Elias's door precisely one hour before the start of the formal gala. He was going to drive us to the event. Previously, I had explained to him what I planned to do, in case he wanted to back out. I didn't want to risk getting him involved or creating trouble for him. I trusted him; I mean, if you couldn't trust the creator of Mickey Mouse, then who could you trust? It was probably safer to leave intricate details of the plan out until we were at the function.

He laughed, smiled, and said it sounded like a grand adventure, as only he could put it. It had been a while since he'd had any kind of excitement outside of the hospital, and he definitely wanted in on it.

We arrived at the Science Ministry just as the band began playing. The event was being catered in the Grand Room, which was located on the first floor. It could hold up to one thousand guests. The floor was made up of white gold tiles with mulberry emeralds interlaced in non-repetitive patterns. I could only imagine what these precious metals and gems would be worth on Earth.

The tables were octagon shaped, and names cards were already set out in an established seating arrangement. Employees of the Ministry paid for their own seats. Of course, none of the employees could afford the price, so the cost was generously deducted from their future pay. I estimated that it would take a mere thirty years to pay off my debt. That was fine with me, since I didn't plan on staying here that long. I was either going to make it back to Earth or die trying.

Gossamers' Wings were playing classical music as we entered the room. I wasn't familiar with the music, but it sounded like a cross between Beethoven and Mozart. A series of large rectangular tables laden with lavish foods was set against to the back wall.

One table contained seafood. Large lobster-like and crab-like crustaceans with exotic looking fish were beautifully displayed. A cornucopia of shellfish was placed in tiny ice sculptures that were carved into the shapes of local and flora and fauna.

Next to the seafood table was a table of savory delicacies such as cheeses and meats that were roasted, baked, broiled, and fried. There were times, especially now, when I really wished I was a vegetarian.

An entire table devoted to salads, fruits, and vegetables followed. Finally, the last table proffered a bounty of desserts. Cakes, pies, ice creams, and cookies were lavishly showcased. Cookies were Erika's favorite dessert. A wave of sadness enveloped me. I had to push it aside; I had a job to do. If I wanted to get back to Earth, I had to focus.

Sensing my momentary gloom, Elias tried to lighten the mood. "If this is just a pre-dinner spread, can you just imagine what the main courses must look like?"

Halfheartedly I smiled and said, "It really is too much food."

"What's the matter, Michael? Don't you like cookies?"

"They are fine. They just remind me of someone."

Elias seemed to understand and said reassuringly, "Maybe tonight will help you resolve that."

"I hope so."

"So what exactly is the plan?"

"After dinner, Dr. Shelly is scheduled to make his keynote speech. I am going to slip into the bathroom and apply the magical eye drops." (I had told him about Merlin's espionage kit.) "Between his speech and the question and answer session, I should have about an hour to investigate the upper floors."

"What can I do to help you?"

"Glad you asked. If for any reason Dr. Shelly leaves this room, and it looks as if he is going upstairs, push the button on this device." I handed him a tiny contraption that resembled a cell phone. I continued, "When this button is pressed, the top button on my shirt, which is also a miniature camera, will turn crimson and start to blink intermittently. This will let me know that the jig is up, so to speak, and I will have to get out of there."

Elias nodded.

I felt someone come up behind me, and heard a familiar voice ask, "What would you like for your main course? Personally, I would try the lobster and soft-shell crab steaks. I hear that they are exquisite this year."

I looked around. Our waitress, Rosalie, smiled and said, "Hello."

I'm not afraid of death; I just don't want
to be there when it happens.

—Woody Allen

When Dorothy looked up into the sky and saw the flying evil monkeys, she knew she wasn't in Kansas anymore. Similarly, Captain Rita Denton realized things were bad; in fact, she began to wish that she *was* in Kansas. *Anywhere but here*, she thought. They were surrounded by at least twenty cy-monks and, as if things weren't bad enough, there were also genetically and mechanically altered giant spiders that seemed to be forming a lively alliance with the cy-monks against them.

The spiders looked like very large tarantulas augmented with machine parts. Their mandibles had been replaced with sharp sickles, and their robotic legs were studded with metallic spikes that radiated outward. These cybernetic arachnids made clanking and hissing sounds as they moved closer.

"This is probably not good," James said.

"You think?" Rita replied sarcastically.

"Okay, what's the plan?"

"Plan? There is no plan. I didn't exactly anticipate this."

The cy-monks started to move even closer. They also seemed to be sending signals to the altered spiders, as the spiders seemed to follow the monkeys.

James scanned the area. There were some rocks and sticks piled near the house.

"We could hold them off for a little while," he said, pointing at the makeshift weaponry.

"Maybe for a few minutes, but I really don't think—"

James cut her off. "I think the cavalry is here!"

With a bit of irony, the people that she and James had rescued earlier—the discarded souls of society—were now running to rescue them.

"What the hell do you think you guys are doing? I told you to hide and wait for help!" Rita yelled.

One of the men, Xavier, replied, "Like hell! We are tired of being pushed around and being scared. If we are going to die, then we want it to be with purpose and dignity. Besides, it sure looks like you can use our help!"

James turned to Rita. "He does have a point."

She replied, "If the chief at VC gets wind of this ... On the other hand, this is kind of an emergency. Okay, everyone grab stones and sticks!"

There were ten men and five women besides Rita and James. Everyone picked up large stones and began throwing them at the approaching cy-monks and cy-spiders. A number of the rocks hit their intended targets. A few spiders started hissing and spitting out a green venomous liquid. They crawled in a circular pattern before collapsing.

The cy-monks were smarter and more agile, easily avoiding the incoming projectiles. One of the cybernetic simians called out. It sounded like a blend between simian and machine. The monkeys and remaining spiders began to retreat and reorganize.

"Great, the chimps seem to be much more highbrow than I thought," Rita said.

James looked confused. "Huh?"

"Smart. It means they're intelligent."

"Right. I knew that. We'd better become more highbrow ourselves before they attack again."

"If I could interrupt," Xavier said. "I have an idea. The one chimp making most of the noise seems to be the leader. If we could take him out, it might confuse the others and give us an opportunity to escape."

"That's worth a try," Rita responded. "But the lead cy-monk seems to be well protected, hanging toward the rear of the pack."

"Leave that to me. I was a marine during the Iraq war. Our unit had special tactical training," Xavier said.

"You are a veteran and living on the streets?" James asked.

"Let's just say our government doesn't always provide for people who have served our country. There is always some lobbyist persuading a senator or two to divert funds for this project or that project—funds that were originally slated to help veterans. Anyway, that's another story, and we need to focus now. I think I can sneak around their flank if the rest of you can distract the main group."

Rita turned to the group. "If the rest of us start making noise and throwing rocks at the main pack, maybe that will create enough confusion so Xavier can sneak around their flank and take out the main cy-monk."

A stream of the black cybernetic spiders started to advance on the group. Being a big Indiana Jones fan like most guys were, James quipped, "Spiders. Why'd it have to be spiders?"

"Very funny, James," said Rita. "But I think the movie line was about snakes, not spiders. Anyway, I think we need to get moving—now!"

Xavier sprinted off to the left of the army of approaching spiders. He wielded a large rock in his right hand and a thick stick in the other.

Rita, James, and the remaining fourteen homeless group members picked up rocks and started throwing them at the approaching black swarm. They yelled and screamed, creating as much noise as their dry vocal cords would allow.

Some of the projectiles hit their intended targets, but many spiders continued to advance. "Be careful," Rita instructed. "I think there is acid on the tips of their pinchers. Stay away from their pinchers!"

They picked up sticks and started stabbing at the arachnids. One of the homeless women slipped and was bitten. The area of dermis around the puncture began to immediately swell and turn green. She started convulsing, and a mauve-colored liquid spewed from her mouth. The others tried to reach her, but she was immediately overwhelmed with additional spiders. The cy-spiders started tearing her flesh apart. In only a few moments, her human form was no longer discernible. All that remained was a skeletal outline of a humanoid creature.

At this point, things got worse. After the spiders finished off the fallen woman, the cy-monks joined the fray and advance toward the group with the spiders. They were making primal cybernetic monkey sounds. Some of the cy-monks picked up rocks and sticks and hurled them at the party. Apparently, they were fast learners and copied the behavior they had seen the humans display.

Rita ordered everyone to form a close circle so they could protect each other. The cy-monks and cy-spiders began to close in on the small group. A number of the homeless people were bitten by the monkeys, but everyone was careful to avoid the acid-filled pincers of the spiders. The monkey bites were very painful, but at least they weren't poisonous. The monkeys' mouths might contain bacteria that could lead to infection, but that was still much better than the green deadly spider poison.

Led by Captain Rita Denton and Agent James Dubay, the small group of vagabonds fought relentlessly. The problem was that there were too many of the cybernetic creatures. As it is in every great story, it looked as if there was no hope.

James turned to Rita and said, "Well, it has been a pleasure working with you. I wanted to tell you that you remind of my late wife. She was also very brave."

"Thanks, James. I'm sure she was a great woman. But remember, it's always darkest before the dawn."

"Well, it's pretty dark, and the dawn is taking its sweet time getting here."

And then, as in every great story, something very strange happened. The cy-monks and cy-spiders stopped their attack. They began to look confused and disorganized. With this newfound luck, Rita ordered the survivors to head south toward the beach. James and the others followed Rita as a deluge of soothing rain fell.

> Be a first rate version of yourself, not a
> second rate version of someone else.

> —Judy Garland

Journal Entry 63

Impersonator

"Rosalie, what are you doing here?" I asked.

Rosalie laughed. "I'm here to help you guys."

Elias took a sip from his aperitif and inquired, "You work for Elvis, don't you?"

"Not so loud. You know there are ears everywhere."

Rosalie sat down at the table and continued in a low voice, "I do work for ASAP. My orders are to assist you two tonight."

"Geez, is everybody a spy here too? I know I'm supposed to be a spy," I said. "Elias, are you also a spy? Is that heavyset woman in that white mink a spy? Are there hidden cameras in the seafood?" I blurted out these questions too loudly.

Rosalie pointed to her ears. "Relax and take a chill pill! You are skitzin' out."

Sorry," I said in a lower register. "Are you?" I said to Elias.

"No, of course not," Elias replied.

"Michael, calm down," said Rosalie. "Elvis already informed me about your plan. I'm just here to help you. I'm not spying on you."

"Sorry. I guess I'm just a little nervous. I was never a spy before, just a science teacher and now a janitor. Maybe I overreacted."

"No worries," she replied.

"Hakuna matata," Elias said with a chortled.

"What?" Rosalie questioned.

"Never mind," I replied. "It's just a joke. It was a line from a movie. After all, he was Mr. Disney back on Earth."

"Okay, whatever," she responded. "I have to get back to pretending to be a waitress, but I'll keep my eyes and ears open in case I spot any trouble. If I do, I'll alert Elias, and he can signal you." She wrote something down on her waitress pad and went over to the next table.

I turned to Elias. "In a few minutes, Dr. Shelly should be making his keynote speech. When he begins to speak, I am going to the bathroom to apply the eye drops. If he leaves before I get back, signal me. Also, keep an eye on Rosalie."

"You don't trust her?"

"I'm not sure. I think I do, but it's better to play it safe."

The crowd started applauding as Dr. Shelly made his way to the stage.

As I was leaving, I could hear Dr. Shelly's icy voice. "Thank you all for coming to our little event. It only increases my resolve when I see so that many of you support our ventures."

I left the grand ballroom and made a left into the lavatory. It was empty, so I pulled out the magical eye drops and applied two drops to each eye. I concentrated on being Dr. Shelly. His icy voice echoed in my ears. I imagined being taller and tried to feel indifference for living beings. I put my head down and looked into the bathroom mirror. The image was not Dr. Shelly, but it wasn't me either; it was more like a blend between the two of us. Panic began to set in. It wasn't going to work. My plan was a wash. I felt forlorn; I had failed. I was just about to give up when I heard Jean's voice, "Things are not always what they seem, silly."

It then occurred to me that, since I knew who I really was, maybe I wouldn't see Dr. Shelly's image when I looked into a mirror. But those who didn't know who I was might see me as Dr. Shelly. There was only one way to find out. I walked out of the bathroom and headed straight for the transportation tube leading to the fourth floor. It was always guarded, day and night, twenty-four/seven. Well actually twenty/seven here.

As I approached the transportation tube, the guard looked at me with a funny expression. "You finished your speech already?" he asked.

I nodded.

"If I were you, I would still be in the Grand Room enjoying the food and the drinks, rather than going up to the fourth floor to do more work. But I guess that's why you are at the top of your field and I'm just a security guard."

I cleared my throat and coughed. I smiled and patted the security guard on the back as I walked past him into the transportation tube. He looked at me oddly. Maybe Dr. Shelly never patted him on the back. But he pushed some buttons, and I was swooshed upward.

Maybe it was because it was my first time in this tube, but my stomach felt a little uneasy. It was similar to the feeling one experiences when an elevator stops suddenly. When I reached the fourth floor, I stepped out of the tube, and my stomach felt normal again. I didn't vomit, which I always considered a good thing, unless I'd just swallowed some type of poison, but that usually didn't happen. So it was a good thing that I didn't vomit.

There seemed to be a skeleton crew working the floor. Most of the employees were probably attending the ball downstairs. I walked past a nurses' station. The head nurse looked quizzically at me but said hello. I nodded a quick greeting back at her.

Curiously, the floor was set up like a hospital ward. There were a few examination rooms, but most of the cubicles appeared to be patients' rooms. It seemed odd to me that there would be a hospital on the fourth floor of the Science Ministry, and even stranger that it would be treated as top secret. The image of Alice's Cheshire Cat popped into my mind.

As I walked down the hallway, an occasional orderly would smile or acknowledge my presence. There were a few surprised looks, but no one seemed to question me or my appearance.

All of the patients were sleeping or unconscious, which I thought was highly unusual, especially early in the evening. I walked into one patient's room to have a closer look. An IV drip was set up and positioned in her left wrist. There was a clipboard at the end of her bed. The paperwork listed her name Cherry, which sounded like a made-up stage name to me. Her hometown was Camden, New Jersey. She was twenty-five years old, five three, 110 pounds, blood type O$^+$, and her blood pressure was 110/80. There were a number of other vital statistics also listed. Surprisingly, the chart gave no indication as to her condition, considering she was unconscious in a hospital room.

As I continued to read her chart, my eyes were drawn to the words *organ donation* and *Cyborg Project*. Within my stomach, a pit formed, and I could feel the bile beginning to swell. A list of her organs was indicated for donation: right eye for Cyborg 235, left hand for Cyborg 178, right ear for …

I stopped reading the chart and placed it back on its hook. Swallowing back the remaining freshly formed bile, I walked uneasily into the hallway. One of the nurses passing by asked if I was all right. I nodded yes. She informed me the final release papers for the recent batch of recruits were on my desk ready for me to sign. I cleared my throat slightly and said, "Thank you. I'll get to them right away."

Immediately, I regretted talking, because my voice sounded like myself and not Dr. Shelly. The nurse looked at me, nonplussed. I pointed at my throat and gave her a mournful expression. For whatever reason, this appeared to work. She nodded and walked away.

I continued to make my way down the long corridor, bypassing most of the patients' rooms. I didn't want to feel worse about what I was beginning to understand as the reasons for the secrecy. Dr. Shelly's office was at the end of the hall.

When I reached his office, a very simple thought occurred to me. How was I going to get inside the office? There was a lock and a keypad, but I didn't have his key or his password. It never occurred to me that, if I actually made it up to the fourth floor and found his office, I would need a way to gain access to it. But you never know, sometimes the simplest solutions are the best. I turned the handle; the door was locked.

In a futile effort, I tried a couple of passwords. I typed in different —*organ, donor, cyborg, crazy, mad scientist, pompous, sick bastard*—but none of these words were correct. And then I remembered the little box that Merlin had given me. I was to open and use it only for extreme emergencies.

Well this certainly seemed to be an example of one.

I pulled out the box and opened it. It contained a verdigris powdery substance and a single marble. There were no instructions, just a greenish powder and a marble. What was I supposed to do with these? Although I was an agnostic by nature, it occurred to me maybe there was actually a higher power with a sense of humor because of what happened next.

I sneezed and some of the powder scattered and landed on the code pad. After I brushed off the powder, I could see the faint trace of fingerprints on the letters A-D-I-N-R-W. It didn't take long for me to realize they spelled "Darwin." I pressed the letters in order, and the door to Dr. Shelly's office opened. It made sense. Dr. Shelly was always talking about how his science would improve people on both worlds. It was "simply evolution at its best," as he would have put it.

Of all the things you choose in life, you
don't get to choose what your nightmares
are. You don't pick them; they pick you.

—John Irving

Journal Entry 64

Irony and Nightmares

As I sat down at his desk, the motion sensor lights automatically came on. I took a quick glance around his office. A cold chill ran down my spine. The room had a Hannibal Lecter feel to it. I could hear Dr. Lecter saying with icy assuredness, "I've no plans to call on you, Clarice. The world is more interesting with you in it."[4] I'm not sure why, but I always thought that quote was memorable and had deeper implications than most realized.

But then again, my favorite scene from the movie *Rocky* wasn't a fight sequence or the training scenes, as it is for most people. My favorite moment is when Rocky is in the Spectrum looking up at the rafters. He notices that his mural is wrong, and he says to the fight promoter, "Mr. Jergens, the poster is wrong. I'm wearing white pants with a red stripe." Mr. Jergens takes a deep puff of his cigar and responds, "It really doesn't matter, does it? I'm sure you are going to give us a great show."[5] Then the music plays and you realize that he knows he can't win the fight. And

---

[4] *The Silence of the Lambs.* Dir. Jonathan Deeme. Writers Thomas Harris (novel), Ted Tally (screenplay). Orion Pictures, 1991. Film

[5] *Rocky.* Dir. John G. Avildsen. Writer Sylvester Stalone. United Artists, 1976. Film.

aside from his wife, Adrian, no one else believes in him either. That same hopelessness Rocky was feeling began to seep into the pit of my stomach a little deeper.

But I had to remember that a lot of movies have happy endings, even if sometimes you have to wait for the sequel. Besides, I knew Walt Disney and the great wizard Merlin both believed in magic, so maybe I should too. I forced myself to continue searching for clues.

There were shelves filled with bottles and jars that appeared to be filled with organs and appendages from various species of humanoids. However the majority of the specimens seemed to be human. There was a slightly nauseating smell in the room—a hint of something that smelled similar to formaldehyde. This was probably the odor of the improved preservative used on this planet.

Three of the walls were painted blood red. At least I hoped it was paint. Portraits of the illustrious scientists Darwin and Newton were hung on the walls along portraits of other people I didn't recognize. I assumed they were similarly prominent scientists from Evion or other worlds. I wondered if Shelly really compared himself to those men. Could he really be that vain and self-absorbed?

On the last wall swastikas were etched alongside pictures of the man who had made this symbol infamous forever in the annals of history. I did not take the bitter irony for granted. This symbol had been used for over three thousand years, long before the Nazis adopted it, according to a lunch conversation I'd had with a history teacher when I was an educator in another universe.

She told me that the symbol originated from Sanskrit and was associated with positive connotations. In fact, the word *swastika* loosely translates into "to be good." The swastika was, at one time, a common decoration that often adorned cigarette cases, postcards, coins, and buildings. Many cultures and religions had used this symbol to represent aspects of reaching a higher, more evolved self. Far from being evolved personally, I didn't have to worry about these elevated states.

This fourth wall was reserved for pictures of Adolf Hitler at various stages of his life, from his early child hood in Austria-Hungry to his decorated World War I picture, through his NSDAP (National Socialist German Workers Party) days, and ending with his rise to power as chancellor of Germany. Below each of the pictures was a plaque on which was engraved a personal quote from Hitler himself, only adding to the sickness of the monster and the man who had hung these pictures.

I noticed a picture of Adolf as a young boy. Looking at the child, I found it hard to see the heinous criminal he would become later in life—until I read the quote below: "Anyone who sees and paints a sky green and fields blue ought to be sterilized."

Adjacent to the childhood picture was Hitler dressed in a World War I uniform holding a medal, the Iron Cross given for bravery. The irony of this award stung me like pouring alcohol on a fresh cut. The quote at the bottom stated, "Demoralize the enemy from within by surprise, terror, sabotage, assassination. This is the war of the future."

Another picture displayed Adolf as an employee of NSDAP talking with fellow workers. The following lines were inscribed: "By the skillful and sustained use of propaganda, one can make a people see even heaven as hell or an extremely wretched life as paradise." Although this quote sickened me, I couldn't help but think he was right. A charismatic person and the right lies could make some people believe and see whatever they wanted. History was filled with examples.

The final picture was a collage of Adolf speaking to a crowd as the chancellor of Germany. As I read the quote, I thought of Merlin and what his reaction would be to these words: "Great liars are also great magicians." It was painfully clear to me that Dr. Shelly was another monster. Maybe monsters stuck together, following a kind of unethical code. I forced back the additional bile and disgust ebbing from my digestive system and moved on.

Below the picture of Darwin was a file cabinet with two large drawers. The top drawer was labeled with the words: *Extension-of-Life Program*. The drawer was locked with a coded pad key. This time, without sneezing, I sprinkled a little of the enchanted dust on the pad key and I could see that the letters E-G-L-M-N were highlighted. It took a moment (and perhaps a bit of magic), but I "saw" the name "Mengele."

Buried somewhere in my hippocampus was a faint memory of a senior-year history class lesson on World War II. Josef Mengele was a surgeon assigned to Auschwitz. He became infamous for performing experiments on camp prisoners. Mengele's reign of terror landed him the nickname *Todesangel*—Angel of Death. Did Dr. Shelly really admire this sick, demented doctor as well? The realization of just how much of a disgusting individual Dr. Shelly was kept becoming clearer and clearer, or so I thought.

It was unclear if the Extension-of-Life Program had been restarted or initiated by Dr. Shelly ten years ago. These experiments were designed to increase the average life span of humanoids. Most of the DNA was extracted from the cells of the test subjects, mainly the homeless humans collected from Earth. Then the DNA was manipulated in an attempt create a sequence of nucleotide bases that would increase the life span of the individual. After the majority of the DNA had been extracted, the subject would have to be sacrificed.

Using most, but not all, of the remaining magical powder, I sprinkled some over the bottom drawer keypad. The letters E-L-M-O were highlighted. It must have been magic this time, because I "knew" the word was "Morell." Later, I would discover that Theodor Morell was Adolf Hitler's personal physician. It was disgustingly obvious to me that Dr. Shelly had a strange fascination with the Nazis, including Hitler himself. Perhaps he was even involved in one of the neo-Nazi groups, or worse yet, was continuing to follow in their footsteps of the original Nazis.

Initially, the Organ Donor Program for Cyborgs appeared to be organ donations solely for the purpose of creating and maintaining cyborgs (simply a way to get spare parts to create cyborgs). One spare right arm for this cyborg, a left eye for this one, and so forth. As I continued to read, it became apparent that Dr. Shelly was bent on creating an army of these cyborgs, which I was assuming he would control.

Why would he need an army of cyborgs? What did he plan to do with them? I had some ideas, but I hoped I was wrong. Maybe he was just lonely and looking for companionship.

I put the organ donation files away. Two things seemed evident after I read the initial files on these two programs. First, at the risk of stating the obvious, Dr. Shelly was not only a brilliant scientist; he was also one severely sick bastard. Second, these programs were probably not funded by the mayor or city council. Even if these politicians were corrupt, I doubted the mayor or his council had any clue as to what Shelly was doing on these upper floors. I wiped the magical dust off the keypads and closed all the drawers.

An unsettling thought crept into my mind. Maybe it wasn't just the good guys who could transmute from Earth to Evion; maybe the bad guys did as well. I thought of Lucky Luciano from The Trades. He had been a mobster and a killer on Earth. Maybe Hitler and other bad guys could also transmute to Evion.

Was it possible that evil also served a kind of purpose in both universes? Did the universes need a balance of good and evil to operate? Could good exist without evil? This concept was too deep for me to ponder at that particular moment, so I concentrated on the task at hand.

On his desk were the final release forms awaiting Dr. Shelly's signature. I looked through the stack of forms.

A number of them had already been signed. Some of the forms contained the names of the subjects listed, although many didn't. Since these poor souls were mainly the homeless, many of them hadn't had personal identification on them at the time they were abducted.

I started to read the release forms. The first form was for Janet Leigh. Seriously? Anyway, under her name was listed the purpose for her abduction. She was currently in room 405 and was scheduled to be part of the cyborg organ donation program. Her vitals were also listed—height, weight, blood type, and so forth. Her legs, one arm, an eye, and one kidney were listed as parts to be "harvested" for Cyborg 57.

The next form was for John Doe Number 3267. I wondered if this meant there were already over three thousand previously abducted nameless men who were used in these experiments. God, I hoped that it was just a code and not an actual number. Under his vitals, it specified he was to be used in the Extension-of-Life Program.

I continued to read through the release papers, making sure to snap a picture of the signature page with my special ASAP button camera. Elvis and ASAP would likely need these snapshots for evidence. Most of the release papers were similar—nameless people designated for organ donation or the Extension-of-Life Program. I finally reached the last release paper on his desk and gasped.

My heart started pounding. It felt as if every neuron in my body started firing at once. No way! This wasn't possible! I read the name on the release form over and over, but the name didn't change. It didn't make sense. It didn't seem possible. The sick irony stabbed at my heart. She was here after all. My heart sank, and I felt ill. The last unsigned release form read, "Erika Nirvona, scheduled for experimentation." Her DNA was to be extracted and used in the Extension-of-Life Program. There was also a note about mutated DNA, but the rest was unreadable because it was written in a code that I couldn't translate.

The greatest escape I ever made is when
I left Appleton, Wisconsin.

—Harry Houdini

Journal Entry 65

Let's Get the Hell Out of Dodge

I took her release form, folding it and placing it in my
pocket. I walked down to room 411. Taking a deep breath,
I walked into the room not knowing exactly what to
expect. I pulled back the curtain surrounding the bed. She
was lying there looking beautiful. She was unconscious.
An array of tubes was hooked to her right arm. I estimated
her age to be around eighteen, based on pictures of her in
high school yearbook that she had shown me.

The chart at the end of her bed indicated that she was
to be used for the Extension-of-Life Program as I had
previously read in Dr. Shelly's office. I still wasn't sure
what the coded text meant, but we were not going to hang
around to find out. As I scanned her vital information, a
clue to the coded DNA became more evident. I noticed
the words "Subject is pregnant with child" and something
to the affect "Do not discard embryonic DNA or stem
cells, slated to be used in mutation experimentation."

I thought for a brief moment. Father! I was going to be a
dad! And then reality set in—not unless I could think of
a way to get her out of there.

The good news was I still had one unused item left that
Clayton had given me from Merlin. Of course, the bad

news was that it was a marble. What was I supposed to do with a marble? It was a marble!

I knew that Merlin would not have given me this object without a purpose. I could hear Jean's voice in my head, "That's right, silly." I was about to experiment with the marble when a nurse walked into the room.

Although slightly startled, I turned to face her. Visions of Nurse Mildred Ratched from the movie *One Flew Over the Cuckoo's Nest* flashed into my mind. This nurse had the same frigid eyes as Dr. Shelly. Her face could have been pretty except for the rigid sternness and angry creases strewn across her cheeks. The words *heartless battle-ax* formed in my mind, and a frosty chill raced down my spine.

"Doctor, is everything all right?" she asked in a wintry, callous voice.

I shook my head yes. She wasn't convinced. "Shouldn't you still be at the ball, schmoozing with our potential benefactors?"

I made a coughing sound, mumbled something inaudible, and pointed to my throat. She started to question me but I dismissingly waived her off. Nurse battle-ax walked out of the room and back to her station.

I pulled the marble out of my pocket. Instead of a solid green color, it had turned translucent. There were wisps of power blue on the inside.

I placed it on the floor and waited for something to happen. Of course, I forgot to say the magic words … "Abracadabra."

Nothing.

"Shazam."

Again nothing.

"Presto."

Still nothing.

I picked up the marble, and it slipped out of my hand. When it hit the ground, a small crack appeared around the circumference. As the air penetrated the marble, it began to transform into a syringe containing a syrupy, clear fluid.

It was at this moment that Elias signaled me that trouble was on the way. I was not sure what was in the syringe, but I was confident that Merlin wouldn't lead me astray. Besides, what choice did I have? I injected the thick liquid into the IV.

After a few seconds, Erika regained consciousness. Quickly, I started disconnecting the tubes as alarms on the diagnostic machines started blaring.

Erika was naturally a little groggy but said, "Michael, is that you?"

With a surprised tone, I said, "You can see me and not Dr. Shelly?"

"Dr. Shelly? Why would you think of that monster?"

"Oh, so you have met the good doctor."

"But you died in my arms in Washington DC. You had no pulse. I was at your funeral, and you were dead! Your mom and sister—"

"I didn't really die. I was just transmuted to this Universe, to the planet Evion."

Understandably, she looked very confused. "I don't understand any of this. Is this some kind of a trick?"

"Erkie do," I said.

"What did you say?"

"When you were a little kid, you told me you would say that to your parents when you wanted to do something on your own."

"Quickly, where did you take me on our first date?" she asked.

"We had a scrumptious dinner at Jo Jo's just outside of Atlantic City. After you stared into my big brown eyes during most of the dinner and were melted by my irresistible charms, I took you see Lucy the Elephant since you had never seen her before."

She smiled but refused to acknowledge my attempt at humor. "And what happened afterward?"

I blushed a little. "You kissed me in the car because I told you I was too shy to kiss you first."

Her devastating smile—that she didn't realize she had—flashed across her face. "Of course, Michael, I would know you anywhere. But you look so much younger."

Hesitantly, I glanced into the mirror. I still looked as I had before, like a mixture of myself and Dr. Shelly, but somehow Erika saw me and not him. I heard Jean laughing in my mind. "Michael, true love can see through any kind of glamour or magic."

I smiled. "Hi, babe. I missed you so much." I creased my cheeks and bared my teeth. Smiling had never been my forte. I handed her a small mirror I had seen on the bedside table.

"Is this really me?"

I laughed. "Yes, we are both younger here on Evion."

"How is that possible?"

"I would love to explain everything, and I promise I will, but right now we need to get out of here."

Although she was confused and still in a light state of shock, she instinctively trusted me.

Pulling out Merlin's ring, I said, "Put this special ring on and follow me. It will make you invisible, so don't say anything if anyone else is around."

Before she could respond, I gently pressed my lips to hers. For a moment we were reliving our teenage years as if we actually had known each other during our youth. Sweetly, softly, and deliciously her lips pressed back. Her arms enveloped my body with a warm and tender embrace.

Momentarily, Erika was kissing me for the first time. We were in Disney World covering our heads as the big drop on Splash Mountain was approaching. We were in Aruba, Las Vegas, and the Bahamas. We were in all of the places we had visited and enjoyed together.

The last thing in the world I wanted to do was stop, but I knew time was running short. Reluctantly, I pulled away and slipped Merlin's ring on her index finger. Within a blink of an eye, she vanished.

"I don't feel any different," she commented.

"Look in the mirror."

"Cool."

"Yes, way cool. Now follow me quietly," I said with a smirk. "If we can make it downstairs to the first floor, Elias and Elvis might be able to help us."

"You don't really mean? Oh never mind. I guess I'll find out soon enough."

We left the room. I wasn't sure how much longer the enchanted eye drops would work or how much time we had before the real Dr. Shelly showed up. However, my

Spidey senses were kicking in letting me know time was not a luxury.

Things appeared to be normal as we walked down the corridor. A few nurses and orderlies passed us, and I nodded hello. Nurse Ratched was at the main nurses' station talking on the phone as we passed by.

The transportation tube was located just beyond her station. I assumed Erika was following me as I reached the tube. The security guard nodded a greeting as we approached.

"Going back down, Doctor?"

I smiled and nodded.

He reached over to the keypad to type in the code to initiate the transporter when nurse Ratched ran over and yelled, "Stop!" She was brandishing a syringe filled with a clear liquid.

The security guard seemed momentarily confused. This gave me an opportunity. With Bruce Lee–like precision, I landed a roundhouse kick to the guard's chops, knocking him backward and dazing him. I forgot to mention that while I was in The Trades at Merlin's Castle, he had taught me some martial arts moves.

Nurse Ratched stopped and was knocked backward, hitting her head against the wall. As she fell, she landed on the syringe and was rendered incapacitated.

"Where did you learn to do that martial arts maneuver, and do you know the code?" Erika asked still being invisible.

"No, but I have an idea how to figure it out. As far as my newfound fighting prowess, Merlin gave me some tips."

I sprinkled the remaining enchanted dust on the keypad.

The numbers 1-2-3-4-8-9 appeared on the keypad. There was no way I could quickly figure out the right combination, even though they seemed eerily familiar, but it didn't matter. Suddenly the transport tube came to life. We stepped in and were swooshed back down to the first floor. As we swooshed, Erika took off the ring and reappeared. Almost simultaneously, the eye drops wore off, and I appeared as my younger old self.

As we stepped off the transporter, Elias was waiting for us.

"Michael, who is that with you?" he asked.

"Believe it or not, this is Erika!"

Elias looked stunned.

Erika looked just as surprised. "Michael, is this Elias? Walter Elias Disney? Mr. Walt Disney?"

"Yes."

"Don't tell me that Elvis is really Elvis—"

She stopped short as Elvis Presley walked in. He was dressed in a navy officer's uniform and was accompanied by Rosalie, who was still dressed as a waitress.

My Father had a profound influence
on me. He was a lunatic.

—Spike Milligan

Journal Entry 66

Doctor Daddy

"This is one of my favorite outfits," Elvis was saying. "It's from a little movie I did called, *Easy Come Easy Go*, and I—"

He stopped abruptly, "Michael, who is this lovely creature?"

"This is hard to believe, but this is Erika Nirvona."

"No way! How did she get here?"

"I don't know. To be honest, I haven't had the chance to ask her. I know that Dr. Shelly must be involved somehow, but I was so busy trying to rescue her and playing the part of a hero, I forgot to ask."

Erika smiled and commented, "My knight in shining armor." She turned to my friends. "Hi, Walter and Elvis. It is a pleasure to meet you both. Walter, I love Disney World. I have been there so many times, my kids call me a Disney Mom."

For a change, I was the serious one. "Sweetheart, the last thing I remember was dying and leaving you in Washington DC. How did you get here?"

Erika went on to explain her meeting with Dr. Reed and how she subsequently awoke in a guarded factory room with a number of homeless people. She paraphrased the speech that Günter had read to the group at the direction of Dr. Shelly. She described how she and the others had been knocked unconscious with gas and then awakened in hospital rooms, apparently in another world. She explained that Dr. Shelly had nonchalantly described his plans for improving science by sacrificing the people that had been trapped in the room.

I confirmed what Erika was telling Elvis by briefly describing the contents of the two files I had found in Shelly's office and the medical charts that I had seen in the patients' rooms on the fourth floor.

"I never reached the fifth floor, but I would guess that the operating rooms for organ donations and DNA extractions are located up there," I said.

"Well, there is only one way to find out," Elvis stated.

Ten members of the ASAP squad walked into the building. I realized it was the first time I had seen their official uniforms. They wore jumpsuits that were half blue and half red. On their sleeves were golden emblems of what looked like an Earth wolf, but this animal was scarier and bigger.

"At the time Elias signaled you, Dr. Shelly was on his way upstairs," Rosalie said. "Obviously the transporter guard was a little confused when he saw Dr. Shelly down here when he hadn't seen him—I mean you posed as him—come back down from upstairs. After he sent the real doctor up, I detained the confused guard."

I looked over at the transporter, which stood unguarded at the moment. I had used all of the remaining magical powder from Merlin.

"Without the guard, how are we supposed to know the code to get back upstairs?" I asked.

"We?" Elvis questioned. "Look, Michael, you have more than fulfilled your end of the bargain, and I will keep my agreement to help, although it's a little more complicated now that there are two of you. But I will try and help both you and Erika get back to Earth, if that's what you both still want, after we conclude this matter. You don't have to go up to the fifth floor."

Erika looked at me. "What arrangement did you have with Elvis?"

"It's complicated, but the long and short of it is that Elvis agreed to help me try to get back to Earth—back to you—if I did some recon work for him," I responded.

"You were trying to get back to me to live on Earth? Is that even possible?" she asked.

"I don't know. Nobody seems to know for sure, but either way I had to try, no matter the consequences."

"Even if you died for real while trying?"

I smiled and nodded.

She reached for my hand and intertwined her fingers around mine. "You don't have to die, because I'm here, and I don't plan on losing you again."

Elvis seemed moved; it was the first time that I had seen the sensitive side of him. He sniffled, blew his nose, and said, "I understand. And the thing that I miss the most back on Earth is my mom, Gladys, and I would …" But he stopped in mid-sentence. A more serious look returned to his face. "We need to get to the fourth and fifth floors," he insisted.

"I am coming with you to help," I demanded.

"Then I am going with you too," Erika stated.

I was going to argue with her, tell her she should rest and wait for me to get back, but I knew the look. It was the look that said, "You can say whatever you want, but I'm still coming." So I just nodded.

"Great," Rosalie said with a wry smile. "So we will all go up together. Before I disposed of the security guard, I was able to persuade him to graciously provide the pass code.

"Okay, we just all need to be careful," Elvis replied. "Or it will be my ass on the line at ASAP headquarters."

Rosalie chimed in, "With any luck, maybe we can still catch that bastard of a father."

We all looked at her dumbfounded.

"Oh, I guess I forgot to mention that Dr. Shelly is my father."

When a man wants to murder a tiger he calls it sport;
when a tiger wants to murder him, he calls it ferocity.

—George Bernard Shaw

Journal Entry 67

Getting Away with Murder

Fourteen of us—nine ASAP agents, Erika, Rosalie,
Elvis, Elias (who insisted on helping us—it was a grand
adventure, as he would say), and I— were transported to
the fourth floor. One of the ASAP agents had to remain
behind to operate the controls of the transporter.

While we were waiting our turn to swoosh, Rosalie
started to open up about her absent, crazy, mad scientist,
sociopath father and her mother. Arielle, her mother, had
been homeless. She was living on the streets near a local
beissel that Dr. Shelly frequented on occasion.

"My mother had long, blonde hair and crystal-clear blue
eyes," Rosalie told us. "She had offers to do modeling
work, but never was interested. I think she was more of
the intellectual type. She worked as an assistant in Mayor
Tremball's office. One day she accidently came across
some files on the mayor's desk. They were important
papers, but she never mentioned what they were."

"I wonder if those files had anything to do with Dr.
Shelly's work?" I questioned.

"I also have wondered if there was a connection to Dr.
Shelly in those papers," she replied. "Anyway, the next

day she was fired. All of her money and credit cards were confiscated. She was kicked out of her apartment, and since she had no relatives, she was forced to live on the streets. Eventually she became frustrated and agitated over her living situation." She took a deep breath before she continued. "Unidentified people—although my mom swore they were from the mayor's office—showed up one morning and injected her forcefully with psychotropic drugs. They repeated this procedure several times over a number of weeks. Eventually, this put her over the edge, and she was remanded over to Andorra's Sanitorium. She spent three years incarcerated at that mental institution before she was released."

"How did Dr. Shelly become involved in her life?" Erika asked.

"Dr. Shelly was kind to her, giving her food and money. After a few weeks, he became very friendly. Slowly, her mental state improved, and she started to trust him."

"Well, he can be quite the charmer," Erika sarcastically intoned.

"Believe it or not, he was a lot different with my mother, at least initially. One night he asked if he could take her out for dinner. At first, she declined his offer. When he showed up one day with new clothes and makeup for her, she thought it was so sweet, and she relented. He took her to the new Italian restaurant that had just opened; it was all the rage in Andorra. People in this city love anything that's from your universe because it seems so new and different."

Rosalie stopped her story for a minute and smiled before continuing. "In her new clothes and makeup, my mother was stunning. Heads turned as she walked through the restaurant to their seats. Dr. Shelly and my mother had a pleasant meal and conversation during dinner. After supper, he convinced her to allow him to show her his estate. Her instinct was to say no, but after he had been so generous to her, she found it hard to decline. During dinner and the ride to his house, he was a perfect gentleman."

Erika laughed. "Dr. Shelly, a gentleman. Really?"

"Yeah, I know it's hard to believe. Anyway, once they arrived at his house, his demeanor completely changed. He became very aggressive. After several advances, which my mother politely declined, he slapped her around and then raped her. When it was over, he silently drove her back to the streets and left her there among the garbage."

"Classy guy," Erika quipped.

"My mother tried to report the incident to the local authorities, but no one would listen to her. Eventually, her mental state deteriorated once again, and she was incarcerated in the sanitarium once again, where I was born."

We all looked at Elvis. "Don't look at me. It was never reported to my office. If it had been, I would have certainly looked into the matter."

Rosalie continued, "After a couple of days, against my mom's wishes, I was taken away and put into the orphanage. I was immediately adopted by a very nice couple. Of course, I had no idea these people were not my real parents. Hell, I even looked a little like them. At least that's what people would say."

"When did you find out that you were adopted?" I asked.

"When I became a teenager, my adoptive parents decided that it was best to tell me the truth. They said it was morally the right thing to do."

"How did you find out all of the information about your mother and her experience with Dr. Shelly?" Elvis inquired.

"After my adoptive parents told me, I went to visit my mother at the asylum on a weekly basis. She was pretty far gone by that point, but every once in a while she would be somewhat lucid. During those brief coherent moments, she slowly disseminated information about her past." Rosalie sighed. "She was in such a fragile mental state, I didn't press her. On one visit she told me that Dr. Shelly was my biological father. Another time she causally described the rape incident. She tried to make it clear that, although I was a child created by a horrific situation, she loved me and had never wanted to give me up for adoption. This was obviously impossible because she was living in the asylum."

"The whole thing was very unfair for your mother," Erika said solemnly. "I can't even imagine how hard it must have been for her."

"Is your mother still there?" I asked.

Rosalie's eyes became placid. "No, she died at the asylum a few years back."

"I'm sorry," Erika and I said in unison.

"The last time I visited her she told me that she believed Dr. Shelly played a major role in her incarceration and her mental state. She swore she had seen him on several occasions talking with her doctors and nurses. When she would ask them about it, they would just say she must have been hallucinating again."

"What do you think?" Elvis asked Rosalie.

"Well, I checked, and there is no record of Dr. Shelly being on staff at the asylum. After joining the ASAP, I interviewed a number of doctors and nurses there. None of them remembered or would admit Dr. Shelly was ever present at the facility. However, there is a man listed as Floda Reltih as a member of the board of directors," Rosalie responded.

"Why does that name sound weird but somewhat familiar?" I asked.

"Yes, it does seem oddly familiar," Erika agreed.

"That's also what I thought."

Just then Erika blurted out, "Adolf Hitler spelled backward, right?"

Rosalie smiled and said, "Michael, she is sharp."

She continued, "I thought that couldn't be just a coincidence, so I did some further checking. Strangely enough, there were no pictures of Floda, as there were of all the other board members. However, I was able to find a description of the man, and it fit Dr. Shelly's physical appearance exactly."

"Why would Dr. Shelly go to so much trouble to remain anonymous as a member of the board?" Elvis asked.

"I think I can take a guess," I said. "It makes sense in a crazy, twisted, mad-scientist, sick sort of way. When I was in Dr. Shelly's office, I found many connections to the Nazis and Hitler. It seemed like he was a big admirer of their heinous work. So it was probably amusing to him, hiding his true identity and using a pseudonym from one of his pernicious idols."

"I also think it has something to do with my mother, and maybe even me," Rosalie stated. "He didn't want any ties linking him to me or my mother."

"He obviously didn't want any connection tying him to the rape of your mother, which I assume is illegal even in this world," Erika added.

Elvis nodded that it was.

"But I also think there is more to it than just the rape," Rosalie explained. "In one of my mother's few lucid moments, she alluded to some kind of scientific experiment he was trying on unborn children, but the information was fragmented and mostly unintelligible."

Elvis put his arm on her shoulders. "Don't worry. We will figure this mess out."

Rosalie continued, "The main reason I became an ASAP officer was to stop these kinds of creeps—mostly people like my father."

"Gee, I thought you joined to make your city a better place to live, work, and play in!" Elvis chortled.

"Well there was that whole patriotic aspect, but it was mainly to pay back daddy dearest for my mother."

It was our turn to be swooshed up to the fourth floor. When everyone was on the floor, we assembled by the main nurses' desk. There did not appear to be any nurses or workers on the floor. There were no signs of any doctors on the floor either.

"We should split up into teams of two and search every room," Elvis suggested.

As we started to search the rooms, two things became sickeningly apparent. Half of the patients' rooms were empty. There were patients in the other half of the rooms, but every one of them had been murdered!

If employment really cared about employees,
people wouldn't have to work until
retirement comes to their rescue.

—Mokokoma Mokhonoana

Journal Entry 68

Rescue

"We have to find Xavier!" James shouted.

"He is probably dead, and we really need to get out of here before the cy-monks and cy-spiders regain their awareness and begin attacking again," Rita replied.

Everyone stopped running and stared at the captain. She stopped and said, "Oh, what the hell. All right I'll go find him. James, you lead the rest back to the shoreline."

James started to protest, but she insisted, "That's an order."

He laughed and then thought, *Hey, who put her in charge?* But she was right. She was less injured than he was, so he said, "Aye aye, Captain."

James led the remaining survivors toward the beach.

Rita ran into the dense underbrush and called out Xavier's name. There was no response. As she wandered through the trees, some of the cy-monks stared blankly at her, giving her an eerie feeling. There was no telling when they would turn aggressive again.

When she was a teenager, Rita Denton was a fan of *Star Trek*—not the older James Tiberius Kirk series, but *The Next Generation*. She remembered that Commander Ricker and the away team on the Borg ship investigated a new threatening species, worried that they might come out of their static condition at any moment. These cy-monks had the same creepy aura—they could come out of their docile state at any moment. She wasn't going to waste any time, just in case.

There was no sign of Xavier, just the cy-spiders crawling in circular patterns and cy-monks apparently waiting for instructions. She was just about to abandon the search when she heard a faint moan about a hundred feet to her left. She ran to the location and found Xavier partially buried under a pile of leaves and small sticks. He was injured but fully conscious. He had cuts and bruises along with a few nasty simian bite marks.

"Did it work?" he mumbled.

"Yes, your plan worked perfectly, but we need to get to the beach and join the others." She pulled the scattered debris off of Xavier. He had been severely battered and bitten, but there was no evidence of cy-spider marks on him. That was good; she had seen what the venom of the cy-spiders had done to that poor woman.

"I don't think I can walk on my own," he said as she helped him up. She put his arm around her shoulder for support, and they started waddling southward toward the beach.

"This reminds me of the three-legged races my daddy and I used to enter in the local fair," she said, trying to distract him from his fear and pain.

"I bet you and your dad were good."

"We were competitors. Took first prize a couple of times. What happened back there?" she asked firmly.

"Well it's a little foggy, but I remember sneaking around their flank. I saw this large cy-monk hanging in the rear. He appeared to be giving orders, so I assumed he was their alpha."

Rita nodded.

Xavier continued, "I waited briefly, and when I saw he was completely occupied with the attack on you guys, I charged at him. At the last moment, he turned and saw me. I had a large rock in my fist and started smashing him in the head. The cy-monk was very strong. He kept coming at me, biting me as I was smashing his head with the rock. Eventually, he stopped, but not before I got pretty bruised and bitten."

"You did a great job and probably saved all of our lives. When we get back to the states, I'm going to see about getting you a job, if you are interested." she offered.

He nodded.

It was an arduous journey, but the two eventually made it to the beach. The others were waiting for them. "Out there, a ship is approaching fast. Do you think it's the good guys or the bad guys?" James asked.

"There is only one way to find out," Rita responded. "If it's the bad guys, then we are out of options anyway."

As the ship got closer, they saw a large symbol on the side of the ship: a giant bald American eagle in a circle with the words *Fleet Forces Command* at the bottom of the circle. Thankfully, it was one of the US Navy emblems.

"I guess the blood protein signal worked after all. I had my doubts, but it really worked," James blurted out.

A small lifeboat was dismissed from the larger ship. Rita, James, Xavier, and the remaining survivors were loaded on to the boat. When they reached the ship, they were greeting by the commanding officer. Captain Allison Sanders was in charge. She was a prototypical military brat. Her father was in the army, and her mother was in the air force so, of course, she chose the navy. Her father was a chemical engineer, and her mother was a doctor.

Captain Sanders was the shortest officer in the fleet and was often the brunt of jokes; that was until recreational time. She was very athletic and often beat her male counterparts in most sporting events. Her ship, the *Fighting Fanatic*, was the only ship with a satellite dish capable of picking up baseball games played by the Philadelphia Phillies, her favorite team. Of course she'd had to pull a few strings and cash in a few favors, but it had been well worth it.

"Welcome aboard. I'm Captain Sanders, and this is my first officer, Lieutenant Thorn."

"I'm Captain Rita Denton. This is Agent James Dubay, and these people are the survivors of a ship wreck."

"This island was undetectable by radar, but we were able to get a fix on you from the blood protein signal that the boys at VC implanted. The signal was just fading when we found you," Lieutenant Thorn said. "That technology is fantastic. The navy could really use it on special recon missions."

Captain Sanders gave what appeared to be a surprised look. Maybe it was legitimate, and maybe it was great acting, Rita wasn't sure. Captain Sanders started to ask a question, but let it go. "We can talk later. Right now let's go below to the galley where our cook has prepared food for you," Captain Sanders offered. Meanwhile, her officers were taking the other survivors to sick bay.

"No arguments here," James replied. "I think I can safely speak for all of us. Chow would greatly be appreciated."

As they walked down into the belly of the ship, Rita whispered into James' ear, "We might have another problem here."

"What, you're not hungry? I know that military food isn't always the best, but I'm sure anything would taste great now," he whispered back.

"Of course I'm hungry. Why do men always think about food? Anyway, that's not it. Lieutenant Thorn referred to VC—Vomit Comet—as part of the operation."

"So?"

"No one on the navy's side was supposed to know about VC's or the OSS's involvement. As far as they knew, it was supposed to be strictly a military search-and-rescue operation. Somewhere, I think we have a leak. There's a mole out there."

"Well, I'm not a fan of moles—I mean people who are moles. The real moles don't bother me unless they get in my house."

"Right, James. Maybe we should just keep our eyes open."

Nothing is more difficult, and therefore more precious, than to be able to decide.

—Napoleon Bonaparte

Journal Entry 69

Decisions

"I'll call for reinforcements," Elvis said. "They can body bag the deceased and have them autopsied, but I'm sure, by the blue coloring of their skin, that they were poisoned."

"Why do you think he killed some of the people and took the rest with him?" I asked.

"I'm not sure, but I would bet the people he took with him had some sort of biological value or genetic importance to him."

We decided to investigate the rooms individually just in case some clues had inadvertently been left behind. We split into teams of two—Rosalie and Elvis, Erika and me, and so forth.

As we investigated the rooms, an execrable smell of death and despair lingered in the air. I surmised that the people left behind probably died painlessly, as most had probably been unconscious to begin with, but this was of little comfort. It occurred to me that these "throw-way people" would never be missed or have a proper burial even on Evion.

Although precious metals and gems were bountiful here, things we took for granted on Earth were not as prevalent. Undeveloped land was scarce, and because of that, there were very few cemeteries. The ones that were available were strictly reserved for the rich and the famous. Most Evionites who died were cremated. Their ashes were placed in small urns or disposed of if there were no family members to claim the remains. It seemed that these people, who had been transported to another universe from Earth and then murdered, deserved a better final fate.

I thought about the quote from Oscar Wilde: "Life is never fair, and perhaps it is a good thing for most of us that it is not." I was fairly sure that, at least in this case, he was wrong.

After we thoroughly searched all of the rooms of the living and missing, we had found no clues or evidence. Dr. Shelly was a true baseborn mongrel, but he was also good at covering his tracks.

"We should investigate the fifth floor just to see what's there. Maybe we can find clues about his future plans," Elvis suggested.

As was the fourth floor, the fifth was also deserted. A clinical, aseptic smell permeated throughout. The floor was divided into two separate sections. One consisted of five operating rooms for the human-to-cyborg organ donations. The other was a large room for the DNA extraction. The operating rooms seemed to be standard; there was nothing unusual about them. As we continued to search for clues, I couldn't stop thinking about how many people from Earth had already been used for these donations.

The DNA extracting room was a different story. There were all kinds of high-tech-looking devices that none of us had ever seen. Elvis remarked about the high level of sophistication and how the lab boys back at ASAP might be able to glean some knowledge from these technologically advanced machines.

As we suspected, it was disappointing because there was no evidence of Dr. Shelly's future plans or current whereabouts, or even how he had escaped. We were about to leave when I noticed a little black notebook on the table. I grabbed it and put it into my back pocket.

Elvis offered us a ride back to the apartment building, but I mentioned that Jimmy and Suzie would be picking us up. At the front of the building, Jimmy and Suzie were waiting for us. As we climbed into the back seat, Suzie said, "Hi, you must be Erika. I can see why Michael was so eager to get back to Earth."

Erika blushed slightly. She looked at Jimmy. "You must be Jimmy, and the voice that greeted me must be Suzie. Sorry I seemed surprised, but back on Earth, cars that can talk have a sterile computer voice and they certainly don't have a charming personality like yours."

The dash illuminated with a slightly pink hue. I guess it was Suzie's turn to blush. Suzie recovered and continued, "So how did you and Michael meet?" The light banter between the two continued throughout the ride home.

Eventually we reached my apartment complex. I think Suzie had been flying a little slower to prolong her conversation with Erika. Finally, we said our good-byes.

We stepped onto the elevator, and I pushed the twelfth floor button. We continued talking as we walked down the hall. I stopped at 1211.

"Interesting," she said.

"How's that?" I asked.

"I noticed that your apartment number is the same as your birthday."

"Yes. You know? The weird thing is that all of the apartment numbers correspond to their residents' birthdates—Walt, Frank, Elvis, and the others."

"You know I don't believe in coincidences."

"Yeah. I know all that CIA training kind of makes you—"

I flashed my ID card, and the door opened.

I stopped abruptly as we both stared at Elvis and his companion, who were hovering above my couch.

The man had a long, white beard and wore a dark-blue robe embroidered with symbols and astrological signs. He looked a few years older than the last time I had seen him, but I recognized the face.

"Hello, Merlin. Don't take this the wrong way, but what are you doing here?"

Erika turned to me and asked, "Is that who I think it is?"

"If you are thinking Merlin, the magical and supposedly mythical magician from Arthurian legends, then you would be right."

"At the risk of sounding a little like Alice in Wonderland, 'curiouser and curiouser,'" Erika replied.

"Michael, don't take this the wrong way. You have a lovely apartment, but I wouldn't have left all of the comforts and conveniences of my castle without a good reason," Merlin said playing on my words.

"I contacted Merlin," Elvis interjected.

"Go on," I responded.

"Maybe you should start," Merlin said to Elvis.

Elvis got off the couch and began pacing. He was wearing a bright yellow blazer and black slacks. He unstrapped the guitar he was wearing.

"*Viva Las Vegas!*" Erika blurted out.

"Excellent. She is real sharp in more than one way," Elvis said to me. "You know I really do miss Ann. She was the only member of the cast who came to my funeral."

Merlin cleared his throat. "Elvis, maybe we could get to the point before my beard turns any grayer and Calygreyhound and Freybug starve to death."

"You're right. Here is the thing. While we were at the Science Ministry, some of the boys at ASAP obtained Erika's medical records containing a DNA analysis, which had been left behind by Dr. Shelly in a secret safe located in his office. The results were somewhat interesting."

"Interesting in what way?" Erika asked.

"I played a doctor once—John Carpenter was his name, but I still had to have the medical boys at the lab explain the term *erythroblastosis fetalis* to me."

Erika looked at me and asked, "Okay, science guy, I remember that Patty mentioned that term but how does that affect me?"

"I believe Elvis is eluding to a condition in newborns called *maternal-fetal conflict*, which is caused by some of the fetal blood leaks into the mother's bloodstream. They can form cells known as *microchimera*. However, the effects of this condition are usually expressed in the fetus and not the mother."

"Right, Patty didn't mention anything about this affecting me. Is the baby in any danger?" Erika asked.

"Yes, we believe that the fetus is just fine," Elvis replied. "In fact, the abnormally fast growth rate the baby was exhibiting at first has slowed down to a normal rate, according to the boys at the lab used," he continued.

"That's a relief, but how has Erika been effected. What did the report say?" I asked.

"Yes, stop blathering and just tell them what we know," Merlin interjected.

"We don't have all the facts, and it is rare, but it appears that the condition that has caused the *microchimera* cells has also generating some genetic alterations in Erika's DNA," Elvis answered.

Erika became concerned. "So I'm like Michael and you guys now?"

"No, not exactly," Elvis said. "Our DNA was created naturally as a result of certain consequences at the time of the big bang. Your DNA has changed as a result of a mutation caused by a possible incompatibility of your DNA and the baby's DNA, which is a combination of yours and Michael's."

"What does this mean?" I finally blurted out.

"We are not one hundred percent certain, but we believe this mutation in the DNA sequence will allow Erika to freely transverse any wormhole between the two universes," Elvis replied.

"So, in a sense, we"—I indicated myself along with Elvis and Merlin—"primarily belong in this universe, whereas Erika really belongs to both now?"

Elvis nodded.

"Is she okay? I mean is this new DNA stable?" I asked.

"We can't be positive without running more tests, but all indications from Dr. Shelly's research, and what little we have been able to analyze, are that her DNA is stable," Merlin responded.

Elvis gave me a look that I assumed was supposed to reassure me.

"We think that Dr. Shelly's Extension-of-Life Program wasn't just to manipulate the DNA sequence to extend the longevity of a person's life cycle; it was also to also create beings who could freely coexist in both universes at any time," Merlin explained.

"We believe he was attempting to create an army of beings that would have this ability. That's why he was so interested in Erika and brought her to this universe. Nature accomplished what he was trying to create, and he wanted to know how to copy this mutation," Elvis continued.

"You see the implications of this mutation, don't you?" Merlin asked.

"I think so. Dr. Shelly could send his own emissaries to alter events on Earth anytime he wished," I answered.

"Or worse still, he could create his own army to attack Earth whenever the mood struck him," Erika followed up.

"That is our greatest fear. We believe that Erika is in great danger. Dr. Shelly will stop at nothing to get her back and finish his research on her mutated DNA," Merlin warned.

"Is she safer here on Evion or on Earth?" I asked.

"That is hard to say, but ASAP believes that she would be safer back on Earth, at least until we can locate and capture Dr. Shelly," Elvis responded.

"But we know that Dr. Shelly has people working for him on Earth," I chimed.

"Yes, that is true, but we also have clandestine special agents on Earth working on our behalf as well," Elvis assured us.

Besides, Dr. Shelly isn't on Earth, and there is no evidence that he has ever been there or can transmute there. It would be much harder for him to find her there and give us time to find him," Elvis continued.

Erika and I looked at each other.

"We have promised each other to never be separated again. You know that 'until death do us part thing'—except for the officially being married part," I said.

Erika rolled her eyes at me. And then we read each other's minds and nodded in agreement.

"Okay," I said. "But under one condition. I get to go back with her, at least initially, so I know she is safe."

The only thing necessary for the triumph
of evil is for good men to do nothing.

—Edmund Burke

Journal Entry 70

Dr. Frankenstein, I Presume?

Dr. Shelly was understandably frustrated by the prior
events. He had barely escaped the Science Ministry
building before that damned Elvis and his ASAP boys
raided his facilities. Fortunately, he'd had advanced
warning from his informant (even though she was
unaware of her role) that the ASAP was in the building
and up to no good. It didn't take a brilliant geneticist, let
an alone a rocket scientist, to figure out it was time to get
out of there.

Fortunately, he was a careful man. After all, if you were
going to be in the mad scientist business and change
worlds, you needed to take certain precautions and always
have a backup plan. The odds were good in this business
that, no matter how careful you were, one day your
operations would be exposed. And so he'd had a special
escape route installed for just such an emergency. When
he realized what was happening, he exited the building
via the special transport tube he'd had clandestinely built
for emergencies.

Luckily, he was also a patient man. Wasn't it Earth author
Jack London who had once said, "Anything worth having
is worth waiting for?" London was an entrepreneur in his
field of commercial magazine fiction. Dr. Shelly at least

related to the entrepreneur aspect. It wasn't that he agreed with London's avocations of unionization, socialism, and the rights of people, but Dr. Shelly did fancy himself a pioneer in his own respect.

Dr. Shelly was an enduring man. Besides priding himself by leaving no stone unturned and preparing for every possible disaster, he never gave up. With this in mind, besides his secret escape route and the foresight to plan for a possible ASAP invasion, he'd had another headquarters location created so he could continue his valuable work. It was true that this lair was not quite as cozy or well equipped as the upper floors at The Ministry of Sciences but it would do. Besides, it could have been a lot worse.

His new headquarters was built in a place that ASAP would never think to look. With the assistance of Weston, the mayor's "right hand man," he had been able to establish these new headquarters a half mile below the mayor's office in the City Council building.

Mayor Tremball had no knowledge of these headquarters. Although he was a little corrupt like most of the politicians on Earth and Evion, he would never have agreed to this groundbreaking work within the field of evolution. The mayor was a little dimwitted, but as long as Dr. Shelly gave him positive reports on the little scientific projects, he asked few questions. Besides, he was too busy attending social functions and kissing babies to realize what was happening right under his big nose.

This new atelier was set up a bit differently than the fourth and fifth floors in the Ministry of Sciences. This was in part due to available space and a shift in priorities. Dr.

Shelly would have to put on hold his cyborg program and, to some extent, his Extension-of-Life Program. He needed to focus on acquiring the proper genetic DNA code that would enable people from both universes free access to both worlds.

Dr. Shelly had furtively been working to find a series of nucleotide bases that would enable the existence of humanoids in both universes. He had serendipitously discovered the perfect blend of DNA sequences within Erika Nirvona's genetic code. But before he'd had time to extract her DNA and analyze it fully, ASAP had crashed the party, and he'd had to leave the Science Ministry.

He had taken along with him the subjects he believed would be useful in this research. Dr. Shelly saw no benefit in leaving alive those individuals who were of no use or for whom he had no room. They would have eventually died anyway due to the degradation of their DNA in this world. Just before his grand escape, he had injected into their IVs a simple concoction made from chemicals very similar to strychnine and cyanide. They had expired quickly and peacefully, so in a sense, he had really been doing those people a favor. *Sometimes I am just too damn thoughtful*, he thought.

Although he still had half of his subjects to work with, finding the right fusion and combination of DNA could take some time. Even with time, there were still no guarantees that he would find the right sequence with his limited resources and limited number of subjects. It really would be best to analyze Ms. Nirvona's mutated DNA make up.

After setting up his new lab and getting each of his subjects comfy, his priority would be to get Erika Nirvona back so he could analyze her DNA sequence and begin his new trials on the mutated DNA. Now that ASAP was involved, he knew this would not be an easy task. ASAP was probably even aware of his special interest in Erika and would do everything to protect her. They would most likely try to send her back to Earth, thus making it even more difficult for him to get his hands on her.

He would need to devise a plan before this happened. The one advantage he had was his informant. And the best part was that she was not even aware that she was helping him.

If you don't know where you are going,
any road will take you there.

—Lewis Carroll

Journal Entry 71

And What Alice Found There

Agent James Dubay and Captain Rita Denton were seated at the captain's table. Captain Allison Sanders was the last to arrive at the table. "Sorry. I just had to make a few calls and let the base in Miami know our ETA," she said.

"Once we arrive in Miami we will need a car," Rita stated.

Lieutenant Thorn interrupted. "We have arranged for a car to be available for you two after we dock."

"We have an hour or so before we arrive, so why don't you two enjoy our chef's cuisine. I know the navy has a reputation about its chow, but I can assure you that Chef Holden is top notch," Captain Sanders proudly announced.

"Well, I am hungry enough to eat a horse," James volunteered.

"I suppose we should eat something Rita commented. "It has been a while since we have had a decent meal."

"We were on a routine patrol when my supervisor said that we had a pickup to make," Captain Sanders explained. "Your island isn't on any map, and our radar wasn't able to identify it. Rather strange don't you think? Anyway, the ship's computer was linked to a satellite by an unknown source, which apparently picked up some signal from that strange place, and we were able to navigate to the island to rescue you."

James acknowledged their efforts. "Thanks for doing that. We really appreciate it."

"My superior, Admiral Myers, didn't give me any insight or explanation as to what you were doing on this uncharted, radar-proof island. Is there anything you can fill me in on?" Captain Sanders asked quizzically as food was brought to the table.

Rita wanted to avoid that subject. "Let me echo James's appreciation for our rescue, but I am not free to really give you any additional intel." Rita looked at James, as he seemed to be very much enjoying a crab cake sandwich and said, "Is there anything you would like to add?"

James almost choked. He took a sip of his drink and looked as if he was about to say something but just added, with a slight smile, "No. I'm good."

Captain Sanders looked a little disappointed, but as a navy brat she had been brought up to follow orders, even ones she couldn't officially question. She thought of Jack Nicholson from the movie *A Few Good Men*: "We follow orders son, we follow orders or people die. It's that simple. Are we clear?"[6]

---

[6] *A Few Good Men*. Dir. Rob Reiner. Writer Aaron Sorkin. Columbia Pictures, 1992. Film

It was clear, just as Lieutenant Kaffee responded in the aforementioned movie: "It was crystal clear." However, something was going on with these two and the others she had rescued from the mysterious island. Some high-ranking politicians or navy officials didn't want this information to be known. Who knew how high this went up the chain of command? She wondered if the admiral knew. Maybe even the president or vice president was involved in this as well.

By her very nature, Captain Sanders was a curious person. She liked mysteries and solving them. Sometimes she even thought she would have made a good scientist. But she was a soldier, a good soldier who played by the rules, at least most of the time. She decided that it was best to play it cool. She had asked the proper questions and hadn't aggressively pursued the noncommittal answers. It was best not to pursue any further unless either Agent Dubay or Captain Denton decided to give her some answers of their own volition.

Rita was a well-trained agent. She knew all the ins and outs of every training manual and all standard procedures. But she also believed in intuition and gut feelings. Every once in a while, she threw out the book and listened to her gut.

That little voice told her she could trust Captain Sanders. It was probably against her orders, but she decided to confide in the navy officer. Rita couldn't reveal every detail, but she could at least tell her something, especially about the mole on her ship. It was true that Captain Sanders could actually be that mole, but Rita's instinct told her otherwise. After lunch, Rita stopped on the bridge and asked Captain Sanders if she might have a private word with her.

They stepped into the captain's private, soundproof office on the bridge where Captain Sanders would occasionally clandestinely slip away to catch a couple innings of her "Fighting Phils." She offered Rita a seat on her red-and-white couch on which the words *Philadelphia Phillies* were embroidered throughout. There was even a picture of the green Phillies' Phanatic mascot on each arm.

On a small coffee table was displayed a baseball incased in glass. It had been signed by every member of the 1980s Philadelphia Phillies World Series Team. Next to the baseball was a small statue of Harry Kalas and Richie Ashburn sitting in the announcer's booth. On the wall behind the table hung a picture of Veterans Stadium next to a picture of Citizens Bank Park, the ballpark where the team currently played.

"Nice couch and memorabilia. I'm taking a wild guess that you are a baseball fan and a Phillies fan to boot," Rita said.

"What gave it away?" Captain Allison Sanders said with a friendly snicker.

Rita just laughed and said, "Oh, I don't know … just call it a wild guess."

Captain Sanders smiled. "Yes, when I'm back home on leave, I try to catch a game or two at Citizens Bank Park. But I'm assuming you wanted to talk about something besides sports."

"I'm a Nationals fan myself. Anyway, you are correct. I'm not at liberty to tell you everything, but I feel there is something you should know about your crew," she responded.

"Please call me Allison."

"All right then, you can call me Rita."

"Rita, how can you enlighten me with news that pertains to my crew?"

"I believe that you have a spy on board."

"And you believe this because …?"

"When you first picked us up, your first officer referred to the Vomit Comet—VC for short. Did anyone inform you that I worked for this program?"

"No. All we were told was that this was a simple rescue operation to pick up two people who had been shipwrecked somewhere in our vicinity. We were to link our computers to a satellite for our coordinates. When I tried to ask for more information, I was told that it was classified and to let it go. I've never even heard of the VC before, and I have heard of lots of things. I don't think the admiral himself knew any of the details or who was running the operation."

"That's just it. If that's all the information you were given, why did Lieutenant Thorn refer to Vomit Comet in the first place?"

"So you think that my first officer might be the mole?"

"He does seem like the logical choice."

"Well, if that's true, then it complicates things."

"Why is that?"

"Because, besides being my first officer, he is also the son of Admiral Myers."

"But they have different last names."

"That's because Lieutenant Thorn took his mother's maiden name after the admiral and his mother divorced. Thorn didn't want to be perceived as getting special treatment by being the admiral's son. He thought by using another name, most people wouldn't associate him with the admiral. I've worked with Lieutenant Thorn for years. He is one of the most dedicated officers that I have ever seen. I can't believe he is a spy."

"Well, there is one other possibility."

Do not underestimate your abilities.
That is your boss's job.

—Unknown

Journal Entry 72

ASAP Headquarters

We were approaching the ASAP headquarters in downtown Andorra. ASAP must have been using some form of "glamour" or magic, because the outside of the building looked to be an abandoned business. To be more accurate, the outside looked exactly what I would expect a merger between a Krispy Kreme donut shop and a Starbucks coffee shop to look like. At first, this was confusing because these two business were usually quite viable on Earth. As we walked closer to the building, Elvis pushed a button in his pocket, and the building appearance changed dramatically.

The deserted warehouse with the Krispy Kreme–Starbucks front turned into an ultramodern, three-story building. Upon entering the building, I was struck by the vast security and surveillance stations throughout the first floor. The equipment looked very sophisticated; in fact, I figured that every inch of the city could be viewed from one of those stations.

I understood the need for security, but I couldn't shake the creepy feeling that Winston Smith experienced in the novel *1984* as Big Brother watching everyone. Looking at Erika, I suspected that she was experiencing a similar reaction.

Elvis noticed our expressions. "I see you two are admiring our extensive visual network system. I can assure you that these cameras are used only to spot criminal and terrorist activities. Our agents are highly sensitive and trained not to interfere with private and personal business that is of no interest to the safety of our city."

Alongside the transportation tube was an old-fashioned escalator and an elevator. The company name Otis was evident in the fancy gold frame around the elevator doors. Elvis explained that he'd had these put in when he took over as head of the ASAP. They were a little sliver of home, and they made him feel a little better about missing Earth and especially Gladys.

Collectively we decided to go old school and ride the escalator and forgo the faster, more efficient transportation tube. The second floor of the building included conference rooms and Elvis' private office. The third floor housed the ASAP training rooms and laboratories. Elvis explained that, in the training rooms, computer-generated holographic simulation exercises were used to train officers.

"Just like in *Star Trek the Next Generation*," I muttered.

"Next generation?" Elvis questioned.

I kept forgetting that, contrary to some popular folk legends, which included supposed Elvis sightings, he had legitimately died—I mean transmuted—in 1977. This was long before the sequel to the original *Star Trek* series.

Elvis remembered the original series. I explained to him that the original *Star Trek* had actually spun off three sequels, *The Next Generation*, *Deep Space Nine*, and *Enterprise*, which was probably the least successful and last of the series. I even had to admit, I had a hard time watching that one.

"To be honest, I was never much of a 'trekkie' I believe the term is," Elvis retorted. "But I did dig those fancy uniforms, and I did like Captain Kirk. He was my kind of fellow, with all the fighting and getting the pretty girl in the end."

"Me too," I said as Erika gave me a look that suggested I was a hopeless geek.

We entered the first conference room and were directed to sit at a golden oval-shaped table adorned around the edges with diamonds, rubies, and opals. An inlay of the ASAP insignia nearly filled the center.

Elvis sat at the head of the table. He was dressed in a pink button-down shirt and blue jeans—the outfit he'd worn during his ninth movie, *Follow That Dream*, which Elvis thought was apropos. Rosalie was seated to his right, and a number of other ASAP officials were sprinkled along the table. Rosalie wasn't dressed as a famous Earth heroine, but rather as a serious ASAP agent. I liked the other looks better. The remaining cast of players included Erika and me, Merlin, Jimmy, and Elias, who had been invited because of his invaluable assistance at the Ministry of Science. Plus, I had requested he be allowed to continue his grand adventure. Elvis had reluctantly relented to this request. He'd said something about some senior officials being unhappy, but then mentioned something like, "Oh well, that's life."

Elvis asked Rosalie to fill in the remaining ASAP officials regarding what had transpired over the last couple of days with Dr. Shelly.

Rosalie stood up and pushed a button on some sort of clicker, and a holographic image appeared over the table. A translucent but colored picture of Dr. Shelly emerged. His vital statistics were displayed—height, weight, eye color, and so forth.

She moved her fingers, and we saw image of the hospital rooms on the fourth floor of the Ministry of Science. She displayed the empty rooms along with the rooms containing the deceased victims. She continued to manipulate her hands, and the image of the fifth floor was displayed. The separate empty labs were shown as they had been left. During this process, Elvis provided vital information while the holographic translucent image appeared in midair.

Finally, an image of Erika appeared in the center. A spiraling image of a DNA molecule rotated angularly around her image. Elvis reiterated that her DNA had been altered as a result of the baby's blood mixing with her own blood. He explained to the ASAP officials that because of this mutation, Erika could basically now belong to both universes.

Rosalie took over and explained that, at this point, the mutation appeared to be stable, but the long-term effects were uncertain. However, they were pretty certain Dr.

Shelly's current main goal with his research was to emulate this mutation. This would enable him to create an army that could freely access both universes. With this crazy, diabolical, but brilliant scientist controlling this army, the ramifications could have a disastrous effect for both worlds.

She paused for a moment as some of the high-level ASAP personnel talked among each other. When they appeared to refocus, she continued. She explained that recent reports suggested that Dr. Shelly would attempt to recapture Erika in an effort to reproduce this anomaly in the DNA.

***

The whole time Rosalie was explaining this information, Dr. Shelly was listening to every word! Rosalie knew she was his daughter. What she was unaware of was that she was also a product of a number of his scientific experiments. When she was a baby he had injected her with the element Evionium (Ev), an element created artificially in this universe. It was now part of her nucleotides. Ev was a stable element that could be used in a process known as beamforming, the transferring of sound waves through a liquid or a gas. In addition, he had implanted a tiny, undetectable microchip in each of her temporal lobes to amplify sound. The combination of the Ev infused into her DNA, and the microchip amplification picked up every audio signal that Rosalie heard.

At the time, it was merely one of the scientific projects he was working on the ability to listen and hear what other people heard in their brains. It had never occurred to him that Rosalie would grow up and join the ASAP, and this micro-audio chip would actually still work after so long.

Just as Shelly had predicted, it was obvious that ASAP's plan was to get Erika back to Earth where he would have a much harder time getting to her and extracting her mutated DNA. The ASAP building was much too heavily guarded to attempt a kidnapping. He decided his best option would be to attempt to waylay her at the transport site that contained the wormhole that would send them back to Earth.

Not only does God definitely play dice,
but He sometimes
confuses us by throwing them where they can't be seen.

—Stephen Hawking

Journal Entry 73

Black Holes, White Holes, and Wormholes

When Rosalie had finished her briefing, everyone agreed the best thing for both worlds—and Erika—was to send her back to Earth. The only problem was that she would not agree to this unless Michael was allowed to accompany her back. They both understood his stay on Earth would be very brief, just long enough to ensure that she was safe. Additionally, they knew she could not return until Dr. Shelly was captured and incarcerated.

Because of her mutated DNA, Erika could travel back to Earth through a number of wormholes, but Michael could not. His only safe passage back would be through the same wormhole he had transmuted through when he left Earth.

ASAP scientists working along with Merlin had created a number of stable wormholes that connected Evion with Earth. There was one major problem. On occasion, the wormholes shifted, and therefore, even if they tried to determine the "original" wormhole that Michael had traveled through before, they might not be able to pick the right one.

As the committee listened, Elvis asked Merlin to elaborate, which he did. "You see, wormholes are really tubes that connect worlds or areas in space. One side of the wormhole opens into a black hole and the other side opens into a white hole."

"I am familiar with black holes," I said. "But I have to admit I am confused about white holes. Are they the opposite of black holes?"

"Basically, whereas a black hole sucks in all surrounding matter, a white hole spits out all matter that travels through the black hole that it is connected to," Merlin responded.

"Okay then," Erika interjected, "the wormhole is a big open pipe that attaches at one side to a black hole and to the other side with a white hole?

"Well, yes," Merlin said. "I mean it is just a tad more complicated, but you get the basic idea."

"All right, assuming that this crazy notion of drain pipes, wormholes, and black and white holes is all true, I'm still a little confused on two issues," I stated.

Erika smiled at me and said, "Go on, science guy, ask your questions, because the pipe thing was as far as I got."

"It is my understanding that the intensity of gravity inside a black hole is so great, any matter that enters it would be crushed instantly. I would assume the same would be true for a white hole if it really existed. How could someone travel through it to reach the other wormhole without being crushed?"

"And your second question is?" Merlin asked.

"If you have actually created stable wormholes, how or why do they shift? Why can't I travel back through the same hole I originally came through?"

"Good questions," Erika said as she winked at me. "I was thinking the same thing myself."

"Let me start with your first question," Merlin answered. "Not all black holes are connected to white holes. In regard to a normal black hole, you are correct—anything that enters it would be crushed out of existence instantly. However, there are rare black holes connected to white holes that can be manipulated by science or the supernatural, whatever term you prefer. In these black holes we can prevent the crushing out of existence all together."

Almost forgetting who I was talking to, I said, "Merlin, are you serious?"

Merlin laughed. "I was only half kidding. It's really more of a blend of real magic and science. You see, most people don't realize the connection between magic and science. The two are much more aligned than most people understand. The alchemists of the Middle Ages and the Renaissance had some basic understanding of the connection between science and magic, but for some reason, that field of study died on Earth long ago."

"So you have devised a way to solve the gravitational problem of black hole traveling?" I asked.

"Yes," Merlin said as he glanced at Elvis. "We can talk about the details of my work on black and white hole antigravity stabilization later if ASAP clears it."

Elvis gave us a noncommittal flustered look.

"As to your second question," Merlin continued. "I believe I can answer that without giving away any national secrets. You see, by their very nature, black and white holes are very transitory. Space is very vast and nonconfining. If a black and white holes happen to come close enough to one another, their extreme gravitational attractions sometimes cause them to intermix. Can you see the implications?"

"I think so. If a black hole mixed with a white hole, you could end up traveling through it and arriving in a completely different world than the one you intended. If a black hole were severed from its original wormhole, then you would be crushed out of existence, as would occur in a normal black hole. If the wormhole remained connected but the white hole was removed and replaced with another white hole, then you would theoretically travel through the wormhole forever, or until you ceased to exist," I postured.

"Excellent. You have a sharp mind. Maybe your talents are being wasted as a janitor at the Science Ministry," Merlin joked.

I looked at Elvis. "I'm sure now that I have fulfilled my original purpose for having been manipulated into working as a custodial engineer, maybe the boys at ASAP can better utilize my talents. I was thinking of maybe going into the entertainment field when I return, maybe even starting my own rock band."

Elvis shook his head. "Sure, Michael. After Erika is safely returned to Earth and Dr. Shelly is captured—whatever you want."

***

Dr. Shelly continued to listen carefully. He laughed, but only briefly. He knew he was a wanted man, but his resources were substantial. He believed capturing Michael would be easier than he thought, especially after he had Ms. Nirvona back in his possession where she belonged— to science and him, of course. Erika was simply too important from a scientific perspective to be allowed to escape back to Earth.

It's hard to tell who has your back, from who
has it long enough just to stab you in it ...

—Nicole Richie

Journal Entry 74

Betrayal at the Aquarium

The *Fighting Phanatic* arrived at the AUTEC Complex
Navy Base, formally known as The Atlantic Undersea
Test and Evaluation Center Complex, located in West
Palm Beach, Florida. It contained one of the world's most
advanced three-dimensional laboratories within the fields
of hydrospace and aerospace technology.

Nicknamed TOTO (Tongue of the Ocean) by naval
personnel, the complex was strategically positioned
between the islands of Andros, New Providence, and
Exuma Sound. Three phases of military testing occurred
there: testing the world's most advanced weaponry systems;
acoustics science; and FORACS drills (Fleet Operational
Readiness Accuracy Check Site). FORACS was important
for measuring the bearing and range accuracy of sensor
systems on ships, submarines, and aircraft. Completed in
1974, TOTO remained one of the most sophisticated and
advanced laboratories in the world.

There were several reasons that Captain Allison Sanders
chose to dock at the AUTEC Complex. It was the closest
naval base to their current location. Additionally, she
thought they might be able to take advantage of the
highly advanced laboratory equipment to find answers as
to why Devil's Island was off the grid, so to speak. Okay,

so maybe she followed orders, but not exactly. Sometimes she took certain liberties in the interpretation of those orders. And last, as luck would have it, Admiral Myers was coincidently making an inspection of the base. His inspection was supposed to be a surprise, but she had a few connections of her own that she occasionally used.

Captain Sanders didn't believe in coincidences. She was superstitious when it came to sporting events. But she was less confident in coincidences. She wondered why the admiral had chosen to spring an unannounced visit at this particular time.

Agent Dubay and Captain Denton would remain with her and her crew at TOTO. The remaining injured survivors would be transferred by helicopter to the naval hospital in Pensacola for medical attention and eventually government assistance. This hospital was among the oldest and most modern medical facilities in the United States.

The current commander of TOTO was Commander Levon Breeze, an old friend. He was the first African American commander of this base. She had met him during freshman year at the Naval Academy in Annapolis, Maryland, and they had dated briefly. Allison had not seen Bree—her nickname for him—for a couple of years; she had radioed ahead to expect their arrival.

After they docked, the injured were immediately airlifted to Pensacola, and the rest of the group entered the complex.

Commander Breeze came to the reception area to greet them, and gave Captain Sanders a warm hug. "Sands, it's great to see you."

Captain Sanders introduced Captain Denton and Agent Dubay to Commander Breeze. She gave him a brief summary of what she knew had transpired in the last twenty-four hours.

Commander Breeze listened intently to her story. After she finished, he said, "Follow me, please."

They entered an elevator followed by Rita, James, and Lieutenant Thorn. The elevator took them downward, toward the bottom of the sea.

"Do you guys have an undersea restaurant?" James quipped. "Because I have always wanted to dine twenty thousand leagues below the sea with the fish."

Allison turned to Rita, "Does he always think about food?"

"Ever since I've known him," she said, laughing.

"Actually, we do have a wet bar and a snack station down in the conference room," Bree said.

"Really?" James asked hopefully.

"Um, no, but it is about twenty thousand leagues below the sea," Commander Bree stated. "And we do have a great view of some very unusual sea creatures that most people never get to see. But the main reason I'm taking you to this underwater conference room is because it is secured. It is far enough below the surface to be free from any outside bugging or listening devices."

The elevator was made from five-inch-thick glass allowing them to view the spectacular sea life on the way down.

As they descended further, James noticed a seven-inch roundish, lumpy-looking brown-and-black creature. Its huge orifice was filled with sharp teeth, and a flexible three-inch "fishing rod" stuck out from its forehead. There was even a light at the end of the rod.

"What in the world is that?" he asked.

"Oh that's just a *Melanocetus johnsonii,* more commonly known as a humpback angler fish. They are pretty common at these depths," Bree responded.

"Well, it looks evil," James said.

"Yes, that's probably why it belongs to a species commonly called the Black Sea Devil," Bree affirmed.

Rita looked out the back pane of glass, "What is that thing?"

"You mean the creature that looks like a twisted shark with a triangular head and very small fins?" Bree asked.

Rita nodded.

"That's a frilled shark. They are very rare and considered to be living fossils. We don't often see them around these parts," he informed the group.

"Maybe it's our lucky day," James joked.

Just before the elevator stopped, a crab-like creature with long hairy arms swam by.

"Those arms kind of remind me of *Big Foot*," James said.

"Close," Bree interjected. "Actually more like a yeti."

"You mean like the one at Mount Everest in the Walt Disney World resort?" James pondered.

Commander Bree laughed. "Not quite. This creature is called a yeti crab, and it was so rare a whole new family classification had to be created to identify it."

James turned to Rita. "See? It must definitely be our lucky day. Maybe I'll play the lottery when we get back."

The elevator finally came to a stop. They exited and walked into a large, glass-enclosed circular room. Admiral Myers was standing there with three of his officers. Each of them had a 9mm gun pointed at the visitors.

Rita turned to James. "Yeah, it definitely must be our lucky day."

Close your eyes and tap your heels together three times.
And think to yourself, there's no place like home.

— L. Frank Baum

Journal Entry 75

Going back to Kansas … I mean New Jersey

Elvis stood. "Okay, we are all in agreement. We will attempt to send Ms. Nirvona back to Earth with Michael. Michael, you understand that you can stay with her on Earth only for a very brief time or your DNA will most likely destabilize, which will cause you to cease to exist."

"Got it. By the way, how long is a brief amount of time? I thought that maybe I would take in a ball game or two when I got back. Your sports are okay, but I miss the old-fashioned rules and sporting events," I proclaimed.

"We are not exactly sure how long you will have," Elvis replied. "Probably no more than a couple days or so. Actually, we are not even a hundred percent positive that your DNA will destabilize, but the odds are not in your favor."

I shook my head and echoed, "Okay then, for only a short time."

"After we apprehend Dr. Shelly, Erika will be free to come back to join you if she wishes," Rosalie added.

"That's assuming her current mutation is stable and continues to allow her access to both universes," I interjected.

"True, but at this point there is no reason to believe anything to the contrary," Merlin pointed out.

"Okay, but there is still the slight problem of actually capturing Dr. Shelly," I mentioned. "I have a sneaking suspicion it will be somewhat difficult, given the fact that he is brilliant. I know he is a twisted, self-absorbed, psychopathic murdering snake who sees himself as a deity-like figure and believes that he has the right to play God and manipulate evolution, but he is still a very cunning bastard."

Erika looked at me and smiled. "Wow, that was quite a speech, but I agree with Michael, since I have had my own personal experience with that creep. It won't be that easy. It took a knight in shining armor to rescue me," she said and stuck her tongue out at me playfully.

"There is also the problem of finding the correct wormhole for me to travel back through," I said. "Merlin explained to me earlier that I would need to travel back through the same one I originally entered this universe from."

"True," Rosalie interjected. "But Enoch has provided us with the proper coordinates, so that should not be a problem. You see, each wormhole gives off a unique radio wave signal. It's kind of like a person's fingerprints. The biggest challenge, I think, will be keeping the operation a secret and getting you two there safely."

Elvis must have seen the look of concern on my face because he cut in, "Don't worry, Michael, we have a plan. There's always a plan." He was trying so hard to be reassuring.

I don't know why—I never really have been psychic like my mother—but I got the strange feeling it wasn't going to be that simple. I felt like Joe Pendelton listening to Mr. Jordan telling him not to worry, that there was always a plan, just before he was shot and fell down the well in the movie *Heaven Can Wait*. Okay, I really did watch too many movies but I couldn't shake the feeling.

Maybe it was the Philadelphia sports fan in me who always subscribed to Murphy's Law, especially when it came to watching sports. Maybe I was an eternal pessimist. Or it could have been the old wise man that everyone is always talking about who said, "Listen to your gut …" My gut told me that it was far from over.

I don't like to commit myself about heaven and
hell—you see, I have friends in both places.

—Mark Twain

Journal Entry 76

Sociopaths, Moles, and Such

Captain Sanders glared at Commander Levon Breeze. He
lowered his head in shame. "Bree, how could you?"

"You don't understand," he replied.

Breeze looked at Admiral Myers, who nodded and said,
"We have a little time for explanation if you want."

"I'm sorry, Sands," Breeze explained. "They have my
family. My wife and little girl are being held captive."

"You're married and have a child?" Captain Sanders said,
shaking her head.

"Yes. It's been a while, and I guess I forgot to mention that
the last time we talked … the last time we were together."

"Men!" said Rita. "So many times they act like real jerks!
They think—"

One of the solders with Admiral Myers stepped forward
and jabbed the butt end of his gun into Rita's side,
effectively stopping her in mid-sentence.

"They told me that if I didn't do what they asked, they would kill my wife and daughter," Commander Breeze said dejectedly. "I had no choice."

"But how did you know that I would bring these people here?" Captain Sanders asked. "And why did you let the others go?"

"We were not certain, but we took into consideration your previous relationship with Commander Breeze and the fact that this is the closest naval base to your location. Then we took a calculated risk," Admiral Myers answered.

"But why did you let the others go?" Captain Sanders reiterated.

"Let go. Oh, yes," Myers replied. "The story about sending them to the hospital in Pensacola was a little white lie. Actually, they also know too much. Those vagabonds were sent to Dr. Reed at Hospital X for some R and E—rehabilitation and experimentation."

"Michael Cardazia informed me about Hospital X before he died," Rita interjected. "It is really an experimentation and torture center, isn't it?"

Admiral Myers laughed. "Died? You think he died? That's funny. Anyway, tomato, tohmaydo, call it what you like. It's really just semantics anyway."

"Father, why are you doing this?"

Again Admiral Myers chuckled. "Father! I'm not your father."

"What are you talking about?" Lieutenant Thorn asked.

"Your mother and I never told you that you were adopted. Your real mother was a junkie living in the streets of Philadelphia. Your biological father wanted nothing to do with her. Besides, he died fighting in the Vietnam War."

Lieutenant Thorn looked stunned. Finding this out made his whole childhood seem like a lie. Everything he thought he knew about growing up was probably a lie as well. What was the truth and what was imaginary?

"But to answer your question," said the admiral. "Why I'm doing this? There are really two reasons. The first reason is obvious, isn't it? Show me the money! Isn't it always about money? If we are being honest, crime really does pay. I know it's a bit cliché, but it's true."

"Of course, it is always about money with criminals," Rita stated.

"Please don't insult me," said the admiral. "There's the money aspect, but give me some credit. I said there were two reasons. The work that Dr. Reed and Dr. Shelly are doing with our test subjects will improve humankind dramatically. Their research will lead to evolutionary advancements that would have taken Mother Nature thousands of years to accomplish. I would just like to play a small role in this grand experiment."

"So the medical advancements justify the killing of innocent people?" Rita angrily chastised him. "You're supposed achievements give you the right to play God and determine who lives, who dies, and how humankind should evolve? The names and faces may change, but the profiles are always the same."

"How's that?" Myers asked.

"Do I have time to elaborate to such a brilliant man?"

"Sure, we a have a little time before we have to leave. Humor me."

"You fit the profile of a classic sociopath that I learned about during my training at the CIA and NASA, as does Dr. Reed and most likely Dr. Shelly, whoever he is."

Myers smirked. "Go on."

"People such as yourself tend to be manipulative and cunning, seeing your own self-serving behaviors as permissible," Rita explained. "You exhibit a lack of guilt and remorse for your actions, not seeing people as important but rather as targets and opportunities. Obviously, you have a grandiose self-image and believe you are entitled to whatever you want, whenever you want it. You are callous and lack empathy for the homeless people, but have no problem taking advantage of them, causing them pain, and allowing them to be experimented on and killed. Lying is no problem, even to the point of pathological lying as long as it justifies getting what you want. I would not be surprised if you could pass any lie detector test because maybe you even believe that your justifications are warranted. And the best part is that you go about your business with a glibness, even a superficial charm."

She took a deep breath and continued, "Your kind is not concerned about wrecking other people's lives or dreams. It is not uncommon for you to lash out with verbal outbursts and physical punishments against people who disappoint you. I would bet that, as I child, you exhibited acts of cruelty to people and animals. You probably—"

Admiral Myers laughed out loud. "Yes, well, that's enough. I think we all get your point, but it's time to get down to business. Let me say that it's a shame you wasted your analytical skills on being a common spy. You would have made a really good shrink, which pays a little better. Anyway, the rest of you have a more exciting journey ahead of you. Some might even say this adventure is out of this world."

"Kreacher said nothing," said the elf, with a second bow to George, adding in a clear undertone, "and there's its twin, unnatural little beats they are."

—J.K. Rowling
Harry Potter and the Order of the Phoenix

Journal Entry 77

Twins, Sort Of?

Dr. Shelly listened as Rosalie laid out the plan to get Michael Cardazia and Erika Nirvona back to Earth. As she deftly moved her fingers through the air, notes and a map appeared on the holographic digital screen that hovered in midair.

***

"We figure that Dr. Shelly has spies, possibly a mole or two within ASAP. Therefore, we have decided to take every precaution. These arrangements will take a day to prepare, so our target date for sending you guys home is tomorrow," she explained.

"I only get one day to show her around the city?" I joked. "You know, show her all the perks that Andorra has to offer—the museums, local cuisines, fine arts and such?"

Elvis laughed. "I get it. Sell the city to her. Make her want to come back after this is all finished. Clever, but I do have some security concerns. I'm afraid I can't allow that. It will have to be a quiet evening at your apartment and an early pickup in the morning."

I smiled at Erika. "Well, I guess there are worse things in both universes than spending a quiet evening alone with you."

She blushed and nodded in agreement.

"Let me introduce Skyler," Elvis stated. "He is one of my assistants. He will take over from here."

Skyler entered the room. He looked human. In fact, he looked to be a perfect human specimen. He was six foot one and had blonde hair and hazel eyes. I estimated he was approximately twenty-three years of age. He appeared to be in excellent physical condition. Skyler was clean cut. He had no facial hair, and the hair on his head was perfectly aligned—not a single strand was out of place. In fact, on Earth, he probably would have been in *GQ* magazine. It also occurred to me that he fit the description of the "master race" Hitler was striving for.

It wasn't that I was jealous of his model looks; after all, I was sort of decent looking myself now that I was many years younger on Evion. I just had a feeling that I didn't like him. I couldn't explain it, but it was like a premonition. You know the feeling you have when your team is winning big and you think there is no way they can lose the game? But in your gut you have the sinking feeling that it is too easy and they end up losing? Okay, maybe I was a teeny bit jealous, but I still had that feeling.

"Thanks, Elvis," said Skyler. "Hi, everyone. My name is Skyler, and my expertise is in tactical planning in the transportation of both dangerous prisoners and high-ranking officials. Enoch has provided us with the coordinates of the wormhole Michael originally traveled through to get to Evion. As luck would have it, there is a closer entrance that would prevent Michael and Erika from having to travel through the Nether Region to get to it."

How convenient, I thought, sounding a little like Dana Carvey as the Church Lady from *Saturday Night Live.*

"The problem," continued Skyler, "is that entrance is located in an unstable part of the city. It will be a little more difficult to secure, but we feel it is an acceptable risk."

"Acceptable risk?" I questioned his words. "You mean like sacrificing the few for the good of the many?"

Skyler grinned. "It's not like that at all. You will be heavily guarded. I just meant that we, the ASAP, believe that, since this location is so much closer than the other entrance, it's the way to go with this operation. As you know, the Nether Region can be very unpleasant this time of the year."

"Don't worry, Michael," Rosalie interjected. "We will have the area secured by tomorrow evening."

"And, in addition," offered Elvis, "we have one more safety feature."

The door to the room opened, and two people walked in. The couple looked exactly like Erika and me. I mean *exactly* like us, down to the scars, moles, and bitten finger nails that we both had. Our mouths dropped.

"Shape shifters?" I asked. "You have shape shifters like on *True Blood* and *Fringe*?"

Merlin interjected, "Not exactly. I have a special TV down in The Trades, and those are two of my favorite Earth shows. These people are called drones. They are not shape shifters but duplicates."

"Where did they come from?" Erika wanted to know.

"First let me explain more precisely what they are," Merlin said. "They are low-functioning doubles of you two. Their mental capacities are just above the serviceable range."

"You mean they are developmentally disabled?" I asked.

"No, I wouldn't use the term *disabled*," Merlin answered. "But they are not very intelligent. They don't have many independent thoughts. They wait for instructions and do what they are asked."

"And in this case?" I politely inquired.

"Isn't it obvious?" asked Skyler. "They look exactly like you and sound like you in every way. Double Michael and Double Erika are exact copies of you except for their intelligence level. They are your decoys. These two double will be sent to the farther entry point of the wormhole. They will leave before you two and head into the Nether Region. If any of Dr. Shelly's people are following you, they will think they are the real Michael and Erika."

"What happens if they are captured or killed along the way?" Erika asked.

"Nothing." Skyler stated. "They would only be obsolete after the mission anyway."

Erika and I looked at each other; I knew we were thinking the same thing. "By obsolete, you mean destroyed, right?" I asked.

"Well, yes," Elvis said. "But that is their purpose, and it is done painlessly and compassionately. Besides, I doubt they really understand what is happening anyway."

"It's wrong to just use them and then destroy them," Erika countered.

"I'm sorry," Elvis said apologetically. "And I understand how you feel, but these doubles are low functioning and wouldn't be able to contribute much more than what they were created for—body doubles. They would create a huge burden on our society's limited resources."

"I think I know the answer, but I have to ask it anyway," I said. "If they are exact genetic copies minus the brain power—and let me add that I am definitely more debonair than my double—where did they come from?"

"When you both entered our universe, a copy of your DNA was made. These genetic maps were stored in the medical branch of ASAP's science labs," Elvis responded.

"So you have a DNA record of everybody on this planet, and it can be used to make exact, albeit stupider, copies of anyone?" I asked.

Elvis looked a little surprised that I would take offense to this procedure. He was probably thinking, after all, he was helping Erika and me. But being a good old Southerner, Gladys had always taught her to be truthful, at least when there was no harm in it.

"Yes, that is true," he stated honestly.

That's because it's from the night,
and the night keeps secrets.

—Maggie Stiefvater, *Lament:
The Faerie Queen's Deception*

Journal Entry 78

Last Night, Silent Night

Jimmy and Suzie dropped us off at my apartment after the meeting with ASAP. After completing the mission of safely returning Erika home, I was going to be coming back to a world I had mixed feelings about. I had no choice but to take Erika back to Earth. I believed she would be coming back to Evion after Dr. Shelly was apprehended, but it was her choice and hers alone. Provided Dr. Shelly didn't have his way, she was the only person we knew who was capable of surviving in both universes. Maybe our unborn child would have the same ability, but that had yet to be determined.

Sensing the realization that Erika might not return, Suzie said, "Good-bye, Erika. I hope I will see you again, but just in case I don't, I wanted to let you know it was really great meeting you, and I wish you the best."

Erika smiled. "Ford and General Motors could certainly learn a lot from you. It was my pleasure getting to know you, but I will be back sooner rather than later. Maybe then you could show me that great parking garage you were bragging about earlier."

Suzie's dashboard lit slightly with a soft-colored hue, and I would have sworn she was blushing ever so slightly.

We said our good-byes. I leaned over to Jimmy and whispered, "Thanks for all of your help. I never could have done all of this without you. You are a true friend, and I will never forget that." I shook his hand and left with Erika.

When we arrived at my apartment, we decided to review the next morning's arrangements. The plan was relatively simple. (Aren't they always?) After breakfast, Elvis, Rosalie, and Skyler were going to pick us up in an unmarked air van. One hour prior to our departure, our doubles would be sent in a similar air van through the gigantic city gates to the Nether Region and through the Acituan Mountains. Finally they would arrive at the wormhole where I had originally entered into this universe.

Although the area of town we were headed for wasn't the most desirable, Elvis promised that ASAP would have it cleaned up and secured before we arrived. I had a feeling I knew what that meant and didn't think it was good news for the people that lived there. I knew that ASAP and Elvis were basically the good guys here on Evion, but their methods seemed a bit extreme and harsh to Erika and me.

After we arrived at the second secret opening to the wormhole that Merlin had helped to develop and stabilize, he would meet us and help facilitate the process of opening the wormhole and sending us back to Earth.

I would have only a maximum of seventy-two hours before I had to return back to Universe Zero through the same wormhole. If I didn't, it was possible that my DNA could destabilize, and I would cease to exist in either world. Since not existing would not help me stay with Erika, I had no choice but to return.

We were told to lie low that night as a precaution. ASAP would provide us with anything we desired for dinner. Although going out of the building into the city was not an option, we were free to visit any of our friends from Earth within the building. Elvis was busy with the final arrangements for our trip, but Elias, Abraham, and Frank were home, so we could visit them and say good-bye. Marilyn, Enoch, and Brace were on another recruiting mission, but they had left their best wishes.

We were not particularly hungry, but we decided it was best to order something for our last meal, so to speak. Interdimensional travel through wormholes on an empty stomach is never a good idea. It was recommended that we eat a decent dinner and then have a light breakfast the morning of our voyage. Since it was possibly our last night together, Elvis pulled a few strings and was able to get us food from Earth. He wouldn't say how he accomplished this, but told us to think of it as a going away present.

Since money was no object, I ordered a two-pound Maine lobster with a twice-baked potato, Caesar salad, and a diet coke. Erika ordered broiled deep-sea scallops with a cup of soup and a diet peach Snapple.

At the conclusion of our meal, which we ate mostly in an unsettling silence, Erika began, "Michael, I know you respect Elvis, but what the ASAP is doing—creating doubles from people's DNA without their permission—is wrong. Even if the drones don't fully understand what is happening, using them as collateral damage is immoral."

"I completely agree with you, and when I get back, I promise to have a long talk with the officials at ASAP. I will see if I can get that practice stopped, but I have a feeling it will take a lot of convincing. In the meantime, my first priority is to get you back safely to Earth."

"Okay, you know I'm still not happy about it, but I guess I have to let this one go, at least for now."

"I promise I will do what I can when I return. I wasn't sure if you wanted to visit Elias or Frank or Abrah—"

She stopped me short with a gentle kiss.

"When I come back, I will have plenty of time to visit with them, but not tonight. Tonight is just about you and me."

I pulled away slightly. "There's nothing in the world I want more than to be with you. You are my heart and soul, and even though I met you later in life, you changed my life. You are my life, and nothing makes sense without you. I used to think I was right even when I was wrong, but with you I see so much clearer. Simply put, you are part of me and always will be. But it is because I love you so much that I can't ask you to give up your life and family back on Earth, to give up everything you have worked for."

She smiled and then gave me a more serious look than I had ever seen before. "Because I love you so much, I chose to give them up to be with you. Because you love me enough not to ask, you don't have to. I admit there were times when I wasn't sure, but losing you once erased any doubts. I won't lose you again."

Erika leaned in, and this time gave me a more passionate kiss. That was it; I was helpless and hopelessly unable to argue—probably for the first time in my life. Whatever the fates had in store, it would be for the two of us together. I would let go. I would give up control and let the Universe do what it would. But I knew that, in the end, we would be together. I didn't know how or why, but I just knew we would.

She held me close, and nothing mattered but the warmth of her skin. Her sweet lips pressed tightly against mine. The curve of her body intertwined with mine, her heart beating in rhythm with mine. Our bodies fit together perfectly as they always had, as I believed they always would. All of these things made me forget our troubles.

I began to realize how quiet and peaceful the night was. It occurred to me how lucky I was to be here in this moment with Erika. I recognized how fragile life was and how it could change in a New York minute. But that didn't matter. I was in the here and now, and it was what it should be. It was what it had to be. It was perfect.

Life hadn't always been fair to either one of us. We each had our crosses to bear in our own unique ways. Both of us carried old war wounds and scars. I knew that, in many ways, life had been hardest for her. But none of that seemed to matter now.

No matter what happened the next day or afterward, in the end it would always be okay as long as I had Erika by my side. And for the first time—and the only time—this world somehow turned out to be my real world. It was all good, and I was finally at peace.

The great temple of fiction has no well-marked
front portal; most devotees arrive through a
side door, and not dressed for worship.

—John Hoyer Updike

Journal Entry 79

The Portal at Stonehenge

"If you have finished psychoanalyzing me," Admiral
Myers said, "which I must add was highly fascinating,
and maybe some of it is true—hell, probably most of it
is true—I think the psycho-babble time is up. Again, I
would like to emphasize that it has been a pleasure. Try
to remember me as more than a simple criminal after
just the money. Try to think of me as a patriot in this
evolutionary cause."

"I'm assuming that you wouldn't mind telling us your
plans for us," James said.

"Of course not! That's all part of the fun. You know us
sociopaths," he said, glancing briefly at Rita. "We so enjoy
telling our victims what we are going to do and then
executing our plan."

"Well, we are all listening," Captain Sanders said.

"All of you are going to be sent through a portal—more
precisely a wormhole—that leads to another universe."

"Right, and I guess afterward we will all be going to
Disney World," James joked.

"No, I think he is serious," Captain Denton interjected.

Looking directly at Agent James Dubay and Captain Rita Denton, Admiral Myers responded, "Yes, I am. Since you two created problems for us on Devil's Island, we can no longer use that portal. But fortunately, we have another wormhole that we can use. It's a bit more of a trip, but on the plus side, I hear the countryside is lovely this time of year."

"I'm guessing, Admiral Myers, that you won't mind telling us where that is," Lieutenant Thorn said.

"What, no more *dad? Father?* Oh well," he laughingly replied.

Lieutenant Thorn just looked back with disgust and contempt.

"Well, since the plans are already in motion, and there is nothing any of you can do to stop them, I guess there isn't any harm in telling you. There's a little county called Wiltshire in England not far from Amesbury and Salisbury. That's where we are all headed in my private jet."

"You don't mean Stonehenge, do you?" James asked. "Well, geography was sort of a childhood hobby of mine."

"Very good, Agent Dubay. Apparently you are smarter than you look."

"I wish I could say the same for—" Before James could finish, one of the admiral's lackeys jabbed the butt end of the rifle into his mid-section.

"Respect, Agent Dubay," Admiral Myers stated sternly. "All I ask is for a little respect from all of you. I don't expect that you can or will appreciate all we will accomplish for humankind. But, at the very least, I feel that I have earned a modicum of deference." He scratched his head. "Anyway, where was I? Oh yes, we were talking about the gateway to the other universe. You see, the people from the other universe established two portals—wormholes— that would allow travel from one universe to the other. One of these gateways was established in the Bermuda Triangle on Devil's Island. The other was established at Stonehenge."

"You really are serious, aren't you?" Rita asked Admiral Myers.

"Yes, of course I am. There is another universe that connects to our own. The great man that I am working for, Dr. Shelly, is currently there. Obviously, you all know too much, so I am sending all of you there to meet Dr. Shelly. It really is a great honor. He has done some amazing groundbreaking work in the field of genetics and evolution. The five of you will have a part in this research. To be completely honest, I am a bit jealous, but I'll deal with it."

"So that's it? Captain Sanders sneered angrily. "You're just going to send us to another universe into the hands of a madman?"

"Madman? You mean a great man! And, yes, that's pretty much it in a nutshell. The details are trivial but simple. My chief medical officer is going to inject you with a rather strong sedative. Don't worry; it's mostly harmless except for a slight headache when you wake up. It should keep you asleep throughout the trip so you won't be too bored during the flight. I've been told that a slight modification has been added to the drug, courtesy of Dr. Shelly. This modification should give you pleasant dreams—or nightmares, I forget which—while you are asleep."

Rita calculated their probability of escaping if they attempted a quick assault on the men holding the guns. They were not very good odds.

As if reading her mind, Admiral Myers quickly added, "If you attempt any trouble, my men will shoot you immediately, and we will kill Commander Breeze's wife and child. But you do have my word as an officer and a gentleman that Commanders Breeze's family will be released and unharmed after you are transported to Dr. Shelly."

One of the guards whispered something to Admiral Myers, and he nodded. "I almost forgot," he said. "Since none of you will be returning to Earth, if there is anything you wish to write or notes you wish to leave, I give you my word as an officer and a sociopathic gentleman that your messages will be delivered to your loved ones. Of course, they will arrive anonymously, but I will make sure they are delivered. I feel that's the least I could do."

Sensing their apprehension and possible resistance, he decided it was best to leave out the part about their DNA destabilizing and that they would not survive very long in Universe Zero, even if Dr. Shelly chose not to use them in his work.

I took the road less traveled by, and
that has made all the difference.

—Robert Frost

Journal Entry 80

The Yellow Brick Road Home through Denny's

We woke up early. I didn't want to. I just wanted to lie
enveloped in Erika's arms. But Elvis had insisted on an
early departure and what he called "a filling but sensible
breakfast." I had my usual vegetable egg white omelet, and
Erika had french toast. As usual, she gave me half. One of
the best things about eating breakfast with her was that
I could always count on getting half of her pancakes or
french toast.

Like the dinner we'd had the night before, the meal
tasted as if it had come from Earth. I wasn't going to
inquire because I knew the response would probably
be something like, "It was magic. Just enjoy the meal
and don't question it." So, we just enjoyed our breakfast
together—me with my coffee and hazelnut creamer and
her with hot chocolate topped with whipped cream.

After breakfast there was a knock on the door. Skyler and
Rosalie were dressed in normal clothing. *Undercover, I
suppose*, I thought. They informed us that Elvis was in
the vehicle waiting.

There was an air van waiting for us. The minute we
entered, the inside turned into a long, black stretch limo,
but the outside still looked like a small van. I had to give

Elvis credit; he did like to travel in style. We sat in the back with Elvis, Rosalie, and Skyler. Elvis was dressed as a United States Army sergeant; I guessed it was the outfit he wore in *G. I. Blues*. "I like the outfit. You know my father was also in the United States Army," I proudly stated.

"I know," he responded.

"You do? Did you know him? Is he also here somewhere?"

Elvis smiled and laughed. "Take it easy, Michael. We can talk when you return, but right now I think we should focus on the current mission."

"Sorry, it's just that I haven't seen my father since I was ... Never mind. Of course you are right."

"Your duplicates left for the Nether Region in the same type of van about an hour ago. So far there have been no reports of any incident," Skyler informed us.

"Where are we going?" I asked.

"The alternate portal through the wormhole is located in a section of the city known as Old Earth. It's not one of the more desirable or affluent sections of town, but last night a crew from ASAP rounded up some of the trouble makers, so we should be fine," Elvis said.

It took about twenty minutes. We drove through a tunnel that separated that part of the city from the rest. The limo landed on a car pad, and we exited the car. We walked over a hill and down a path to the heart of the district. I was instantly taken back by the appearance of the small town.

It was as if the 1950s from Earth had exploded everywhere. Vintage cars were parked along the streets. For a moment I thought I was in a scene from *Happy Days*, and that Arthur Fonzarelli would appear any minute with his thumbs pointed up recanting, *"Aaaaeeeyyy!"* or *"Sit on it."*

I noticed a 1950s red Chrysler Newport adjacent to an orange Ford Thunderbird. Parked across the street was a spectacular silver Cadillac Eldorado Brougham. There was also a blue Studebaker Commander Starlight, a grey Packard Clipper, and a green Hudson Hornet parked in a lot across the street. It was a rich man's car-collecting dream.

The people walking on the streets looked to be mostly human. They generally ignored us but seemed to be a little intimated when they saw Elvis. The men were mostly clean cut and conservative wearing charcoal grey flannel suits, single-breasted with two or three widely spaced buttons, unwaisted, with no back vent. They wore what I believe were called "penny loafers," a slip-on shoe with a cut-out apron into which one could fit a penny, and hence the name. Some of the men sported crew cuts, but in general their hair was kept short and neat.

The ladies wore clothes with tight bodices and flowing or fitted skirts, and high heels. Some sported jackets that nipped the waist and skirts that were either full or fitted. Their sleeves were shorter, allowing them to better show off the bracelets and gloves that most wore.

Younger girls wore poodle skirts, bobby socks, saddle shoes and ponytails. Some of the women were wearing tight sweater sets or blouses and skirts emphasizing the waistlines. Others wore dresses with flowing skirts in bright colorful fabrics. I noticed that fabrics like organdie, chiffon, and tulle were very popular among these women.

There was a sense of innocence emanating from the streets. I could smell popcorn and cotton candy as we walked down the main street, which was coincidently called Main Street. A faint hint of burnt charcoal, hot dogs, and hamburgers was present.

As we walked, Erika noticed there didn't seem to be any children anywhere—just men, women, and a few teenagers. I realized she was right.

Every street corner we passed was named after a tree. There were Maple, Oak, Cedar, Elm and Pine Streets. There was a pharmacy with soda counter inside, a hardware store, and a diner, each located on street corner. On one corner, an advertisement for a drive-in movie had been pasted on the old-fashioned lamppost.

I turned to Elvis, "Okay, I really have to ask, what is with this town? Did we suddenly transport back in time through a *Happy Days* time machine or something?"

Elvis smiled. "You mean because the town appears to be a typical small American town circa 1950?"

"Yes, that's exactly why I'm asking."

"We still have a little time," he said, "Why don't we all sit on the park bench under the large elm tree, and I will explain."

When we were settled, Elvis continued, "When I moved up into an important role at the ASAP division, we needed to create some alternate access points to some of the wormholes. I had these towns created. Some of them contain alternate routes to the wormhole entrances."

"I get these alternate routes to the wormholes to save time and the secrecy part, but the *Happy Days* theme?"

"Oh, I see what you mean. The answer is simple. We needed to create a district that most Andorrans wouldn't want to settle in. That was the only way we could keep them secure. Most of the citizens like more modern surroundings, so the majority stayed away from Old Earth."

He continued, "Since my heyday was the 1950s, as it was for Marilyn and Frank and to some extent Walt, I decided on that theme. It was a special time for me. Just think of some of the important events of that decade—NASA was created, the DNA molecule was discovered, the first modern credit card was introduced, color television became available, drive-in movies were popular, Disneyland was opened and—"

"The first issue of *Playboy* magazine starring Marilyn Monroe was issued," I interjected. Erika gave me one of those looks.

"It was a happy, ideal time for me. I realize that there were also some unpleasant events, but overall, I have very fond memories. Besides, being a high-ranking official at ASAP does have some perks, you know."

"But you mentioned there were some trouble makers and undesirables who also settled here in Old Earth," Erika said.

"Yes. Well the best laid plans of mice and men … At the time we didn't anticipate that the out-of-the-way location and nostalgic atmosphere might also attract some of the less desirable elements. Fortunately, their numbers are not overwhelming and easily controlled when necessary."

We walked another block or two, and Elvis stopped, "Well, here we are."

I looked up. I was staring at the doors of an old-fashioned Denny's restaurant.

I have noticed even people who claim everything
is predestined, and that there is nothing we can
do about it, look before they cross the road.

—Stephen Hawking

Journal Entry 81

Out of this World

Captains Denton and Sanders looked at each other. They
realized they had walked straight into a trap, and trying to
escape at this point was futile. Captain Denton's survival
training at the Agency had taught her there was a right
and wrong time to try to make an escape. This was the
wrong time. However, if she was patient enough, the
right opportunity would usually present itself. The best
thing they could do was to play along for now and wait
for their chance.

Captain Sanders seemed to understand this, and they gave
almost imperceptible nods to each other.

"We won't give you any trouble," Captain Sanders assured.

James seemed a little reluctant but realized that Rita had
a plan, or at least he hoped she did. He decided to exhibit
self-control, which went against his instincts.

"Good then. I am glad that you will cooperate," Admiral
Myers stated. "It always makes things much easier and a
lot less messy. Oh, by the way, I was being sincere. If there
are any messages you wish to leave with a loved one, you
have my word that they will be delivered."

"It's nice to know that you are a man of honor," Rita quipped.

A guard raised the butt end of his gun again to strike her, but Admiral Myers waived him off. "I do appreciate a sense of humor, to a point," he said. "In a minute my men and I will exit the room. A colorless and odorless gas will flow from the vents into the room. I assure you that it is completely harmless, but it will render you unconscious for a few hours. When you awaken, you will be in another country, and the rest will be explained to you then."

James began to twitch as if he was ready to make a move, but Rita shook her head, sending him a silent signal: "No, not yet. The time may present itself, but now is not that time." He seemed to understand, and he relaxed his muscles.

Admiral Myers saw this restraint and smiled as he and his men left the room.

"We can't just stand here like sitting ducks!" James exclaimed. "We have to do something!"

"What do you want us to do?" Captain Sanders responded in frustration.

"I don't know, but something—anything!"

Captain Sanders turned to Commander Breeze, who had been very silent up until this point. He looked a little shell-shocked, "Is there any way out of this room?" Captain Sanders asked.

Breeze thought for a moment and then shook his head. "Unfortunately, no. This room was designed for top secrecy. The navy spared no expense. We are too far below the ocean for any cell phone signal to work. The glass is thirty inches thick, and even if we could break it, the pressure at this depth would crush our lungs within a few seconds. The ventilating system is too small for anyone to crawl through. In addition, we are too far down to reach the top of the ventilating system before they release the gas. The door and lock are coated with a steel alloy that is virtually unbreakable."

"Well then, I guess our best chance for escape will be after we get to wherever they are planning on taking us," Captain Denton said.

Everyone in the group began to feel sleepy and a little dizzy.

"I don't smell or see anything, but we must be feeling the effects of the gas he was talking about," James mentioned.

Within two minutes everyone was sleeping.

***

Admiral Myers was watching them from a translucent hidden camera embedded in the windows. When he was confident that the drug had taken total effect, he had his men collect the sleepyheads and load them onto a plane.

After five hours, the small cargo plane landed at Bournemouth Airport in Southern England. Originally a Royal Air Force airport known as Hurn Airport, it had begun operations during World War II. It was used for paratroop training and as a glider base for the North African landings during the middle stages of the war. Hurn was also an important drop-off site for supplies to aid the French Resistance. The hardened runways of the airfield saw extensive use by United States Army and Air Forces in the preparations for D-Day and the subsequent Battle of Normandy.

To this day, the United States military maintains a small presence there, so it was not unusual for a United States military plane to make a landing. Bournemouth Airport was only thirty-five miles from Stonehenge, Admiral Myers' intended destination. There, the portal to the wormhole would be opened, and the group would be sent to Dr. Shelly in Universe Zero.

The Fab Five, as Admiral Myers had jokingly dubbed them, had been loaded into five separate oxygenated sealed crates. They were more valuable alive than dead. Günter had met Admiral Myers at the airport and would help facilitate the transport from the plane to the deportation site.

Günter extended a welcome. "Sir, it's good to see you again."

Admiral Myers replied, "As it is good to see you, old friend. The packages are all secured and ready for transportation."

"Good. I trust all went well. My men will accompany us to Stonehenge. In addition, we have placed road blocks around the facility indicating that Stonehenge will be closed today to the public for routine maintenance and governmental scientific testing."

Gunter and Admiral Myers retired to a pub that was located adjacent to the airport. On Devil's Island in the tropics, Günter's preferred drink was a piña colada, but since he wasn't in the tropics, he figured when in Rome ... He would try the local cider, which was made from apples and contained a heavy dose of alcohol.

He took a large gulp and said, "I think the locals call this scrumpy."

"You know, my old friend, you really drink too much. Before you know it, you will need a new liver," Admiral Myers remarked.

"You're probably right, but I do enjoy it. And you know that I have so few vices. Besides, Dr. Shelly can probably give me a new one from one of the test subjects when that day comes anyway."

As they both laughed and enjoyed their beverages, the last of the crates containing the new Fab Five were loaded into the Ford E series van.

Nothing says despair, broken dreams and poor
life choices more than a Denny's at 3am.

—Unknown

Journal Entry 82

**Skip the Grand Slam Breakfast; Two Tickets Home
Please**

"You are kidding. The way home is through a Denny's!
Did they even exist back in the 1950s?" I asked Elvis.

"Actually, they did. The first store opened in 1953, I
believe. I had just turned eighteen years old. The first
store was open in Lakewood, California, and it was called
Denny's Donuts. The next year they expanded their menu
to include sandwiches and other items. In the late 1950s
they expanded further and changed their name to just
Denny's, although they didn't introduce the Grand Slam
Breakfast until 1977. You know, Michael, you are not the
only one who watches *Jeopardy*." He gave me one of his
famous smiles.

I laughed nervously. Something didn't seem right. "Gee,
thanks for the history lesson. Hey, wasn't that the year—
1977—you died, I mean transmuted?"

"It was, but not before I got the chance to sample that
culinary delight. It's been so long, would you guys mind?"
Elvis asked.

Apparently this Denny's was special. It contained all the
original menu items, and all the menu items ever served,

right up to today's current menu. There were the original donuts and initial sandwich items along with today's modern menu featuring over 106 choices, and that wasn't including the appetizers, drinks or desserts. I wasn't going to ask how that was possible. I just assumed that magic, or his special connections had something to do with it.

Elvis went to get us a table.

"We have a little time before you two leave," Rosalie stated. "It really has been a while since we have been here."

The five of us sat down at a booth. The interior of the restaurant was similar to the exterior, with that *Happy Days* feel to it. The waiters were dressed in all white and they wore "soda jerk hats." The waitresses all wore floral skirts and had tied their hair back. People were sitting at the front counter ordering soda pop and root beer floats.

Our waitress came over to our table. She looked a little bit like the actress Erin Moran, and her nametag said Joanie. She winked at Elvis, and Rosalie gave him a dirty look. "What can I get you folks?"

Elvis quickly responded, "I'll build my own Grand Slam. I would like bacon strips, buttermilk pancakes, eggs cooked over easy and, of course, some grits."

She looked at Erika, "For you, honey?"

"Just a cup of hot chocolate with extra whipped cream, please."

Rosalie was next. "Just a bowl of oatmeal and some water."

I looked up at Joanie. "I'll have a cup of jamocha with some creamer."

She looked back at me, "You know, honey, we have real Earth coffee here."

"Of course, I would prefer that instead. Thanks."

Skyler ordered a Moons over Hammy, which was kind of nasty to me because it contained ham. I didn't like ham. In fact, to quote a line from the character Newman in *Seinfeld*, it was a "vile weed," although he was talking about broccoli and not ham. But the logic still applies, I think.

In the corner was a 1950s Seeburg MC 100 jukebox. The exterior of the 1953 model had been used in the credit sequences of the TV show *Happy Days*, according to Elvis. It was capable of playing up to fifty forty-five-rpm records. It was a colorful jukebox with chrome and glass tubes on the front, mirrors in the display, and rotating animation in the pilasters.

Elvis noticed me admiring the jukebox. He handed me a quarter and told me to play a song or two. I walked over to the machine and deposited the coin. I selected three songs, all from the King himself. The first song I selected was "Burning Love," my favorite Elvis song. The second I had never heard of but thought it seemed appropriate, "Happy Ending," which I was hoping for eventually. And the third was what I hoped was a surprise for him.

"While we wait for our food and drinks, let me run through the plan with you two," Elvis said. He smiled as "Burning Love" started playing. He mentioned that it wasn't one of his favorites, but knew a lot of people liked it. "After we eat, the head chef and manager, Maurice, will pretend to give us a tour of the kitchen. He is one of our undercover agents. Maurice will lead us back through the kitchen into a secret ASAP office. Inside the office you will be provided with equipment for your journey to Earth."

"Burning Love" ended and "Happy Ending" began to play. I listened to the words, written by Ben Weisman and Sid Wayne, and thought they were relevant: "Give me a story with a happy ending, when boy meets girl and then they never part again but live forever happily like you and me." That's what I was hoping for, although my Spidey senses were kicking in again letting me know it wasn't going to be that simple. Something was wrong, but I couldn't quite pinpoint what was bothering me.

Rosalie continued, "Inside the office we are going to equip you each with a specially designed jumpsuit."

"Is it one of the official ASAP blue suits with the wolf symbol?" I joked.

Erika rolled her eyes, and I shut up.

Rosalie giggled slightly but continued, "The suits are designed to make your travel through the wormhole more comfortable. In addition, they have a tracking device built in so we can keep monitor you guys. Also, there is a small supply of condensed food and water, just in case."

"Just in case of what?" I asked.

"The very small, small, chance that something goes wrong, which, of course, almost never happens. In fact, wormhole travel is just as statistically safe as your airplane travel on Earth. I believe there is only a 0.000089 percent chance of an accident."

My mind immediately thought of Don McLean's song "American Pie," which was about the tragic plane crash that killed Buddy Holly, Ritchie Valens, J. P. (Big Bopper) Richardson and the pilot, Roger Peterson.

"Michael, I almost forgot," Rosalie said. "Inside the zipper pocket on the right side of your suit are special instructions for your return to Universe Zero. They contain the location and specified time of your travel back. Everything you need for your return trip is contained in the envelope. However, for security reasons, please don't open the instructions until you have arrived safely back on Earth."

The third selection in the jukebox began playing—"Peace in the Valley"—and a small tear ran down Elvis' cheek. "That was Gladys' favorite song. How did you know?"

"I have my own sources and have learned a little bit of magic myself during my time here," I answered him, smiling.

Rosalie waited a minute, letting Elvis enjoy the song and memories. Then she spoke. "Skyler will give you the final instructions."

Skyler put his hand to his earpiece and said, "Please confirm." He listened and said, "Thanks. Message received." Then he turned to us. "I have just been informed that your doubles were killed. Apparently, Dr. Shelly's men blew up their vehicle when it was on the way through the Nether Region. We should be good to go now because Dr. Shelly will believe that you two were stopped from leaving Evion."

"But won't he be angry?" Erika pointed out. "That doesn't make sense! He wanted to analyze my DNA. Blowing up what he thought was me is counterproductive to those plans."

"I agree," I interjected. "It is very difficult to retrieve DNA from an explosion."

"That's true on Earth, but not here," Skyler responded. "Our methods are a little more advanced in the field of genetics. We have methods for extracting DNA, even from explosion sites.

"Well, if that's true," Erika said, "he has gotten what he wanted. He can analyze the DNA of my drone and get the secrets he's after."

Elvis cut in. "No, that's not correct. Although the drone looked exactly like you, the DNA wasn't an exact copy. He won't be able to deduce the genetic combination that enables you to travel freely between universes."

"Well, at least that's good but those poor doubles," Erika stated sadly. "They were just created to be sacrificed."

"I understand," said Elvis. "But it was in your best interest and the best interest of both worlds. Is it really that different than raising cows and chickens on Earth for the sole purpose of being slaughtered and eaten when they reach a certain age and weight?"

I thought, although it wasn't exactly the same thing, there was a certain undeniable logic to his thought. Was it really much different than how we humans treated some animals on Earth?

Skyler continued, "Once the jumpsuits are tailored to fit your bodies exactly, we will escort you through the office down through the catacombs where the wormhole is located. Merlin—I believe you know him—will be waiting for us down there to help with final instructions on the suits and with the transport to Earth. You will not need to put the wormhole suits on until we are ready for transportation"

When you reach the end of your rope,
tie a knot in it and hang on.

—Thomas Jefferson

Journal Entry 83

Ropes, Strings, and Things

My father died when I was nineteen. I remember he would carry with him a small notebook containing quotes. I guess he loved quotes. Some of them I understood immediately and some I didn't understand until I was older. One in particular always stood out to me. It was a Mark Twain quote: "When I was a boy of fourteen, my father was so ignorant I could hardly stand to have the old man around. But when I got to be twenty-one, I was astonished at how much the old man had learned in seven years."

We would be back on Earth soon. One of the things I had wished was that my dad had transmuted and not died. I had hoped that I might be able to meet him there on Evion, but so far, I had not. No one seemed to have any information about my father.

The book of quotes reminded me of the little black book that I had picked up on the fifth floor of Dr. Shelly's lab before we left. I had almost forgotten about it. I had planned to leave the black book with Elvis before leaving Evion. I hadn't even had a chance to look at, it and I had forgotten about it until now. I would come to regret not taking the time to read what was written in those small pages.

***

The Ford van carrying the Fab Five arrived at Stonehenge twenty-five minutes after leaving the airport. Dr. Shelly wanted the group conscious when they were transported through the wormhole. However, Admiral Myers had realized they would not go willingly, so before he had the travelers put in their individual crates, he'd had their hands bound with a right-angle knot, which provided extra security. This particular knot was harder to undo than most. He'd learned how to perfect the right-angle knot during his training as a Navy SEAL.

The crates were unloaded and opened. Each of its occupants was still unconscious. They were each injected with a stimulant containing a small amount of epinephrine. The members of the Fab Five were instantly revived. Admiral Myers pulled out a scanning device and aimed it at the Heal Stone. Instantly a panel on the side of the great slab of stone became visible. He input the secret code, and a door inside of the Leaning Stone became visible and opened. Myers led the captives down a series of dimly lit spiraling underground stairs, which seemed endless. The air became stagnant and unusually warm as they dropped deeper into the bowels of the Earth.

As they reached their final steps, the reason for the increase in temperature became more apparent. They were staring at an elongated giant tunnel that was emitting a large amount of heat.

The hands of the captives were still bound, but their feet were free, and they were not gagged.

"What kind of device is that thing that looks like a giant cigar?" James asked. "It looks like one of those huge water caves that dip deep below the surface of the bayou back off of Honey Island Swamp. I visited there as a kid." Admiral Myers gave James a dirty look, but James continued, "Maybe Freud had it wrong after all."

"Funny," said the admiral, "psychology was my minor in college. What was he wrong about?"

"Well, I guess sometimes a cigar isn't a cigar after all."

"Tape his mouth shut," Myers ordered the guards. But he quickly regained his composure and waived away the guards. He smiled. "That cigar-looking device, as you call it, is actually a wormhole that will allow me to transport you to another universe where a colleague of mine, Dr. Shelly, will be your host."

Up until now, Rita had been pretty sure this other universe was just a hoax, but looking at this peculiar device, she wasn't so sure anymore. The trouble was they were sort of tied up—literally. She needed time to think of something. Maybe she could stall a little bit by asking about the machine. Admiral Myers was a narcissist and loved to talk about himself and his plans. She spoke up. "Since you obviously have the upper hand, maybe you could at least share with us how it works. I'm sure someone as accomplished as yourself could explain it to us in layman's terms."

He laughed. "You do have a propensity for stalling and toadying, but I take no offense and will at least honor your request, being that it's probably your last. To be honest, I don't completely understand the whole process, but I can give you the *Reader's Digest* version of what I do know."

Realizing Captain Denton was probably stalling, Captain Sanders jumped in, "That would be great! I've always thought we were not alone and that there must be other universes or dimensions out there somewhere."

Admiral Myers continued, "I am sure you did, my dear. Here is what I can tell you. It has something to do with strings."

"You mean the concept of string theory?" James asked.

Everyone looked at James with surprise.

"What are you implying?" he said. "I took a couple of electives in college, you know."

The admiral continued, "Yes, I think that's it. Because all matter, whether light or dark, is made up of tiny strings. These strings can vibrate at different frequencies; each of the two universes vibrates at its own unique frequency. I don't recall the actual numbers, but they are slightly different, out of sync as it were."

Captain Sanders chimed in. "And since the vibration frequencies are different, each universe can exist separately from the other."

"That's correct. This machine enables the wormhole to match the frequency of your universe with that of the other universe and thus allow transportation into it through the wormhole," Admiral Myers explained.

I buy all my socks with holes in them. Otherwise,
how would I get my feet in them?

—Jarod Kintz

Journal Entry 84

Where Lost Socks End Up

Skyler led us through a secret compartment in the office.
We walked down a long, slender corridor. The walls were
sterile, painted white and had no remarkable features;
there were no dents, scrapes, or markings. At the end of
the walkway, we reached a metal door. The words painted
in blue said, Authorized ASAP Personnel Only.

Elvis placed his eye to the door, and a retina scan
confirmed his identity. Rosalie and Skyler did the same.
Each time a laser beam scanned their retinas. The door
opened to a platform. A series of winding steps led down
to a vast array of tunnels and vaults.

As we walked along, I was comforted by the discovery
that these catacombs did not contain any dead bodies
or caskets. Actually, this subterranean passageway was
pleasant. Surprisingly, there were no cobwebs or large
sewer rats running about. There was no foul stench or
stale air typically found underground. In fact, there was
a quiet ventilating system pumping in fresh air. However,
this air did not seem to have the same hypnotic effect as
I had experienced in The Trades.

The walls of this subterranean chamber were decorated
with paintings from both worlds. In addition, some areas

contained sculptures, statues, and ornaments apparently depicting the history of both universes.

As we walked, Rosalie mentioned this area of the catacomb had been designed after the famous Camden Catacomb in subterranean London during the nineteenth century. I noticed what appeared to be numbered horse stables being used as storage units or some type of vaults. I turned to Skyler and asked, "What is being stored in those units?"

Skyler looked at both Elvis and Rosalie, and they nodded back at him as if to say, "It's okay. He's one of us, and you can tell him a little."

Skyler hesitated but began, "Some of these units are used to store lost treasures from your old home."

"You mean you guys rob Earth?" Erika asked.

"No ... well not exactly," Elvis replied. "Some of these lost treasures were brought to this universe illegally from your old world. We have recovered some of these treasures and are keeping them safe until we can figure out a way to have them returned without suspicion or the wrong hands getting their hands on them."

"Okay, I guess that makes sense," I said. "Just out of curiosity, what is in the storage unit labeled number one?"

Rosalie winked at Elvis and said, "Let me field this one since it relates to Daddy dearest. The Amber Room is being stored in the first unit."

"That's impossible!" Erika replied. "It was destroyed in 1943."

I looked at Erika and asked, "You know what they are talking about?"

"I remember reading about it during one of my training sessions at the CIA," she said. Erika never ceased to amaze me. She continued, "If memory serves me correctly, the original treasure room was a set of extraordinary wall panels made from the purest amber backed with gold leaf and mirrors. These panels were installed to create a room that was effectively coated with amber and gold. I forget who designed, it but I think that in the early eighteenth century, the king of Prussia, Friedrich Wilhelm I, gave it to the ruler of the Russian Empire, Tsar Peter the Great. This act was to seal an alliance against Sweden." She looked at Elvis and Rosalie and asked, "How am I doing so far?"

"It was designed by Andreas Schlüter," Rosalie remarked, "and constructed at the Charlottenburg Palace in Prussia by the renowned amber specialist Gottfried Wolfram of the Royal Court of Denmark, but you are doing an excellent job. Please continue."

"That's it!" said Erika. "Now I remember the rest of the story. The room was considered to be unique and priceless, and it became the central showpiece of the palace and famous in aristocratic Russian circles. When the Germans invaded in 1941, the Russians tried to move the room, but the walls started to crack, so they tried to cover them up with wallpaper. However, the Germans were not fooled. They dismantled the entire room. It was rumored to be packed into twenty-seven crates and shipped to Königsberg, near the Baltic Coast, where it was put on display. In 1943, it was stored at Königsberg Castle until it was officially destroyed in a World War II Allied Forces bombing raid."

"Excellent," Elvis responded. "Except for one thing. We found significant evidence that suggested it wasn't destroyed, as previously thought. It was actually shipped out of the city in the latter months of the war and taken to be hidden along with many other treasures acquired by the Nazi regime."

"And that 'significant' evidence was?" Erika asked.

Elvis laughed. "We found parts of the Amber Room being transported into this world illegally by some operatives we believed were working for Dr. Shelly."

"What would Dr. Shelly want with the Amber Room?" I asked. "In this universe, gold and jewels are abundant anyway, aren't they?"

"Yes, these precious metals and gems are common, but amber isn't," Rosalie responded. "In fact, amber is very rare, and it can be used for a number of different purposes in this universe, one of which is placing a person in a state of suspended animation for a long period of time."

"Besides the extraction of the amber," Elvis said, "the Amber Room is conservatively estimated to be worth over a hundred seventy million Earth dollars."

"And that kind of cash could fund a lot of operations and pay a lot of operatives on Earth," Erika mentioned.

"Exactly, that was our thinking as well," Elvis quipped.

"And don't forget Dr. Shelly appeared to be such a big fan of Hitler's monstrous work. Maybe he wanted something he thought his hero would have wanted," I added. I thought for a moment. "Hey, Hitler, hasn't transmuted, has he?" I asked with a dreaded feeling.

"Honestly, Michael," Elvis responded, "you have to stop being so paranoid. Not everybody transmutes."

I noticed that he hadn't directly answered my question though. "Why haven't you arrested Dr. Shelly for stealing this artifact from Earth?"

"Two reasons," Rosalie answered. "First, technically it isn't illegal to steal artifacts or treasures from Earth. But more importantly, we were never able to find enough information linking Dr. Shelly directly with the heist."

"But given Dr. Shelly's obsession with the Nazis and Hitler that I discovered while searching his office, it seems obvious he was responsible for the theft," I interjected.

"Yes, yes, you are probably right," Elvis responded. "But without direct evidence, and not to mention his personal connection with the mayor and local politicians, it was decided it would be best to focus on his other operations and not the thefts from Earth."

I wasn't happy with the answer, but at this point it seemed less important than our current mission. However, letting things go had never been my strong point and so I retorted, "Okay then, let me take a guess at what's behind doors number two and three. I'm guessing that there's the Ark of the Covenant behind door number two and possibly Blackbeard's treasure behind door number three."

Elvis gave me a surprised look as if to say, "How did you know that?"

"You've got to be kidding! You mean you actually have these things? Never mind, I don't want to know."

"I think that would be for the best."

We all walked in silence for a few minutes. I continued to look around at the storage rooms, imagining what else could be hidden in these vaults.

Skyler must have assumed we were interested in a history lesson of the catacombs. Maybe he was using this as an excuse to change the subject and to get me to stop thinking about what treasures might be stored in these rooms, because he proceeded to give us the *Reader's Digest* version of the history of catacombs.

"Did you know the first place to be referred to as catacombs on Earth was the system of underground tombs between the second and third milestones of the Appian Way in Rome where the bodies of the apostles Peter and Paul, among others, were said to have been buried?" he asked.

Feigning interest, I said, "You know, I had no clue."

Obviously missing the sarcasm—hey, maybe I was losing my touch—he continued, "Well the name of that place in old Latin was *catacumbae*, a word of obscure origin, possibly deriving from a proper name, or else a corruption of the Latin phrase *cata tumbas*, 'among the tombs.' The word referred originally only to the Roman catacombs, but was extended by 1836 to refer to any subterranean receptacle of the dead, as in the eighteenth-century Paris catacombs."

I whispered in Erika's ear, "Is that what I sound like sometimes?"

"Well …"

"I'm so sorry. I'll really, really, try and work on it."

She smiled. "It's okay, it's just a part of you, and we all have our own flaws. You accept me for my imperfections, and I accept you."

I smiled back at her. "Love is patient, love is kind. It does not envy, it does not boast—"

She cut me off, "Okay, don't push it."

"Right, gotcha." And we both laughed.

At the end of the stables was a lazy river. Two small channel boats were tied to a small dock. Skyler, Erika, and I got into the first boat, while Elvis and Rosalie got into the second boat. Elvis told us that these boats would take us on the last leg of our journey. For a brief moment I felt that I was in Epcot taking the El Rio Del Tiempo boat ride in the Mexico Pavilion. It's not that there were tiny dolls dressed in Mexican outfits or a tour of the countryside with the three lost caballeros reuniting in the end for a grand performance, but it was a dimly lit gentle boat ride through a part of the catacombs. They seemed reminiscent of Mexican pyramids. Of course, it could have just been my overactive imagination playing tricks on me again.

I glanced behind us and noticed that Elvis and Rosalie were hand in hand. She was gently leaning into him, and I was thinking of a quote from *Saturday Night Live*'s Church Lady, "Well, isn't that special?" Actually, it was nice. I had come to associate Elvis with much sadness and pain. He tried to cover it up by changing his outfits and exercising his sense of humor. Maybe Rosalie made him happy and, to some small degree, helped to ease the loss of his mother.

As we approached the end of the lazy river, Erika reached for my hand. I smiled. "I think everything will be okay once we get to the wormhole. It's a different mode of travel—kind of wild actually—but maybe you'll like it."

"I doubt it. What does it feel like?"

"Well, you came through one, don't you remember?"

"Actually, I'm not sure if I was awake, because I can't remember much about traveling through any type of portal."

"Strange. Anyway, it's kind of like Aerosmith's 'Rockin' Rollercoaster' but faster and more out of control."

"Great. You know how much I love that ride."

I laughed. "I'm just kidding. It's really not that bad. But just to be on the safe side, maybe they can give you something for the ride."

"That's okay," she said. "I'll take my chances."

Skyler turned to us and said, "It's time for me to explain the process of getting the two of you home. When we reach the end of the river, we will walk about a quarter mile to the device that will send you back to Earth. Merlin will be meeting us there and assisting with the transport back."

This is not the end. It is not even the beginning of the
end. But it is, perhaps, the end of the beginning.

—Winston Churchill

Journal Entry 85

End? Since It Hasn't Worked Out, It's Not the End!

Admiral Myers looked at the Fab Five and extended his
right hand to shake each member's hand. The ropes had
been removed from their hands, but the admiral's men
still had automatic weapons trained on the group. Maybe
it was human nature, or it was the shock value of this act
that seemed so strange, but each of the Fab Five accepted
his handshake.

The admiral smiled. "Good. I see that there are no hard
feelings. In a little while, you will be transported through
a gateway to another universe. I trust you will be in good
hands. And speaking of hands, we will have to leave you
unbound for the transportation process."

"You trust us?" James asked sarcastically.

"Nice try. Actually, Dr. Shelly has developed a type of
control serum, which will be administered to all of you
just before your journey. It is a derivation of sodium
pentothal, which is what you call truth serum on Earth.
Dr. Shelly's version of this serum, Serapanol, not only
makes you tell the truth, it also makes a person very
controllable and open to suggestions."

"You mean you can tell me to act like a duck, and I will start quaking?" James asked.

Admiral Myers laughed. "Actually, yes. We could suggest you do stupid pet tricks or command you to make weird animal noises after the drug is administered. However, I like to think of myself as a professional, so I will keep our relationship strictly business. After we give the five of you Serapanol, I will simply give you a suggestion to remain calm and follow all of my orders. However, in your case, James, I might bend the rules a bit, just for fun."

James looked as if he was going to say something to make it worse for himself, but Rita quickly shot him a look. He could just imagine her saying, "You'd better shut up before he really does make you do some stupid pet tricks or something worse. Besides, you don't want to make it worse for all of us with your jokes."

Admiral Myers continued after pausing for James to make another joke. "Oh, yes, there is one more thing that I forgot to mention. While Serapanol is an extremely useful drug, it is not one hundred percent perfected."

"I may regret asking this question, but what exactly does that mean?" Captain Sanders inquired.

"A good question," Admiral Myers answered in an almost condescending and enthusiastic childish manner. "You see, this drug works perfectly in about eighty percent of the patients that we have used it on in our trials."

"You mean that this drug has only been used on test subjects and not real people?" Rita asked.

"Well, technically yes. You will be the first group to experience this particular batch of Serapanol outside of a controlled lab setting. But we have great hopes it will work similarly to the way the other batches worked in the lab setting," Admiral Myers responded.

"Okay, getting back to the point that the drug is only eighty percent effective. What happened to the other twenty percent—the ones on whom it was not effective?" Rita asked.

"Naturally there were some unfortunate side effects," Admiral Myers answered.

This time James responded. "Okay, I'll bite. These side effects were?"

"You know the usual headache, nausea, dry mouth, fever, chills, anal seepage, and hair loss."

"Hair loss?" James asked nervously putting his hands through what was still remaining of his thinning hair.

"James, seriously, hair loss? Is that what you're worried about and not anal seepage?" Rita quipped.

Admiral Myers chuckled. "Don't worry, I was just kidding about those side effects. They are pretty rare."

"That's a relief," James said with a sigh.

"The much more common side effects are brain damage, stroke, and anaphylactic shock, which usually causes death."

"Well, I guess that's better than hair loss or anal seepage," James wisecracked.

***

We continued to walk toward the wormhole that would send Erika and me back to Earth. For me it would be only a temporary visit, but the important thing was that Erika would be safer back home than she would be here. The closer we got, the warmer the air became. The portal must have required a great deal of energy, as we began to sweat just a little.

"Don't worry, we have a force field around the gateway that acts as a pocket of cooler air so you won't fry when we finally reach the device," Skylar said.

"Great, so I guess I won't need my SPF thirty after all," I kidded.

"What?" Skylar asked.

"Don't worry. It's just Michael trying to be funny," Erika said.

After we walked another few feet, the air became a bit cooler as we reached the final entrance that would lead us to the wormhole.

Elvis approached the door, and a retina scan confirmed his identity. Rosalie followed, and finally Skylar. Apparently, all three retinas in the proper sequence were needed to open the bay door leading to the wormhole.

As we entered the lab room, we were immediately greeted by Merlin. This time he appeared more like the Merlin I had read about from classic Arthurian legend. His beard appeared snowy white, and it was very long, almost touching the floor. His face still appeared a little older, and it showed a bit of strain. He wore an old, weathered wizard's hat that was reminiscent of something Gandalf would have worn. It was blue and covered with gold stars. He also wore a long blue robe that was embroidered with pictures of scenes from the Harry Potter movies. Calygreyhound and Freybug were at Merlin's side. When they saw me, they came running over to greet me.

I knelt beside Calygreyhound and Freybug and started to pet the big lugs.

"Michael, what in the world are those two animals?" Erika asked.

"They are Merlin's pets and guardians. Calygreyhound and Freybug, this is Erika," I said.

They both walked over to Erika and extended their paws to greet her. She shook both their paws. "Nice to meet you," she said to each of them.

"Ah, I see that my companions like you," Merlin said to Erika. "I have found these beasts to be excellent judges of character."

Curiously, I noticed that Merlin looked over toward Skylar after making that comment.

"I like them too," Erika replied. "They are a little different than what I am used to back home. I usually like smaller dogs, but these guys do seem sweet."

"They are sweet," Merlin said. "But they can be fierce if they feel that I am being threatened. Both of my babies have been my companions for a very long time. Anyway, I see you noticed my robe. I have just recently started watching the Harry Potter movie series, and although there are many discrepancies that most real wizards would find disturbing, I have found the stories to be very entertaining and amusing— hence the robe."

Elvis gave Merlin a look that suggested time was starting to run short.

"Elvis is quite right then," said Merlin. "Enough about my movie preferences. Our optimum window for transport is arriving shortly."

Clayton flew into the room and landed on Merlin's shoulder. He sang something into Merlin's ear.

"Thanks," he said to Clayton. "I almost forgot the jumpsuits given to you back at Denny's are specially designed wormhole traveling. They will give you some added protection as you travel through the wormhole."

When no one was looking, he whispered into my ear, "The suits also have some magical surprises included for you two, but let's keep that our secret for now."

I started to protest and was about to ask Merlin why all the secrecy, but he gave me a wink and a look that said, "Just shut up and listen to what I say."

The suits were powder blue with specs of silver, gold, and platinum laced throughout the fabric. The sleeves and legs were equipped with multiple zippered pockets, and when I touched the suit, it felt as if each contained a discretely placed item. These suits were designed to fit comfortably over our clothing.

"Can I see something in another color?" Erika asked in jest.

I laughed. "Now that's something I would say—I mean if it was possible for a guy to ask that without looking stupid or sounding too girlish."

"Sorry, I don't know what came over me. Just a momentary bout of corniness I guess," she responded.

"Let's just leave the corny jokes to me then," I said.

Our ASAP team was beginning to look very impatient, so we slipped the wormhole suits over our clothes.

Rosalie handed me a small device that resembled a smartphone and explained, "This is a digital database holographic machine—DBH for short. It contains instructions for your pick-up point and return information.

It includes an emergency list of our contact operatives on Earth should you run into any trouble."

Elvis walked over and handed me Caliburn. "Please take her with you. I have instructed her that, for the next couple of days, you are her master. She is to help you in any way possible."

"Thanks, but I really don't think that's necessary. It seems like this operation should be pretty routine. Are you sure that you are not trying to keep tabs on me? Afraid I won't come back?" I joked.

"No, I have no doubt that you will come back. If you don't, your DNA would eventually destabilize, we think, and then you wouldn't be any good for Erika, being dead and all. Think of Caliburn as a good luck charm. You never know."

"Thanks. As soon as I know that Erika is safe, I'll be back." I tried not to sound like the Terminator.

"Okay then," Merlin said. "We have two minutes before we initiate the transfer back to Earth. Now would be a good time to say your good-byes."

I shook Merlin's hand and thanked him for all his help. Rosalie gave me a big hug and wished me luck. She said to stop into the club and have a piña colada on her when I came back. Elvis game me a brief hug and assured me that they would continue to look for Dr. Shelly while I was gone.

Calygreyhound and Freybug rushed over and gave me a big lick on my face.

"I like those two big guys," Erika said, "but I'm not kissing you until you wash your face."

Finally, Skylar shook my hand and uncharacteristically patted me on the back. In addition, he gave me an odd wink and smile.

Erika said her good-byes as well.

"Okay, so what do we do now?" I asked.

"In twenty seconds, slowly begin to walk into the wormhole," Merlin advised. "And enjoy the journey back to Earth!"

We took a deep breath, held each other's hands, and slowly began to step into the wormhole. As we entered the maw of the portal, I turned to Erika and said, "Just think of it as quick ride down Splash Mountain."

"Piece of cake, right?" she replied apprehensively.

I smiled. "I love you," I said.

I had barely finished those words when we were swooshed into the wormhole. We tried to hold together, but something was different. Something was wrong this time. We were traveling faster, and we seemed more out of control than I remembered being on my previous trip. I remembered seeing a flash of light and hearing the sounds of commotion coming from the opening of the wormhole the moment we were swept away—right after I had told Erika I loved her.

I thought I'd heard Press say, "Skylar, what the hell did you do?"

And that was it. Our connection to that world was detached. We were gyrated in contorted motions, and I began to lose my orientation. I couldn't tell up from down, left from right. A wave of nausea ensued. I could taste the bile swelling up the peristaltic muscle of my esophagus, but I was somehow able to keep from vomiting.

We traveled for an indeterminate amount of time. The more experienced wormhole travelers know that time obviously works differently in wormholes, but it was all new for the less experienced like Erika and me. I lost sight of Erika just before we were suddenly spit out of the maws of the wormhole.

We landed much harder than I had landed in my previous experience. Erika ended up with a number of scrapes and bruises. I wasn't as lucky. My left ankle was injured. It felt broken or at least severely sprained, but we had reached our destination. We were back on Earth together.

Erika ran over to me. Her face was ashen. We both noticed a terrible stench of burning and rotting flesh. It was freezing cold, and a light snow was falling. We scanned the area around us. She spotted two large German shepherds that were obviously on patrol.

Next to us were railroad tracks that led into a nearby encampment. Next to the tracks were two large buildings.

One looked like a railroad station complete with a large wooden clock. Another looked like barracks of some sort. A twenty-foot-high fence topped with barbed wire surrounded us. There were other weathered wooden shacks that looked as if they were also barracks. I couldn't tell the total number from our vantage point.

In the distance we heard voices yelling at us in a foreign language. I wasn't sure—maybe German? "Halt! Keine Bewegung oder Ihr werdet erchossed! Wer seid Ihr beiden?"

Normally, I would be inclined to make a corny joke like, "I don't think we're in Kansas anymore." I couldn't. Not because I was mostly sure we weren't in Kansas, though I had never actually been to Kansas, but because my heart began to sink. I turned to Erika, who looked white as a ghost, and said very solemnly, "I don't think we are home."

We looked up at the gate entrance as the guards and German shepherds were approaching rapidly. We nearly fainted. Perched high above our heads was the infamous sign Konzentrationslager followed by the word *Auschwitz*.

To be continued …

About the Author

Caden is an accidental author. He is not sure if he was born on this world or another, since he was adopted and knows little about his birth parents. As a junior attending the University of Montana, he became a Walt Disney World intern. Caden is currently unemployed as he begrudgingly moves from town to town. At this time, he has won no writing awards and never meant for these journals to be published. Caden loves animals and hopes that one day this craziness will end so he can meet a nice girl and settle down with a wife, pets, and future children. Presently, his whereabouts are unknown.